CITY AT MY FEET

MANNAHATTA SERIES
BOOK 1

THOMAS MORE

CITY AT MY FEET

Published by Mannahatta Press—*History Rewritten*™

An imprint of New York City Dreams Publishing House

© 2023 by Thomas More | thomasmorewriter.com

SECOND EDITION, 2025

Library of Congress Control Number: 2025920037

ISBN: 978-1-942947-55-4 (ebook)

ISBN: 978-1-942947-56-1 (paperback)

ISBN: 978-1-942947-57-8 (hardcopy)

ISBN: 978-1-942947-58-5 (audiobook)

Printed in the United States of America

NYC DREAMS

PUBLISHING HOUSE

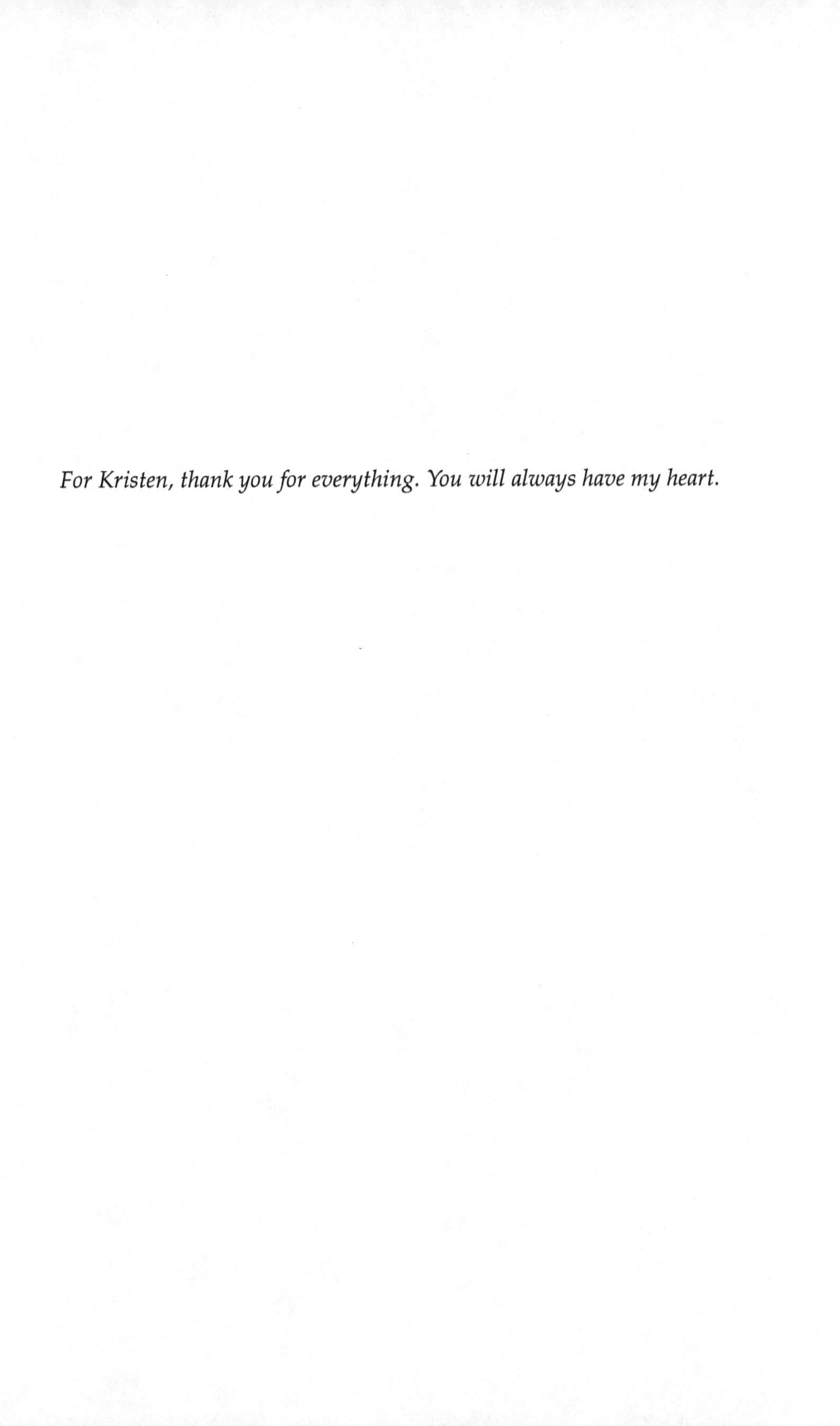

For Kristen, thank you for everything. You will always have my heart.

CONTENTS

PART ONE
MANNAHATTA

CHAPTER 1

A loud crack of a large branch snapping hit Sakima Tamanend's ears like a punch. Something big was in the forest with her—and close. She heard a low, deep growl. This was clearly not a small, cute creature who made small branches snap. This was something else, something big, and it sounded displeased.

Sakima immediately raised her bow and fitted an arrow onto the string with a single, swift motion. She flexed her arm and chest muscles as she pulled the bio-engineered gut string taut. Standing still, every muscle tense, she did not make a sound. She heard the shuffling of enormous paws across fallen leaves, and then out of the shadows the creature emerged.

It was a mechBear, *mechmàxkwi*, and it lumbered noisily into view on the path ahead. She quickly studied the threat. Less than twenty feet separated her from the beast in the thicket. Sakima's finely tuned senses picked up the animal's lab-made odor—sulfur and the slight hint of burnt rubber—and its radiating mechanical heat. She concentrated on the cracking twigs and crunching leaves as the mechBeast stomped from one side of the path to the other back into the dark overgrowth of *Tèkëne* forest. The angle was wrong, and so was the distance. So she did not let the arrow fly—not yet.

She anticipated the mechBear would reappear soon on the path as it wandered around in search of food. This time, she would be ready. After the strike, the mighty animal would give up its chem-fur and bioMeat and simBones to help one of the True People of Mannahatta. This would be its greatest sacrifice and Sakima intended to accept this gift with gratitude and grace.

Sakima focused on the scent of warm fur, the barely noticeable snap of the smallest twig. Her hunting skills gave her the ability to zero in on certain sounds and movements. More than focus, what she needed was time.

She swiftly swept the bow and her body around to face the rear from where the beast had suddenly emerged behind her, surprising her once again. Yet, on this occasion, she was ready. She had already strung an arrow in the bow. Another dangled from her shooting hand, ready to load in right after she let the first one fly.

She froze. The taut string, holding all the energy in the world, quivered with the promise of relief. Nothing happened. Beads of sweat dotted Sakima's face, above her lips and on her forehead. Her arms trembled from the exertion of keeping the bow and string apart, using all her strength.

Unable to let the arrow go, she slowly released the tension on the string and then turned and sprinted. She jumped over small boulders and around thick oak trees and straight through bushes. Many of them had pointy branch ends where traveling animals had snapped them off. Then she remembered.

Her knees went weak at the thought of being with him, kissing him. How could that have even happened? He was too beautiful for words. He never spoke to her or said "Hi."

Who cares? she had thought back then at twelve years old. *I am better off on my own. I do not need a boyfriend trying to kiss me when I am working on my archery skills.*

But Apatschin, her Pat, had come into her life—real and wonderful. Kissing him above the banks of the *Shatemuc* River had been so much more glorious than she'd imagined, as they held each other and watched the sparkling river flow over the edge of their world, into the dark mystery of space.

Sakima stopped to catch her breath, tears stinging her eyes at a different, horrible memory from nearly five years ago. First, a splash of blood; next, a fast stream of it. Flesh being torn, a body being slashed open. A scream.

Sakima shook her head to rid herself of the memory. There was no blood and no screaming in the now. She lifted her bow up to her face again. *Thank the Spirits that the mechmàxkwi has not seen me yet.* She'd had the luck to be downwind from the creature, so it couldn't pick up her scent. At least not at that distance.

Blood everywhere. Skin torn open. The screaming!

Tears filled Sakima's eyes as she fought against her memories and her guilt. Back in the present, she nocked an arrow into her string again. She blinked to clear her vision, to focus on the mech-Animal now in front of her.

She swallowed to stop the choking wave of grief building up in her throat. This was no time to cry. She needed to be as brave as she'd ever been.

Sakima steadied her arrow and concentrated, closing one eye to aim. The arrowhead, shining blue with targeting energy, gave an almost imperceptible whine from the tip as it prepared to go. A similar but lower-sounding hum came from the feathers, which also now glowed a bright cyan. These components tested the air quality, humidity, and wind as they calculated the distance and the perfect trajectory, as Sakima waited to release the arrow toward the target.

The *mechmàxkwi* turned and spotted her. The bear's eyes blazed red; the metal wheels embedded in its back became a dull crimson as they powered up and spun around, preparing for an attack.

Sakima heard the screams in her ears as clearly as she had that terrible day, almost three years ago…

> *"Sakima! Help me!"*
>
> *That awful noise of Pat's voice, a usually sweet sound, was now in tandem with horrible shrieking. It came out as a kind of whooping from where the rip in his throat was. A hollowing death-wind roar.*
>
> *"Shoot!" He tried to scream the words. Sakima understood him, even though the screech from his open, bleeding throat and the growling of the mechmàxkwi drowned out his voice. She couldn't let the arrow fly and potentially kill the boy she loved. So she shut her tear-filled eyes while the sounds of screaming grew dim.*

Here in the present, not in her memories, Sakima launched an arrow from her bow with a loud snap of the bowstring. It traveled with such velocity that when it hit the bear's shoulder, it drilled through the muscle and straight out the other side. Blood pumped from the mechBear in spasms, but the animal did not slow down or veer from its target.

Not only the hunt but also rage and pain motivated the mech-Beast. It blindly flew toward her, growling. Then the mechBear slammed into the large, coarse trunk of a sycamore tree, skidding to a painful stop. Sakima jumped out from behind the trunk and shot a second arrow into the bear's back, then nocked again and loosed yet another.

The bear roared with pain and rage, twisting around again to face its adversary. Sakima dashed away as fast as she could. She knew the beast's injury should have felled it. Then it stood up, seemingly unaffected, and pursued tight on her trail once again. She knew it would catch up to her in seconds. And that there would be no time to shoot an arrow of any kind.

Sakima pulled a ten-inch blade from the leather belt attached to her waist. She dodged left and then right, then twisted to face her pursuer. The mechBear's paw was bigger than a large rock and more deadly as it swept down at her. Sakima stayed out of reach. She felt the slight breeze as the paw swiped past her, nearly slicing her face in half.

She jumped behind the wide trunk of a pine tree as the mech-Bear, weakening now, attempted to follow. But Sakima's radius around the tree was tighter, quicker. The *mechmàxkwi* skidded in the underbrush, slipping and falling on one knee. Sakima rushed until she was behind the creature now. She gripped her knife in both hands. Screaming a battle cry, she plunged the blade deep into the animal's hide, aiming for the heart far beneath the muscle and fat. She jammed it in as far as her strength would allow. Then she pulled it out and tore off running.

A tree branch hung just above her head a few yards farther on. She arrived at the spot below it and leaped high, grabbed the branch, and swung herself up. She climbed swiftly, despite the small, spiny branches cutting into her skin and blocking her way. When she finally reached the top of the tree, she allowed herself to stop, breathe, and study the forest below her.

The mechBear was not following her—not at the base of the tree, not in its branches. Sakima adjusted her position so she could look deeper into the forest. There she saw it, not far from her. It lay on its side, nearly dead, its chest moving up and down in shuddering, shallow breaths. Its enormous paw clutched Sakima's quiver, its claws deeply embedded in it. She hadn't felt it being ripped off her back as the adrenaline had carried her toward and into the tree's welcoming arms.

She waited to be sure the mechBear would not get up again before she lowered herself to the ground. Then, with cautious steps, she made her way to the bear. She hesitated as she heard the creature's breathing, loud and labored. Blood oozed out of multiple wounds.

As she stood above the mechanical beast, Sakima said a quiet prayer thanking the *Wematëgunis*, the Wood Spirits. Then, kneeling down, she slit the bear's throat.

CHAPTER 2

The mechBear was dead, its warm, damp smell slowly changing as Sakima waited. She took a deep, long breath in the surrounding quietness. With her eyes closed, she silently thanked the universe's spirits for their generosity and protection. Sakima thanked the bear for giving up its life, feeling honored to be there with the creature in its final moments.

Sakima opened her eyes with sudden alarm and gazed around her. She knew there were scavengers and predators everywhere in the ominous shadows of the forest, some probably just feet away. She could not allow herself to become lost in thought and prayer for too long—another creature could attack while she was vulnerably unaware.

But Sakima knew—or wanted to believe—that she was a warrior, too skilled a tracker and hunter to be snuck up on like that. Sakima removed her knife from its sheath on her belt and held it in front of her like a holy object. This blade was her prize, her pet. She sharpened it daily on a stone with two drops of mech-oil. First one side, then the other, and then the first again. The blade could cut a raindrop in the air.

She adored her knife, *"chessi,"* short for *"chesimus,"* meaning "brother." This was how she thought of her blade, as her tough, trustworthy little brother, ready to strike at her enemies and defend her. Like a miniaturized Tommy, her actual older brother.

Hìtami, whom she and all her family called "Tommy," had been a true warrior in the Mannahatta military before a treacherous squad of enemies betrayed and slaughtered him. Tommy was a glorious hero, and Sakima loved him with her entire heart and hated that he had passed on to the other land, the Land of the Dead.

She'd never known him; she was still inside her mother's belly up to the very day of his murder. Her mother informed Sakima that Hìtami had set aside this knife especially for her. He said to present it to his newborn sister on her twelfth birthday. He wasn't around to hand it to her himself. Her mother had given Sakima this special knife with a befitting ceremony at age twelve. Still, Tommy was gone, and she would never know him—not in this life, anyway.

Gone just like her first ever and only boyfriend, Apatschin, was gone forever. Sakima had prayed to the Tree Spirits, the Water Spirits, and the Spirits of the Wind. Not a one of them would bring him back or answer her prayers to see Pat's smiling, handsome face, to know that he was all right in the Land of the Dead with her brother and others.

Sakima wiped a tear from her cheek and rubbed the wetness between her fingertips, lost in thought. She wanted to believe that she was stronger than this. She took a deep breath that ended in a sigh. Sakima desired to be strong, to fight, and to protect. Yet here she was, in tears.

What is so different in this, in my pursuit, in my dreams? How come the one thing that makes me happy makes everyone on this island miserable? Why must I be hated and scolded and ridiculed for being myself? For wanting to be, and training myself to be, the first female warrior in my world.

The loud cawing of crows flying overhead sucked Sakima out of her reverie and back into the now. The knife in her hands and the dead mechBear below her—stretched ungracefully in the dirt and dry leaves—surprised her at first. She stared at *chessi*, contemplating her love for the small, sharp weapon.

Hours of rubbing with oils, holding, and caressing had smoothed the mechBuck horn handle. As had hurling it through the air into a tree trunk until she could slice the leg off an ant and leave the rest of the insect unharmed. Embedded in the handle were shiny bits of oyster shells that were luminous in their shimmering beauty.

Sakima lifted the animal's back leg and took her time deciding where to cut first. She felt around near the groin, then up the stomach and back along the spine. She knew how to do this, and she'd done it before, but never with an animal bigger than a squirrel. Squirrels were easy; you could stab anywhere, then peel off the skin and fur in practically seconds. This bear might take hours to prepare.

"Sakima!"

For the third time in less than an hour, Sakima's heart jumped, and because she was in an awkward crouching position, she almost fell backward.

"Oh!" she said, cursing her inattentive ears.

As she stood up and turned toward the familiar voice, she sheathed her beloved *chessi* knife with care, shut her eyes, and gritted her teeth.

"Sakima. We have been looking everywhere for you," her father shouted. He crashed out of the underbrush with the grace of a malfunctioning mechBoar. "Your mother is very worried about you, my daughter!"

Nimàt, Sakima's younger brother by a little over two years, followed next. He tripped on a tree root and flailed his arms to keep from falling. Sakima rolled her eyes without thinking and looked away from her brother, who was now on the forest floor doing pushups. He was trying to cover the fact that he clumsily fell by pretending he had intended to hit the ground and do a quick set of ten. It fooled no one, least of all Sakima. But nobody ever called Nimàt on it.

Sakima turned her face to her father and addressed him. But not with the full respect that he deserved with his station as the ruler of her world—the king, the *Gegeyjumhet*—and as both an Elder and her father.

"Why?" she asked. "What is bothering her this time?"

"Watch how you talk to me." Her father stopped walking toward her and stood in the clearing, glaring at her. "And most certainly check how you speak about your mother."

"I am sorry, Father. I—"

"Your mother told me you had gone running off to the forest again, by yourself. Which is an extremely dangerous, and stupid, thing to do."

"I did not run. And I go to the forest all the time, practically every day."

"She saw you heading for *Tèkëne*, alone. She immediately summoned me and Nimmy to come find you and get you home safely. I had assumed you'd run into the woods to be alone and play out your warrior fantasies. I wanted to get to you before you got too deep into..." His voice trailed off. It was only at this moment, remarkably, that he noticed the mechBear on the ground, all its lights gone dark.

"What is *that* doing there?"

"Do not worry, Father. It is terminated. Although I have to say it nearly clawed me to death before I was able to elude it and shut it down."

"Well, I can see it is a terminated mech. What I mean is, how is it that a dead *mechmàxkwi* lies there in a patch of sun, flies buzzing around its wounds?"

"I killed it," Sakima said, standing proud and smiling.

Takachsin stared at her disbelievingly.

"I destroyed its CPU and internal networking system. That is why the bioFlies are there, released automatically upon termination. Proof!"

"*You?* That's the biggest bear I have seen in quite a while," her father said. He pondered the situation for a second. "Well, at least this close-up."

"*You, Sakima? No way!*" echoed her brother, getting up from the ground and clapping dirt and pine needles off his palms. "Then again, maybe so. A big bear, taken down by a big pain in the ass!" He laughed loudly.

"Son," Takachsin said, giving Nimàt the side-eye. "Give it a rest."

"Yeah, *këlulël!* Screw you, man." Sakima's mouth was down-turned, her eyebrows drawn together. But her love for her brother was in her eyes. "Had this mechBear been after *you,* Nimmy, you would be as dead as it is now."

Her father laughed. "I don't question that," he said. "Son, you have certain skills, but staying out of trouble is not one of them."

"I'd have killed it. Sakima just got lucky. She said herself the thing nearly killed her, nearly clawed her to death. I'd have shut it down before any danger. She got lucky."

"Not luck. *Skill,*" Sakima countered. "I only told you how close he got to show you how amazing my escape and my ultimate victory was. You would have cried like a baby, Nimàt."

"Enough," Takachsin said before Sakima's brother could lift his jaw from where it had fallen. "We need to get this beast home. It is getting late, and we must prepare to keep the mechWolves and mechCoyotes and the repliVultures from making your victory theirs."

Sakima drew in her lips tight and frowned. *Here we go again,* she thought. She put her hands on her hips and breathed out her anger hard through her nose.

"Hear me out, my daughter," her father said. "I know you think you are a warrior. I know you practice shooting tech arrows and throwing your optiKnife—*Kishelë* knows why! But there is no such thing as a woman who fights. A woman against a man? That can't be considered."

Her father, Takachsin Tamanend, known affectionately within the tribe as "TeeTee," stood with his arms crossed and his chest pushed out. It was a posture of his that Sakima was quite familiar with. He rarely used it at home, and not with her—only occasionally with her mother. It was his "stance" when addressing the members of Sakima's clan because TeeTee was their leader, their Sachem. Her father slowly shook his darkly tanned head back and forth.

"It is unfair to both the man and the woman," Takachsin went on. "Because the man holds back and does not use his full killing powers. The woman will die a quick, embarrassing death. By dying, she brings shame to the male warrior my god, Sakima, listen to me, would you? It would bring shame to his people, his village, his clan."

When he had finished talking, he hung his head, as if mimicking the ridicule such an incident would inflict on him and his family. Behind him, his son, Nimàt, was distracted by a butterfly dancing past on an unpredictable flight path. Nimàt turned to watch it and before long he had wandered off into the woods to follow it with wonder and love.

"I killed it," Sakima said in a sharp whisper, "so it would not kill me!" Tears filled her eyes, making her dark brown irises shine more than normal. She fought back the tears and her familiar sorrow, sorrow caused by the constant pushback by all against her being a warrior, a fighter, a hunter. Any of the so-called "male only" abilities.

Her father squinted at her as if waking from a dream and slowly realizing what was happening. "I am glad you are not dead, Sakima. What I was trying to say... and I am not a man whose words flow freely when talking to his daughters... is that I wish you were not here, um, with the bear. I would prefer if you were home making fry bread with your mother. If you must have your strolls through the forest, I wish a real warrior, a great man like Machto, your brother-in-law, was here to protect you!"

With that, Sakima let out an exasperated yelp and flung her hands to her sides.

"What?" her father said. "What did I say wrong?"

"You should know Machto as I do!" Sakima spat on the ground. "Please, leave me. I am fine. Let me strip this bear. You can help carry the reusable components and bioMeats back home."

"No, Sakima! It's forbidden. I forbid this language you use. I will not allow you to keep talking in this way like you're a man! You are a *shiki skixkwe*, a beautiful young woman. You ought to be gardening, harvesting, making food to eat. Not slaughtering mech-Beasts. Not skinning and butchering and cleaning them. That is man's work. Sakima, listen to me: you must stop this. You have got to give up this *tèpahtu*, this stupid idea!"

Sakima stomped away, nearly growling. She shoved past her brother, who had just returned cradling the butterfly in the temporary cage he made with his two cupped hands. When she bumped hard into him, his hands separated and the insect escaped, flitting into the upper boughs.

"Ah, Sakima. Look what you did!"

She didn't answer him; she just kept moving, from a stomping exit march to a jog and finally to a full run. Through the bushes and trees, branches slapping her legs and arms and face. She didn't care. She wanted to get as far away from them—from *every* man— as she possibly could.

Sakima mostly followed the trail that she and her people used, a trail created by bears and deer. Sometimes she used shortcuts through the trees and bushes off the path.

Sakima's thoughts drifted to her father. *Why can he not see me?* she thought. *He has known me forever, and he says he loves me, but he does not act like it. He treats me like a child, and I am almost twenty years old. Well, in two and a half years, anyway.*

Sakima ran on, her steps slowing a bit after a while.

And Mother. I am tired of her always picking at me, of her never understanding me. I should run away from home. Yes, that is what I will do. I mean, I am a little old for the actual "running away" part, but I can go, pack up my stuff, and get out of here. Go to the other side of the world. Maybe some other clan will accept me. Maybe even our hated enemies? I do not care anymore.

Sakima took a deep breath to calm her nerves. She stood in a small clearing now, listening to the birds singing in the trees while a pleasant breeze caressed her back. There was saltwater in the air. It was one of her favorite things, the sea. Cooking clams and oysters and eating them by the crashing waves. She missed that. Her family hadn't been to see *kitahikàn shohpe*, the seaside, in years. Father was always too busy running the clan. Mother helped him with that, while also tending to the crops and taking care of the children. It had not been an easy time.

Sakima peered into the bright blue sky. From up there somewhere had come the Star Walkers, the *Alànëmëskat*. The Mannahatta legends called them the People Who Fell From the Sky. They arrived from the multiverse with marvelous technologies, magical elements, and deep scientific knowledge. They changed everything on Mannahatta for the better, and forever.

My ancestors of long ago lived in humble houses built from branches, Sakima thought and smiled. *Wîkëwams and longhouses. Our best technology is comprised of just stone arrowheads.*

But the *Alànëmëskat* and Mannahatta cultures interconnected in their equal love for the Spirit World. The True People and the Star Walkers communicated with each other through Vision Quests. Thus, the two cultures shared visions of the future even though they did not yet have a shared language.

CHAPTER 3

Sakima trotted along until she finally burst out of the *Tèkëne* forest and into the middle of *Tùkwsitàk* village where her home was located. Taking what she hoped would be a shortcut, she passed through a neighborhood she knew all too well: the outer edges of the *Tùkwsitàk* village. Her sister, Amimi, lived there with that disgrace to the Wolf Clan, Machto Pequonitto, and their new baby, Mimëntëta.

The sun shone brightly now that the clouds had parted and the brief rain that had started minutes ago had stopped. Sakima passed the row of monuments to Lapowinsa, the glorious Chief of the Mannahatta from ancient times, and then past Moskim's statue, the Rabbit Hero of myth. She smiled at the funny character as she walked past some other famous faces, both human and animal.

The air felt cooler, carrying the scent of wild gardenia, which she loved. Her grandmother's garden had overflowed with them—the off-yellow ones and various shades of white and cream. Her grandmother had sometimes filled her living room nearly floor to ceiling with those blossoms in what seemed like hundreds of vases. As Sakima jogged along, breathing deeply, the flowery bouquet became overtaken by another, stronger scent. Sakima crinkled her nose in disgust: manure. The stench wafted over from the cornfields across the open meadows of grass and flowers.

Artificial excrement from the digestive tracks of *sisilieyòk*, mechBison. In the past, this included metal shavings from operational gears and levers in the mechBison migrating to the digestive tracks of the beasts. This resulted in the minerals from the shavings leeching into the root system of the *xàskwim* stalks, then into the ripened corn later harvested that the people ate.

But a team of scientists and graduate students had fixed the problem of the metal shavings ending up in mechBison spoor, making all harvests clean and safe again. That was a noble victory, and Sakima fondly remembered the ceremony of thanks and the big celebration after. Her smile faded. The party had taken place a year after her Pat had died, and now she felt that sadness all over again, fresh in her heart where he still lived.

A few minutes later, she turned the corner and headed across a large field of grass toward her home. There, she spotted her little sister, Tangetta, sitting on the bottom step of their porch, playing a game of pretend with her homemade figurines. Tangetta preferred these over many of the modern manufactured dolls she owned. Scattered around the small child were her pickup sticks and cup-and-pin toys of varying sizes and colors.

Sakima grinned at her little sister as she approached the back-yard and neared the porch. She found it funny that Tangetta once again wore her ridiculous mechBear cub suit, even though it was now two years old, tight, frayed, and worn. She noticed the dirt on the knees and elbows. The outfit, pajamas really, had fake fur all around and the hood had plastic bear's ears sticking out on each side. Tangetta's real left ear peaked out from the hood where the bear's ear had loosened and tipped away.

"What are you up to, Tangetta?" Sakima said, now with a big smile on her face.

Tangetta twisted around to look at her big sister, not at all surprised that she was there with her now. "Okay, I've got a city all figured out," Tangetta said. "See?"

Sakima removed her bow and placed it on the ground, then squatted next to Tangetta. "Oh, you have a city, do you?" Sakima's smile grew even bigger as she stroked the top of Tangetta's head. "Come on and tell me about it."

"You see," Tangetta said, getting up and rushing to the setup she'd created on their front lawn. She smacked her lips for a second and then licked her top lip, which was chapped, preparing herself for the serious dissertation she would deliver. "These are the buildings, for example." She reached over and pointed to various stacks of clamshells and oyster shells.

"And these are us!" Tangetta walked a couple of paces to gesture at some shiny, smooth stones positioned in a circle at the center of the stacks of seashells. "You, Mommy, Daddy, and Nimmy."

Tangetta walked along a bit further. "And that's Mimi and Uncle Machto and their new baby, Mimëntëta." She waved at three small stones about two feet from the center of the "city." Then she walked over to the steps where Sakima crouched and sat down.

"Is that all?" Sakima said. "I see more things. For example, those big rocks. Which buildings are they?"

Tangetta tilted her head and nearly folded herself in half from her waist down. "Those," she told her sister with a very serious tone, her lips squeezed tightly together, "are the monsters." She jabbed her small finger toward the three large rocks with sharp edges. Moss, like a beard, grew on top and down one side of the biggest rock.

Sakima remained still, her eyes wide, surprised by her sister's revelation. Then she spoke. "Monsters? What are you talking about, Tangerine? There are no such things as monsters." Sakima hoped she sounded convincing. She tried to laugh, but something like a cough came out instead.

"Don't say it like that!" Tangetta shouted, standing up and

staring at Sakima. "Of course there are monsters, Sakima, everybody knows that!"

"Okay, okay. Calm down." Sakima smiled as she put her arm around her sister. "I just do not want you to worry about those types of things is all."

"But I have seen them, Sakima. I have! At night, out my bedroom window."

Must be nightmares, Sakima thought. "Okay, look. If there are any monsters in the world, they cannot hurt you. You know why?"

"Why?"

"Because I will not let them!"

Tangetta appeared to contemplate that notion for a moment, squinting up thoughtfully at the dark storm clouds collecting again in the sky. "But Sakima, they do stare at me in my bedroom. I close my eyes and pull the sheets over my head so they can't see me. When I look again, they're still there. Only closer..." Tangetta took in a sharp breath.

Sakima felt chills on the back of her neck. What her kid sister was describing sounded so real. "Okay, fine. But do not be scared. They will never get you, I promise." She moved down closer to Tangetta, giving her sister's shoulders a quick, tight squeeze. It surprised Sakima how tense her sister's body was, like hugging a stone statue instead of a girl.

Tangetta wiped her nose with her tiny index finger. Sakima couldn't tell if her sister's drippy nose was just because she was a little kid—as little kids seem to always have drippy noses—or because Tangetta had been crying.

"Easy, there, Tangerine. Take a deep breath." The two sisters pulled apart gently to look at each other. "You will be fine, I promise. You know I will protect you—forever!" Sakima patted the quiver of arrows on her back, then stood up. Sakima picked up her bow from where she'd placed it before. She mimed shooting it, holding it up near her face and pulling the string again and again.

"Zoom, zoom, zoom. The monsters are dead! One after another.

Look, a great big ugly one! What a stupid face it has! It thinks it has a very scary face, but I think it is just dumb—*tèpahtu*—and I laugh at it." Sakima fired imaginary arrows at the tip of a pine tree across their yard, high above them. "Zoom, zoom, *zoom*! This freak needs many arrows before it will fall! And many more to kill it. There, it is dead now. No *tèpahtu* monster can defeat your mighty Sakima!"

Tangetta laughed out loud and hopped up to hug Sakima, her thin arms wrapped around Sakima's waist. "Thank you, Sakima, thank you! I knew you could defeat them!"

After Tangetta released her tiny hug, Sakima said, "Well, I have to go inside now. Mother is waiting to talk to me."

"Will you be going monster hunting after that?"

Sakima's eyes widened in surprise. "Hah. Tangetta! Why would you even ask that? No, that is not what I am planning to do!" Sakima winked at her sister.

"What if you run into a scary monster one day and it wants to kill you and eat you all up?" Tangetta made growling noises, exposing two rows of tiny, white teeth.

"I will shoot it down with my arrows; that is what I shall do! And slice it up into pieces with my trusty knife, my *chessi*! Then I will eat it—turning the tables on it. What do you think about that idea?"

Tangetta's face turned pale as a ghost, her eyes filling with small tears. Sakima knew that she'd gone too far with her monster-killing tale. "No, no, Tangetta. I misspoke. I mean, I would use my knife to pin its tail to the ground. Then I would come get you and show you that the monster was a threat no longer."

"Okay, Sakima, I would like that. Then I could take your knife out and stab, stab, stab!"

Sakima's mouth fell open, and she gaped at her sister. *Had she, Sakima, just created a monster?*

"And he would say, 'ouchy, ouchy'!" Tangetta said, laughing hard, her eyes squeezed tight with joy.

Wow, there's a lot this miniature human doesn't understand, she thought. "Gotta run, kid," Sakima said.

"Can you teach me arrows?" Tangetta asked her, surprising Sakima again as she headed up the steps.

"Well, I do not know. Why?"

"So I can be brave like you and fight the monsters."

"Look, Tangetta," Sakima leaned over and put her hand on Tangetta's tiny shoulder, "You should let Mom teach you what you need to know. I can only teach you things you will never use, that will get you into trouble."

"No, Sakima, I can do it! I'm good at it, like you! You don't get into trouble."

Sakima chuckled. "I do, though; I do all the time. Okay, now I really have to go."

"Okay, Sakima. When you come back, you teach me arrows, okay? Promise?"

"Wow, Tangerine, you stay on point, right?" Sakima laughed gently. "I will think about it. How does that sound?"

"What's 'think about it' mean?"

"I will weigh on the one hand…" Sakima said, sticking her left hand straight out in front of her, palm up, "your desire to learn about warrior skills and the affairs of men. Knowledge that will make your life miserable and your mother and father very sad indeed. On the other…" she said, doing the same with her right hand as she had with her left, "what if I do go ahead and train you in all that I am the best at. What if you were to become better than me? I could not allow that!" Sakima laughed.

"I will never be better than you, I promise! Okay, Sakima? I'll stop myself from getting any better right before I'm almost as good as you. Okay? So, *pleeeease…*" Tangetta batted her eyelashes, holding her hands in a prayer-like supplication.

"I showed you my two hands, Tangetta. That means I will consider it but I am not promising anything. You get me?"

"Fine, fine, I get you, Sakima. You still have to tell me what hand becomes the winner. Okay?"

"Deal," Sakima said, stretching out a fist toward her little sister. Tangetta bumped Sakima's strong fist with her little one, as hard as she could.

"Got to run. For real this time," Sakima said in her softest voice. "We can discuss all this later. Deal?"

"Deal!" Tangetta hollered, reaching her fist up toward Sakima, this time initiating the bump.

Sakima paused and then tapped the small fist, chuckling quietly to herself. "You are quite something," she said, shaking her head.

"So are you," Tangetta said, giggling and flopping herself down onto the grass to return to her "city."

Sakima felt a couple of raindrops and raised her palm to test the air. "Looks like rain's coming again. Seems like bad news on the way…"

CHAPTER 4

Sakima entered her house through the backdoor. As she made her way down the hallway toward her bedroom, in the background she could hear her mother banging away in the kitchen working on dinner. It smelled wonderful.

She entered her bedroom and paused in the middle of it, silently saying goodbye to her childhood. She sighed deeply as she scanned the room, as if she were studying a museum recreation of her life. As far as she was concerned, it was now time for her to go prove herself, well, somehow. Despite everyone telling her that being herself was the wrong thing to be. That there was no such thing as a woman warrior. That she would fail and embarrass her family. *Why live, if you can't be who you were meant to be?* At seventeen, she felt she had already waited too long to do this; there was no time to contemplate further. She needed to leave—and soon.

First, though, she had to get organized. Sakima paced around her room. *Now, what shall I take on this initiating mission? What will I need?* She noticed two of her older quivers of arrows, no longer in use. She'd stacked them together in the corner of her room near her window. The small and faded pale red quiver held a dozen arrows.

The other quiver stood taller, and wider, and was a deep brown in color.

The larger quiver held all the arrows Sakima had over time examined and rejected, one by one. These were the arrows that, no matter how carefully she calibrated them, would never fall within the narrow spectrum of strength and straightness required to hit a target. Her adjustments to the arrow's built-in electronics and CPU for distance settings, flight trajectory, and power on impact never fixed what was wrong with these arrows.

What good is an arrow—regardless of how hard it hits or how far it can travel—if it cannot fly true, if you cannot be certain it will hit the target you have taken aim at? Sakima thought. *No good at all.*

Sakima smiled broadly as she grabbed the full quiver and leaned it against her bed. When she returned from this journey—*if* she returned—she would try again. Maybe she'd missed a step when she attempted to recalibrate the broken arrows in the past.

But if she was unable to do so, she'd take them up to her favorite place in the world: the peak by *Nagatamen Mùxul Allanque,* the Trusted Starship. She'd shoot them off the top of that high point —the highest for miles—just for the fun of it. Watch them fly and dance along their ridiculous anything-but-straight trajectory. It would be a fitting way to deploy those defective arrows. To send them flying through the forest to strike wherever they might.

Next, she examined her bows—she had three in total. The first was small and rose-pink. Her father had given it to her when she was a little girl of eight, back when he hoped Sakima's interest in archery was merely a phase. She outgrew that bow quickly, as it only shot short arrows with blunt tips. It was designed to be aimed at flimsy paper targets made especially for children. Safety Archery Kit, it said on the box. "For real warriors."

Sakima's mother had presented her next bow, a gorgeous gleaming gold color, on her twelfth birthday. Like her father, her mother also assumed Sakima's desire to be a warrior was only a preadolescent thing and that she would soon outgrow it. Yet, her mother enjoyed how much Sakima loved her archery games and practice sessions. She couldn't help indulging her daughter with that gift, for the last time, though. Her mother hoped Sakima would, after this and at last, put away her youthful, harmful dreams.

The third bow, Sakima's pride and joy, was the one she'd used earlier in the day—the one she always had with her. The bow was gray and black, with touches of burnished copper throughout. It looked fierce and serious. It stood tall and strong, almost muscular somehow, and capable of the best tricks. Sakima had once shot two arrows at the same time from it, but only that one time. Sadly, she could never recreate that incredible feat of hitting two targets side by side with a single pull of her bowstring. Endless practice had so far not reproduced that extraordinary result.

Sakima grabbed her bow-cloth and perched on her bed with the bow. She lovingly polished the wood and metal with a cloth, cleaning off old dirt, rain spots, and bits of grass. She dabbed a second, smaller rag in the wax and ran it along the string a few times until it shone. Then she returned to buffing her cherished bow, quickly bringing a fresh glow to it, as if it were lit from the inside. As her last task, she applied leather polish on the bio-leather strip of the bow's grip and massaged it in so that the handle would remain soft and flexible.

Sakima said, "Tuner, please," and a small computer the size, width, and shape of a maple leaf in autumn floated off her wall to hover about chest-high in front of her. She touched the front panel with a well-practiced finger pattern. Purple-pink ripples echoed out from where she had tapped the screen. The waves increased in size but decreased in intensity as they reached the edges of the computer's touchscreen.

In reaction, the top and bottom tips of the bow responded by glowing and pulsing, first only slightly, then with a purple glow so dark it was almost black. As the ripples on the gadget bounced from Sakima's fingertip to the edge of the device, over and over, the bow tuned itself to perfection. Finally, the tips glowed a cyan-turquoise hue. Sakima finished bringing both the bow and the string to perfect conditions, with no overstretch in the string and no weak points in the bow.

As the maple leaf technology floated slowly back to its perch on the wall, Sakima placed the bow on her shoulder and slid it around to her back. She did the same with the quiver, setting it carefully behind her other shoulder.

As a soft summer rain began to plink against her open window and pattered on the sill, Sakima strolled over to her knife collection. A display case on the wall over her headboard held five knives, each with its own unique capabilities. She lifted the clear cover, and it stayed raised up in position.

The first knife in the row was tiny—about two inches long and pink. This had also been a present from her father, this time when she was only six years old. The blunt blade couldn't cut anything, but at the time, the younger Sakima had thought it was the finest gift ever.

The knife next to it was blue and had two closed blades; the larger blade opened on one end and the smaller one across from it on the other. This knife could cut, but not well, and the "big" blade measured only four inches long.

The third of the blades lay in a sheath, and unlike the previous two knives, didn't open or close but was always available. This weapon was the first of this type Sakima had ever owned, and it was given to her by her favorite uncle, Uncle Pahòke. It was five and a half inches long and fine for cutting small things like thin branches while also pretty good for throwing—but not great.

The fourth was a tiny bit larger and had been Sakima's first to contain built-in electronics, which she found amazing at the time. She could set the target or the distance, and it would fly true from her hand and never, ever miss. This kind of accuracy made the young Sakima feel like a fearsome warrior with true abilities. This was also a gift from her father, and she loved showing off with it. It had a boomerang setting that let her toss it through the air, the weapon returning to her palm safely each time, slowing down before softly touching her hand.

The fifth blade was already in the sheath at her waist: *"chessi,"* her favorite. Her parents had presented this one to her as well, also on her birthday. It was the posthumous gift from her brother Tommy. He'd wanted it to be hers and that was why it meant so much to her. Sakima patted the handle of the knife gently, like petting a tiny cat. As her eyes misted over, she worked carefully, so as not to trigger the nano-defense system that would target the nearest threat. Once in Sakima's grip, the knife was programmed to find the best insertion point for inflicting various levels of damage, up to and including death.

She'd take *chessi* with her, naturally, as well as the one her father gave her, with its targeting and return-to-hand features. She retrieved that one from the display case. Then she turned, walked over to her bookshelf, and removed the matching sheath off one shelf, then slid the blade into it. She attached it to the belt on her waist, directly across from *chessi*.

The drizzle outside increased, changing from intermittent drops to a steady downpour. Lightning carved through the sky, reminding Sakima of the laser scapulas in the school lab when she used to examine small bio-animals last year.

Almost ready.

Sakima approached her nightstand, where she kept a small tree branch embedded in hardened clay which she'd made when she was twelve. Hanging from it were two necklaces. The first, a cherished gift from her now-gone boyfriend, Pat. It had a lovely fake gem set against burnished wood. A thin leather strip formed the necklace. She still loved that choker, but for many reasons, she would not take it with her.

The other necklace had belonged to her mother. Sakima slipped that strand off the short, narrow branch it was draped on. She smiled as she watched it flow through her fingers until it dangled below her outstretched hand. This one was made of braided silver. A shiny disk displaying the Mannahatta symbol for *kishuxa,* the moon, hung at the end of the chain. Her mother told Sakima she should always reach for the moon and never give up.

Don't worry about that, Mother, Sakima thought. *I will reach even higher than the moon, further into the galaxy. And your daughter will do just fine as a warrior—the one thing you do not want me to be. But I know you love me.*

Sakima was about to slip the necklace around her head and onto her neck, but with a swift motion, she raised the moon to her lips, kissed it, and dropped it back again onto the branch.

Do not want to lose you, she thought with a sigh. *Well, there is only one more thing to do. Say goodbye to Mother and Tangetta and I will be on my way, at last.*

She hurried through her bedroom door as it slid silently open for her.

CHAPTER 5

Sakima made her way through the house and over to the warm kitchen filled with the delightful smells of stew and bread. The pristine walls of the room were bright white. Gleaming metal appliances filled most spaces. She found her mother by the stove, busily preparing dinner. Sakima picked up a shiny apple, casually examined the fruit, and then crunched into it before speaking.

"Hi, Mom. Dad said you were looking for me? Well, here I am. What is up?" Sakima said between chews.

Her mother, Wùnita, chuckled, focused on the contents of the pots and pans simmering on the stove in front of her. "Cooking, cleaning, shopping, taking care of my family. You know, the dream life. What's up with you?"

"I have decided I am going on a quest."

"What's that, honey?" Wùnita said, bending slightly to adjust the flame under the largest pot.

"A quest. You know: an adventure. It is well over time that I set out alone to test myself. A Vision Quest!"

Her mother slowly turned around, and to Sakima's surprise, she looked at her with tears in her eyes.

"Mom…? What is the matter?"

Wùnita hesitated for a second. "Nothing, nothing, sweetheart. Onions," she said and sniffed. She wiped at her eyes with the back of her hand and then smiled bravely at her daughter. "So, what is this quest? Or should I ask, which boy are you questing with?"

"Mom, seriously! It is nothing like that!"

"Okay, okay. So…" Wùnita paused to take a deep breath. "What *are* you up to, then?" she said. She exhaled, a look of exasperation on her face—like she'd been here too many times before.

"Well, Mother, I cannot tell you. I cannot reveal anything. Not yet anyway."

Her mother sighed again.

"But I *will* tell you everything, when I return. Promise!"

If I ever do, Sakima thought. *That's the thing with Vision Quests; they can take you to far away, enchanted places with dangers unknown. I'm a great warrior and I know I will survive. Nothing is written in stone, it is only written on the wind.*

Sakima picked up a snack bag of mixed nuts, grabbed another apple, and then stuffed both of them into her side pack.

Her mother dried her hands on a small towel. Dropping the damp cloth on the counter between her and Sakima, she said, "Tell me what's really going on."

"All I am at liberty to reveal," Sakima said in a conspiratorial whisper, "is that I am traveling to *Tèkëne* forest, deep into it. The farthest I have ever gone!" Pivoting to the fridge, Sakima grabbed a water bottle and attached it to the loop on her belt before turning to face her mother again. "But like I said, I will be back as quickly as possible."

"Is this, um… " Her mother frowned, pulling her lips tight until they nearly disappeared. "Is this your 'warrior' fantasy again, honey? I thought we settled that. Didn't we? You are seventeen now, my daughter. Isn't it time you gave up all this 'girl warrior' *kèpchat*—this foolishness?" She twisted her mouth as if she had just smelled something terribly offensive.

"You never listen to me!" The sudden outburst from Sakima surprised both her and her mother; her emotions had become unexpectedly strong. "You do not understand me!" She pivoted away, jostling the statue of *Kishelë*, the Great Spirit of Mannahatta and the Creator of All Things. The two-foot-high, terra-cotta-and-shell edifice wobbled for a second and then pitched off its shelf. Sakima caught it, feeling the tiny chips of clam and oyster shells sticking into her palms. As clumsy as she first felt, she had to smile at how quickly she had reacted to catch the statue of the religious idol as it began to plummet.

Many years ago, the sculptor pressed the shells into the wet clay of the statue. The pieces completely covered the statue and gave it a dull but pretty shine. It was her mother's favorite object in the entire house, but Sakima glared at the thing in her hands with a level of anger at the moment that surprised her. She wished the stupid thing wasn't just an idol but actually *Kishelë*—she was sure the Great Spirit would understand her and why she had to do this. To go to the forest and test her skills. *It is time,* she thought, *to prove myself at last, or retire my dream of being a warrior forever.* The forest was full of predators, and she needed to show that she could survive in there. Show herself, if not anyone else. Because no one else seemed to care.

"No, Sakima, it is *you* who refuses to listen to reason!" her mother said, snapping Sakima out of her reverie, rushing over to snatch her precious idol out of her daughter's hands to reposition it carefully in its wall alcove.

She marched back to the stove to attend to dinner again without saying another word. The family favorite, *salàpòn*—fry bread— sizzled in the pan while soup of lab-grown venison, corn, beans, tomatoes, and spices bubbled next to it in a towering *mpoalonium*-powered kettle.

The yummy aroma was so strong that Sakima grew furious at

the soup, with the sweet memories it fostered of laughter and love and family. It called her to remain home, stay safe, and not go off to discover her destiny, to learn whether she was talented enough, strong enough. With no wars on Mannahatta for decades now, testing herself against the odds in the forest was the only way to truly know.

Wùnita stirred the stew, making a *tch-tch* sound at herself for having let dinner nearly burn. She stood there facing away from Sakima, stirring the bubbling stew and adjusting the heat.

"But you must admit, Mom, our traditional ways, as important as they are, only help keep men in power and women 'in their place.' It's been that way since time began." She took a deep breath and pulled her shoulders back. "I want to be a warrior, Mother. It is not only my dream, but the very core of my being. I know it! To be a warrior just like Tommy! I was born for this; it is as simple as that. I feel it in my bones, in my soul, and in my heart. My whole life. I cannot turn away from that calling. I cannot be anyone but who I truly am. Why can you not believe in me?"

"Of course I believe in you, Sakima!"

"Well, it doesn't always seem like you do. Anyway, I do have to get going—"

"No! You are not going anywhere. Do you hear me?" Sakima's mother slammed the wooden spoon onto the counter, her back tense. "Are you being thick-headed or are you just being cruel?" Wùnita said, raising her voice. She spun around to glare at Sakima. Her face was crimson and dappled with tears. "They murdered your brother! And you know why? Because he lived the life of the warrior!"

Stunned, Sakima took a cautious half-step back. She spoke softly as if to counter her mother's loudness. "Mom, that was a battle with a renegade group of Mannahatta enemies. A surprise, a cowardly ambush."

She cleared her throat and swallowed with some difficulty before continuing. "They shot Tommy in the back with three arrows. Slaughtered the scouting party that accompanied him, too. He never got a chance to fight." Sakima sniffed noisily, her eyes full of tears to match her mother's. "Father told me all about it..." she whispered.

Her mother bit her lower lip but said nothing.

"Well," Sakima said, taking a deep breath. "That is *not* going to happen to me. No one will sneak up on me. I will never hesitate to fire at a threat! A threat to me, to Tangetta, to Father. To you, Mother."

Her passion surprised her, and she hoped her mother didn't notice that her hands shook. Her mother, though, had already returned to her cooking, her posture stiff.

"Don't be so childish, Sakima. You know nothing of those days, of what happened; you were not yet born when your brother left us. So, you have no right to speak of it." Then she wept hard, her hands on the counter and her shoulders shaking.

"Mother," Sakima whispered, her eyes wide.

"If you were to be a female warrior... I can't even say those two words together. *Xkweyòk ilaok*: female warriors!" Wùnita wiped away fresh tears that had flashed out of her eyes and rolled down her cheeks. "There is not even a Mannahatta expression for that, my daughter, don't you see? If you pursue this path, you will no longer be in control of your fate. I'm certain that you will be killed and at a young age. Just like Hìtami, my sweet, innocent Tommy!"

Sakima stared silently at her mother, watching her face melting into sadness, her lips slowly parting. Then Sakima spoke, nearly silent, "If you think that way, Mother, then you do not believe in me."

Sakima turned abruptly and stormed out of the warm and fragrant kitchen, again crashing into the effigy of the God of All Things. This time, however, it crashed to the floor before she could attempt to catch it, her reflexes overtaken by her emotions. The sacred idol shattered into a hundred fragments.

"Sakima!" her mother yelled in disbelief, covering her mouth in horror.

Sakima stomped to the foyer where shoes and jackets were neatly arranged. She glanced at the Mannahatta symbol for *tulpe*, the turtle, painted in pale silver on the wall about three feet wide and tall. It welcomed and blessed all as they entered or departed their Tamanend home. Sakima leaned against it, fuming as she slipped on her leather boots.

"Would you mind not touching the art?" her mother scolded, arriving at the front hall, her face bright red from both anger and the heat of the stove. "It's delicate, you know," she said so softly Sakima barely heard her. "It scratches so easily…"

Sakima exhaled slowly, trying to collect herself, to rise above her anger and hurt feelings. "Mom, I—"

"The traditional ways keep our clan, our tribe, our family, together; do you understand? Without them, we'd have nothing to guide us." Wùnita sighed, releasing the sharp edges of her anger. She approached her daughter and affectionately played with Sakima's quiver, adjusting it on her daughter's shoulder a bit better.

"You've knocked your quiver all lopsided," she said as she straightened the arrows in Sakima's quiver. "There!" Reaching behind Sakima, Wùnita stealthily added a brightly colored arrow from the umbrella stand into Sakima's quiver. "For good luck," she said with a mischievous smile.

"I appreciate that, Mother," Sakima said, smiling herself and calming down a bit, too, matching her mother's new tone. It amused Sakima how her mother attempted to pull a fast one. How her mother put so much faith into that ridiculous "lucky" arrow. To Sakima, it was the dumbest-looking thing she'd ever seen.

Whenever her mother managed to insert that arrow into her quiver over the years, Sakima had always found a way to take it back out. Despite her mother's intentions, the odd arrow spent far more time sitting in the umbrella stand by the door than it did in Sakima's quiver.

"Mother, I must go," she said, kissing Wùnita on her cheek.

"I know," her mother said, with a look of love and fear on her face, her lips trembling. She reached out and pulled Sakima close, squeezing her briefly before letting her go. "Be safe, my little one. More than that, be smart." She returned a kiss to her daughter's cheek.

They hugged for a moment and then Sakima ran straight outside, the front door "whooshing" shut behind her. She rushed off as fast as she could across the rain-soaked glen to get to the puddled streets and on to the neighborhoods that would take her to the opening of *Tèkëne* forest.

"Goodbye, my child!" She heard her mother's voice call out to her across the long and wide field behind her. "Be careful. Watch and listen for the mech-predators in the forest. And please, don't let it happen again; do what you must do to survive!"

Sakima dared not turn to look at her mother by the door because she knew she'd lose her resolve and run back to her, cry onto her breast, and never leave her childhood home.

But on the other hand, it had been almost three years, and Sakima wanted to forget it forever—the day she failed. Unable to let her arrows fly, she failed to save him. Now the rage was back as hot and dark as it had been when she and her mother fought in the kitchen.

Mother does not know what she is talking about, she fumed. *She has no right to remind me of it.* Maluwe—*damn it!*

CHAPTER 6

To distract from the sad memories falling darkly around her, Sakima forced herself to study the various homes and businesses she passed. While doing so, she saw a familiar sight: a house with a tall spire rising high into the sky, just like the one at her family's home. This one sat atop the house owned by the Winkalits, where her aunt and uncle lived. As her parents had done with her house, the Winkalits had implemented a design known as "modern longhouse."

SimGrass, along with chestnut and elm simBark, made up the thatched roof. Saplings of simTree materials formed the skeleton of the rooftop atrium, as well as the porches along the side of the longhouse on the upper stories. The tops of these saplings had been carefully bent and interwoven to create a dome-like shape. Grass and bark shingles created a natural-and-sim cover from the rain and hot sun. Sakima smiled, thinking about her aunt and uncle—an old-school couple, well-meaning and full of love for Sakima and her family.

Picking up her pace, Sakima darted through fields of corn and long grasses and wildflowers and soon found herself on the very outskirts of her village. Lost in thought, she entered *Tèkëne* forest. Crows mocked her from tree branches deep in the wood as she ran her hand across a natural hedge of boxwood, flicking the raindrops out in a semicircle back into the denser brush behind. A distant rumble of thunder made her look up to the sky, although the brief storm had long since passed.

She kicked a rock down the footpath and it landed in the nearest small puddle without joy in its bounce. A squirrel chittered nastily at Sakima from above, just out of her reach. As she gazed up at the creature, ready to give it her best stare-down, the fuzzy thing leaped from the branch it was on to another, showering Sakima with an unwanted extra dose of raindrops.

"Maluwe!" she said in her native Mannahatta tongue. "Damn it!" Sakima spat to take the dirty taste of the old tree out of her mouth. She licked her lips and found that the rain itself, however, tasted so good. As she wiped her forearm across her face, she heard a sound, the crack of a branch yet again, and sensed eyes were upon her.

She stopped and spun around, ready for battle. But the trail behind her was empty. She stared into the dark brush on both sides of the path, squinting to make out the shape of perhaps *xinkwtëme*: a wolf. Or even *kwèn'shùkwënay*, a mountain lion. Her vision always strong, she focused on the shadows hidden within the shades, but she discerned nothing frightening. She had traveled far from home now, beyond the outskirts of her village. Not unsafe—but not that safe either.

Sakima turned around again and peered on ahead where the pathway led deeper into the forest. A red cardinal swept low across her field of vision and then drifted up into the trees. Sakima took that as a positive sign and chuckled at her seemingly unfounded nervousness. She continued hiking, daydreaming about her brother, Nimàt—only younger by a couple of years—and the fun they'd had playing tag, chasing each other through the tall grasses and the wide bushes by their house when they were kids. Then, a vigorous slap on her shoulder brought Sakima quickly into focus on the now.

"No!" she gasped. She swung around, confused.

"Hey there, Sakima!"

Sakima's face hardened from fear to stone-cold hatred. She bared her teeth reflexively. *"You!"*

CHAPTER 7

"The one and only."

A tall, overly muscular man stood before her, hands on his hips. Clearly, he had experimented liberally with bioMech muscle formulas, including the black-market *wchètahsën,* or "stone muscles." *Wchètahsën* produced *"kèpcheonkèlët* rage," which could make someone act deranged at times, driven by anger and ego. The person who stood before her needed no chemical or biotech enhancement to act crazy because he already was.

She stared at her brother-in-law, Machto, who'd married her older sister a year earlier after he'd gotten her pregnant. The marriage had not been his idea, but rather the decision of their two clans collectively, who also enforced it. An old-fashioned *"tànkamikàn"* or "spear" wedding.

"What are you up to, sweet 'suhk eemuh'?" Machto sneered, trouncing her name into two words. He took a step forward and Sakima detected with repulsion the fox gland oil on his skin that Machto used to "attract the ladies," as he often declared. She hated that stink; it reminded her of death. The poor little fox. *Òkwës* should not be hunted like game; they were fellow hunters to be respected. No mechFoxes could yet produce this oil, so it always symbolized to her the passing of an endangered natural fox.

"What are you doing out here, Machto?" Sakima said. Despite trying to suppress her contempt, her lip curled with disgust.

"I followed you, my 'sister,'" he said, winking. He forced a smile, but it tilted south to become more like a drunken leer.

What is wrong with this idiot? Sakima thought. "You *followed* me? What are you talking about?"

"Yeah, sure. I saw you heading for *Tèkëne*. I sought you out for your own protection. You do know there are wolves and bears and wild piggy *mech-kwëshkwësh* out here? You should know that, as the big hunter-warrior *man* that you are, right?" His leer grew bigger as he leaned in to seize Sakima's right bicep. "Ooooh! That's solid. A true man's 'muscle.' Well, I got one too." He grabbed his crotch with his other hand and winked lecherously.

Sakima slapped at his hand on her arm. "Get lost, you weird creep." She wrinkled her nose. "Leave me the hell alone."

"Ah, is that any way to treat your savior? I came here, at great personal risk, to make sure *you* stayed safe and sound." He winked again, like he had a twitch.

"*Phwit!* Bullshit," Sakima growled.

"Again with the insults! Well, you have no gratitude, girl. That's right, no gratitude at all." He reached out, this time with both hands, to grab her by her shoulders. He made sure he brushed her breasts as he reached for her shoulders.

Sakima didn't feel it, though, because she wore a leather and steel vest for protection whenever she planned to head into the woodland. She wore it for another reason too: because the vest had once belonged to her brother, Tommy. It had taken her weeks to repair it and rework it to fit her much smaller frame. The garment had ceremonial markings of Mannahatta symbols. It required another two months for Sakima to weave in filaments of the sacred energy—*mpoalonium*—given to her people by the Star Walkers. She had woven in two strands, one down each side of the vest, running in parallel wavelike shapes.

Sakima pulled away from Machto's grip. "Let me go, you asshole!" she said, her voice rising in anger.

"Nope, you like it when I touch you. Am I right? Of course, I'm right!" He licked his lips suggestively.

"Screw you, Machto!" Sakima shouted. She turned and hurried on further into *Tèkëne*, her forest, her sanctuary, her escape. Before she had taken ten steps, she felt Machto's arms slime around her and form a tight bear hug. She tried to scream, but Machto had already reached up and covered her mouth before she could even try. Sakima, eyes wide open, dropped down and sent her fists hammering fiercely between his legs at his groin.

He wasn't a bad fighter, though. Sakima recognized this as he sidestepped the worst part of her strike. He tugged her closer and she smelled the *wëshkiyëm* on his breath because, of course, he'd been drinking whiskey in the middle of the day. Then, to her horror, he licked her neck with hideous and exaggerated slowness. Sakima kicked and squirmed to free herself. Finally, she bit down on his hand as hard as she could, but he quickly yanked it from her teeth, laughing.

"You're a feisty one! Damn right!"

But it was all the time Sakima needed. "My sister knows you're here?" she cried out with such anger that she sprayed spit into the air. Machto stalled. Then he let her go, giving her a hard shove as he did so.

"Shut the fuck up," he snarled.

"She'd love to learn about what you tried here. You *sànkweyòk*, you weasel!"

Sakima straightened her vest and pulled her quiver around to her back again. She bent over to pick up her bow where it had fallen when Machto violently grabbed her.

"You are nothing, SUCKima. I could kill you here, you know that? Easy. Your sister would never hear of what happened. You'd be dead, and nobody would care. Not one single person would give a shit about some little man-girl warrior. Not even your parents."

"Try it," Sakima hissed, teeth clenched, her eyes nearly slits, her jaw pushed out. She clenched the handle of her knife, *chessi*, at her waist, where she'd been unable to reach it earlier. "I would *really* like you to try it." She said this last in a hoarse whisper, her lips pulled tight. Sakima instinctively bent her knees and leaned forward slightly like the brave cat, *kwèn'shùkwënay*, ready to pounce. All muscles tense—if only she had fangs and claws!

Machto hesitated, his hand now on the handle of his knife, too. After a long pause, he let go and gave a loud laugh, his hands raised in supplication. "No, I don't need to kill a nothing, a complete nobody. I'd rather have you live your stupid life in shame: the Man Queen. The Lady King. You are neither a woman nor a man. You are an unnatural thing that the Spirits hate to look upon." His eyes grew dark, his sneer a grimace of loathing. The large vein in his neck throbbed. "You are too dumb to realize that this world you wish to escape from is *man's* world. Men do the hunting, fighting, killing. Men take whatever woman they choose and make them do anything they want. You're something like a girl, but I'm not totally sure, with your girl muscles and your angry face. Ha, ha!"

Sakima couldn't control her anger any longer. She stepped up to him and spat in his face. Then she spun around and sprinted as fast as she could into the forest.

"You bitch!" he yelled after her.

It is always 'bitch,' Sakima mused. *This is what they always say.*

"I'll deal with you later; you can bet on it," Machto hollered after her, but she was already out of earshot.

CHAPTER 8

Sakima sped on through the brush, tears stinging her eyes. How she hated those tears, being seen as weak and helpless—the *nshawësi xkwe*—"weak woman."

She pushed on through the thicket, oblivious to the pain from the small, thin branches whipping at her legs and stomach. Blind to the bugs that dinged off her face, then scuttled into her mouth. She spat them out, wiped her lips off, and kept running. After a few minutes of reckless running, she slowed to a stop and peered back over her shoulder.

The path was empty. Machto was gone—as if he'd never been there.

She stared for a long time—she wasn't sure how long—and then a white *òpinkwinakwsu* with its long snout and pink tail crossed onto the path halfway and stopped. The opossum must have thought better of it. It turned around and reentered the safe shadows of the undergrowth.

From far away, Sakima thought she heard her mother calling her name. Or maybe it was the wind playing tricks. Turning swiftly on her heel, still gripping the handle of her knife, she darted deep into the darkness and safety of her sanctuary forest.

Her mind wandered away from Machto's attack. He was dangerous, but a fool. *I will deal with him one day, and he will no longer be a blight on the Tamanend family name*, she thought. She grew satisfied that the moment would come when he would have to answer for all he'd done. Sakima couldn't think about that right now or about the inevitable conversation with her sister, Mimi, that she would need to have when she returned from her quest.

Sakima knew she had to get to the mountaintop, her refuge, the place where she could think and be at peace: Òhchu Peak. There, the visitors' monument rose high into the sky, *Nagatamen Mùxul Allanque*, the Trusted Starship. It should be easy to spot, glistening like a giant gem in the sunshine. So, she would go to the peak and rest there, maybe have a snack and drink some water. Sakima figured once she reached the very top, she'd determine the correct navigation to continue her quest.

She had the general direction of travel in mind—north and then west, toward what would soon be the setting sun. From the summit, she counted on making a more precise orientation. It would take fifteen minutes to slog through the rough terrain and dense forest of *Tèkëne* to get to Òhchu Peak.

The air had cooled down quite a few degrees thanks to the day's thundershowers. She caught the sweet scent of honeysuckle now that she'd entered the forest and traveled deeper into *Tèkëne*. The sharp, refreshing scent of pine and cedar came next, and Sakima took it all in with joy.

She kept the croaking of the frogs to her left. With the wetlands on that side, she knew Òhchu was on the other. She had her eyes peeled for predators, even though it was too early for most of them to be out hunting yet. She patted the knives on her waistband while feeling the reassuring weight of her quiver as it bounced rhythmically on and off her back as she ran.

She moved through the brush slowly, lost in thought about Machto's motivations and plans, her family, her few friends, and Tangetta. Before Sakima knew it, the path leading up to Òhchu Peak appeared, and she began her slow climb. Facing upwards as she went, she soon caught the glint of the *Nagatamen Mùxul Allanque* up ahead. It was often referred to by its acronym, NMA, pronounced "Nemma," which was a play on the Mannahatta word meaning "the thing to see." Sakima reckoned she'd be at nemma straight away.

She climbed through more sparse forest now, hillier than the area by her family's longhouse. She continued the challenging job of scaling up the side of the steep slope. At the summit, the woods thinned out to almost nothing, just large boulders, some bunches of grass here and there, and a handful of stubby bushes.

Sakima stopped to stare at the structure that had changed everything: "*nemma*." The gigantic disk-shaped object was about fifty *shaèk* (about fifty yards), across from bow to stern, or in this case, from top to bottom. About a third of the craft—sixteen *shaèk*—remained hidden in the dirt. Nemma had chopped the nearby hills almost in half when it screamed through the skies of Mannahatta out of nowhere, centuries earlier. The buried disk was wedged vertically where it had crashed, like an immense axe blade driven deep into the ground.

Even with a good chunk of it hidden underground, the ship was still an impressive thirty *shaèk* high, just over seven stories, another three of which were permanently embedded in the dirt. Small bushes covered the bottom of the disk where the structure had planted itself in the earth. This flora grew to about three feet high and about as thick across. Beyond that point, moss clung to the metallic craft mostly on the north side. Where the moss had not yet grown, she could still make out strange markings. These were not like early Mannahatta symbols that Sakima knew so well, yet they were similar. As if the people who had constructed the flying disk had spoken a comparable language to Mannahatta, and perhaps had a somewhat related culture. How that could be, she had no idea.

She wondered what it was like to fly such a spacecraft, where it had come from, and how it found its way through the Many Worlds, to her people. The Mannahatta had never built a ship like that; no one had ever been interested in such flight, what with the portal, the *Skontay Chìpilësu*, enabling people to travel to strange new worlds. But local flying machines—the hovercraft found everywhere on Mannahatta—were more than sufficient.

Still, the military forces had developed a virtual space flight training system that simulated all the tech that Mannahatta scientists had been able to develop. Because of her position in society, she had also had some training on the controls. Though it was more like a space camp than true training, she nonetheless studied it all intensely, because it if felt important to her to learn all those virtual dials and screens and controls, both hands-on and voice activated.

Sakima had taken to her spaceship controls simulator like a *namès*, a fish, to water. She spent hours in there, often having to be kicked out by her father when she was little, so that the actual warriors could get some practice. The simulated flight through virtual outer space was something she loved. Her shooting accuracy, flying and navigational abilities, and hours logged were the highest scores achieved so far. Though it could never be, she fantasized about controlling a real spaceship through all the galaxies within reach.

Sakima dropped to the ground and fell against the starship, panting. She pulled her quiver and bow off and laid them down beside her. After she'd eaten one apple and a handful of nuts and then took a few long sips of water, she realized that, despite her best intentions, she couldn't travel any more tonight. So much for great plans. Tomorrow would be different—she'd continue to new places, new discoveries.

She lay down, using her quiver as a rough pillow for her head, her hands clasped over her stomach, ankles crossed. As she watched the stars, her eyelids slowly fell, and she drifted into dreams.

CHAPTER 9

Tangetta lay in her bed after a delicious dinner—although she mostly ate only the fry bread. Her mother had read to her a story in a sad voice, although the tale wasn't sad at all, and had cut reading time short to announce that it was now bedtime. However, Tangetta wasn't sleepy. She had already explained that fact to her mother and her mother said it didn't matter at all. Seven-year-olds needed lots of sleep.

That might be true of every other night, Tangetta thought, *but it is not at all true for tonight.*

Tonight felt different, with how Sakima and Mommy had fought and how Sakima had been behaving. The broken statue that made Mommy cry. *They did not know I was listening,* Tangetta thought, *standing at the front door, peeking in through the screen.*

Tangetta pulled off her covers, which wasn't easy because her mother had tucked her in "as snug as a bug." It was more like she'd been strapped into place, and as if the straps were screwed into the bed frame. After rolling and kicking and flipping from side to side for a bit, Tangetta freed herself. She sat up and pushed away the rest of her sheets and blankets that still covered her middle and her legs.

She squirmed around until she was up on her knees on her bed, and leaning forward, she placed her elbows up on the windowsill. The bed was just the right height to do this. She rested her head on her arms and let the breeze caress her face.

Outside, she heard a big-eyed *kukhus* somewhere nearby going "hoo, hoo!" and a *tëme's* lonesome cry on some distant hill. It was so distant, Tangetta barely detected the lonely song of that young wolf. She heard it, though, because she had amazing hearing. Sakima had told her that once. So had Daddy.

Tangetta watched the trees swaying gently and scanned the skies, hoping to spot comets or spaceships, but the sun was still out since it was late summer. The sun would set soon, and then she'd see the space objects—she was sure of it. She continued to think about her sister.

What is Sakima doing? she wondered. *What secret adventure has she gone away to find? Has she gone off to fight monsters and will she ever come home again?*

Tangetta wished she could be just like Sakima, with arrows and knives and a brave heart. *I want to be like Sakima! Then she and I could go on adventures together.* An enormous smile grew on her face, and her eyes nearly sparkled in her darkening bedroom.

I wish I could walk beside her, have a bow of my own, and be a "worrier," too. And fight and jump and punch and shoot! Tangetta gazed up toward the night sky again. Closing her eyes, she made a wish to the Spirits.

Tangetta fell quietly to sleep with a smile on her face as she thought about her sister and all the cool things they would one day do together. The following morning, Tangetta hopped off her bed and planned her next actions. She wandered around her room, examining her stuff and humming as she went about her business, putting some things down, keeping others.

She stood very still in the middle of her room as she'd seen

Sakima do when she would get ready to practice her skills in the yard. Tangetta raised her tiny fist to her chest and with as much pomp and drama as she could summon, hit the area just above her heart with a mighty thud and then arced her pudgy arm to her side. *Exactly how Sakima and Father do it!* she thought, smiling.

Tangetta grabbed her favorite straw doll off her bed and tucked it into the waistline of her shorts. Then, taking a big, brave gulp of air, she signaled for her bedroom door to open. Tangetta ran downstairs and hurried to the back door. She slipped out of the house into the backyard.

This is going to be the best day ever, she thought. *Today, I become a "worrier"!*

CHAPTER 10

As the early morning sun just barely crept over the horizon and the blue jays squawked and crows cawed loudly, Sakima awoke, stood up, and gathered her belongings. Stretching with her arms high overhead, she peered down into the forest. *Where to now?*

With the sun still low in the sky, she discerned only vague outlines of the tallest trees. Slowly, the details of the distant landscape emerged: the individual trees, the largest of the boulders, all intertwined in morning mist. She wanted to squint to see more details, but she knew that would make things worse.

Sakima turned to face north. Her knowledge of the stars told her which way to stand. *Alànkok Luweyunk*—the North Star—slowly disappeared as the dark sky grew blue. She witnessed a streak, a comet, flying from one side of the sky to the other. Sakima smiled, amazed to see such a sight when it wasn't the middle of the evening. She nodded in respect to nature and the universe when the sudden snapping of a branch somewhere on the hill down below her startled her back into the here and now. *This forest is not empty,* she thought. *It is filled with a variety of creatures that can kill me.*

Sakima relaxed as she realized that the twigs snapping sounded small, and whatever was walking on them must be little, too. Like the furry, masked thief, *nahënëm*, or the dam-building worker, *tëmakwe*. Neither would be this deep in the forest. *Something else.*

Suddenly, she heard a noise like a squawk or a chirp from some small animal. *No, it is a bird, definitely,* Sakima thought. *It sounds like the giggling of a little kid. How could that be? A child here, deep in the wood and high on the mountaintop? That's a crazy possibility.*

Then she saw what was making that sound. A large, crow-sized woodpecker with a prominent red crest along the top of its head. A *kwèhkwès*, also known as a pileated woodpecker. Famous for the cackling it made that sounded like a child laughing.

Sakima smiled but also reached down and touched her knife, chessi, knowing that small birds and animals and even bugs were only a small part of the creatures living in the forest. She needed to stay aware and ready for trouble, just in case.

Time to move, she thought.

She proceeded down the mountain and reentered the forest. As she walked, she sometimes heard faint footsteps behind her, but nothing too disconcerting. It was likely *pupukwësh*, quail, or *tschikenum,x`* turkey. Sakima kept her eyes and ears wide open, and her grip on her knife tight. She'd throw it if necessary, but she'd rather not. Better a stab than a toss because it was harder for an animal to dodge, as opposed to an object flying through the air.

CHAPTER 11

Sakima squatted to pick up a stick and drew a crude outline of a *tulpe* in the dirt: a circle for the shell, as seen from above, and an oval for the head. Two small ovals represented each of the front legs, two larger ones for the back limbs. Then a narrow triangle for the tail. The turtle shape always calmed her. The solid shell meant home and safety; its slow pace meant confidence and deep reflection. Her family and her village were a part of the *Tulpe* Clan. She would rather have been of the *Xinkwtëme* Clan. While she had definite turtle-like qualities—bravery, loyalty, and stubbornness—Sakima knew she was more like the wolf: strong, fast, and deadly. A warrior.

Sakima stood up and breathed in again, deeply. She smelled the sweet scent of the jasmine flower and smiled. She opened her eyes and realized that she had no idea where on Mannahatta she was. With a slight tickle of panic, Sakima decided it didn't matter. She had her knife, her bow, and her arrows. This would be an adventure. She chose a tight, overgrown trail ahead and jogged toward it, confident she could handle anything.

Then, she was out of the forest, from shadows into light,

standing on a spot she did not recognize. Sakima had crossed from the rough *Tèkëne* trail onto manicured grass on the flattest piece of ground she'd ever seen. No hills—not even a bump or two. The perfume of gardenia and rose blossoms filled the air. Everything appeared staged, perfect, and located "just so." The grassy area where she now found herself stretched out further than many cornfields put side by side. The flat green carpet of it swept forward to end at a trail that was not sand or dirt but something black and smooth as glass. An enormous sign with white letters against a burgundy background squatted about fifteen feet away on the lawn. A garden of short-stalked flowers, including marigolds, surrounded the post. The writing on the sign formed these words:

LËPWEICHIK ÈLIKHATINK MANNAHATTA

The Technology and Research Campus of Mannahatta. Sakima recognized this place with a smile. So, this was the "back way" in, then. Through the forest to a probably off-limits alternative for entering the campus. In other words, a security problem.

Her father worked here. He used to bring her with him sometimes when she was little, but she hadn't returned since over a decade ago. She remembered he had hoped she'd take an interest in research, experiments—or whatever it was they did here.

Why spend your life sitting indoors on a chair under fake lighting? Where's the excitement in that? Still, her father told her there were discoveries to be made—more thrilling than any battle a person could ever be in.

Many more buildings populated this site now than back when Sakima visited as a young girl. At the time, there had been only one building with two more in the early stages of construction. Today she counted eight. Probably even more hidden from her viewpoint. The campus was now at least three times the size that it had been when she was a child. Sakima allowed herself to be impressed with both the place and how it had grown. With her father for being a part of it.

But fond memories would be of no use to Sakima right now. She needed to figure out exactly where she was geographically. She returned to studying the trail. It wound its way to a massive structure that jutted up into the sky like a small mountain. Neat and symmetrical, built from glass and metal. Sakima peered over at the structure. It was like nothing else on Mannahatta or any of the buildings in her village. It was taller and wider and more serious.

Yes, that is it. This is one serious building.

It both imitated and honored the classic longhouse design of the ancestors, but recreated in steel, glass, and oak. Carved Mannahatta words on the front of the edifice, above the immense doors, stated:

WĬKËWAM SHAWKEN OBROA

This was the Mannahatta Science, Research & Technology building. She tried to remember what they'd taught her in school: scientists doing important work, her father always insisting it was amazing. There were displays inside about old legends—mythical monsters, not real, just projections in glass cases. But she always wondered what else went on inside, beyond what anyone ever talked about.

She continued to survey the area, taking in the symmetric and geometric hedges and the groomed trees all about. A few benches lined a secondary path that appeared to Sakima to follow the perimeter of the grass field all the way around. No trail she could distinguish led into or out of the forest, other than the overgrown and long-since-abandoned pathway she'd stumbled onto.

No, this is interesting. She'd heard stories about the history of the visitors from beyond the world of Mannahatta. Strangers who had seemed friendly at first, like the *Shëwanahkòk*—the pale people— had been. Things changed the more these people saw how beautiful, lush, and full of game and other treasures the lands of Mannahatta held. She remembered one of the times her father had talked to her about the days when the change came.

Her father told her that, in the time of the peacekeeping, before the arrival of the Alànëmëskat—the Star Walkers, the People Who Fell From the Sky—were already in danger.

Idiocy and greed had become the two great pillars of almost all societies on Earth, he had said. People obtained what they wanted, no matter the cost to people, animals, vegetation, and to Mother Earth—*Kahèsëna Hàki*. No one cared about how they destroyed the planet for riches.

Soon, there'd be nowhere to build their fancy houses, her father had informed her. There'd be no place to shop, and no fine dining, should the world cease to exist in an unending state of destruction. Stupid did not care about consequences. Stupid just wanted to be rich and to party and have expensive things and show it all off.

When the Alànëmëskat, the Star Walkers, came; the *Shëwanahkòk*, the white people, disappeared. They took their guns, their greed, and their stupidity. Why? She recalled the look on his face, his eyebrows rising up with the question and then crashing down with the answer: Because they wanted our land, they wanted to take it from us one way or another.

When the Star Walkers, the People Who Fell From the Sky, brought their *xinkwi tàmahikàn*—their gigantic machines—they stopped all the madness. This ended the destruction of *Kahèsëna Hàki*, Mother Earth. The arrival of the Star Walkers brought peace to all the True People of Mannahatta.

Sakima couldn't help but smile as she remembered her father's story. Was it true or just a myth? It almost didn't matter.

CHAPTER 12

Sakima's focus returned to what she could see from where she stood: the front of the building and part of one side. She had wisely ducked back in among the shadows. She crouched behind a bush with its public-facing side trimmed to perfection, but its back, where Sakima now hid, as wild as the woods. Sakima kept still in the shaded area. She waited, gazed around her, and then with a start, she realized she wasn't alone. Someone else was cloaked in shadows about fifty yards away, up against the wall that faced the forest.

It was Machto!

He crouched by the lone window on the lower back of the wall. Machto had an animal with him at his side, but the shrubs and vines between where she hid and where he crouched partially blocked Sakima's view. Anyone who might come strolling up the path would likely not notice him there. Machto then took his knife out and worked it slowly along the bottom of the window sill and then up one side.

She wanted to move closer to the action. She spied a great place to hide much closer to where he worked: another big cluster of bushes and shadows. The problem was that she would be exposed if she were to run across the flat grass to reach it. So Sakima backed into the forest to try to approach Machto from that direction, under the cover of the forest. Sakima planned to reposition herself about six *shaèk*, or roughly twenty feet, from Machto—about a quarter of the distance which now separated them.

She glanced back at Machto, who had gotten down on a knee, pushing his knife like a wedge into the gap where the seal gripped the window. By the way he struggled, he seemed to be leveraging most of his upper body strength. Sakima couldn't see for sure, but if that *was* his knife, and it wasn't bending or breaking under the pressure, it could only mean one thing: that the blade was made of the same material as her knife, *chessi*, *mpoalonium*, the gift of the Star Walkers.

Sakima dove quietly back into the embrace of the woods. She didn't see a trail leading anywhere near her target destination, so she'd have to push through the thicket. It didn't appear to be too dense; it was mostly soft growth—fiddleheads and fern below the low branches. A few blueberry bushes and other plants filled some gaps, vying for sunlight. If she could force her way through all of that, she'd arrive in time.

As she progressed into the brush, she noticed a small opening close to the ground. It led to a trail that would give her better mobility. The bandit-masked, bushy-tailed *nahënëm* with its tiny black mittens probably created the path. Sakima crouched down on her hands and knees and moved through it. It soon became too low and narrow for her to continue in this way, so she lowered herself flat and snaked along.

After a short while, an exhausted Sakima stopped for a minute to lay on her stomach on the coolness of the forest floor. She blinked a drop of sweat off her eyelashes. The subtle perfume of blueberry blossoms drifted in the air. A bright yellow and orange caterpillar at her eye level seemed to stare right in her face.

"Hello, sister," Sakima whispered, smiling. "How are you today?"

The creature raised itself up on its many hind legs and continued to stare at Sakima. Then, assured that this young Manna-hatta woman represented no danger, it lowered its body again and crawled along the small branch, then deeper into the bush.

Sakima inched forward herself, plucking a pill bug from the dirt on the path. She lowered her head until her left cheek nearly brushed the ground. She made slow, steady progress until finally, she took a quick peep out of the brush.

She pulled herself immediately back under cover. *You fool. Use your ears, not your eyes.*

Sakima had miscalculated, misdirecting herself. She hadn't ended up a safe distance from Machto, which had been her plan. Instead, she found herself in the brush almost directly opposite him and beside a spot where someone had cut the fencing and bent it out of the way.

The sound of suction breaking with a *pop* caught Sakima's attention.

"There! We're in!" Machto whispered to himself, loud enough for Sakima to hear.

She dared to peek out between the rough branches of her hiding place. The yellow forsythia leaves grew thick there, providing her with excellent cover. She watched as Machto pulled the window from its casing and lowered it to the ground, laying it flat on the grass.

Then he lifted the little animal—maybe a pet wolf pup?—and lowered it through the window opening and onto the floor where she could no longer see it. There was something familiar about that pup, but Sakima couldn't quite put her finger on it, and she was still too far away to see real details. Machto then lifted himself into the opening, legs straddling the gap, one foot outside and the other in.

Sakima sneezed. *Oh, maluwe. Darn it! All this dusty dirt by my face.* She shut her eyelids and made herself as still as she could, listening for footsteps coming her way. Thankfully, none did.

She opened her eyes. Machto remained straddling the window opening, staring in Sakima's direction. She determined he was peering too far above her, though—thank Kishelë. Machto gazed for a while about the center of the bush, three feet above Sakima. Then his gaze drifted higher.

He's looking for someone who's standing or crouching here. Not some fool flat on the ground in a gap barely big enough for nature's small thief, *nahënëm.*

Sakima watched him shrug. Then he disappeared through the opening.

Once Sakima was certain Machto wasn't suddenly going to leap back out, she extracted herself from the bushes. She raced the short distance across the lawn, careful not to be seen. She waited for a second and listened. She heard no sounds of activity or talking or any such thing. With one last look around her, she climbed up through the window and into the building.

The strong and off-putting scents of different intensities of various cleaning solutions assaulted Sakima's nostrils. The disinfectant smell grew stronger as she reached the end of the short hallway she had landed in. Around the corner stood a mop bucket surrounded by orange cones. She looked up and down the hall before crossing it, continuing on her way. That's when she smelled the ammonia, NH_3. It wafted up from under the door of a room labeled LAB-12. Sakima had no idea what took place in LAB-12, but whatever it was, it needed a lot of ammonia to clean it up. Or perhaps the NH_3 was a byproduct of the experiments happening inside.

She hurried along the hall, trying to make as little noise as possible, and then turned the corner into a wide-open space. It was gigantic space, bright white, with bluish lights around the entire circumference about six feet from the floor. The arena, or whatever this might be, stretched farther up and across than any modern longhouse Sakima had ever seen. The ceiling was glowing, adding additional diffused ambient light.

In front of her was some kind of model, a full two stories high. Sakima estimated this cathedral space at about three times that height. The disk-shaped structure had lights of all around the outer edges. A few additional lights ran across the bottom. The disk itself tilted slightly and had windows at what Sakima took to be the forward face of the thing. From where she stood, she detected miniature seats and what might be control panels inside the craft, if that's what it was. It appeared to her to be a ship that traveled vertically, cutting through the air like a knife, instead of horizontally like a plate or saucer.

CHAPTER 13

The Mannahatta scientists in the room were the best in their field, the brightest minds in the entire tribe. Each of them had at least a master's degree and a Ph.D. One had two of each, and the oldest of the group had three Ph.Ds. They sat in the meeting room, while the talking whiteboard, the Nimbus Think & Draw 2000, guided them through their thought processes.

"Brainstorm session active: Problem 1171b-3," the whiteboard announced. "Please submit an alternative explanation for recent system breach."

"Well," said one scientist, "these cages are old. The technology hasn't been updated for over half a millennium."

"But that's an argument *in favor* of them not deteriorating," a second expert said. "Their tech has worked perfectly for every one of those five hundred years." She glanced at her watch nervously. According to her calculations, the breach shouldn't have occurred, yet it had. She took a deep breath. If someone had broken into our systems, *Kishelë* forbid, then that would mean the end of everything. All that they had built and protected—the advanced technologies for conquering disease and exploring the Many Worlds—

would be torn apart. "It's not a system malfunction, gentlemen," she said over the noise of the debate among the other scientists. "We have been hacked."

"That is patently absurd, Adrianna," a third scientist said.

"It's Dr. Cherryh," she said.

"Dr. Cordwainer, what do you think? " the man continued. He turned to face the other man while ignoring Dr. Cherryh's objection to his using her first name. "Hacking? Ridiculous."

"I agree. This is an impenetrable facility," said Dr. Cordwainer, smirking. "No one can get in who doesn't work here. Everyone has had a full security check. We update quarterly with new checks, searching for any compromised individuals. The network is completely isolated and impossible to hack. You'd have to be a brilliant programmer and a talented actor to carry it off. With an impeccable and unimpeachable background. Who would that person be? What Mannahatta would desire the destruction of his world? Absurd. These things, these monsters of our ancient legends, have no remorse. What drives them is an insatiable desire to kill. It's all they know."

"Regardless of the reasoning," Dr. Cherryh continued, "we need to face it, as impossible an option as it might appear to be. The only interpretation is that our systems have somehow been infiltrated."

"Nonsense!" The fourth scientist rose to his feet and slammed his fist on the table.

"No demonstrations of emotions, please," the whiteboard stated firmly. "No physical threats or threatening gestures. Rule 19a, page 147 in the Meetings Handbook, version 12.4.9."

"I apologize," the scientist said, remaining standing. Then he gestured at Dr. Cherryh like a parent reprimanding a child. "But to suggest that a system which has functioned superbly in defending against all attackers and malicious code might have failed—after all these years, centuries in fact!—it's insane" He paused long enough to allow his brilliance to sink in. "Our benefactors were not stupid people, Adrianna. They designed the software, the hardware, and the security mechanisms to perform flawlessly and they did so with perfection." He then sat back down with a triumphant sneer on his face.

Fervid whispering initiated among the team of scientists.

"Do we agree that we reject the validity of the premise that we were hacked?" the Think & Draw 2000 voiced. The machine drew a large X through the notes it had taken on the topic of system infiltration.

"Yes."

"Absolutely."

"Without question. Done. Over."

"*Këlulël*! Dammit! Wait a minute." This time Dr. Cherryh stood up. "I'm only asking you to keep an open mind. You're scientists, right? So, let's apply scientific methods here and not dismiss a theory before thorough analysis. Instead, we should try to disprove it." She strode to the door. "Will you all join me in a walk to the incarceration area, Area 21?" She opened the door. "Let's conduct a few more tests. You say there is no malicious code in our programs? Well, let me play devil's advocate then. Regardless of how well-crafted the intrusion is, it's not a matter of if we'll find it, but when."

General grumbling commenced. After a moment of this, the scientists reluctantly left their seats.

"Fine, fine," Dr. Cordwainer said. "For the last time, however. We've spent enough thought and energy already on this wild goose chase."

"Wild geese are easily caught and killed," Dr. Cherryh said. "I've never grokked that expression, frankly."

The T&D 2000 announced, "System infiltration re-added to the discussion list for tomorrow morning's meeting. I have sent materials to your notebooks. Please sign after you've reviewed it. Have a productive day!"

All notes and diagrams evaporated from the screen as the four scientists, led by Dr. Cherryh, marched out of the room and down the hall.

―――――

Sakima heard footsteps approaching. *Machto? No.* Because she could make out the melody of a woman talking and the quick, distinct tapping of her heels on the floor.

Sakima plastered herself against the wall. The surface was cold, but not uncomfortably so, and extremely smooth. She listened as the voices grew louder—one woman and at least two men. Panicking a bit, she surveyed the surrounding area.

There were a few doors down the corridor to her right, lining the outer edge of the cathedral-like room. She rushed to the first and stopped in front of it, but it would not open, nor did the glowing panel to the left of it respond to her waving hand or her touch.

The voices were dangerously close now, and Sakima stood exposed. She scurried to the next door, and this time heard the *whoosh* she had hoped for as it glided open to accept her. She dashed inside the room, the door barely finishing whooshing closed again as the sounds of talking and footsteps arrived. She crouched down in a dark corner. *Thank* Kishelë *I had not activated any lights or devices*, Sakima thought as she held her breath and waited.

The small group passed directly past the room where Sakima hid, apparently without taking any notice, and continued on their journey. Sakima stared at someone's lunchbox left on the table before her and a pencil on the floor as she waited for them to pass. Then a booming voice addressed her:

"Would you like to brainstorm? The Nimbus Think & Draw 2000 is ready whenever you are!"

"Who's there?" Sakima shouted, jumping to her feet, prepared for battle. Against what, she didn't know. She scanned the area hoping to figure out who was suddenly talking to her.

"Here, let me get you started!"

It was the whiteboard up front. An overly cheerful, somehow feminine—and quite loud—whiteboard.

"I'll draw a Venn diagram and you fill it in, okay? Does that work for you?"

Sakima noticed the whiteboard on the wall in front of her glowed with a slight purple tint. On it, a large feather-shaped cursor skidded across the center of the board to draw a set of ovals in the shape of a Venn diagram. The labels on each of the circles pulsed, like the heartbeat of an animal. Waiting for Sakima to tell the *Ntite Pikchëlhe*—the Think & Draw 2000—what she wanted for each label.

Sakima's mouth turned sideways, and she let out a long breath of air to calm herself. *Just a talking wall. No menace, except for how loud the stupid thing is.*

"Maybe next time," Sakima said.

She inhaled and listened at the door to determine if anyone had heard the commotion—someone who might pose an actual threat to her. Once she was sure the people had gone down the hall and weren't coming back, she exhaled and reached for the door. The shiny metal panel quietly slid open. She hurried through and toward the immense arena ahead of her.

CHAPTER 14

Sakima stood in awe of the vast atrium space and all that was alien to her. While she knew her mission was to track down Machto and figure out what rotten thing he was up to, she couldn't help herself. She *had* to investigate these mysteries.

Sakima strode down five wide steps, taking her deeper into the room where she surveyed the place. Ten large windows covered opposite sides of the circular arena. Sakima strolled up to the first one. It was a diorama of a strange being a little shorter than Sakima. Next to this being stood two shorter ones, which she presumed were children. *What else could they be?*

The taller being, the "adult," looked somewhat Mannahatta, only with far fewer clothes on. Sakima studied the being's pinkish-purple skin, striated with cyan veins running up and down its body. The skin had a slight glow to it as well, in a much subtler shade of blue.

The being—and that's how Sakima considered it because she felt she couldn't call it a true person, not a Mannahatta—stood about five feet tall. Sakima couldn't discern their gender because their clothes were nondescript.

A gray cloak covered the creature from shoulder to below the knees—or what Sakima assumed were knees. The material tightly followed the contours of the being's body, without clinging to it.

There were circles cut out of the cloth along the front of the frock. The initial circle was at chest level and about three inches across. The next was below it at about where a human stomach would be. These circles revealed hairless shimmering purplish sections of "skin."

Sakima stepped closer. The mouth of the alien being was closed, so she couldn't learn about its teeth or tongue or even if it had such things. Its nose was little more than a flap-covered hole. Its eyes, large and bulbous, had no eyelids. Sakima moved in closer still, to verify that her initial observations were correct. They were.

She noticed, due to her proximity to the being, that it had transparent inserts in its ear holes. These implants fit nicely into the ears while also covering them. They were roughly an inch larger than the openings, in a disk shape.

In its hand the being held a transparent, flat, dish-shaped device. It gripped it by the base, which also acted as a kind of handle. It used all of its nine fingers of that hand alone, including both thumbs, Sakima noted. The top of the device was a clear disk about seven inches across. She saw no buttons or switches or triggers of any sort. Sakima understood somehow, without having to analyze it further, that this thing was a weapon.

Sakima next turned her gaze to the two children—as they seemed to be. They lay on the ground, seemingly asleep. Their eyes were missing, though. Upon further study, Sakima realized the eyes were still there, only the creatures' foreheads covered them. The foreheads appeared to have lowered over the eyes using a hinge mechanism, similar to the human jaw. They covered the children's eyes like lowering the lid of a chest to close it.

Sakima tilted her head slightly to study the scene more. She glanced away from the children to the full diorama. Trees that were comparable to those on Mannahatta filled the set—birch, elm, oak, pine, and spruce. The background was lit by a silvery light simulating the nocturnal glow of the moon. A small moon had been etched onto the back surface painted a deep blue and black with few stars. Below the sky, simulating distance, stood small trees. The forest reminded Sakima of the one she had so recently been sprinting through: *Tèkëne.*

She shrugged and moved on to the next item of interest. As she wandered throughout the vast atrium area, she noted various items sitting on tables, a single piece per table.

The first that she came upon was a white cone. It sat in the middle of a glistening white table. Sakima examined it briefly before reaching up to touch it, at which point the white cone vibrated. She jumped back, and the cone went still. She raised her hand to it again, and again it shook. Sakima kept her hand raised to see what might happen. The vibration increased, faster and faster. Then the cone rose from the tabletop.

When it had risen to about twelve feet high, it made a slight clicking noise. Next, a laser beam from the apex of the cone cut a perfect circle around the enormous room. It swept in an up-and-down pattern as it headed in Sakima's direction.

Startled, Sakima lowered her arm and sprinted toward the hallway. Immediately after she had dropped her arm, the cone ceased firing its laser. It floated gently back down to the table, landing as silent as a spirit.

Oh. So that's how it works.

She peered about, listening hard, checking whether someone had picked up the noise and was perhaps coming to investigate. There was no commotion anywhere else, other than what she herself had caused.

Sakima glanced at the walls where the lasers had hit. She could see a continuous cut less than a sixteenth of an inch deep, if that, but that was all. *What are these walls made of, anyway?*

The laser had etched so exact a pattern into the wall it appeared as if the walls had been manufactured with the design already on it.

There were no burn marks, no smoke, no residue. Only a nice, neat pattern.

Impressive, Sakima thought. *I can see how a thing like that might come in handy. If I could learn to control it, at any rate. I wonder if there is a hand motion to increase speed or intensity? Or perhaps make it shoot more than one laser beam at a time. Or maybe in many directions?*

Sakima proceeded to the next table. It was clear, and upon it sat a transparent pink disk. The disk had several holes cut into it. Sakima looked. *Where have I seen that pattern before?* Then she remembered: on the shirt of the bigger being in the diorama. The one she'd assumed was the mother or father of the smaller sleeping ones at its feet. It had an almost identical arrangement on its cloak. These matched the circles, large to small, that ran along the face of the disk.

Sakima held her hand up to the disk. Nothing. She waved. No response.

"Rise!" she said. It didn't rise. "Okay, fine, whatever." She snapped her fingers in a dismissive gesture.

She continued to the next table and its curiosity. As she did, she had a distinct feeling that someone was watching her. She swung around, hand grasping her knife handle. About an inch from her eyes, the clear disk with the three-hole pattern hovered in the air as if it were staring at her.

"What in the world? Oh! " Sakima suddenly grasped that the signal to start this weapon must have been the snapping of her fingers. So, she snapped her fingers again, and the device silently floated back onto its pedestal. "Well, I'll be!" Sakima said under her breath.

Seems dangerous if these devices respond to anybody at all who waves their hand or randomly makes snapping noises. She wondered if it responded to just anyone. Or if there was something special about her. She hoped it reacted only to her. Not any old jerk. Especially not Machto.

Speaking of which, she needed to get back to hunting him down. He didn't break into here to have a nice walk around this museum. He broke in to cause havoc, to release monsters, to run away. "The coward," she whispered.

Sakima's eye caught a mysterious object on the last display table. The other tables were round, column-like things. This was a black rectangle. The item on it wasn't white or transparent or bluish, as all the others were. It was burnished gold and brown. It was tube-shaped too, narrower on one end, and not a disk. It looked almost like a *tëpinxkèpi*—an archer's cuff.

CHAPTER 15

Sakima lifted her hand up and waved it around in front of the device. It just sat there, exactly as she expected it to. Moving closer, she saw that there were three jewels embedded into the cuff. There was a green jewel closest to where the wrist would be when worn. The next up was blue, and the third was red.

Sakima reached over and picked it up. Nothing happened. No laser beams, no problems. She smiled and slipped it onto her left arm, delighted that the cuff fit her perfectly. She lifted it up closer to her face. On further inspection, she realized the jewels were not in a normal setting, as she had expected. Instead, each stone was in its own unique setting.

The emerald-like jewel sat in an opening the shape of a *tulpe* as seen from above. She could just make out the little head, feet, and tiny tail. The gem itself made up the shell. She understood why the green stone was in the *tulpe*-shaped setting. And for some reason, it made perfect sense to her.

The middle stone, the blue one, was in a set in what seemed to be the paw print of the *xinkwtëme*. The blue of a wolf's eyes. *Pretty.*

The red, garnet-like jewel rested in the center of the three-toed foot of the wild *tschikenum*. It was only then that Sakima comprehended the meaning of the shapes. They corresponded to each of the clans of the Mannahatta people: Turtle, Wolf, Turkey.

Then all three gems took on a beautiful, light blue shimmer. She could no longer discern the individual hues. Only this new, mysterious glow. Sakima laughed.

Good thing I'm not standing too close to that laser cone, she thought. *Who knows what strange action a shaky hand might make that device do? But then she grew serious again. How could all these foreign technologies have anything to do with her people, her heritage? Why would this unusual contraption have Mannahatta symbols on it?*

Sakima drew a deep breath and studied this strange cuff perched on her arm. She hesitated, tilting her head slightly and squinting her eyes. *Wait. A. Minute!* The two things appeared to be identical—like they belonged together. *Perhaps it is my destiny to wear this curious new cuff.*

Sakima didn't know what to make of it all. She brought the strange cuff up toward her face again, to appreciate the glowing gems. She noticed they had just the slightest bit of interior glow. She'd never seen expensive jewels up close like this. She'd read that the best gems have that inner shine.

She reached out to caress the green jade of the turtle. When she did so, the internal glow of the stone became very much external, as if it emitted a bright light. The light didn't travel anywhere; it stayed within the gem as if electricity ran through it. Sakima was not afraid, and she instinctively pressed down on the gemstone.

Then, a three-dimensional, transparent wireframe image appeared of the room she was in. She touched the gem again, intending to shut the map off. Instead, it increased in coverage. She could now see a schematic drawing of the entire first floor.

"Èchei!" She gazed through the map projection all around the room. Her eyes widened, and an enormous smile emerged on her face. "Wow… èchei!" Sakima said, exhaling.

She explored the area, using her new virtual, see-through map system. Before she could get very far, she heard the voices of those scientists once again. Sakima ducked behind a display cabinet in the middle of the gigantic room.

Seconds later, the group walked past the opening of the grand cathedral space. The woman did most of the talking. Sakima watched as the committee in their white coats passed. They spent some time before a massive steel door, chatting. Then it opened with a low grinding noise.

Must be incredibly heavy. No whoosh at all, just that scraping sound.

The group passed through and the huge door ground shut again. After a safe pause, Sakima approached the door. It was a thick, solid structure, with only a small square window at about eye height. The window was thick too, so dense that it slightly distorted the view of the inside area. It didn't seem like a window that you could break with a hammer.

Sakima bobbed side to side, hoping to force the door to let her in, but nothing happened. She held her hand up to the control mechanism on the left of the door. She tried her palm, her fingers, her thumb, and then she just waved frantically. Still nothing. She bent over and placed her face as close to the instrument as she could. She opened her eye as wide open as she could make it. No success.

Giving up, Sakima meandered around the immense space. As she did so, she saw that the yellow sphere in the wiry map moved with her. *That's me!*

She wandered absent-mindedly back to the massive metal door the scientists had just gone through. Then, four bright blue orbs appeared on the virtual map the cuff projected. It had to be the scientists on the opposite side of the gigantic door.

Sakima noticed a cluster of four in the center of the space. Then two more off in one corner. As she drew closer to the doors, she suddenly saw a large, dark gray blob off to one side. Not an orb, but very much blobbish. Almost as if it didn't have a defined border.

Sakima had no idea what that meant. Was it a plant, perhaps? Plants are life-forms and would not show up as human. But a gray splotch? It seemed more like an amorphous energy source.

As she came closer, a second gray blotch showed up on the map that hovered above her cuff. Then a third, then a fourth. She realized they were all lined up on the left wall of that research or lab space or whatever it was.

Sakima observed that the outsized gray spots stood equidistant from each other, as if they existed in separate, restricted spaces.

She turned slightly as she neared. Now four more blobs appeared on the right side of the virtual map. These matched the size of the first set, distributed across the opposite side. Two parallel rows of big blobs separated by—*what?*

The large globules floated around—not staying in one place, but not moving beyond a limited distance, as if they were being stopped by walls.

Why are these globs so big compared to the human ones? Represented on the map at about ten times the diameter of the little blue human dots. They moved back and forth like pendulums, but not in sync with one another. It indicated restlessness to Sakima.

Then, one of the globules traveled outside of what Sakima had assumed to be its prescribed perimeter. This dark gray globule advanced swiftly for the blue orbs, which appeared to rush to the front of the room, according to Sakima's virtual map. Sakima heard a commotion near her, then loud banging and the sound of the huge door being activated.

The scientists, she thought. *They're right here. That was where they were running: to the massive door.* She pondered that for a second or two. *Hmmm… I must not have the map hovering correctly.*

Then the horrible screaming began. Sakima stumbled back a couple of steps. She wanted to cover her ears, but she stood frozen in fear. Then she saw the blood oozing out from under the enormous door, then through the metal capillaries in the floor that were part of the door's opening-and-closing mechanisms.

The screaming grew louder and more horrifying. Sakima could almost feel their pain. She was momentarily shocked into inaction by the wave of grief she felt. Then she pulled herself together. *This was what I have trained for all my life! I have to get in there and do something.*

"I don't care who you are, you *maluwe*, you damn gray blob. I'm coming after you!" Sakima shouted. Her jaw set, her right hand gripping the handle of her knife, she worked the door again. She tried her fingerprint, then her retina print. The sounds of suffering became increasingly unbearable. Still, the door refused to open.

Then it struck Sakima: her new arm cuff. *Could it… ?*

She tested the wolf button. No luck. Then the red turkey. No results. Sakima knew just what she needed to do, as if some mysterious supernatural force silently dictated it to her: *tulpe* the turtle, strong like the door and *xinkwtëme* the wolf, for taking action.

Sakima pressed both the turtle and wolf jewels at the same time. She heard a faint beep from the other side of the door, and then it opened. The system acted sluggishly, and the door only cleared a few feet wide where it then came to a stuttering stop. It bounced an inch or so as if something jammed in the tracks kept it from opening completely.

The bodies that had fallen against it. That's the problem. She pushed against the door with all her strength to assist it, and after significant effort on her part, the door opened entirely. When it did, it spilled mutilated bodies onto the slick floor before her.

Sakima screamed, her hand flashing up to hide her mouth, eyes wide. She turned away from the sight and leaned over, breathing deeply.

Come on, Sakima. Warriors don't squeal when things turn weird or confusing or disgusting. Get it together, girl!

She pulled her favorite knife, *chessi*, out of its sheath and prepared to go after whatever monster or man had done this. But she found nothing.

No adversary. No gray blobs.

Only four scientists dead on the floor in a large, sticky pool of darkening blood.

CHAPTER 16

Sakima sidestepped the ghastly corpses without gazing at them any longer. Bypassing them was not difficult to do because the opening stretched as wide as ten ordinary doorways. She made her way cautiously into the space and then stopped cold.

First, she knew her initial impression of the place had been exactly right. The room she'd entered looked to be a research area. It was as massive as the museum-like space she had just left. What she hadn't expected to see were the giant enclosures that she assumed were some type of cages. Or perhaps even prison cells, based on their structure.

These spaces evenly lined both sides of the interior. Each cage was constructed of some sort of "living" glass panels, or whatever these immense boxes were. The glass made Sakima think of a living thing because it had veins. *Veins of... what? A solution of some kind? A liquid that glows?*

Sakima didn't know the answer, but the effect was as if the panel rippled. It glowed with that pinkish-purplish tone. A hue she was beginning to understand as the color scheme of this whole place. She wished she could gaze straight through these panels and discover what was hidden behind them.

Sakima remembered her cuff and pushed only the *tulpe* button. The map popped up again and hovered over the cuff as before. The blue orbs near her no longer showed up. She realized that other black blobs lay beyond each murky panel, just on the other side, information from the cuff's virtual map told her so. Either these mysterious blobs were silent or asleep, or those glass-face enclosures were soundproof. Because Sakima neither heard nor saw anything.

Why can't I see any additional blue blobs—especially the ones representing the humans by the door ten feet behind me?

Oh! I think it senses only living things.

Sakima had that revelation, but she couldn't concentrate for long because the black spot materialized once again. That huge blob she'd witnessed while separated from it by the enormous door. Now another section had appeared on the hovering map as Sakima moved along.

That's where the blobby thing has gone to. Sakima jogged to the far end of the area, her senses on high alert. She came to a sudden stop.

The cage or cell where she now stood was empty, and shattered glass was everywhere. Sakima studied the outline of the enclosure. It was roughly twelve feet by twenty by twenty—or using *shaèks*, four by five by five. Liquid filled the bottom of the space held in place by a short wall maybe three feet high. The floor all around her, she now noticed, was damp. Some kind of solution had passed over it recently and drained out somewhere.

Sakima peered up at the signage she had just noticed for the first time. The big sign read:

DANGEROUS CREATURES

Beneath that, in smaller letters:

NOT LEGENDS, BUT REAL

Beneath that, in even smaller letters:

DO NOT FEED

A smaller brass placard, just to the right of the demolished cage, contained a single word:

YAKWAHE

They're real. The terrible monster she'd heard of only in stories. She shuddered at the possibility of the humongous, hairless maneater of nightmares being real. She tried to absorb this shocking new information, but she couldn't take the time to ponder it because she had urgent things to attend to.

A loud, monstrous shriek filled the room like a siren going off. Sakima fell hard against a murky, opaque window and covered her ears. She tried not to yell from the pain the horrible sound caused her. She squeezed her eyes tight. When she opened them, she couldn't repress her reflex to scream any longer.

Staring at her were the blood-shot, bright green eyes of—*what?* Each orb was twice the size of Sakima's head. They stared at her with menace, looking directly into her soul. Whatever face held these eyes, she could not say, as the milkiness of the window had only cleared where the creature's eyes seemed to hover.

My Kishelë! What barbaric experiments do they do to innocent creatures in here? Turning them into these abominations.

Sakima grew angry at the injustices she perceived the scientists to have inflicted in this room. She noticed, however, that the monster's piercing scream had created a tiny crack in the cage's glass wall. As she examined the break, the panel suddenly vibrated furiously. The brute was trying to use the initial crack and make it bigger, attempting to escape its high-tech prison by banging its insanely large head against the glass.

With horror, she realized, *It's trying to get to me!*

Sakima knew enough about cracks in glass to know they only become larger. This one did just that, the original break now tracing a deeper, longer fissure. It cracked along from the thing's head down to the middle of the plate, like a break in thin ice.

Sakima stumbled backward, bumping into the tables crammed with lab equipment behind her. She couldn't make herself look away to see what other damage she might have caused just then. She swallowed rapidly and clapped her hand over her mouth as the glass warped and the ungodly thing bellowed.

Then something remarkable happened. The rippling, multicolored veins in the glass, or whatever they were, increased their vibrations and grew thicker—like white blood cells on the attack. New smaller veins swarmed around the fissure, and right before her eyes, the crack healed. In minutes, the panel was back in perfect condition, despite the fiend banging its head into it, again and again. Sakima stood up straight. *So, that was how they kept mythological monsters trapped! The glassy cages they were in were laced with nanobots and nanoparticles.*

Many things on Mannahatta were produced with nanotechnology embedded. These were different—they were defensive and built to protect against the escape of the imprisoned behemoths.

Only one thing mattered: the constant flow of electricity through the walls of these cages to keep the nanoparticles active. So, Sakima realized, that is most likely what Machto did—he shut down the power to a cage when he passed by. Intentionally or not, setting one of these monsters free to inflict horrible murder upon the Mannahatta and maybe the entire Many Worlds.

Since the Split almost five hundred years ago, the Mannahatta had created nanobots, mechBiology, and hovercraft technology. All of these were the direct result of the inherent abilities of *mpoalonium,* or "Mp." Mp was a magical, "supernatural" substance—or at least that's how it seemed. The prefix *"mpoa"* meant "power from the Spirits."

The visitors from space, the Alànëmëskat, had presented the element to the Mannahatta people during the Big Event in the Sky. The *Xinkwi lè Mushhakunk.* An incident that took place during the Mannahatta Year of 10,609 which corresponded to the Land Below Year of 1609 A.D.

Sakima, with her jaw set and her fists in tight balls, forced herself to race back through the giant room, eager to get away from the horrors here and out of this building as fast as possible. She tried to ignore the other monstrosities now, who all beat their heads against the walls of their prison cells as she ran past them. The thumping damaged the glass with fine hairline cracks. The nanobots responded immediately, sounding like swarming bees as they performed their repairs. The surreal landscape made even more horrific by the mound of lifeless bodies at the opening of the space, toward which she sprinted full speed.

CHAPTER 17

Outside, Sakima slowly came to a stop, breathing heavily. She had panicked and she knew it. This was not how warriors behaved, and it was completely unacceptable. Embarrassed, she moved stealthily across the trimmed grass back behind the large holly hedges and tried to pull herself together. As she collected herself, she peered through the gaps in the leaves and branches and spied a tall man in formal attire, striding purposefully out of the building she'd just fled from.

Sakima couldn't quite discern who it was. Then when he passed almost directly in front of her and dangerously close, she recognized him. It was Elder Manunsko. He glanced back and forth in a nervous manner. Then he abruptly turned before quickly disappearing into the shadows.

Interesting. What that was all about? And why was Elder Manunsko acting so strange? She shrugged and returned her attention back to the entrance doors but saw no one else leaving or entering. It was strangely quiet, as if everyone had taken the day off.

Sakima raised herself to her full height and left her hiding place. She headed cautiously toward the building's entrance. As she approached, she noticed something odd: the walls of the big building seemed be coated in reflective technology. She could see the sky behind her and the clouds moving slowly in the sky. A hawk swooped smoothly from a high branch to a lower one in another maple tree across the path.

She strode up to the wide front doors, which still reflected the entire landscape behind her. Oddly, not her own likeness. It was if the technology deleted humans from the reflected image. Sakima felt like a ghost, a spirit drifting across space and time, unseen by human eyes. A visitor from the Land of the Dead. Then the background vanished, and only her reflection could be seen on the building's wall surface. Once again, a flash, and she was gone, and so were the trees. Only the sky and clouds reflected there—nothing else. Sakima had a sudden epiphany as she realized the implications. Machto, in breaking into the site, must have short-circuited the building's cloaking technologies. It was working, but not exactly as designed.

She shrugged it off and concentrated on the problem at hand: the monster or monsters roaming free in the building in front of her. A few feet from the entrance, Sakima strategized how to get in, or more likely, how to break in. Right then, her cuff beeped. Then, as if an invisible doorman were present to guide her into the building, the doors slid wide open for her. Sakima stalled for a second or two, suspecting that maybe it was a trap.

Realizing her cuff had been nice enough to open the door for her, she glanced down at it and smiled. Then she stepped into the building as the doors behind her remained open. Once she'd passed through the second set of doors, these stayed ajar too. Sakima didn't have time to concern herself with the peculiarities of the electronic doors as she found herself once again in familiar territory (although she wished it wasn't, wished she'd never been here). Less than five *shaèks* in front of her: the museum again, or whatever it was. Where she had inadvertently activated those strange weapons. She proceeded to that area but then paused, reminiscing on all that had occurred there mere minutes ago.

Sakima continued toward the laboratory. She noted as she approached that the gruesome pile of dead bodies had already been removed and that the enormous doors were in the open position. She assumed that a robotic cleaning system had kicked in. *So much for forensics and crime scene investigation,* she thought. Senses alerted, Sakima crouched a bit before sneaking further into the massive laboratory / monster prison.

Further on, she passed that empty pen, its glass front wall still lowered down. Sakima pondered how someone, or some automated system, had moved the bodies elsewhere, yet this cage hadn't yet been re-locked. *Perhaps it got damaged,* she thought, *and couldn't be reset without repairing the mechanisms or the software, which might require human intervention, or at least a combined human-nanobot repair effort.*

Sakima heard a sudden scream—muffled and in the distance. It startled her so much that she dropped her knife to the ground where it clanged noisily and slid a foot away from her. While maintaining her gaze straight ahead, she squatted, felt around for her *chessi,* and picked it up. She stood upright, her focus never leaving the area of the lab where the screaming had come from.

Clenching *chessi,* Sakima took a cautious step forward and then another until she was at the back of the "prison" section, next to the enclosure where that horrible creature's gigantic eyeballs had glowered at her with inconceivable hatred. Sakima picked up the faint cry again, almost like the call of a frightened baby bird.

She knew that a close-fought battle with her wielding the knife could very well be too little too late. So she returned her cherished blade back to her belt and yanked the bow from her shoulder instead. She would need the protection of distance. She pulled two arrows from her quiver, then snapped the first onto the bowstring, pulling the string back to half-tension. The other she held in her shooting hand, dangling there but ready to reload and shoot.

She crept further down the hall, moving with care. She could see up ahead that she had a blind corner to turn through. Not good. Anything could be there. She might stare into the eyes of death, the red-rimmed glower of some hideous monster, the mesmerizing glare of an evil spirit eager to rip her apart.

Sakima inched on, her back against the nearest wall, her bow taut and fixed to shoot. She drew a deep breath and held it for a moment, listening to the silence while preparing for the worst. *Please Sakima*, she told herself, *be ready, and be strong. Don't look away.* She swept around the corner, moving fast and with deadly purpose, prepared to release her arrow without hesitation. Instead, she froze. What forced her to stop also made her skin crawl.

The face of a demon. Through the gauzy haze caused by the destruction of the equipment, its eyes emerged. Then its nose, its mouth, and finally the creature's entire sickening face. Because neither fur nor skin covered that hideous surface. The muscle, gristle, and here and there, the bare bone of its skull fully visible. In a few patchy spots, she could see where the skin still clung, and sometimes, there was thick, black fur stuck to that skin.

Staring in disbelief, she watched the glowing eyes withdraw again into the mist. They rose to ten feet high, then twenty. Then, incredibly, it was almost thirty feet above her in this cavernous room that must have been four stories high. Even then, she got the feeling that the beast was still not fully upright, hunched over in the dark space. Then the nauseating face reemerged from foggy obscurity, and Sakima suddenly realized exactly what she was seeing: a thing of nightmares. It was a devil straight out of Mannahatta myth.

It was the mythological creature—or at least until just this second, she thought it to be mythical—the man-eating giant, the hairless bear that tore men limb from limb and ate their hearts. A Mannahatta person eaten by this demon would never see their family again—in this life or any life. This horror she'd only learned about in legends—stories meant to teach the young how to behave right, to stay on the good side of things. The Mannahatta "bogeyman."

It was Yakwahe: the furless bear monster, standing there on its hind legs as if ready to consume her soul.

Sakima stumbled backward, crashing into the shiny metal tables lining the hallway. She couldn't look away, unable to catch her breath.

Suddenly, a tiny voice called out from the darkness, seemingly from nowhere.

"Hi, Sakima!"

It was Tangetta's voice. Sakima looked over from where the voice had come from and saw her little sister waving cheerfully to her big sister. Tangetta skipped around happily in the wide hallway like nothing was wrong and it was just an ordinary, and very fun, day.

Tangetta! How? No!!

Sakima could hardly speak her sister's name. "Tan… *Tangetta…* " she gulped, concentrated, and suppressed her horror. "What are you doing here…? I need you with me. Quickly!" Sakima reached out both her hands and, crouching slightly, started toward her kid sister.

"I was looking for you and I found Uncle Machto in the forest!" Tangetta said, smiling a big smile. "He helped me get in through the window. He said it was his secret entrance."

"Okay, that's fine, doesn't matter," said Sakima. "What I need you to do, right now, is come over here to me, okay, Tangerine? I'll step towards you, you step towards me and then we will—"

At that moment, there was a deafening shriek, so loud that Sakima grimaced at the pain it caused her ears. She did not look away. But this time, she did not close her eyes.

A gigantic shape passed from right to left, arcing between herself and Tangetta. Sakima heard, even above the horrible noises that seemed to be everywhere, her sister's tiny squeal, calling to her as the massive paw swept her away.

"Sakima!"

Then, nothing. No noise, no monster.

No Tangetta.

Tangetta had been taken by that thing that had escaped the inescapable. The cage the engineers no doubt designed to work flawlessly forever. Thanks to Machto, the pen had been compromised, allowing the abomination to escape—the horror that now held Tangetta's life in its gigantic, furless paw.

Sakima gritted her teeth and took a deep breath. She then pulled the bow taught again, to the farthest position her strength would allow. *I will not be a witness to this tragedy. I won't let it happen.*

She set off, sprinting in the direction to where the creature had lumbered away, from which they may never return.

CHAPTER 18

Sakima sprinted around the corner into a short hallway and then into yet another enormous space, with tall clear windows lining every wall, climbing to over twenty feet high, halfway to the ceiling. The ceiling was glass, too. It felt almost as if she'd stepped outside again. Sakima instinctively recognized the area in which she found herself, though. This was where they developed new species. Each room held a different set of material and equipment, another potential new bioMech creature, part of the unique, lab-made species.

She recalled what she'd learned about the lab in school. She remembered that the process for each animal began the same. First, they would create an alloy skeletal system. Lab-made muscle and sinew were then grown over the metal frame using living organisms and nanobots. Next came the mechanical biosystems for digestion, blood flow, and so on.

Part metal and part living biology, these manufactured machines appeared to the average Mannahatta as nearly identical to their original source models—the deer, bear, and coyote. However, the mechBeasts possessed visual clues that were easy for the trained eye to pick up on, such as an unusual glint to the eye or a strange but subtle glow right beneath the fur. This allowed you to quickly identify these creatures as not fully biological animals. At close range, a metallic whirring and clicking would also provide strong proof.

MechBeasts leveraged a highly sophisticated AI-OS (artificially intelligent operating system) to maintain all standard functions. AI also controlled reflexes and reactions and responses to stimuli using the five familiar senses of sight, smell, hearing, touch, and taste. Heart and nervous systems were automatic and *mpoalonium*-powered; they could potentially last forever.

However, and against all odds and initial designs, these machines became able to reproduce. It took decades before the BEPs—birth end products, or simply babies—would survive. Those that did live failed after only a few weeks, as they had significant defects. But that was a hundred years ago.

Now, BEPs were as perfect as any in nature. BioMech machines made new bioMech babies. Even the predators created offspring.

BioMech creatures such as mechLions and mechBears had additional bio-mechanical features such as laser tracking eyes and super strength. The only way to kill these predators or any of the other artificial lifeforms was with specially designed weapons. These included some of the arrows that Sakima carried—purpose-built weapons that could initiate a permanent OS shutdown.

The meat of these laboratory-created animals was completely edible. That was a large part of the reason they had been built. Their fur was as usable as that of any natural animal. All hardware, plastic, specialized materials, and liquids were all reusable. Thus, a brand new mechBeast could be built from the remains of a fallen bioMachine. High school students studied these "animals" in mechBiology class. Sakima gritted her teeth as she remembered dissecting the small animals as she stopped in front of yet another massive door, this one nearly as enormous as that at the front of this research area. *Same access procedure, I bet.*

She understood just what to do and pressed the *tulpe* and *xinkwtëme* jewels simultaneously. Behind the thick wall, mechanical gears ground together as pulleys and weights groaned. The large door scraped open with a noise like pushing a massive block of granite across cement. Ten seconds later, Sakima strode into another enormous room. This one, however, was entirely different from the previous spaces.

Banks of terminals and controls lined both sides of the sparkling clean space. There was a surprising amount of noise from them, buzzing and beeping. Not loud, but constant. She moved forward and stopped again. She stood in awe of a gigantic device deep at the back of the room. She stepped toward it as if in a trance, as if she were being guided to approach it.

Sakima stopped a few *shaèks* away from edifice, dwarfed by it. The structure of it was shaped in a half-dome, with the apex more than thirty feet from the floor. Although it was obviously high tech and composed of the latest materials, it also had components created from carved wood. All around the face of the arch, Manna-hatta symbols shimmered on both the metal and wooden parts. They gleamed with such subtly, Sakima could barely make them out. If she took only two or three steps back, the pictographs would seem to disappear altogether.

Sakima had never seen artistry and technology merged in this way before. It was beautiful and reminded Sakima of a holy place of communion with the Spirit World. Similar, in a way, to the sweat lodges she'd secretly observed (women were never allowed in these special places; they were for men only).

Sakima had been in quite a few such locations without getting caught. She'd even completed a Vision Quest of her own, with no help from the tribe. She'd discovered so much but could not tell anyone what she'd learned. She'd say nothing about the Spirit Animal that visited her: *xinkwtëme*, the wolf.

Sweat lodges had a similar hybrid of natural and manmade substances. They were comparable in application to the oak, maple, titanium, and *mpoalonium* integrated here in this gigantic archway. The arch before her towered much bigger, more impressive, and more stunning than anything Sakima had ever witnessed. Sakima studied the markings on the surface of the archway, above what looked like an altar. It certainly resembled a sacred place. She recognized these symbols well, and their meanings. They were warnings, and they were meant to be taken seriously. Across the top of the arch was etched:

SKONTAY CHÌPILËSU

Its meaning could be interpreted as either "the dangerous doorway" or the "exciting passageway." In common terms, it meant "the portal."

Had the monster that killed those poor scientists been anywhere in this space at this exact moment, Sakima would be dead because she hadn't paid attention to anything but this ornate, enormous archway. She stood transfixed by the sight of the gateway, now that she understood what it was. She'd heard of this portal, but she had never believed that such a contraption could exist. Yet here it stood right in front of her.

Steam and mist poured out from the black space in the middle of the portal. That phenomenon made little sense to Sakima, but then she didn't understand the workings of the device. They rarely taught or even discussed interdimensional travel in school, aside from a brief history of this gate. The lesson to remember forever was that no one should use the portal because it was dangerous, with no guarantee of returning from wherever it might take you.

Yet, here Sakima stood facing the mysterious portal, pondering if a man and monster had recently activated it, that they might have forced her kid sister to travel through it with them. She knew it was her brother-in-law, Machto. He had "joked" about doing this for a long time. To escape to the Land Below and make his fortune there. And then return as the new Mannahatta king.

But how could Machto lured the mythological monster into the Skontay Chìpilësu, *the portal?* she wondered. *Why did he beam himself down with it, across the multiverse, if that was, in fact, what he did? How could he possibly believe that he could control it? What the hell did he think he was doing? The* tèpahtu—*the stupid jerk.*

Sakima shook her head, both in disbelief at Machto's stupidity, but also to snap herself out of her trance. It was time for action.

A bug in the system listed Machto's destination as the Land Below, a mythical place in a parallel universe. The people there were called "primitive" because of their dependence on fossil fuels and disrespect for *Kahèsëna Hàki*, Mother Earth.

Where had Machto gone in the Land Below? Would she ever locate him and bring him back? More importantly, would she ever be able to find and rescue Tangetta and bring her home?

CHAPTER 19

The dials, diagrams, and monitors in front of her overflowed with information, but it told her nothing. Some were labeled using Mannahatta symbols, some with technological words she could barely pronounce, and others with numbers. Sakima stood there, ready to go, bracing herself, and with no idea how to begin.

Then, when she snapped out of her reverie, she glanced to her right. There she noticed that a series of electronic readouts were furiously blinking on a variety of pënael'ntàmahikàn screens, the wall filled with flat LCDs. She strode over to the wall, her head turned slightly away, as if she feared the entire thing was dangerous to look at.

She read the displays. More warnings, but also something else. A screen that said:

DESTINATION STATUS:
SET

And another that displayed:

TRANSPORTATION STATUS:
ACTIVATED

And on a third screen:

DESTINATION TARGET:
MËNATINK OHËLËMI

Mënatink Ohëlëmi—the Land Below. The mythical land her ancestors referred to as "Manhattan" in some of her textbooks. Somehow, the two versions of Mannahatta had split apart with the arrival of the People Who Fell to Earth, the Alànawènik. This event caused the Dutch, the English, and other European settlers to abandon the lands of the Mannahatta. At least that was how the legend was told and passed down to each new generation.

But this was only a myth and nothing but, and Sakima knew it. *There was no such place as the "Land Below." How could there be?* But it had been fun to grow up hearing tales of this imaginary place and how different it was from her land.

Anyway. There is only one real Mannahatta in the entire universe. Mine.

Then, the transport screen flashed briefly and then new messages displayed:

ENTITIES IN TRANSIT:

LIFEFORM: ONE ADULT. HUMAN
LIFEFORM: ONE CHILD. HUMAN
LIFEFORM: ONE UNKNOWN

Sakima took a step backward in horror. Mannahatta Law forbid the use of these transports without authorization, a decree enforceable even by death, or so she had been taught. Sakima's eyebrows rose. Yes, Machto had done the unthinkable.

Worse, he'd accidentally or on purpose transported a fearsome monster with him to a place whose inhabitants, whoever they were and wherever they lived, would now certainly die. Thanks to Machto, that monstrosity was speeding toward the unsuspecting and unprepared people in some alternate world, invaded by a dreadful aberration that had escaped its cage—or more likely, been freed by Machto.

She noticed just then that her cuff gave off a slight turquoise glow. She reached over and pressed the *tulpe* button again. The turtle icon seemed to have something to do with travel: slow and with a house on its back, but still...

However, this time, not even a map appeared. Nothing at all to assist her. The other gems, the fierce noble *xinkwtëme* and the wild bird, *tschikenum*, struck Sakima as not having much to do with any of it. The black matter, the enchanted matter, the wormholes, the multiverse. The Many Worlds.

With a shrug, she pressed the wolf button next. Nothing happened. At least not that she could tell. No sound, no light displays, and no vibration from the cuff. Yet something was happening on the panels in front of her.

Lights blazed on at various places on the wall. Connections beeped. Gears revolved. Small monitors woke up to reveal strange graphs showing interwoven spinning ellipses connected by lines of triangulation.

Waveforms slithered across a larger monitor above her head. Sakima gazed about her. It struck her that the *Skontay Chìpilësu* took more than one person to operate it. Probably a team of *how many?*— she counted the workstations surrounding the portal—well, at least a dozen.

She scanned the room as a multitude of electronic devices and instruments came to life. As she stared in awe, the portal gate rotated. Two halves—metal and wood—spinning opposite each other. Slowly at first, and silently, but then gradually faster and louder, to such a degree that Sakima had to cover her ears. The circling portal arches had a hypnotic effect on her, too, so Sakima shut her eyes too.

Sakima kept her eyes and breathed deep. This was it. Her moment to prove herself. She could leave here and go back, assemble the warriors, and then they could deal with it. And she would remain here on Mannahatta, safe and secure and go on to live her life as an ordinary woman, not a warrior.

Or I could go myself, kill this vicious thing, and bring my little sister, Tangetta, back to her homeland. And of course, that's what I will do. I have a mission now. One of life and death. I will not fail!

Sakima opened her eyes and stepped forward with intense determination. Now she understood why she had been brought here and what she needed to do. She must go through the portal and save Tangetta and the people of the Land Below. In doing so, perhaps make a name for herself at last.

Sakima didn't enter any codes, pull any levers, or trip any switches. She did not step through the portal gate. She did not walk up steps or past a certain line on the ground. She just stood there as the *Skontay Chìpilësu* operated at full velocity again, courtesy of the wolf button on her cuff that seemed instinctively to understand how to activate all systems.

She closed her eyes again and once more covered her ears. As she did so, Sakima felt the room quiver and then shake violently, as if she were caught in an indoor earthquake. The noise was deafening, and for one quick moment, Sakima feared she might pass out.

Then, it all ceased. The screeching, metallic sounds of mighty winds, the topsy-turvy sensation of the floor. All peaceful again. As soon as it had begun, it returned to stillness.

Had the portal malfunctioned? Did her cuff only take a guess and didn't know with any certainty what it was doing?

Sakima sighed, sadder than she'd felt in a very long time. Her little sister was gone and almost certainly dead. The monster, Yakwahe, and the human monster, Machto, vanished to a world that was on the verge of destruction. She had the feeling that the entire universe collapsed on top of her, as if it were all falling apart everywhere.

Sakima was too disappointed and exhausted to be upset, to succumb to anything close to tears right now. Instead, she took a deep breath and tried to center herself. *I'll just try again. I'll get to Tangetta, somehow. I must do this.* She realized she still had her eyes squeezed tight, her palms suction-cupped against her ears.

She cautiously drew her hands away, only to hear some very unusual voices. None of them were speaking Mannahatta, or Munsee, or any Algonquin tongue. Instead, the cadence of a hurried, alien language caught her ear. She heard a word repeated here and there as she listened: "Yanqui." And another: "Metz." And still another: "Nix." Then she heard a sound that was unfamiliar to her, a strange tone, neither flute nor drum. Similar, though, to the honking of geese. Curious, Sakima opened her eyes.

And immediately snapped them shut again.

PART TWO
THE LAND BELOW

CHAPTER 20

The brightness had blinded her, frightened her. Sakima paused for a second to collect herself before slowly opening her eyes again. She peeped through the thick lashes of her half-closed eyes.

Lights flashed here and there, and strange symbols covered many surfaces, some on very big surfaces, and some changing to reveal a new set of symbols every few seconds.

The people of this strange world propelled themselves past her at surprising speed. They appeared quite different from the True People. They were strangely dressed, with odd face paint, and standing about in unnatural ways. Thousands of these individuals moved as one but in all directions. A massive but indecisive army of ants.

Speeding boxes with wheels sputtered by, like primitive versions of the magnetic hover-vehicles on her world. These were where the goose-like sounds emanated, Sakima realized. One of the yellow boxes bore the markings: "T-A-X-I." Another one read: "M-T-A." She recognized these as English-language letters from her *Mënatink Ohëlëmi* language classes back in school.

Sakima stood, unable to move. One more soul in a crashing ocean of people, all laughing, talking, shouting, and gesturing to each other or into the devices in their hands. *Handheld technology. Like on Mannahatta.*

She realized with a sudden start the truth of what had happened to her. She had expected portal travel to involve some spinning through chutes or tumbling through slick, rubbery membranes to pass across the multiverse. Instead, she was here now, instantaneously and without fanfare. *But where…?*

She remained motionless, stunned in the brilliant, warm summer sunlight on a strange world filled with the noises of engines and equipment. There were exotic smells, many of which were new to her. The tallest structures she'd ever seen in strange styles touched the sky. Odd moving vehicles of peculiar design inched along before her, traveling in two directions only.

There were hundreds of individuals of all sizes, shapes, colors, and dress. More people all in one place than she'd witnessed up until that point. For the first time in a long while, Sakima stood immobile. The sight of the strange, old-fashioned buildings. The way these people dressed. The tones of their skin—most so different from hers—from ivory to midnight and everything in between.

Finally, Sakima pulled herself together and got going. She strode along, hoping she blended in, but knowing how she looked made her stand out. Not just her Mannahatta clothes but also her bow and arrows, the knives at her waist, and her Mannahatta-style makeup.

Yet, as she marched along, the people nonchalantly passed right by her. Sakima realized they were not noticing her, just going about their business. Some were talking, some not; others were in a great hurry, and others seemed to have endless time. Although no one looked at her, Sakima felt strangely shy, like she didn't belong.

She breathed in the bouquet of perfume mixed with the scents of flowers and something like the smell of burning oil. Although she recognized some odors, she couldn't identify all of them. The scent of roses was familiar of course, and lavender too.

Sakima moved further north, unsure of what to do next. Meanwhile, her confidence had returned. As she hiked past the odd buildings on her route, she observed that they had enormous windows, similar to the buildings back home on Mannahatta. Then her eye caught what was on the other side of the glass: a row of dazed women.

Sakima stopped and stared, amazed at how different these women looked, not only from her but also from everyone on the sidewalk with her. As still as granite, their hands on their hips or in front of them in awkward poses. They wore tight, impractical dresses along with shoes not designed for hunting or tracking. Their faces had more makeup than Sakima'd ever seen, although she wore similar decorations on her eyelids and her lips. She studied the women, her fingers absently brushing her knife handle, until she realized at last that these were lifelike statues, not actual people.

As she relaxed, her focus moved from the statues to her reflection in the window. Sakima had braided some of the hair at the top and sides of her head and had pulled some of it back into a loose ponytail. The rest of her jet-black hair fell to her shoulders. A gentle breeze caused a few strands to dance across her forehead and her high cheekbones. Her large, expressive eyes were brown with long black lashes. She had a strong, straight nose, and full lips just like her mother's. As she considered her image, she had to accept reality: she was a stranger here.

The screaming in the distance snapped Sakima out of her reverie. She grabbed the bow off her back and raced toward the commotion, dodging people and evading obstacles. She soon left the overcrowded sidewalks and ran across a metal grate into the street. Passing the grate, she heard a loud rumbling like a stampede from deep below. On the road she made better time, avoiding the machines with ease because now they all were at a standstill.

She saw a marker on a pole. The curious symbols on it named the street, Sakima deduced. This long road she was on seemed both familiar and unfamiliar. The immense width of it and the way it cut north in a straight line reminded her of the long, broad trail called *Wickquasgeck* that ran north and south on her Mannahatta.

As she sped across an intersection marked "5 8," a machine blasted her with the goose sound. The man inside the metal box shook his hand at Sakima. He shouted something that she knew was not complimentary because his mouth went crooked like a snake and his eyes burned like small fires.

She approached a wide-open space that felt familiar to her, as if she'd been there before, but that seemed impossible. The area was in the shape of a giant circle, filled with more vehicles and people. A tall monument sprang up from the middle. At its peak stood a statue of an oddly dressed man.

At the epicenter of it all, a monster of Mannahatta legend: Yakwahe, the massive hairless bear. Even hunched over, the creature was still as tall as the shorter structures in the vicinity. The beast had fur and skin missing here and there. Where the skin was absent, the muscles, veins, and even bone showed through.

Without breaking stride, Sakima nocked two arrows, raised the bow, and stretched the bowstring to her eyes. Yakwahe was busy grabbing people with its huge paws and chewing the screaming victims, eating them alive. Sakima jumped onto the front of a slow metal machine, and from there, she leaped into the air. Sakima felt as if she hovered in space, as if time itself ceased to exist. She aimed, and without hesitation, she let those arrows fly. They spun through space toward the terrible monster, and as they did so, their tips opened and a cyan blue propeller emerged, spinning madly. When they hit the creature, they dug in and entered deeper and deeper into the brute like industrial drills.

The behemoth howled in pain and reached down with one paw, clawing the arrows out, ripping its own flesh. The arrows dashed to the ground where they exploded. These micro-bombs were designed to go off once the arrow tip had found essential tissue, such as heart or lungs or liver.

Without blinking, Sakima nocked again. Staying as still as those women in the window, she took aim. Before she could free the arrow, the monster spotted her, glared into her soul, and then it swung its other paw around. Sakima thought she was ready for anything, but she wasn't ready for this sight. In the other paw: Tangetta. Her sister's face was red with tears and emotion as she cried for help with a voice of pure fear.

Sakima didn't let her arrows fly this time. She couldn't. *Not again,* she thought. *Oh, dear God, dear Kishelë, not again.*

Sakima! The voice echoed in her head. *Shoot, Sakima! Why won't you shoot?* Sakima heard Pat's voice and saw his face. The entire memory flooded into view again in her mind's eye, making her feel weak and so very tired.

Sakima, save me! The voice this time arrived in her mind so loud and near it stunned her. Must she relive this all over again with such realistic detail? *No! Please, this can't be happening.* Sakima thought, frozen inside.

"Sakima!"

But this time it wasn't Pat's voice she heard. Not her crush, her boyfriend Apatschin, "Pat," but a younger, female voice. Sakima refocused: Tangetta was there in the paw of the colossus, staring directly at her. This was happening now; it was not a tragic memory.

"Sakima-*aaaaaa!*" Tangetta screamed, her cheeks covered in tears. "*Wichëmil! Wichëmil*—help! Help!"

Sakima sighed. She wanted more than anything to let her arrows go, kill the thing, and save Tangetta. She couldn't do it and not just because she was haunted by demons from her past. Even though her quiver was full of smart arrows, they weren't that smart. They wouldn't be able to differentiate between two tightly overlapping targets. They might hit her sister as easily as the monster.

Sakima couldn't take that chance. She removed the arrows from her bow and put them back in her quiver. Then she flipped the bow around her shoulder and ran, faster than she'd ever run before, straight at the enormous freak.

She didn't know what she would do once she passed that crowded circle of machines and people and reached the creature, but that didn't worry her. Sakima knew she'd do something to save her little sister, but unfortunately she currently had no clue what that would be.

CHAPTER 21

Machto Pequonitto cracked his knuckles by interweaving his fingers together and then brutally pushing his arms away from himself. He rolled his neck, feeling the relief as he heard a popping. Machto stood up and strolled to the window, deep in thought.

Minutes earlier, he lay on his bed, staring at the ceiling, thinking about how life had screwed him over. How was it the accursed Tamanends were in positions of power? It made no sense. Second, that power should be his and his alone. He'd strategically married into the Tamanend family, but the marriage had gotten Machto nowhere in terms of prestige. Marrying Amimi Tamanend was supposed to bring him closer to ultimate authority, but it did not.

It irritated Machto that he was not in the line of ascension in either his clan or Mimi's. He had not one, not two, but *three* older brothers and no sisters. No ascension route. Then there was Mimi's line. Initially, there were two males in that family. Then, a miracle occurred, and the son they called Tommy was killed in an ambush. The younger brother, Nimàt, wouldn't represent a challenge. When the time was right, he would easily dispose of him. Machto snickered with pleasure.

Even with Nimàt gone, he could not envision a single honest path to power with either clan. He would arrange to have Mimi "disappear," leaving him as the sole rightful heir. Now, with Sakima in the picture, this venture seemed hopeless. Machto understood that he'd have to take what he wanted by any means necessary. That brought him here, to the land of abundance, including the availability of every imaginable weapon and a pool of greedy and deceitful men from which he could forge allies. He was intent on getting a few good soldiers and weapons to start the military training process.

Restless, Machto stared out the tall windows to the streets below. He caught sight of a woman dressed like no other New Yorker, sprinting up the boulevard below him.

She appeared slender but athletic, with defined muscles in her exposed arms. Her face, like her arms, was deeply tanned. He was excited; he'd love to have a woman like that. Not to be married to, but to have whenever he chose and then send her away. He wanted his very own harem. Harems weren't a Mannahatta thing, but he'd heard of them from stories of other cultures as told by his Kanyen friends, his true brothers. Machto reflected with approval how this band of Kanyens weren't weak, like Mannahatta men. Rather, they were brave and bloodthirsty, like him, and cared about nothing but victory. They would be instrumental in his overthrow of the Tamanends in the near future, but first, he had to finish his work here on *Mënatink Ohëlëmi*.

He continued watching the woman running along, admiring her behind, how it swayed as she moved. When she reached Columbus Circle, Machto took a step back and blinked in surprise upon seeing her face. With immediate rage, he knew who this was: Sakima.

That bitch. Oh, how I despise her. Now she is here? At my base of operations!

He squeezed his mouth into a tight line. Her death would come earlier than intended and in the wrong world. But did not matter to him where and when she died. Only that she did.

Machto's followed Sakima as she picked up the speed, screaming at the top of her lungs. That's when he spied it: the colossus he'd freed from its electronic cage. Yakwahe had somehow made it here. Machto had only intended for the creature to attack the Mannahatta people and destroy his homeland; that would make it easy to conquer Mannahatta upon his triumphant return.

This, he realized now, was actually so much better. Let the fiend decimate New Yorkers. He'd take credit when it was all over. Demand millions from the city—no, *billions*—for his guarantee not to release any more monsters, whether he so did or not. Then he'd leverage the cash he would make to secure weapons of every type, design, and quantity as he returned to Mannahatta with an unstoppable crew of mercenaries.

He watched Sakima race directly at the behemoth, without a weapon in sight, other than her bow and quiver of arrows. She'd fastened them to her back instead of using them either offensively or defensively.

She jumped up onto the hood of an abandoned taxicab, then on to its roof, vaulting from there to the top of a brown delivery truck. She then hurtled through the air to attach herself like a tick to one of Yakwahe's enormous, hideous legs.

CHAPTER 22

Kieft Willem checked his phone: three recent messages and five texts. It wasn't even 7:00 a.m. Yet his primary investor and main pain-in-the-butt was on him once again about the new product, harassing him about release dates and additional features. Kieft stood at the corner and gazed up at the traffic light. Still red. Yellow taxis and white-and-blue delivery trucks rumbled past him, filling his nose with the stink of diesel smoke.

Then, the crosswalk signal gave him the go-ahead. Kieft crossed as his phone buzzed again. Another message from Viktor Azog, the head of the venture firm backing Kieft's latest project. Kieft's company developed sophisticated "defensive" weapons. His current undertaking was so top secret that no communication occurred outside the secure firewall the team had set up. Or in special circumstances, like today, in person.

Kieft stepped up on the sidewalk and hurried past a loud construction site. Dust flew in the air, jackhammers rattled, and the stench of warm tar wafted over him. His phone vibrated in his pocket as he jogged a few more feet and then tapped the earbud in his left ear to answer.

"This is Kieft," he said, unconsciously leering at a passing woman in a short dress.

"Kieft Willem, my man! Viktor here." Viktor Azog's voice boomed so loud, Kieft had to yank his earbud away from his ear a bit. "Hey, buddy, we're on a tight deadline. You realize that, don't you? I'm getting concerned."

"Viktor—" Kieft took a deep breath, preparing to give his usual, lengthy explanation. *How many times will I have to keep explaining to this moron the reality of product development?*

"Get in here right away. Bring coffee. Grande. Black"

Kieft jerked his head back as if he'd been slapped. "Did you just tell me bring coff—?"

"Is there a problem?"

Kieft hesitated, swallowed, and said, "I'll be there in ten."

"Make it five." Azog hung up before Kieft could utter another word.

Kieft stepped inside the next Starbucks he came to and got in line. Five minutes later, he returned to the noisy pavement, a single caramel latte with extra milk in one hand and a black coffee in the other. He sipped the scalding drink while the sticky-sweet aroma caressed his nostrils. Then he headed for a towering office building on Broadway between West 60th and 61st Streets for his meeting at Gnaden Hutten Investments, Inc. GHI also involved itself in funding gun-smuggling in the Third World. You wouldn't find that devil of a detail in their quarterly reports. Kieft entered the elevator and pressed the button to take him to the twenty-fifth floor.

"About time," Viktor Azog said as Kieft walked into Azog's office. "Where's my brew, my man?" Azog's artificial use of casual street language only made Kieft dislike him more.

Kieft handed the coffee across the desk, pulled out a chair, and sat down opposite Azog. He then propped his briefcase on the desktop, snapped it open, and withdrew an impressive stack of papers.

"What you got there, dude?" Azog showed a big fishy smile. His bulging watery eyes, slick fat lips, and pale bald head added to the grotesque effect.

"What I have here are the latest stress test reports, and it's looking good. Got the defect count down from over 200 to less than fifty." Kieft smiled and continued to reference the report in his hands. "The weapon of the future is here, minus about a week or two to give my team time to bring the defect count," he cleared his throat, "the bug count, in other words, down to a reasonable number. Say under ten. We can start shipping the first of the... " Kieft stopped and stared at his latte in the other man's hand.

"Are you drinking my—?" He hadn't noticed until just that moment that Azog had pulled Kieft's coffee over to his side and taken two sips.

"What the hell are you trying to pull, Kieft?" Azog said, cutting him off. "Do you think fifty bugs is a victory? I need zero, bro', zero. You follow? ZEE-row!"

"Look, this is how it's done," Kieft said, ignoring what he took to be the rude appropriation of his drink. "You're not appreciating the monumental achievement here at all. It's unheard of to have eliminated two-thirds of bugs after only one month's testing. The track record in these cases is a defect closing rate of like 10% not 66%. Takes time and—"

"I don't give a shit what average projects achieve. Or what average people are doing out there. At Gnaden Hutten Investments, we maintain our one hundred percent success rate." Azog took another sip of Kieft's coffee. "*Mmm.* Anyway, buddy, there's a bug-closing percentage for you. How do you like that? One hundred. Sound good? Well, you might want to shoot for that number: zero bugs."

Azog banged his fist down and pushed himself away in anger. He spun himself out a foot or two from the table on the small wheels of his chair. He swiveled to peer out the enormous window behind him, a satisfied smirk on his face.

Kieft, meanwhile, fumed and tried to stare holes into the back of Azog's head. He was familiar with being mistreated and disrespected, but this was a whole extra level. "That has to be… " Kieft said, his voice a throaty grumble, "the most uninformed rant I've heard."

"What did you say?" Azog turned to glower at Kieft. Kieft cleared his throat as Azog's spinning chair came to a creaking stop.

"Um, what you just said, I mean," Kieft stumbled on. "Dumb. I mean, in terms of product development. Something you don't understand at all. I mean—"

"Are you calling me a dumb ass, you *mofo*?"

Kieft cleared his throat again to prevent his voice from rising any higher before he spoke. "What I'm saying is that my team is crushing the entire development cycle. That's all." Kieft scratched at an itchy spot at the back of his neck and diverted his gaze.

"Well, guess who's not crushing it?" Azog said, pronouncing the word "crushing" as if he'd taken a bite of rotten fruit. "You know who? Well… " He slammed his hands onto the table again and jumped to his feet. "It's you!"

"Look, Viktor, I know where you're going with this, but I think—"

"No, that's just it: you don't think. You putter along in your slow-witted way, reporting to me this and that. Never taking action." Azog raised himself to his full height. "You know that clause in our contract? The clause that says if the stakeholders at GHI—which includes me—determine that this project is in danger of failure because of ineffectual elements—that would be you—all money invested reverts to GHI. As does all ownership of the IP, meaning your military-use technologies. All of it."

"Say that… " Kieft squeezed his groin muscles like the male version of Kegel exercises. "Say that again." This came out as more of a question than a command.

"It's all mine now," Azog said, a twisted smile sneaking across his face. "Leave the paperwork and get out." His arrogant sneer melted to curiosity and after to fear. His eyes widened. "What's that? What are you doing?"

"This? This is my baby." Kieft pointed what appeared to be a red toy gun from the 1950s at Azog's forehead. "The weapon you've been paying for but which I'll never deliver to you. Not now. Not ever."

Azog laughed. "That?" he said as he got a better view of the gun. "It's a freaking water pistol!"

"I assure you, it's not," Kieft said. "Don't push me; don't say another word or I swear—"

"Ah, what you gonna do with that baby water pistol? Squirt me?" Azog threw his head back and laughed. He stopped as a whirring noise filled the room. "Hey! What do you think you're doing?" he said, waving his hands palm out in front of himself. "What's going on?"

"What's going on? I'm glad you asked, bro. What's going on is I'm about to realign the molecules in your body with this 'baby water gun.'" Kieft pressed a touchscreen on the side of the shiny red weapon. The whirring noises grew in intensity. Small concentric circles rippled out of the device. These became larger as they left the barrel and headed toward Azog.

"Okay, that's enough! Joke's over!" Azog yelled, beads of sweat appearing on his upper lip. He stuck out his hand, palm up. "Give it up."

But it was too late. Viktor Azog trembled as the bright cyan ovals entered his body, one after another. He quivered as his insides convulsed. His eyes registered shock, and then he exploded. Dripping-wet pieces of flesh splashed through the air and smacked onto the walls and furniture and Kieft.

After a minute, all these scattered parts vanished. At first, they became and more transparent. Then they vibrated again, emitting odd hissing noises and thick blue smoke. Finally, the last bits of

Viktor Azog disappeared, as if these fragments, and Azog himself, had never existed.

Kieft gathered up his papers and snapped his briefcase shut. He ran his fingers through his short hair and then brushed off his shirt and pants with quick motions. With a smile, Kieft headed out the door. He couldn't help but reflect that this spontaneous beta test worked out far better than he could have hoped.

CHAPTER 23

On the leg of the horrible beast, Sakima had no time to plot or plan. It was all action and reaction now. All or nothing. She clung to the limb, the smell of putrid flesh overwhelming her senses. The exposed muscles and bones made Sakima want to vomit.

Instead, she squished her features to narrow her nostrils and hide her mouth and fought that urge. She reached up and grabbed the thigh bone of the monster, as if traversing the rocks up the face of a mountain, something she'd done since she was a little kid.

The familiarity of the technique helped normalize the situation somewhat for Sakima. She was, in some weird sense, comfortable with the challenge. Using rock climbing techniques, feeling for handholds and footholds, she worked her way up—finding a chip in the thigh bone to wedge her foot into, discovering a small hole in the wet muscle to slip her fist in for a classic handhold. Bit by bit, she climbed higher and higher up the monster's rotting body.

But the creature ignored her. While this helped Sakima immensely with her task of scaling the monster—not being swatted at or picked off and eaten—she also found it disconcerting. She wasn't invisible. Although small by comparison to the hideous freak, she wasn't the size of an ant or mosquito.

She lifted her head up to determine what the beast was doing, but its skull was too far up there. She couldn't see much more than the clumps of skin and fur immediately above her. So maybe that was why it hadn't yet attacked her, Sakima realized. She was too lightweight for the monster to feel her creeping up its leg. Too small for it to perceive her, at least not without it having to lean all the way over.

Around her, Sakima saw towering edifices, some under construction. These had tall mechanical devices attached to their sides to lift supplies to the higher floors of other buildings. Below spread a tapestry of vacated cars and trucks. There were virtually no other people around anymore, since she'd first bounded onto the beast. What had started as an ocean of panicked residents had wound up being a still, quiet moment in the heart of a very big city.

A flying machine hovered high overhead. Sakima had no idea where it had come from; she hadn't noticed any new sounds. Then it moved toward Yakwahe, a direction which, by default now, included her and Tangetta.

She wondered what kinds of weapons it had on board and how surgical or general these weapons might be. Were they here to blow this creature to another dimension in bloody pieces? Or would they put an arrow through its skull and topple it where it stood?

The flying box was close now, a few yards away. Sakima could make out the English letters "N-E-W-S" painted in blue and orange across a surface of white. It moved closer to her position by the second.

Sakima sighed, resigned to the stinky task at hand. She was well above the middle of Yakwahe's thighbone. She decided to work her way around to the back of the beast, to maintain the only advantage she had—the element of surprise—which could turn out to be worthless. Sakima finally reached the creature's hip bone, which was fully exposed but covered in the slime of mortal decay. Then, she inched her way across the gigantic bone toward the back.

Unfortunately, the flying machine decided that exact moment was the right time to be swatted out of the sky by the bloody paw of Yakwahe. The twisting of the beast's pelvis required for it to take that wide swing caused Sakima to slip off its hip. She did not have a good handhold, but her feet were locked in place in a couple of small crags in that ancient, putrefied bone. Sakima hung in agony upside down with her hands flailing about trying to find something to grip in thin air.

Her ankles felt as if they would break, but Sakima refused to succumb to the pain. Instead, she concentrated on squeezing her abdominal muscles together. After about thirty seconds of extreme contraction with no outward physical effect, she finally could feel herself rising by a fraction, then a fraction more.

At a pivotal point midway between upright and upside down, Sakima stretched her arms forward on either side of herself, reaching for nothing but needing every ounce of assistance her body could provide. Finally, Sakima's heroic efforts beat inertia, defeating gravity. She reached out for the bony parts of the creature in front of her and grabbed on tight.

The news machine, after much spinning and swooping, plunged into the asphalt and exploded into flames. Sakima looked away and shut her eyes. She had seen the look of horror in the faces of those people trapped inside the flying metal capsule right before it crashed, seeing death staring them in the face. But Yakwahe, the evil mythical Mannahatta monster could never really die. Sakima had hoped it could be stopped, and perhaps, in the process, explode into so many pieces it wouldn't matter whether it was dead or alive.

The behemoth kicked into motion at last, as Sakima knew it must do now. It started out moving slowly, but she sensed it would soon be at a full gallop—or full scuttle—or however hairless bear monsters run when fleeing with three paws and a front one busy holding a screaming child.

Sakima recognized this might be her only chance. She lifted her arm with the alien cuff and selected various combinations of the bejeweled buttons. The cuff seemed to have a consciousness, or if not that, then communication abilities with forces beyond Sakima's understanding. Finally, one combination responded, as if the cuff had waited for Sakima to push the correct, seemingly random sequence.

Circular bright blue-purple beams shot from the cuff. These reminded Sakima of the waves created by her bow-tuning device. These beams rippled away from her cuff through the space between her and the beast. Reaching its shoulder, they penetrated in an unexpected way. At first, they drifted gently into the monster's body, like an X-ray passing through a patient in the hospital. Then she saw the creature's minimal fur and skin tremble. Soon the muscles and bone did the same. Then it exploded.

A hole the diameter of Sakima's entire body materialized where there once was a solid section of the oversized creature, effectively a window through which Sakima could see the burning helicopter and all the emergency vehicles surrounding it. The monster, suddenly aware of the new opening in its body, shrieked and roared. Then it rushed on at full speed—furiously and without clear intent.

Flailing, Yakwahe made its way around Columbus Avenue. It crashed into the statue Sakima had noticed earlier. The sculpture toppled off its high pillar and shattered into a dozen large chunks when it hit the pavement. The head, still intact and recognizable, continued, rolling furiously across Columbus Circle. The head's facial features chipped off as it was ground into an ovoid, unmemorable shape. It finally rolled to a stop in the middle of the street where a truck, speeding up to flee the chaos, crushed it into dust.

Continuing without taking any interest in the damage it inflicted, Yakwahe knocked over an enormous, silver globe. The orb spun madly at the smoldering wreck of the flying machine. Yakwahe then smashed through the corner of the first five stories of the building where the sphere had been stationed. The whole destructive incident might have killed Sakima. She managed to escape solely because she was at the rear of the beast, not the front where the impacts occurred.

Up ahead, Sakima noticed multiple flat surfaces, wood held up by metal poles, flanking the facade of the building. *Well, this will be the end of me right there*, Sakima thought, *if Yakwahe crashes through it. I am not safe at this level, no matter what side of this beast I'm on.*

The change in the wind now that they'd left Columbus Circle blasted the putrefying stench of the creature directly into Sakima's face. It flooded her sensory system with a disgusting rotting-meat-sprinkled-with-manure smell. Then, Sakima nearly fainted from unbridled fear because the behemoth finally found her and started to reach down to pluck her out from its body, as if she were an annoying thorn.

With a complete lack of interest, Yakwahe tossed Sakima away. She tumbled like an out-of-control missile to a certain, painful end. *I have seen death too*, she thought between moments of screaming and unconsciousness.

The monster veered into Central Park as Sakima somersaulted past windows on the twenty-fifth floor, moving in the opposite direction. Had it not turned when it did, the beast would have destroyed the scaffold there. The very structure which now cradled Sakima like a metal-and-wood angel. Smacking into the scaffold was painful for her, but not as painful nor as permanent as crashing into the street many stories below.

Sakima thought about death and dying and her little sister. She fell into unconsciousness, the world shrinking into a dark hole. Not before reciting a quick prayer for Tangetta: an appeal for protection and blessings and luck.

But Tangetta would need a thousand such prayers.

CHAPTER 24

A teenager, whom his parents named Mike Biehn, but his friends called Blue, piloted his skyboard around the corner and stopped to hover about ten feet above where there had been, until thirty seconds ago, a large, skeletal, metal planet Earth. Like the globe over in Queens on the site of the '64 World's Fair featured in that classic movie, where men dressed in black suits took down an alien they referred to as a "bug."

The fallen globe sizzling in the wreckage of a news helicopter was smaller, yet somehow still ostentatious. It was cheaply made, proven by how swiftly it partially melted in the flames of the downed chopper.

Right before that, Blue had witnessed a woman dressed in a haute couture leather outfit, pirouetting through the air on Central Park West. He watched her as she crash-landed into the scaffold of a building under heavy renovation, which recently had that large metal globe along its south side.

Blue then turned around as his board gently bobbed in midair and waved to the others in his small band of friends who were hovering toward him with increased speed.

First to meet up with him was "MaryJeezus," whose given name was Alice Tiptree, but who went by "MJ." Her pink hair, always in a ponytail with bangs obscuring her eyes, was her signature style. She had twelve piercings in her ears and a tiny tattoo of Mother Mary on her neck. Upon catching up with Blue, she smiled. They fist-bumped.

Next was Curly, who had perfectly straight hair that he wore Beatles-style and dyed bright, sanitary white. Curly, whose birth name was Charles "Chuck" Benbova, hated dirt of any kind. Sometimes he wore purple dishwashing gloves so as not to touch the handle of his skyboard directly, let alone any of the disgusting objects and people all around him every day. Before today, Curly had thought he'd seen the most hideous, filthy things imaginable in New York or anywhere else on the planet.

But that beastly, nearly thirty-foot-tall Elephant Man took the prize. If Curly died right now, he could do so with a clean conscience. Emphasis on clean, because he knew with total confidence that there was nothing more disgusting than that monster he just saw devouring pedestrians at Columbus Circle.

The fourth to join the group was Janie Jones, who went by, well, Janie Jones. What she lacked in imagination with her nickname was offset by her actual name being the title of a Clash song, which was her favorite retro band from back in the day.

Janie Jones wore her straight black hair in a long bob. She was Asian American on her grandmother's side, who had come to the USA from Vietnam in the seventies. Her grandpa was a white American serviceman. Janie Jones understood it was a cliché, but she was okay with that.

The four friends hovered just beyond Columbus Circle, watching the monster disappear into Central Park in the general direction of Sheep Meadow. Well, not so much disappear as trample down trees and plow on toward the East Side. It had traveled far inside the park before they could no longer make out its repulsive head above the tree line.

"You want to go check if she survived?" he asked MJ. As the leader of the foursome, it wasn't actually a question.

Sure, MJ said, but with a sharp head nod, no words.

"Let's go, then" Blue said, looking over at Janie Jones, who hovered next to MJ, and then he turned to Curly behind him to make eye contact.

The four sped to the scaffold, drifting up higher as they moved closer until they were on the twenty-fifth floor. They hovered there in space, bouncing gently, and watched the unconscious woman, each lost in his or her own thoughts.

Thoughts like:

I wonder if she's alive?

I wonder who she is?

What's with the arrows and the arrow-holding thingy?

Nice hair!

Now what?

"Let's find out if she's still breathing, to start with," Blue said. He guided his skyboard onto the faded plywood and stepped off. His board hovered about three inches from the wooden surface. Curly did the same after considerable jockeying for space on the narrow, long scaffold.

Blue bent down and held his hand near the girl's nose, hoping to feel her breath. Nothing, or at least nothing he could discern. He leaned in closer, listening for something, anything, but no luck. By this time, Janie Jones and MJ had floated over and landed their boards on the platform too.

Janie Jones gently walked over, squatted down, and picked up the lifeless woman's wrist. "Oh, cool!" she said. "Look at this thing on her arm! What are these?" She pressed a couple of the buttons, but there was no reaction. "Pretty jewels is all, I guess," she said, twisting her lips in disappointment.

She placed the exotic person's arm back down and lifted her other wrist. "Pulse!" she yelled. She did a fist pump with her free hand. "Real strong pulse. Wow, this girl is fit!" Janie Jones gazed down at the young woman's exposed stomach. "Real fuckin' fit, damn! Wish I had abs like that!"

"Let me see, move over," MJ said, elbowing Janie Jones gently. "Shit, she's gorgeous!" MJ said as if saying a prayer. "That face, it's so pretty. Those lips, perfect!"

"Yeah, she got lucky in the gene pool," Janie Jones said. "But you need to back off a bit."

"Whatever, jerk," MJ said. "All I was saying was—"

"Okay, now what?" Blue said, ignoring the girls' discussion. "I wonder if we should try to take her to the hospital or something?"

"Probably," Janie Jones said, still focused on the woman's face. "Might be a good idea. We could just drop her at Columbia Med on 58th and we can leave—"

The mysterious woman stirred, groaning. She sat up and immediately put both hands on her head. "Ow, *owww!*" She dropped one hand to her shoulder and rubbed it as she opened her eyes and peered around, confused.

CHAPTER 25

Will this nightmare ever end? Sakima thought as she let out a long breath filled with despair. She stared past the girl's pink head of hair to the blue-streaked hair on the boy behind her.

Now I have to fight some renegades before I can go after Yakwahe gain, she thought.

"*Tëta hèch Yakwahe?*" Sakima asked the group.

"'Yuck-your-way?' What…?" the teenager with the pink-streaked hair and the many pieces of metal inserted in her ears and nose said. "What the hell are you talking about—"

Sakima interrupted her to try again, enunciating slower and with more care. "*Të-ta hèch Yak-wa-he?*"

The teens searched each other's faces, confused.

"What are you saying?" MJ said. Then, slow and loud: "We. Do. Not. Under. Stand. You." She made motions with her hands that mimicked sign language, finally pointing to her own temple and shrugging.

They do not speak my language, Sakima realized. *Of course not. Why did I not remember that from school?* She reached over and tapped her cuff a single time on the *tulpe* and *tschikenum* gems, both of which were currently glowing brightly.

"Where is *Yakwahe*? That's what I was asking. I am looking for that monster," Sakima said in English. Sakima's eyes widened in surprise until she realized it was the cuff that had given her the ability to speak and understand English. She watched, a small smile growing on her face, as the gems dimmed.

The *Alànawènik* cuff had given her the ability to understand and speak this strange new language. It accomplished this by sending a brainwave-like *mpoaolonium* beam to her anterior cingulate cortex, which acted as a "wetware" universal translator. The process leveraged her brain's youthful neuroplasticity.

"Where is it?" she asked again. "*Yakwahe.*"

The eyes of the pink-ponytail girl grew wide, and she let loose a slight smile. "Oh, the monster! I get it now. Well, why didn't you say so?" She turned to her friends and said, "She means that big fuckin' Godzilla!"

"It is not a god or a 'zilla.' It is what my people call a *manëtu*. It has formidable powers," Sakima said. She attempted to get to her feet, her aching etched onto her grimacing face. "But first," Sakima said, "you and I must battle."

"Um, okay," the other girl said, the one with the black hair who looked like she could fit in on Mannahatta quite well. She walked over and offered Sakima her hand. "Can I at least help you to your feet before we, I guess, 'battle?'"

Sakima hesitated at first, but a quick study of her features reassured Sakima the raven-haired one posed no threat. Sakima took her hand, letting the girl help her stand.

The other girl, the one with the piercings, handed Sakima the quiver she had just picked up from the scaffolding floor. Then she also gathered up three of Sakima's arrows. There were two more on the next floor down; the rest lay scattered about on the sidewalk far below.

"Shouldn't there be some kind of bow to go with these?" MJ asked Sakima, pointing at the arrows she held.

"What?" Sakima said, a little confused, and then with urgency, "What? Where?" She looked all around herself frantically, peering back and forth across the scaffold floor they stood on. "What have you done with my bow?" she said with alarm.

"We didn't do anything. We're just trying to help," the boy with the blue hair said. "However, I'm guessing your missing bow is up there, if it's anywhere." He pointed slowly upward to the plywood floor above, his mouth twisting as if he were suppressing a laugh.

Sakima leaped up onto the metal frame behind her and scampered up one story in a demonstration of perfect parkour technique. "It is here!" she called out from overhead. "Thank the Spirits. It is here and unbroken. *Kishelë* is good!"

"That was a cool trick, girl," one of the girls shouted up to Sakima. "Based on that monkey-move up the side of the scaffolding and your relative coherence, I'd say a trip to the hospital ain't necessary."

"She might have a concussion, though," one of the boys said. Sakima peered down from the platform she stood on and saw the one with the white locks shrugging his shoulders.

"Who's the President of the United States right now?" the girl with the metal and the ponytail yelled to Sakima.

Sakima, puzzled, observed the four of them and saw that the girl talking had repositioned herself so she could gaze back up at the mysterious stranger.

"What is a 'president'?" Sakima asked. She shrugged her shoulders in imitation of the white-haired boy.

"See? She's fine. That's the right answer. Who cares, in other words," the girl said to her friends.

"Let's get going," the blue-haired boy said. "The cops will be here any second." He glanced at Sakima. "You have a skyboard or anything?"

"What is a 'cyborg'?"

"Never mind. If you want to come with us, you can ride with Curly here; he's got the longboard. Rest of us have the standard model. Not a whole lot of room for passengers."

"I do not know," Sakima said, climbing back down and jumping onto their platform into an athletic squat position. She stood up straight, this time with much less pain and no grimace at all. "Are we not to do battle? We must achieve that first before we can accomplish any other thing."

"You keep saying that," the blue one said. "Why do you keep saying that? What battle? Us? We don't typically 'battle.' Especially with someone we just met and don't have a good reason to fight."

"Well, you are against me, correct? Or at least that is what I feel I must assume in order to protect myself." Sakima said, now rubbing her neck, which felt like a twisted knot.

"We are not what they might say in the common parlance as 'pernicious'," the boy said.

"Parlance..." the other boy said, chuckling. "You use the craziest words, man. What does that even mean, 'parlance'?" He chuckled again before resuming his awkward way of gawking at Sakima. He made her uncomfortable, so she kept a wary eye on him in her peripheral vision. "For that matter, what does 'pernicious' mean?"

"You are not a friend, so I must assume we are enemies until proven otherwise." She beat her fists together attempting to simulate aggression or anger, neither of which she was feeling any more.

"Well, I have no idea what you're talking about," the blue-haired one said, "but nice to meet you! My name's Blue, she's MJ, and that's," he pointed, "Janie Jones. Not just Janie, by the way. She insists everybody use both those names, but don't ask me why; ask her if you need to know. And that guy, my bro, is Curly Benbova. But he's fine with your using just Curly."

"Are you trying to trick me?" Sakima frowned. "Or are you being plain *tèpahtu*?"

"What is 'tar pay, too' mean?"

"It means stupid."

"Whoa, slow down," MJ said. "It's all just some kind of weird misunderstanding. Tell us your name, and we'll all be good."

"Yeah, chill," Janie Jones said. "We're friendlies." She smiled at Sakima with the innocent eyes of a kitten.

Sakima analyzed their amiable faces and had to admit that none of them appeared threatening. "Okay, sorry for overreacting." Sakima said as she cleared her throat. "So, um, I am Sakima. Sakima Tamanend. Nice to meet you all. Now that I have had some time to think about it, you are right. There is no need for battle."

"I agree," MJ said. "Absolutely."

"Good to know you, Sakima Tamanend," Janie Jones said, blushing.

"Yeah, hi, Sakima," Blue said.

Curly just waved a bit and ran his hand through his thick, white shock of hair, which immediately fell back into place like ruffled feathers.

"So, let me guess. You're not from the city?" Blue said.

"I am from the beautiful Mannahatta, the greatest planet in all galaxies!" Sakima said."

"You mean, *Manhattan*? That's where we are right now..." Blue stopped himself from correcting her. "Nah, never mind. That's enough with introductions." The sound of sirens screaming filled the air, growing louder every second. He looked down the street toward Columbus Circle and then back at the group. "Let's roll."

They all hopped quickly and easily onto their skyboards, Sakima jumping up behind Curly as if she'd done it hundreds of times before.

"Everyone, switch on your beacon, just for now. I know it lets our parents spy on us, sure. But for the next little while, we need to know where we all are, in case we get separated."

Everyone but Sakima pulled out what appeared to be an ordinary phone. The four tapped their way through a couple of apps until a three-dimensional beacon showed up above their phones in a pale, transparent blue. The metaphor was a lighthouse, and the bright beacon of light spun about in a slow circle. Sakima was struck by how much it resembled the map her cuff could create.

Having taken care of that, they quickly put their devices away. Then the five dropped down to just above the first story as suddenly as opening a trapdoor. As they jetted across Columbus Avenue to Central Park West, zipping over the short walls surrounding the park, Sakima cried out and pointed.

"Over there, in the tall trees… I see it! Fuckin' Godzilla!"

CHAPTER 26

Once Kieft Willem's meeting concluded satisfactorily, he exited the high tower building near Columbus Circle and stepped out into a world of chaos. People ran in every direction, the air filled with sirens and screams. Then, he caught sight of an inexplicable event unfolding right in front of him.

A woman in strange clothing—Iranian, perhaps?—jumped straight into the air. As if by magic—or by those cable-and-pulley "wires" used on movie sets—she sailed along. She instantly clung to the side of the optical illusion like a magnet thrown at a metal wall. That's how Kieft tried to rationalize what he witnessed.

A large 3D projection perhaps? A new-tech invisible movie screen displaying an oversized image of a monstrous beast? Or maybe it was an advanced type of hologram. There was no doubt in Kieft's mind that this was a publicity stunt. An expertly executed trick. He worked his way through the crowd, drawing closer to the show.

The woman progressed up the beast's leg as if she were rock climbing—a convincing illusion. Kieft wondered how they pulled it off. Smiling, and enjoying the spectacle, Kieft was less than a block away when the stench hit him.

Holy crap! He covered his nose and mouth. The stink had the retch-inducing repulsiveness of an open barrel overflowing with baby diapers.

He turned his back on the spectacle before him, and the smell lessened a bit. *It's emanating from the projection of the monster, Kieft* thought. *Brilliant! Whoever was behind this must have some amazing talent and unlimited money. I wonder if this is for the new superhero movie?* He tried to remember which movie that might be, as there seemed to be another supergroup film coming out every week to avenge some injustice or another. He spun around again, his hand still firmly cupped across his face, and examined the woman from afar.

He thought that maybe she was the latest strong female super-hero character. Her costume didn't look familiar, nor did the archery gear. Kieft made a mental note to check out the comic book websites and find out the name of this heroine and what the movie was called. Should be easy to figure out: she had kind of a native American vibe, especially with the bow and quiver strapped to her and the fringe along the bottom of her vest-like shirt. Cue the soundtrack of heroic super-music. Yet she appeared to be from someplace else not American and not a native.

He watched her jump off the leg to the back of the creature, right above its buttocks. He gasped involuntarily, as she was at least four floors up when she did this, and it was a long way down to a certain death.

Okay, he thought, *obviously there are cables holding her. I'm not a dummy. Still, kudos to the team for keeping the wires so well hidden; I don't see them at all. Or for that matter, thought Kieft, rubbing his chin, where is the production crew? Where are the sound people, the camera crew, and the lighting pros? The director and all the people that stand next to the director? Where are all the goddam semi-truck trailers? For a production this ambitious, there should be at a minimum a half dozen trailers and electric lines everywhere.*

There were none of those normal components of a special event like this. *Hmmm,* Kieft thought. *That's mighty strange.*

He didn't have time to puzzle over the issue for long, though, as a news helicopter swept into view out of nowhere. Nice touch, Kieft thought. The chopper pulled nearer to the demon or whatever it was supposed to be. An alien? Kieft could see the crew in the helicopter, mics on poles, and huge camera lenses extending out beyond the door opening.

Without a warning, the behemoth slapped furiously at the helicopter, sending it spinning out of the sky toward the street. Too transfixed by the copter crashing, Kieft didn't notice that the woman had made her way almost to the mechanical CG-beast's shoulder. He returned his focus to her as she got closer to what appeared to be a little girl.

Kieft realized that the girl looked like a miniature version of the lady doing the climbing. At that point, the special FX monster—or could this be gigantic practical FX?—turned and bolted northeast toward Central Park.

How are they making it seem to do that? Kieft wondered, almost breaking out laughing at the genius of it. He had been essentially at the thing's feet when that had happened, close enough to suss out the trickery, the ghost in the machine. He'd seen nothing. No cables, no stands, or pipes or rope or anything to indicate artifice. As the creature began to gallop, the Earth shook with each enormous step. *Great effect!* Then he saw the woman raise her left arm. On it sat some kind of cuff. She reached up and played her fingers along the top of the cuff. *Pressing buttons there,* Kieft assumed, but he wasn't sure.

Then, a loud explosion occurred. Kieft saw a bright blue-green beam emitting from the cuff as the girl held her arm, pointing it at the beast's head. The monster-illusion screamed so loudly and so oddly, Kieft switched the hand from his face to his right ear instead. He whipped his free hand up to protect the other ear.

As Kieft kept watching, he saw the thing grab the woman and throw her high and far through the air. He saw with shock as she thudded into the building he'd just walked out of. This was no act or stunt, he finally realized. He refocused as if waking from a hypnotic state and heard a multitude of sirens rushing to this spot.

What the hell was going on? Kieft thought. He scanned the scaffold along the building where the woman was violently pitched. Before he could find her, some hoverboys swung into view, looping around from Broadway and heading up Central Park West. The four of them had now stopped, bobbing like buoys overhead, a few stories above Columbus Circle. The leader in front and gave them a signal for them to catch up and follow. They headed toward the scaffolding where, presumably, the mysterious woman lay dead or dying.

CHAPTER 27

From his penthouse above the city, Machto enjoyed the spectacle. He watched the explosions, heard the sirens, and reveled in the screams of agony. A smirk metastasized on his face. He loved this. His inadvertent introduction of Yakwahe to this land somehow already bearing fruit.

He focused on Yakwahe, from the comfort of the thirty-fifth floor, as the creature plowed its way deeper into the park, from the west side to the east. He rejoiced as the trees toppled, as explosions flared into the sky where the giant bear pulled electrical systems free from street lights. The beast plowed across asphalt and dirt, through puddles and piles of leaves. It was like a grotesque ballet. Most of all, he gloated at the death of Sakima—and being able to witness it.

Machto grinned wider. He had to admit he was a certified genius, without qualification. No one, not any other Mannahatta past or present, could do the things he could do. He'd planned this attack since he was sixteen.

That had been a memorable year, like a prelude to his journey today. That year he'd learned two things. First, his uncle, who was a maintenance worker at the *Lëpweichik Èlikhatink Mannahatta* campus, taught him that the buildings there weren't dusty emporiums of relics from the past or secret locations of alien technologies. Most of which proved to be useless, especially the so-called weapons, which included a ridiculous "cuff" with no apparent purpose, aside from perhaps fashion.

It turned out the site was more than that, it was also a permanent prison for all of the "evil" spirits from Mannahatta myth. These myths, taught to all Mannahatta children, were supposed to scare bad thoughts and behaviors out of each new generation as they approached adulthood, to frighten them away from the truth and power. Machto was unimpressed with the mythology because power was everything to him. He'd remained unimpressed until that day two years ago when his uncle taught him monsters were real and alive, here and now.

The second thing he learned from his uncle was how to break in somewhere. This man was the only Mannahatta Machto had ever seen with male pattern baldness and a potbelly and was also the only one with any guts or fight in him. He'd taught Machto the detailed schematics of the place, pointing to where his crew had repaired the HVAC. He had shown Machto where a person could enter undetected through a window hidden in the shadows by the forest. Because his uncle had shut down the electronic security grid, this window would no longer set off the alarm. Equally essential, it wouldn't show itself as being unarmed on the systems. It would appear on all screens and diagnostics as working perfectly, even when removed from the window casing.

A year later, he also disclosed the multiverse portal to Machto and taught him how to use it. It was sacred knowledge to be given only to the most important people. As head of maintenance, he had also been entrusted with this information. He taught Machto how to program the portal to go through the multiverse and back again.

Machto excitedly had asked his uncle why all the sabotage and destruction. His uncle simply stated, "Because you never know,

Machto, you just never know. Let me tell you, boy, you only get one opportunity in life to make a difference."

So Machto began taking clandestine journeys in the middle of the night, undetected, to the *Mënatink Ohëlëmi*. There, he slowly learned the language spoken in the Land Below: English. He also studied investment science and had successfully grown his wealth through shady investments and backroom deals.

He had done this by leveraging what he knew of the black arts, summoning help from the demon world, working the system against the white man with native knowledge. He took their money as their ancestors had taken Mannahatta treasures from Machto's people in this parallel universe. The white man raped and murdered an entire civilization. Not just the Mannahatta, but all tribes and clans, sending them far away forever on a trail of tears.

Machto would have fought back; not surrender easily, as his people had done. The Mannahatta laid down and stayed down. Not Machto. He knew this because his heart told him so. He had become a threat, a force to be reckoned with. Fuck what his father had said, how his father laughed at him and pushed him around.

Well, I will have the last laugh, Machto thought. *Father is gone forever, and I have grown bigger, stronger, and fiercer than my father ever was!*

Another smile crept across Machto's face, even as he wiped a stray tear from his eye. *Must be the air-con*, he thought. Then he laughed out loud for a long time. *This would be good!*

You want a real leader, a Sachem? He sneered, *I will give you that, then, damn it. The greatest Sachem of Mannahatta for all history! The Conqueror of the Whites and The Destroyer of Mënatink Ohëlëmi.*

Machto beat his left fist against his chest three times, tears of anger and joy streaming over his high cheekbones and down his face.

CHAPTER 28

Kieft contemplated all he'd seen—the monster, the exploding helicopter, and the strange woman scaling up the creature, before she was violently thrown through space. *Incredible.* He shook his head as he thought about it, a twisted smile growing as he did so. He was astounded by the weapon the lady had employed. Whatever the contraption was, it blasted a gaping wound through the creature's arm like a laser through butter. It was a powerful result, considering she'd just pushed some buttons on the cuff on her forearm. The beast had let out a sound that was more an explosion itself, than a roar.

He nearly snorted, not because he imagined the dumb beast's pain, but because he was thinking how wealthy he would soon be. Grab that woman, take that thing off her arm, then bring it to his tech guys back in New Jersey. reverse engineer it, make it even better—*sure, why not?*—and then sell it to the highest bidder. Kieft didn't care about politics in any normal way, nor did he have much loyalty to the country he'd been born in.

The device he and his team were building, in his former relationship with Gnaden Hutten Investments, was quite something.

Well, not his team, to be honest—just some hired guns. He was paying them a king's fuckin' ransom for their coding, engineering, and manufacturing expertise. They were developing a "defensive" weapon, which they'd market as a shield.

In reality, it had already been reconfigured behind the scenes and in secret to be a very deadly weapon, a device never seen before. Any person or country with this device or certainly hundreds of those devices could rule the world. It had virtually unlimited range, all in the palm of your hand.

It was all his: his device, his dream, and his vision. Sure, it had many defects, but eventually all bugs could be squashed. *How dare Viktor Azog try to take it from me?* Well, the man got what he had coming. Yet Kieft knew that his own invention that he had shown to Azog was nothing compared to what he'd just seen that woman use. He estimated the new weapon would, if he could get his hands on it, make him a billionaire many times over.

"Hey, watch it, dumbass!" someone yelled, jostling Kieft sideways.

Kieft popped out of his reverie. "Sorry, I... "

The man standing before Kieft stood taller than him and was built like a bodybuilder. A thick strip of hair swept down the center of his scalp with his head shaved on both sides. He grimaced at Kieft with the face of a natural-born killer. However, the whole package, the way the man was dressed, threw Kieft off. The man sported a fashionable suit in the darkest gray that somehow had the faintest blue shimmer to it. Easily many thousands of dollars for a suit like that. The shoes he had on, brown with black highlights and a slightly reddish shade to them where the sun hit, cost a few thousand dollars too. His silk shirt and Rolex completed the look, but he wore no tie.

Kieft said nothing at first, then finally said, "Shit, did you see all that? Apocalypse, right now!"

The man squinted at Kieft for a second, as if trying to decide whether to speak with him or punch him in the face. He decided to talk. "I saw the chopper looping in the sky from my window. Couldn't see where it crashed or what was going on. I ran down here to check it out."

"Yeah, well, you missed some crazy shit. There was this hideous monster—it had no skin!"

"You don't say," the man said, unsurprised.

"Yeah, a hairless King Kong. A bear, though, not a monkey. The most disgusting thing I'd ever seen!" Kieft's jaw hung wide open. He froze like this, with his hands out in front of him. Then one hand dropped to his side, the other reached out toward the other man. His expression changed to a big smile and bright eyes—as if he'd flushed his previous face and personality down the toilet. "Name's Kieft," he said.

The other man hesitated for a minute, staring at Kieft suspiciously. Then, squeezing out a wicked smile at recognizing a kindred spirit—or an easy victim—he spoke up.

"Machto."

"Cool," Kieft said.

"So. Where's this alleged beast of yours now?"

"Well, it ran off, howling. It had a burning hole in its arm, up by the deltoid, you know?" Kieft patted his own shoulder to demonstrate. "That girl sure surprised him with that shot. BOOM!" Kieft giggled at the memory.

"You were saying? About this girl?"

"Well, you know, like, the wound in that colossal creature. She did that, this babe. She was wearing buckskin. It must've cost a fortune. She was using an impressive bow and arrow system. She shot a crapload of arrows at this creature, whatever it was. They had no effect on it, so then she kind of messed around with this strap on her forearm, like a brace.

"Then, *bam!* this blast comes out. The monster squeals and there's smoke coming out of this big-ass puncture in its shoulder, and it throws her into that building over there—"

"She did that?" Machto interrupted. "With that thing strapped on her arm?"

"She sure did. I'll tell you what: I will track her down, take that weapon from her, and turn it into money."

"It won't be hard to take it away from her, friend; she's without a doubt dead. Just need to find her body."

"Really?"

"Really."

"Okay, that makes it easy then." Kieft paused. "So, about me. I'm a weapons guy. It's what I do. I produce firearms, state-of-the-art, and I sell them at a ridiculous profit margin."

Machto looked at him, his face twisted into a quizzical expression.

"Yeah, reverse engineer the thing from her arm. Improve it, manufacture it, sell it. I can do all that easily. I'm between resources right now. To do this, I need money, an investor, or two or three."

"Well," Machto said, a giant smirk blossoming on his face, "you've come to the right place."

"Interesting," Kieft said, beaming. "You're a money guy? I like the sound of that."

"Rolling in it. I live right over there." Machto pointed up to the top floors of the expensive tower directly across the street from them. "Care to come on over and talk about this?"

"You know I would, buddy!" Kieft suppressed an urge to squeal with joy. *What an amazing day this was turning out to be!*

Machto slapped Kieft on the back, grinning like a mad dog. "The best is yet to come, my friend," he said. "Yet to come. This way... "

They strolled together across Columbus Circle with no concern for traffic. Even though it was rush hour in New York City, there were no cars or taxis anywhere near the circle. Lost in conversation, they sauntered toward the apartment tower that once, long ago, trumped all others as the epitome of luxury, wealth, and taste.

CHAPTER 29

Sakima and her new friends from the Land Below skimmed through Central Park, dodging downed trees and destroyed playgrounds, following the path of destruction the monster left behind.

Before long, they caught the hideous shape of the thing up ahead beyond Sheep Meadow. They could see the sickening bear's head and upper torso above the tallest trees on the eastern edge of the field.

Sakima peered up over Curly's shoulder. She could make out the tiny shape of her little sister in the behemoth's grotesque paw. She couldn't imagine how scared Tangetta must feel. Or how disgusting it must be to be stuck inside of that bloody, hairless, skinless paw with that stench all around her, without those who love her.

"Hurry, " she mumbled into Curly's back.

"What's that now?" Curly said.

"*Hurry up!*" Sakima shouted. She hadn't intended to yell; she'd only meant to speak louder. She seemed to have only two speeds right: nervous, suppressed anxiety, or out-of-control fear. Fear was winning.

"Hey, Blue. She said to attack!" Curly said, pointing ahead to where the monster had stopped.

"Roger that," Blue said. His skyboard nearly doubled in speed with just a gentle twist on the accelerator handle.

"I didn't say to attack," Sakima said. "I said to hurry."

"In this case, it's the same thing," Curly said, turning his face toward her. "Considering."

They arrived, slowing up their skyboards like cowboys pulling the reins of their horses to rear them back. The boards bucked a little.

"Now what, boss?" Curly said.

"How would I know? This is my first monster hunt," said Blue.

"I wasn't talking to you," Curly said. "I'm talking to her." He shot his fist over his shoulder, thumb pointed at Sakima.

"Fly me up to its face!" Sakima hollered.

"I don't know about that, Sakima. I just don't know."

"Do it!"

"Okay, boss, I hope you know what you're doing. Please say you've fought monsters before and that you won and that there were no casualties."

Sakima ignored him, though not deliberately. Because as they approached the face of Yakwahe, it turned its repulsive head. Its red eyes burned into hers.

Sakima didn't feel scared, which was odd, because she had felt nothing but terror this whole time. Now, she felt anger, and with that anger, determination. She nocked an arrow. Tangetta was out of harm's way—well, at least harm from Sakima's assault. Now was the time. She pressed herself against Curly's back for stability, focused, and loosed the arrow.

Sakima watched the heat-seeking arrow whiz through the air as if in slow motion. She had aimed squarely at one of the demon's eyes, gambling that the deadly, self-directing, cornea-drilling arrows would meet its mark.

To her relief, her arrow hit Yakwahe directly where she'd aimed: right into his red, dripping eye. Perfect shot.

With a weak thud, the arrow bounced away.

The projectile hadn't penetrated. It didn't begin drilling in its quest to reach the nearest soft tissue, which meant the monster's brain. No, it ricocheted off the beast as if it had hit bulletproof glass or armor. Sakima stared in disbelief as her arrow twisted awkwardly to the ground like a pod off a maple tree.

Yakwahe roared a sound synergy of every terrible noise ever made in the history of mankind. It was so horrible and loud, Sakima wondered if her eardrums would survive—if they weren't already torn and bleeding.

The beast reached out in one swift move for the skyboard she and Curly rode on, like a bolt of lightning. Curly, it turned out, could outride the whirlwind, dropping, dodging, swerving, and banking out of the creature's slimy reach.

When they resurfaced from that wild ride, they were thirty feet away, hovering about ten feet above the head of the monster. Tangetta's childish face appeared then in the beast's clutches as if drawn by magnets or fate. Her eyes met Sakima's, with a dead look, failing to register Sakima was even there.

Sakima glanced to her left: Janie Jones and Blue. To her right, MJ.

"Take me back in again," Sakima said to Curly.

"Um, I doubt it."

"Do it, Curly. Please!"

"Your super-arrow did nothing, Sakima. Zip, zero, nada."

"I don't recognize the language you're now speaking, and I don't care. I have a plan."

"Does your plan involve some sort of gigantic bomb or something? Because if not, then no."

"As a matter of fact, yes it does. Only that first arrow failed, but

I have others. That one was a drill-arrow. I have exploding ones, as well. Time to use them."

"Will they work?"

Sakima shrugged. "I don't know."

"I mean your first arrow literally couldn't scratch the cornea."

"My others will be much more effective. Trust me. We must try again."

"Okay, sister, I'll give it a try. I must be completely out of my mind, and it might be the last thing I ever do, but..."

"Just go! Go now! It's looking away. I think it's getting ready to charge off again."

"Okay, okay." Curly revved his skyboard and shot down to the level of the creature's skull and slipped in sideways like a car drifting. The side of the board was now parallel in front of the monster's face. This lined Sakima up perfectly to aim, leaning on Curly again to steady herself. While they were in motion, Sakima nocked two exploding arrows into her bowstring. As Curly slid into position, he came to a complete stop. Sakima only needed another half-second to aim and let loose.

"Let's get out of here!" she screamed after releasing her arrows. Curly didn't need to be told twice. He sped away as fast as his skyboard could travel.

Even so, the explosions nearly threw the two of them off the skyboard. Yet they hung on as the board dove towards the ground at a breakneck, twisting pace.

The way down was deadly, dizzying, and rapid.

CHAPTER 30

"**P**lease, sit." Machto swept his arm in a semicircle in front of him. "So, what's all this about an arm-based weapon, *shëwanahkòk?*"

Kieft took a second to decide and then plopped down in the center of the white leather couch. "This is quite the place, I'm impressed," he said, nodding. "So, that girl I was telling you about, with that thing on her arm. A cuff… "

"Tell me what you know about that cuff then, um, Keith."

"Kieft. Sure, no problemo, amigo. Yeah, the cuff thing or whatever." Kieft draped his arm along the back of the couch and put his foot up on his knee, looking right at home. "See, from what I can tell, it can shoot a wave, you know? A beam that is really powerful —invisible rays of doom—which nearly knocked that giant, ugly thing on its ass. Ha!" He looked at Machto but received a stern expression.

So, Sakima has a weapon that can violently affect a giant monster? Machto thought. *Where did she get it? Who cares! I desire this cuff— soon. I'll make it mine if I have to chop it off her arm to do so.*

"How is it activated?" Machto said. "Could you tell?"

"That's easy. She pressed some buttons on it. At least that's what it looked like."

"A key code is what you're saying."

"Yes, a key code. She definitely entered a key code."

"*Hmmm.*" Machto paused to consider this. "Okay. Excellent information."

"So, let's go get it, right? And you're covering all development costs? Are we in agreement?"

Machto nodded slowly.

"I have people: programmers, scientists, and project managers," Kieft continued. "We can dismantle that cuff and reverse engineer it. Get all its secrets. Build our own version. Only stronger! We'd own all the codes. Sell to the highest bidder. You get me, now?"

Machto stroked his chin. "That is interesting," he said. "Your team could make a better cuff device that only we could use?"

"Exactly."

"And we wouldn't require the codes that Sakima has?"

"That her name, Sokeemer? Yes, we'd hack in, steal the tech, and make our own clone. But like I said, so much better." Kieft held up his hand in the air, palm facing out at Machto, and waited.

Machto stared at the hand, then at Kieft, and then back at the hand. "I am not high-fiving you, white man, '*shëwanahkòk*,'" he said, thrusting his right hand toward Kieft. "Shake the old-fashioned way. I know you '*kòks*' stick by their word if there's a handshake involved. It's a contract, for life, that nobody will break." Machto winked, an unpleasant smirk squirming across his face. "As if… " he pronounced slowly, squinting at Kieft. "For real, though, *shëwanahkòk*; you break our gentleman's agreement, and this gentleman will hunt you down and slit your throat."

Kieft Willem stood up, a confused expression on his face, which he quickly shrugged away. "No worries there, man. Deal's a deal!" he said. Smiling, he shook Machto's hand.

"Good," Machto said, yanking his hand out of Kieft's too-tight grip. "I'll provide every dollar you need. You get your team to create the cuff."

"As good as done," said Kieft. "By the way, where does your funding come from? Venture capital? Inheritance… stocks?"

"I made a deal with the devil!" Machto said with an overexcited giggle. "But seriously, Keith, we'll need to get that cuff, ASAP, and get the fuck to work."

Kieft puffed his chest out. "I'm your man!"

CHAPTER 31

Smoke curling from an electrical malfunction drifted through the darkening interior. Chunks of metal and concrete covered the floor like industrial confetti. Sakima's father, Takachsin, and her mother, Wùnita, and the various experts who worked at the LEL campus looked around while moving en masse. Heads turned and twisted in all directions, fingers pointing everywhere.

One of the scientists, Professor Winkalit, involuntarily blurted out, "Oh, my Kishelë!" He scratched at a patch on his head where his hair only grew a few millimeters because of a scar there.

"I know," said Wùnita, shaking her head slowly back and forth. "It's worse than we thought, now that we're taking the time to inspect it closely."

Takachsin nodded. He glanced down at the floor, near one corner. "What's that?" He pointed, and the others peered over.

"Don't know," said a second respected scientist and Takachsin's closest friend, Dr. Pahòke. "A stain—might be rust."

"Not rust," said Winkalit. "I've seen that enough at accident sites, injury sites. That's blood."

"It can't be," said Takachsin. "Too big. Someone would have to bleed out almost entirely to make a stain that large."

"They tried to clean it up, did well. Stain so faint, I'm surprised you saw it, TeeTee," Winkalit said.

"Many people," Takachsin said.

"What are you saying?"

"The bloodstains. It's not from just one person. Four, five people, who had all fallen close together."

Pahòke took another glance over by the door. "I'm guessing the exit was shut," he said. "They were trying to get out but couldn't. Then, something terrible happened."

No one spoke for a moment, then Winkalit said, "Where are they?"

"Where are who?" Pahòke said.

"He's saying," Wùnita said patiently, "where are they? The dead. Their bodies."

"Indeed, where? They must have a proper ceremony; a proper burial, this is clear and known," Takachsin said.

"True, TeeTee, true. Yet the question remains," said Pahòke, "Where have those bodies gone? Did someone take them away— and if so, who? And why? And why have they cleaned up and taken the bodies away and presumably hidden them? Because they aren't anywhere around here—not any place obvious."

Takachsin and the others kept looking at the ground, shaking their heads. "It's unknown. We will find out after we talk with the maintenance team. But first, we must figure out why the alarm was sounded."

"I think that can be known, if I may speak," said Professor Winkalit, stroking his chin. He sighed loudly. "Someone broke in here and caused destruction. Murdered people."

The others nodded and grunted in agreement. Before anyone could continue the line of thought any further, Dr. Pahòke, who had wandered off, called out from the back wall. "Look here! It gets worse!"

The rest of them, who had congregated up by the entrance initially, now moved like a gloomy cloud toward where Pahòke stood.

"What have you discovered?" Takachsin said.

Pahòke lifted his arm and pointed. All eyes followed him and stopped when they saw the open glass cage. Some mouths fell agape.

"This can't be!"

"Impossible. The cages can't be opened."

"What is going on?" Winkalit said.

"This cage door," Takachsin interjected, "has not been forced open, either from inside or outside. Look, no damage." He jabbed his finger at the murky glass and the metal connection points. "It has been proven that it is impossible. This glass is unbreakable. Tested to -4000(o), +4,000(o), +/-12x gravity, and to pressures up to 10,000 pounds psi (per square inch), 4,535.92 kg, to put it another way exactly."

"No matter, damaged or not, the doors can't be forced open," Winkalit said with authority. "I know because I helped design the upgrade. The security system is triple failsafe. Impenetrable security; electrical non-dependent; safeguarded against natural disaster. These cages haven't been compromised in nearly 400 years since they were first constructed. No breaks, no break-ins, and no mistakes. No problems."

"Until now, " Takachsin said somberly.

"This is wrongheaded," Dr. Pahòke said, his voice an angry squeak. "These doors simply do not fail!"

"Yes, but they can," Wùnita said. "It's clear they've been opened—human error, perhaps."

"What do you mean?"

"Look, if all failsafe mechanisms are in place—and these are indestructible—then there's only one other possibility: human. Someone let the monster out."

"Preposterous," Winkalit said loudly. "No one would ever do

such a thing. Look, that would be demented. Okay, if such a demented person wanted to release a monster, then why? More than that. There are obstacles."

"Like what?" Takachsin said.

"Well, getting onto the grounds undetected, for one. The site is laser-swept for heat signatures every ten minutes."

"Maybe it didn't pick up the heat signature of a person. Maybe it was a mech. Besides, a lot can happen in ten minutes."

"Perhaps. Okay, let's say that's the case. Let's suppose that they managed to avoid the lasers after shutting down the grid for the fence. Then they cut through the uncuttable fencing material and snuck onto the campus. Let us also posit no one laid an eye on them and they evaded the security cameras, too, somehow."

"It could happen, " Wùnita said. "It's not impossible, no matter how unlikely."

"Okay," Winkalit continued. "How did they get in? Getting through the front door requires two types of biometric confirmation. Eye and voice."

"Well," Takachsin said, joining the game of 'what if.' "That could also be explained by a something giving off low heat patterns. A mechBeast, as was stated earlier."

"Fine, let's go with that for a minute," Winkalit said, a self-satisfied smile on his face. "So, the mech crosses onto the property, gets to the door, has some sort of bio-forgery system, and gains entrance. A mech animal. Thinking, acting. Not possible, and certainly not possible to go unobserved with all the personnel moving about this campus: scientists, guards, maintenance crew, and so on—"

"Over here!" Pahòke called. "It just got even worse." The voice came from around the corner, out of sight of the crowd in the prison hall. They followed the voice, reluctantly but with curiosity. The group turned at the first intersection and then the next, to see where Pahòke had yet again wandered off to. He stood at the entrance of the portal. The device smoked slightly, as if an electrical impulse of some type had caused stress and fire.

"It's been in use," he said. "And recently. Look." He nodded at the control tower to his left. All readouts showed it had been set for *Mënatink Ohëlëmi*.

"Oh, Kishelë!" Winkalit blurted out, as had become his habit. "The Land Below! How is that even possible?"

"That's not all," Pahòke continued. "The portal wasn't used only once. I checked the log. It was used at least twice, a few minutes apart."

"Then they've gone," Takachsin said. "Somehow, they knew how to use the system, how to program it, and how to select the *Mënatink Ohëlëmi*, to get there." He breathed in sharply. "They will be destroyed."

"The monster and whoever set it free?" someone asked. "How?"

"No, not them. The people of the Land Below. They have no defenses against our monsters. Even we don't have defenses in place and we've been preparing to face them for thousands of years."

"Taka!" Wùnita called out, her voice tense, loud.

"I think we have to find a means to warn—" Takachsin continued.

"Taka!" Wùnita cried out again, interrupting Takachsin's train of thought.

"What?" he said, irritated, his mouth bunched up in one corner. "Seriously, I'm in the middle of something important. Can it wait? Can we discuss…?"

His wife stood by the opposing wall, the one they had all run past in their eagerness to get to the portal. There, he could clearly see the arrow embedded into the surface of the wall at least a third of the way up the shaft. It had been shot with urgency and anger and had also managed to eat deeply into the concrete. The drill-head had been selected and activated too.

More than that, there were the feathers from the arrow's fletching, with an unmistakable color pattern. "Sakima," he whispered.

"Your daughter?" Professor Winkalit shouted from further back. "Are you telling us your daughter's been here? Did she… is this all her fault?"

Takachsin spun around. "Let me assure you before any rumors start. If Sakima was in this building at all, she was here to help stop whatever was happening." But on the inside, his thoughts swirled. *Curse it all, Sakima! Why can't you be a lady and not a warrior for once?*

"How do we know for sure she did not cause all this? The same questions apply, such as how did she get in here and for what reason? If not to do mischief, then why?"

"The next person who implies that my daughter could be responsible for something like this will be challenged to prove it with their strength." He prayed in his mind: *Please, please don't let this be Sakima's fault.*

There was silence for a minute, and nervous shuffling about, and some people muttering things that no one else could hear.

"We must fix the portal," the large man, Dr. Pahòke, said. He was the first to speak the obvious truth. "And then we immediately get a war party down to the Land Below. Save those people, if we can. Save ourselves from the monster returning."

More silence followed.

Takachsin was lost in thought, his eyes staring unfocused at the walls. Then he saw it: the little straw toy, one of Tangetta's dolls. *Her favorite, I believe,* the thought.

"Oh god. Sakima came here for a reason. A terrible reason." He turned to stare at his wife, his eyes watery with shock and fresh worries. He bent down and lifted the little doll up near his chest. When he had straightened out and peered back at his wife, she had her hand over her mouth, her eyes as wide as oyster shells. Tears poured down her cheeks.

Takachsin reeled about to stare at the crowd that had formed around him.

"We have to find them!" he muttered, teeth clenched. "We must get our best warriors off to the Land Below. *Now!*" His eyes shut and his hands slowly curled into tight fists.

CHAPTER 32

The world whirled around Sakima, everything a large blur as she twisted down to what she knew would be her death. One hand clung to some part of the skyboard, another to some part of Curly—his ankle, she realized hazily. She heard her own screaming, but the sound seemed to come from far away, as if from a dream or a memory. Curly's own surprisingly high-pitched howl interwove with hers in a dirge harmony. This was it: utter failure. She couldn't kill the monster, be the hero, or save Tangetta. Now, she would be dead in mere seconds. She picked up a familiar but repugnant scent. Somewhere in the back of her mind, a part of her that managed to stay perfectly calm through all this, she analyzed the odor without thinking and knew what had happened. Curly had vomited and the projectiles and vomitus were in the air around her as she spun toward certain death.

As they plummeted to earth, Sakima, in her near-conscious state, next smelled the powerful scent of pine. A second later, she realized why. Immediately, her body felt the stinging whip of branch after branch as they crashed near the outer edges of a giant pine tree, while still high above the ground. Sakima cried out in pain as a large pinecone sliced across her face, scratching hard against her cheek.

While she concentrated on that fresh pain, she felt a firm hand on her shoulder. *Curly? Had he fallen off the skyboard and now clung to her?* She opened her eyes, which she hadn't noticed were closed. Sakima saw the dark, blurred shape of Curly. At that same time that—and maybe it was hopes and wishes—the spinning feeling seemed to slow. That is, the spinning itself eased from a crazy death spiral to a more moderate, but still deadly, looping. Then this swirling became gentle, curving through the air.

Then, miraculously, they stopped in midair, about ten feet above the ground, having spun their way through the highest trees. Light drops of rain patted her head as she suddenly noticed Blue hovering next to them. She realized that he must have grabbed Curly's board and that's what had stopped her and Curly's swirling descent to an inevitable crash landing.

Regaining her senses, she watched large thunderclouds fill the pink sky as New York City entered twilight time. More lights in windows and all along the street flicked on, contributing to the lights already blazing in the storefronts and hotel lobbies. Then she looked at Blue, who was staring at her with a twinkle in his eye and a self-satisfied smirk on his lips.

"You good?" he asked her. "You were spinning 'right round.'" His smile got bigger as he impressed himself with an old musical reference that was lost on Sakima.

"I'm good, yeah," she said, squinting at him as if trying to see through him and decipher his motivations. "Look." She pointed her finger at him, inches from his face. She surprised herself with this gesture; she'd never made that finger-pointing move in her life, not even with Tangetta. "Thank you, all right? Thank you for saving me."

The rain increased a little, with a drop every five seconds instead of every ten. "You can go now; you all can. This isn't your fight." She retracted her forefinger. "And it is not something you should risk your life for. You get that, don't you? That you might die like we all almost did?"

It surprised Sakima how matter-of-factly she could talk about her own near-death experience. She felt something had changed within her, that there was something new there that hadn't been there before. *Was this what courage felt like? Like nothing?*

"Yeah, I get that, we all get that," Blue said.

"Get what?" Curly said as if waking from anesthesia, his grip still tight and sweaty on the handlebar of his skyboard.

Sakima noticed two things then. The aromatic scent of cut grass the wind stirred up far below her. The odd funk of Curly as he corkscrewed his body around to peer at Blue and Sakima. It was a bouquet of sweaty body odor and puke, mixed with the overpowering scent of a strong teenage cologne. These smells assaulted her nose like ammonia under her nostrils, and she felt simultaneously awake and sickened. Curly's sweat-activated fragrance and his underarm deodorant had both kicked in with a vengeance when they tumbled through the air.

"That we don't need to be here," Blue said. "That we don't have to risk our lives." As if on cue, the monster screamed from somewhere in the distance.

"Yeah, no, we get that," Curly said. By this time, both MJ and Janie Jones had hovered over. Curly looked from face to face. "We want to help. We want to stay, right?" His eyes seem to plead for them to contradict him. The tone of his voice communicated that he was prepared to get the hell out of here—if they were ready to go too. He wouldn't fight them on that if they were to insist on leaving.

"Yes, we know we can go. We're here to the bitter end," Janie Jones said.

"But why?" Sakima said, the dizziness in her brain finally subsiding enough to even think about fighting again. She waited for an answer as their boards floated out of the monster's current reach.

"Because," Janie Jones continued, "We love this city. No ugly monster from outer space will mess NYC up, not as long as we have anything to say about it." She and Blue slapped the palms of their hands together. "Also, the city we love doesn't love us back. Well, the city does, but many people don't. This is our chance to show what we're capable of. We can save our city and maybe reset the prejudice against us."

Sakima was struck by her new friends' similar motivations. She wanted to prove herself, too—and that everyone was wrong—to gain affection where misunderstanding and anger were. More than that, she wanted to save Tangettta and bring her home to Mannahatta.

"Plus, your sister is just a scared kid," MJ said, joining in and motioning to where Tangetta was being held tight in the monster's fist. "That girl was me, not too long ago. Human monsters and also monsters existing only in my head. Not in real life, like that crazy freaky thing."

At that, they all turned to look in the direction of the beast who'd roared and fumed, gearing itself up for, perhaps, one last battle.

"Let's go," Sakima said in a calm, self-assured tone. She nocked two drilling arrows and activated them in one graceful movement that left Janie Jones captivated.

Curly sped the skyboard back toward the creature, and everyone followed, zooming with fierce determination toward potential doom. Sakima let loose both arrows the exact second they were close enough, but neither had any effect. She'd aimed for the eyes, but the arrows not only didn't drill in; they didn't even penetrate. They fell once again to the ground.

"Oh, *maluwe!*" Sakima said.

No one on the team spoke an Algonquin tongue, let alone the Mannahatta-specific Munsee variation of the language that Sakima used—a tongue they'd never heard before now. Yet, they understood the sentiment perfectly.

CHAPTER 33

Sakima followed the arrows as they twisted their way back to the ground, hitting the paved path with a hollow tapping sound. She peered up at the monster, realizing that she'd overestimated both her attack and the strength of her arrows once again. Earlier, she had used her basic drill arrows, but these were explode-then-drill. They'd exploded as designed but had done absolutely nothing. She'd set the fletching for the monster's eyes as the target for the AI navigation system. That had also worked as designed. Problem was, they had built the system for normal bioMechs—the kind that roamed the forest on Manna-hatta, not for mythological demon-monsters.

Sakima sighed, disappointed with herself. She gazed at her cuff. She'd hoped to take the monster down with her archery skills and bravery, as well as the help of her new friends. She'd failed again due to pride. She didn't want the cuff to get the credit for the victory. She and the cuff were one, and Sakima would have to get used to that. To learn to work with the cuff and leverage its myste-rious powers.

Sakima would not fail a third time. With new resolve, she

touched the turtle and the wolf gems simultaneously. They glowed intensely. She aimed her arm at the monster's chest. A shrill tone emanated from the cuff as a laser-like ray pulsed out, touching the behemoth's torso where, in an ordinary creature, the heart would be. A tiny missile shot from the cuff and tracked along the beam directly into the beast. *Well, that's new,* Sakima noted.

In another second, an explosion tore a hole in the creature's chest. A perfectly round wound and a complete through-and-through, as if made using the world's biggest cookie cutter. For a moment, before the blood flowed, Sakima could look straight through the beast, a view of the trees and dark sky behind it.

But no blood or oozing of smashed body parts came. Sakima watched with astonishment while the gaping wound healed. In seconds, the hole vanished, with no evidence that it had ever been there. The thing's body had figured out how to heal from this kind of attack. As it easily repelled arrows, it adjusted to this new type of danger. Sakima realized it would not be long until it worked out how to block the effect of the cuff's bombing technology too.

"Sakima!" Blue yelled. "Look out!"

She had been concentrating on viewing the phenomenon of the monster's healing process and now she whipped her head around, just in time to see the beast's huge paw swiping toward her and Curly. "Down, Curly, now!"

As if he'd been in battle all his life, Curly twisted the left handle. This dropped him and Sakima instantly, almost to ground level. Then he swept up again high above the beast's head and well out of its reach.

"Everyone get back! Let me deal with this! You can't do anything against this beast. It can't be stopped!" She waved frantically at her new friends, who didn't need to be told twice to get out of harm's way. Everyone elevated yards away and up as high as they dared.

"Pull back and let me try something," Sakima said to Curly, pointing to a row of hedge-like bushes. "Put me down over there.

Then go, do you understand? You all must leave here, imme-diately!"

"I don't know, Sakima. I think that's a terrible idea."

"I didn't ask for your tactical opinion of my strategy, Curly. Please," she said with a smile, "do as I say."

Curly shrugged and then arced his board down toward the shrubs and hovered about three feet from the ground. Sakima jumped off and dashed into the shadows behind the bushes. He revved his skyboard and quickly joined the others about forty feet above the park.

In the near darkness hiding in the thicket and out of view of the beast, who now hollered and threatened her friends, Sakima exam-ined her cuff. With a shrug, she concluded that she had no choice but to press every jewel on it in all the combinations that she could think of. She aimed her arm at the back of the creature. She pressed the slow-and-steady *tulpe* with the wild lucky bird *tschikenum* to see what she got.

An arc of blue flame filled the space between her and the monster. The behemoth's minimal skin and fur instantly caught on fire. The demon screamed like tortured souls. It then turned around to face this new threat. It couldn't pinpoint Sakima behind the bushes but ascertained the origin of the flames as being pretty much where Sakima had hidden. The monster raised its huge hind paw and smashed down with all its strength into the ground. The result was demolished shrubbery and a small crater in the bushes where Sakima had been sheltered.

However, Sakima, anticipating a counterattack, had already abandoned her original spot. She had moved quickly to a location about five or so *shaèk* further east. There, she concealed herself behind a small grove of young trees.

Sakima attempted to stay as hidden as possible as she once again readied herself to take aim at the angry, stomping fiend. She burst out of her cover to risk another attack. Even through the sound of the rain and the monster's unbearably loud bellowing, she heard her sister calling out. She had awakened—Tangetta was alive!

But there was something different about Tangetta's tone. As Sakima aimed, she more intently listened to her kid sister's voice. Could it be? Her sister was not crying, or calling out in fear, or moaning in pain. She was *cheering*.

From high above, clutched in the monstrosity's paw, Tangetta encouraged her to fight.

"Go, Sakima! Kill it! Kill the monster, Sakima, like you told me you would!"

Reinvigorated by this unexpected support from her little sister, Sakima tried a new tactic and pressed the wolf and turkey buttons together. This combo appeared to do nothing at first. Then, Sakima noticed an almost imperceptible movement in the air and realized that something was happening at the subsonic and subatomic level.

The humungous creature trembled, slightly at first, then with more and more violence, shaking so fast its edges blurred. Then it screamed. But it was not the only scream.

Oh no, Tangetta! It's hurting her too!

She let go of the button combination and the beast fell to its knees, screeching in agony. Then, she could see the small shape of her sister as it floated like an angel's feather in slow motion to the ground. Only she wasn't floating; she was falling, fast and sudden.

Because of what Sakima had done, she realized, the monster had lost control of its muscles and let go of her sister from its grip. This allowed Tangetta to plummet to the ground as the colossus buckled to its knees, howling.

Sakima was up in an instant, running as fast as she was able, despite the pain that seemed to be resident in every part of her body. However, it wasn't quick enough; how could it be? And what was Sakima's plan to catch her sister from a thirty-five-foot fall? That's four stories. Tangetta would crush Sakima, killing them both in one horrible moment.

"Yeah, Sakima! You did it!" Tangetta hollered.

Wow. Sakima had the same thought she had at her house before leaving Mannahatta. *This kid had absolutely no sense of death or danger.*

Before Sakima reached where she'd calculated Tangetta would crash, the monster's paw swept in to grab her sister out of midair. Tangetta, oddly, still cheered Sakima on, in lieu of screaming in fear.

When Sakima arrived at the spot one second later, sliding in on her knees across the grass, there was nobody to save. Sirens continued to pierce the air behind her. Dogs yelped and howled off in the distance. Red and blue lights flashed from far away, barely penetrating her consciousness as she slid through the mud, the puddles, and the pouring rain.

"No!" she cried, thunder providing a nearly harmonic backdrop to her screams. Before she could have another thought about losing Tangetta to the monster again, the beast's other paw slapped into Sakima with painful force.

The paw instantly yanked Sakima high into the air above the park. The thing now had both Sakima and Tangetta in its grasp, one Tamanend sister in each paw.

Drool poured from its horribly distorted muzzle, like that of a ravenous wolf preparing to attack a rabbit. The slobber was a deep brown-green color and seemed nearly as much solid as liquid. It was gooey and goopy and as the monster drew Sakima up to its gaping teeth, she could smell the putrid stench. The creature stank of rotten vegetables and rancid eggs. The combination of all these odors made her feel seriously nauseated.

Yakwahe continued bringing both of its paws closer and closer to its hideous mouth, but Sakima could do nothing to save her sister or herself. She couldn't move. Her bow and arrows were on the ground far below her, and her cuff was squashed between the monster's palm and her own thigh now. *No doubt being crushed to bits,* Sakima figured, *as both she and her sister would soon be.* Sakima was trapped and had no access to any of her weapons. She could barely breathe, her lungs being squeezed inside her chest by the fiend's crushing grip.

She peered over at Tangetta and realized that her little sister was unconscious for the moment, slumped in the evil beast's gigantic hand like a rag doll. Sakima detected that Tangetta was breathing, just barely. Sakima's vision constricted, her view narrowing more and more, like a camera lens closing. Sakima knew she was passing out and that her life hovered dangerously close to being over. Again, she had failed, more miserably than before.

Her last thoughts were about her sister, her family, and the strange group of new friends who had tried to help her in this impossible, lost task. She wondered, as the world around her disappeared, if they were all safe. If they might survive and escape all this. She hoped they would. Her final feeling was of utter sadness at her predicament and her sister's, as well her new friends.

All for nothing, her brain said in a slow message as she faded into emptiness.

CHAPTER 34

"Take your pick," Machto said. "Whatever suits your fancy." He swept his hands majestically in front of himself, like a chef inviting diners to a feast. Below him on the couch were three big cases, all opened and lined up end-to-end. In each case, there were a variety of weapons, from pistols to machine guns, and everything in between, then some things not in between, like a petite rocket launcher.

"Holy shit," Kieft said, following his exclamation with a low whistle.

"Impressed?" Machto said, laughing. "Like I said, take your pick. You a Beretta man or a Glock man? Help yourself." Machto picked up an AK-47 for himself and examined it proudly. He mimed shooting it across the room until he arrived at Kieft, the barrel pointing right between Kieft's eyes. "Bang, bang, *shëwanahkòk* white man. You are dead."

Kieft said nothing, his face a frozen mask.

"Hahaha," Machto laughed out loud. "Just messing with you, man!"

"Yeah, yeah," Kieft said, a crooked smile etching itself

nervously across his countenance. He reached down and selected a Beretta because it was familiar to him from movies. He tucked it into his belt at his back, as he'd learned from watching gangster films. Then he chose an automatic weapon—an Uzi submachine gun.

"Nice. Well, let's pack up," Machto said. "Put your Uzi in one of those." He pointed his thumb at various cases propped up by the door. These included a violin case, a mandolin case, and a couple of guitar cases. "Make sure you select something that fits. That gold guitar case is mine, by the way." He laughed again, shaking his head in appreciation for his own genius. "Ammo's in there." Machto indicated the closet door with a nod. "Choose what matches your weapons, as much as you want."

Kieft pulled the door open. "Well, well," he said. Boxes of ammunition filled the closet floor to ceiling, every shelf packed with as many cases as it could hold. Kieft wedged a few compact packages of 9mm bullets for his Beretta, then headed over and picked up the case for a mandolin.

"When you're ready," Machto said, "we can go find her. Dead or alive."

"Two shakes," Kieft said, closing the case and clicking it secure. "Done."

Machto stared at the man. *Not ideal, this partnership, he thought. But necessary. At least for now. Once we've got Sakima and the cuff, we can—what did this white guy call it? Reversing it? Once we have it reversed and can control it, no need for my "business partner" anymore. Or for Sakima.*

Machto's musings drifted to what Sakima would say when they caught up with her if she could talk at all. He gleefully anticipated seeing the dumb look on her face. She'd probably try to fight at first, in her girly, pathetic way. She'd beg for mercy. *Then, and this is just how girls are, Machto thought, she'll offer herself to me and do anything to stay safe. I can't wait, Machto reflected, snickering to himself.*

"What's so funny?" Kieft said.

"Don't worry about it, man." Machto locked in a more serious expression. "Time to leave."

"Right. So, what's the plan?"

"Catch and kill, Keith. That's the plan."

Kieft didn't correct him on saying his name wrong this time. "Got it," he mumbled.

"Keith, my boy, learn this: if the bitch is alive, she's dangerous," Machto said. "I hate to admit it, but she's got some balls on her. And she's pretty good with her bow and arrow, let's face it. Then there's that cuff you're going on about. I know she has no chance against me, and with you at my back… " Machto said and flashed Kieft his most solemn expression. "We are unbeatable. So, I'm not worried. She might pull off a lucky shot or two, but I ain't planning on taking any chances. If she gets feisty, I'm taking her down. I ain't hesitating." He tapped the gun at his hip with one hand and reached out playfully with the other to slap Kieft on the cheek. "You get me?" He smiled and winked.

Kieft's mouth flew open to fully expose his teeth and his eyes watered. The slap had stung.

"Of course, man, of course," Kieft said, showing some swagger as he strolled toward the door "Yeah, I've been here before; let me tell you. I thrive in a war zone. That's my world, man. Of course I get it."

"Good boy," Machto said, picking up his guitar case. "Let's get the fuck out of here."

CHAPTER 35

The sun trickled through the dappled leaves of the forest. Sakima rested peacefully against the trunk of an enormous maple tree. She slept as tranquil as an angel, a slight smile on her face, her chest rising and falling gently with each breath.

A bobwhite trilled from bushes behind her while a red-tailed hawk cascaded through the candy-blue air high above the canopy. White cotton laced the sky and butterflies sang their butterfly songs, "tra-la-loooo-la-lay."

All her worries had melted away; she couldn't imagine what trouble there might possibly be. *Were there any problems in this world? Were there things that vexed a person?* That seemed impossible. Sakima's smile grew bigger.

Yet, it troubled her. It didn't feel right. Everything seemed perfect, except for one thing: a feeling Sakima couldn't put her finger on. Even as she observed herself from above as she slept, something nagged at her. Things seemed dreamlike, out of alignment.

Sakima cuddled into herself under the flawless tree, on the ground that felt spongier than any bed she'd slept in. The air around her was clear, and it held and caressed her as she slumbered. But Sakima wasn't asleep. She knew this as she studied herself lying in the half-shadow of the great maple. Something kept her from giving in to sleep all the way, from letting go.

A soft rustling in the bushes grew closer. Sakima stopped studying her sleeping self and peered over at the slight noises, a gentle *wëlàxën* wind heading her way. As she gazed across the bountiful flowers and shimmering green leaves of the idyllic forest, a brightness came into view, and it surprised her with its calming effect. Not a searchlight, but a glow, like a candle or campfire when it's almost dead. She watched it grow wider and taller and brighter. Now it was a sparkling blue light with an enchanted feel.

A beautiful being stepped into the clearing where Sakima slept and where Sakima also watched, awake. Although she didn't walk as much as floated, with the glowing light behind and around her, the woman drifted on the gentle breeze toward both Sakimas.

She was the most beautiful lady Sakima had ever seen. She had long, thick, black hair floating around her as if each strand were being lifted and lowered by invisible strings. It was as if she were in an upright bath, her hair rising and lowering in the warm water. She had alluring brown eyes surrounded by long black lashes. Her cheeks were high and bold, just like Sakima's. Her lips were full and shapely, also like Sakima's. The fringed cloth that draped her body appeared somehow opaque and transparent at the same time. Breezes caught the flowing skirt to reveal and then modestly hide the woman's legs again and again as she drifted closer.

The woman wore a cuff like Sakima's. Her other arm hosted a variety of bracelets, some of solid metal, others made of strings of *kèkok*. Around her neck hung a set of stunning necklaces. Gorgeous, shining earrings dripped from her ears. She had some makeup on but in a style Sakima didn't recognize, with a dab of yellow on her forehead and lines of dark green across each cheek. Shiny silver dust covered her eyelids. The glistening cyan blue painted on her lips was nearly transparent.

Sakima knew suddenly who this was: Nuhëma Shaoneyunk. The Grandmother from the South of the legends and stories.

Although images of the Grandmother depicted Nuhëma as an elderly woman, Sakima recognized the stunning young woman in front of her as the Grandmother of all Mannahatta. The bringer of life, the creator of spring, and the one who ended the winter months.

Nuhëma drew closer to Sakima. Rather than address the Sakima who stood smiling before her, Nuhëma bent down and addressed the other Sakima who slept innocently beneath the shade of the loving *ansikëmès* tree.

"Awake, my child," she whispered. She pursed her lips and softly blew onto the face of the Sakima who was asleep. Then she spoke again. "You must wake up now, sweet one; your sister needs you. This is no time to drift away from the Land of the Living."

Slumbering Sakima stirred as if hearing news she was not interested in knowing. She twisted over toward one side. Some more of the singing butterflies flitted by on their way to nowhere.

The Sakima who watched wished the Grandmother would leave them both alone. It was time, that's all. Time to flee, but not back to Mannahatta or to this strange new land where she had chased Yakwahe. Somewhere else. Somewhere where there were no worries, no exhausting fights, no fear at all.

But Nuhëma continued. She brushed sleeping Sakima's hair and tried again. "You can save her. You can destroy the monster, this abomination, Yakwahe."

Sakima was startled when a sleeping Sakima answered her. "No, I can't," she said without opening her eyes. "I don't want to. Leave me alone." She rolled over onto her other side, fitfully. The Sakima who observed the scene smiled at her response. *That is good,* she thought; *that is right. Stay asleep, Sakima.*

"Sakima, my love," Nuhëma said, speaking loud and clear now, no longer gently whispering. "I can't help you if you don't help yourself. Now, stop running away. Stop drifting to the light. Stay with me as I tell you how to defeat the demon. It can be done. You have the power."

One Sakima awakened. The other Sakima waved her outreached hands frantically back and forth, trying to dissuade the sleeping one from waking, to send her on her way to joy and freedom and peace.

"I can't, Nuhëma. I am not strong enough. I am no warrior. I was incorrect about that. So very, very much so..." Sakima's last words deflated into a soft mumble as she drifted off to nowhere again.

"Sakima, you have to do one simple thing. It may seem counter-intuitive, but it is the way. You must embrace the monster's squeezing clutch. Push yourself into it. You can't wriggle free, but you can push your arm—your cuff—into its palm. Do you understand?"

Sleeping Sakima muttered something unintelligible.

"This will awaken the cuff, sending all the gems into a rippling sequence. It only works if you push against the monster's grip right now, with all your strength."

Sakima smiled and said, "Yes, Grandmother Spirit, but I'm so tired, so tired. You are wrong, I'm not in the grasp of any monster. Ridiculous. Can't I please sleep now? And forever?"

"No, Sakima. This is not your time to depart. It's your time to fight and save yourself. Save Tangetta. Get up and follow the path to return to her!"

Sakima's eyes flickered open, and she peered vaguely around, as if heavily sedated.

"I can't stay any longer, Sakima," Nuhëma said, returning to her gentle whispering. "I have to leave. Please return to the fight, and be ready. Do what I've told you, and you will triumph. I promise." Nuhëma leaned into Sakima and kissed her softly on the forehead. "Off now, my dear. Down the path."

"Okay, okay. Maybe. I mean, I will," Sakima said. She yawned, stretched, and slowly stood up. Her eyes followed Nuhëma's hand to where she pointed toward a narrow trail nearly hidden by brush.

"Resist the temptation of the light, Sakima. It is foretold what you will do, what you have already done. Only you can make it real, to live the life before the legend. Go, be strong, and save the day. It is your right, your destiny." As she spoke, the Spirit of the Grandmother faded away into the sparkling breeze, vanishing back into the deepest part of the forest. To a place where Sakima had never ventured.

Sakima took cautious steps toward where the Grandmother had pointed before she disappeared. Down the pathway, Sakima told herself, don't let the light tempt you. The awake Sakima and the just-now-awakened Sakima merged into a single girl as if tuning an image back into focus.

Sakima spotted a bright, happy light ahead that was so compelling and magical. A pink unicorn pranced about in the field of many blossoms on which the intense light shown. The bright, joyful, mysterious silver beam that Sakima found herself suddenly in love with.

No, no, I must not, she thought as if coming out of a magician's hypnotic trance. *Go to the path. Be the legend. Save Tangetta!*

She tried to look away, but the pink unicorn with its rainbow-colored horn was so interesting. Then the unicorn spoke.

"Sakima," the unicorn said. "Do you want to ride? Ride the unicorn? Do you want to journey to the stars? You and me, Sakima!" It shook its head cheerfully, fluffing out its pink mane. "We can be friends forever, for all time eternally!"

"Of course I do!" Sakima said out loud, laughing. "I'd have to be crazy not to!"

But then she saw it wasn't the unicorn who spoke but the rider upon it. Somebody who appeared as if from the fog of memory.

It was Pat—Apatschin! Her first love. He was alive, as if he had never left.

She smiled at him, and he smiled back. He waved to her to

come closer, to join him. Patting the back of the unicorn, Sakima turned and skipped toward them, into the bright, loving beam. As she drew closer to the magical creature, and Pat, the light took on a visceral quality, becoming like a gooey syrup with the texture of dried blood.

As Sakima got closer yet, she noticed something quivered on Pat's beautiful head. Perhaps a breeze through his hair? Sakima slowed down, still joyously hurrying to her long-lost love, but a little slower now. It was not the skipping she'd done a second before. Something wasn't right.

She witnessed with growing horror as Pat's scalp moved, peeling apart from the top of his skull. The reason became instantly and appallingly clear to Sakima in the next instant: *maggots.*

As the maggots squirmed and undulated, the boy's scalp twisted completely off, falling to the ground like cow dung. The worms wriggled out of Pat's head and ate away at Pat's face, as he continued smiling, still gesturing for her to be with him.

Sakima screamed, loud and long.

CHAPTER 36

The gentle tapping of rain on her face, like tiny kisses, brought Sakima back from the beyond, from near death. She opened her eyes. The sky was inky now with no stars, just black clouds. Sakima felt weak like a thousand arrows had shot her. In a few seconds, the sound of screams came to her. There was shouting in the distance and people nearby calling her name, pleading with her to awaken.

"We can't help you, Sakima, unless you help yourself!"

"Sakima, please wake up!"

The roar of the monster went from the hum of a mosquito far away to a buzz-saw noise. Then to the full bellowing shriek of the brutish creature.

Sakima forced her eyes open, barely able to breathe, hardly able to stay conscious. She remembered what the Spirit Grandmother had said, in the peaceful forest on some other world. Push. She should push further into the grip, not try to wriggle away, despite the risk of contributing to her demise.

She did this now, trying to force the cuff on her arm into the monster's boney paw. A sudden and eardrum-piercing electronic noise exploded into the surrounding air: like the biggest amplifier sending explosive feedback into a crowd.

The giant hairless bear toppled, its eyes rolling back into its head. It released its grip on Sakima as it fell, and she tumbled down along with the beast. She twisted as she fell, bouncing off the monster's arm safely to the ground. She collided with Curly and Blue, who together helped soften her crash landing.

Now, the beast fell toward them like a giant redwood tree, Tangetta in its hand, about to squash them all to death. Collapsing through the air, a toppled building, a floundering cruise ship. The behemoth blocked the lights behind it as it dropped, casting a deep shadow over the young team even darker than night. Without help, Sakima and her new best friends were as alone as if they floated in outer space. Meanwhile, the crashing meteor of Yakwahe continued its unstoppable, unchangeable, crushing trajectory.

Janie Jones screamed and covered her face in a classic pose, palms facing outward, her face turned away, crouching as if about to run, but not moving. Curly cursed out loud while Blue wanted to dash over and cover MJ, which would have done absolutely no good. This would only keep her alive for one second longer than Blue before she, too, would be crushed. The shadow of the beast grew bigger and bigger still, like a black ocean filled with murder. Before it reached them, they felt the rush of air in front of it, being pushed at them by the sheer size and weight of the giant monster. When the blast hit them, it felt strangely comforting. It was more of a soft summer breeze on the beach on Long Island than the wind of doom.

As they all cringed and cowered, frozen with eyes closed, they could almost count the nanoseconds remaining. There was no time to whisper "I love you" to the ones they cherished inches away. Then there was a strange sound, like the popping of the largest balloon ever inflated. Then nothing.

No crash, no slapping of dead monster skin against their own.

No crushing blow, no ground-exploding bang. Just a deafening "pop" followed by silence.

MJ peeked first, and her eyes grew wide. Janie Jones was next. Moving no other muscle, she opened one eye and peered through her spread fingers into the air. There was no monster hovering there, ready to extinguish her life.

"Um, guys?" she said. She relaxed a bit and straightened her stance. "You need to see this. Not that there's anything to see."

Blue and Curly looked up from their position as Sakima's impromptu mattress.

"What the heck?" Blue said.

"What in the world?" Curly added.

Sakima was the last to open her eyes and comment. "Thank you, Grandmother," she said, whispering it in her native language: "Wan'shi, Nuhëma."

No one spoke for a minute. Then they slowly regrouped, standing up or rolling off, as the situation required. Once they were all upright and looking around, Blue was the first to speak.

"Where'd it go? Where did that ugly son of a bitch disappear to?" He spat out a few random bits of grass.

"Sakima," Curly said. "Did you do this? Was this something from your cuff?"

Sakima reached over and dusted some bits of dirt off Curly's shoulder as she talked. "I think so. The Grandmother told me how."

"Your grandmother?" Curly said.

"Not my grandmother. *The* Grandmother. The Grandmother of all the True People, the Mannahatta. She makes the buds appear in the spring. The flowers grow. The warmth arrive and stay."

"And she's great at making big ghastly things go bye-bye!" Curly said.

The entire group laughed, glad for the opportunity to have a moment where they weren't scared, confused, or afraid of dying.

"So your grandmother talked to you. Is that it?" Janie Jones said. "In a dream? While you were dying. Right?"

"Exactly, yes," Sakima said. "It was like a Vision Quest, only the Grandmother came to me, to save me—to save us. An animal spirit did not come to me. No coyote, *tëmetët*; no eagle, *òpalanie*. A woman. That's what made it different."

"A visit from another dimension. Believe me, I totally understand," Janie Jones said.

"She's like that," Blue said, the others nodding in agreement. "She sees things, from the Spirit World or the 'beyond,' or whatever you want to call it." He paused, gazing about with little focus at the area around them. "What happened to that monster, though?" he said. "I mean, seriously."

"My guess is that we have dispatched it to… " Sakima caught herself. "Hey, wait a minute! Where's Tangetta! Where is my sister?"

"Who?"

"Sakima's kid sister is missing," Janie Jones said.

"Right, right. Sakima I… " MJ stopped in mid-thought, seeing the tears flowing from Sakima's eyes and the look of absolute terror on her face.

"No, no," Sakima said, in a whisper at first, then a scream. "No, *no!*" she cried. "She disappeared with the monster. It held on to her, took her with it! If Yakwahe is dead now, so is Tangetta." Sakima cried loudly now, the pain and loss too much to endure.

I'm the one who killed her, my little sister, my xwisëmësa!

CHAPTER 37

The buzz of welding torches punctuated the space where teams repaired the destroyed portal, *Skontay Chìpilësu*. Electric drills and small saws answered in a kind of call-and-response, like jazz improvisation. The smells of burning metal, smoke, and lumber dust filled the air.

Takachsin paced back and forth in front of the portal and the group of villagers laboring there. "Any progress on evaluating the condition of the system?" he asked Professor Winkalit.

"We are still trying to figure it out. The structure itself was damaged, as you can see. We're working to weld it back to its original strength, but it's going to take some time."

"I was talking more about the electronics, the software, circuits, chips," Takachsin said. "The ghost in the machine."

"Well, unfortunately, we're far from knowing that either. Almost all of the circuit boards were fried. A lot of the wiring, too, the connectors."

"What about the *mpoalonium*?"

"Yes. Some of that is still intact, a bit banged up, but it survived. Except for one."

"One? Which one? Don't tell me it's the crossover component, the critical… "

The scientist with the long gray hair made a face as if he'd tasted something bad.

"No," Takachsin whispered. "Please, no."

"I'm afraid so, TeeTee," said Dr. Pahòke. "But we think we can repair it. It's only been cracked in two places near the surface. It is a remarkably strong substance. Because we are planning to cut away the damaged parts it will be smaller, yes, of course. It should still work, in theory. However, I can't be sure what kind of power it contains or how far into the multiverse it can take us. I'm certain it will perform at some high level of functionality, though. We'll have to wait and see."

"You are our expert in this area, my friend. So I trust your judgment. If, when you and your team work to restore it all, you cause any further damage, then my daughters are doomed. Do you understand? Without the *mpoalonium*, of which Mannahatta is in very short supply, the portal will not operate. There will be no more traveling. We all will stay on Mannahatta forever, with my girls destined to spend their final days on whichever of the alternate universes they've landed on."

Winkalit nodded gravely.

Takachsin looked at the ground and ran his palm across his forehead, then through his thinning black hair. "Keep me informed, okay? If you have any doubts about how to proceed or, for that matter, whether to continue, call me over, all right? We can discuss, and I'll give you my opinion. We'll avoid mistakes that way. It's critical that this component survives." Takachsin started to walk away, but he turned back to face the senior scientist with whom he'd begun the conversation. "Oh, and good luck, Professor Winkalit. May the Spirits be with you." Then he waved to Dr. Pahòke and moved slowly toward the exit.

Wùnita, his wife, worked diligently in another corner of the room, in a space segregated from the rest of the large area. Workers had installed a plastic barrier, as well as filtering devices, to make the space as dust-free as possible.

Takachsin flipped the plastic curtain at the doorway out of his way and stepped into an antechamber. He then unzipped the door to the next chamber, entered, and rezipped it closed. Here, he was sprayed with a fine mist of disinfectant and dust remover. This was followed by a loud vacuuming noise coming from the top and sides of the little area. He slipped paper shoe covers over his feet and a paper hair cover over his head. He unzipped one more door and walked through.

At a table covered with assorted circuit boards, wires, and spools of solder, his wife Wùnita toiled away. She removed various destroyed or damaged chips and soldered in new replacements. In a few cases, she had had to recreate a broken board from different parts entirely. As Takachsin approached her, he picked up the warm scent of the soldering gun. It was a good, honest smell.

"How is it going, my sweet?" he asked her when he reached her chair. He touched her hair gently but briefly.

"Slow. It's going slow." She sighed. "Look at all this." She swept her hand toward the tabletop full of parts. "This will take days, weeks." Her eyes filled with tears of frustration. "The longer this all takes, the more likely Tangetta and Sakima will be, will be... "

"I know, I know. You're tired, it's hard to keep going like this. I've got more help coming, and soon, I promise you, we'll be ready to go after them."

She nodded slowly.

"The women are in the fields at the moment," he continued. "And it's a critical time for the first harvest. I can't jeopardize our whole community's sources of food. They'll be here one by one as they finish their work. Twenty women and, what—two hundred circuit boards? That's ten each. Once they get here, it will be hours, not weeks." He squeezed her shoulder encouragingly, and Wùnita smiled. "We'll begin the assembly process for the portal as each board is tested and ready. Piece by piece, we'll get that structure up and running again."

"Okay," she said. "We'll see. The sooner they arrive, the better, though."

"Of course. So how is my woman doing, in light of everything?" He softened his voice. "Are you all right?"

"You know, honey, not good. My babies… after all this time, after losing Tommy…" She sniffed and forced herself to sit bolt upright, proud, and strong. "We need to be leaving now, going through the portal at this moment. I can't stand waiting. We can't be sure we can repair this enormous, complicated thing." Wùnita closed her eyes and took in a deep breath. "We have no Alànëmëskat's assistance this time; their bloodline and DNA have been long integrated into our Mannahatta world. There are no more pure Alànëmëskat among the Mannahatta, now that the original Star Walkers have passed away. This is their knowledge, their technology, the makings of what the People Who Fell From the Sky had brought to our people, but they are no longer here to guide us."

"We can only try to do our best," her husband said in hushed tones. "To apply what we were taught, what our ancestors first learned."

"But what if our best is not good enough?" Wùnita said. "Who can we turn to? If we can't fix it, we're done. The warriors can't get through to rescue the girls. What then?" She blew her nose noisily on a tissue. "Honestly, Taka, I believe I will die if we are here on this side, helpless, hopeless."

Takachsin gave this some thought, struggling to figure out a way to say something comforting, positive, but also realistic. He couldn't come up with anything. For the grief she felt, he felt, too. Finally, he simply said, "Let's not panic. You are working on the most critical components, other than the *mpoalonium* resurrection. You are our specialist for this." He sighed, a heavy weight on his heart. "Understand this: we'll be fine. We've made great progress already and—"

"I know, I know. I am beside myself with worry. I can't eat. Look at my hands!" She held up the hand not holding the soldering iron. "It is shaking like a leaf in a breeze."

"More like in an earthquake, Wù. There is much trembling!" Takachsin said.

Wùnita smiled, more broadly now. "You idiot," she said. "It's not that bad." She took a deep, slow breath. "Taka, what if Sakima could save Tangetta? I've been trying to convince myself that perhaps she can. She's trained for this her whole life, in her own obstinate way." Wùnita chuckled warmly at the thought. "She might be capable of pulling this off."

"Let's not grasp at straws and false hope. She is not a warrior!" Takachsin stiffened and stopped leaning into Wùnita. "She's just a young woman. So what that she trained herself on some skills that she guesses a real warrior needs? That is not the same as being a fighter. She's never fought in battle. She doesn't even have experience with deadly hand-to-hand combat. Everything for her is fantasy."

Wùnita exhaled loudly, letting the soldering iron slip from her grip. "Do you suppose I do not know that Taka?" she whispered. "But you spoke the same things about another young woman once years ago, and she proved you wrong."

"She got lucky," he said, smiling, his back relaxing a bit. "You got lucky."

"No, not luck—skills. And heart. Lots of heart."

"Well, Sakima will need much heart and all the luck in all the multiverses to defeat such a monster."

"I agree. I also think she has more heart than any dozen warriors out there combined."

"Hmm. Well, I don't mean to discourage you, Wù. I'm trying not to go off into dreamland. Once we get the portal fixed—which might be any day now, perhaps even today, Spirits willing—then we send the warriors. Me with them."

"And me," Wùnita said softly.

"No, Wù, my love. I cannot allow you to go. This mission is for warriors only. Trained, experienced, strong men. Warriors."

Wùnita returned to her work as she swiped her hand across her nose, sniffling. "Leave me. I have work to do until the other women arrive from the fields."

"Okay, I'll let you be. Do not worry over the portal any further, yes? We'll get *Skontay Chìpilësu* working again. We will save our daughters. You have my word." He pressed his closed fist against his chest. "You carry on, Wù. I'll be back later to check on you and perhaps bring help."

They kissed quickly, and Takachsin went out the way he came, leaving the hat and shoe covers in a small bucket by the first door.

CHAPTER 38

Sakima wished that her brilliant idea to manufacture "tank suits" for warriors had made it beyond the proof-of-concept stage. She'd love to climb into one of those mechanical outfits right now and blast Yakwahe—and maybe even Machto—into oblivion. Neither were gods, but the device was meant to battle gods of evil as well as attacking warriors and mythological monsters.

Sakima remembered how hard it was to develop the mechSuits —the *mechakgilik*. Not just the technology, which was as close to impossible as anything the Mannahatta's best quantum physicists had ever tried, even though it was based on the papers and models created by the Star Walkers. The Elders, engineers, and almost everyone else also resisted, making the task more difficult.

Her father, Sachem Takachsin, and her Uncle Lippoe—Dr. Pahòke, as others called him—had been the leads on the engineering team for the *mechakgilik*. Dr. Pahòke was a gentle, heavyset man and her father's closest and oldest friend. Sakima fondly remembered the battle the two had over the concept of designing a mechSuit. It happened at the monthly meeting of the Elders the first time she brought up her idea to the council. Her father had invited her as a special, onetime-only guest to the council meeting to present certain scientific findings that she and her father had been working on for weeks.

———

"The topic is: 'New Uses for Mp.' It's the gift from the gods," Sakima said. "'Mp' on the Periodic Table of Elements. Atomic number 111. Atomic weight of 333. That's a little refresher for you all on *mpoalonium*." Sakima smiled, pausing for a second before continuing. "We should devise a thing—a weapon or vehicle— impervious to attacks and resistant even to *mpoalonium*!" She leaped from her seat, a huge grin on her face. "That would make it the ultimate defensive gear, along with all of its offensive capabilities!"

"TeeTee, that's ridiculous," Dr. Pahòke had said, turning away from Sakima to address his friend who sat across from him. "There is simply no such phenomenon as anti-*mpoalonium*." He gazed around the table at the other Elders there on the council. This group was originally called by its Mannahatta term, Lupwaaeenóáuk. A few years after the arrival of the Alànëmëskat, the Star Walkers, they renamed it Council of Elders, after the *Alànëmëskat*'s home planet of Eldëror.

"Antimatter," Takachsin whispered.

"What?"

"Antimatter?" Takachsin said, more of a question itself than a response.

"That's not how antimatter works, TeeTee," Pahòke said, shaking his head. "You can't create antimatter that stays around to be, you know, anti-anything-specific. Especially anti-*mpoalonium*. It's the nature of antimatter to disappear, almost upon its birth."

"But we create antimatter right here in our laboratories."

"This is true. "

"But as you said, Sachem," Winkalit said. Professor Winkalit wore his white hair in the traditional style. He was a somber man, soft-spoken and of few words. He and his wife were good friends with Sakima's parents. "It disappears as fast as we produce it. It's 'anti,' as Pahòke said. Its very nature is not-to-be."

"We can make it, though, right?" Takachsin said, holding his hand up in gentle resistance. "Which is something, a 'fact'—thought to be impossible a few short years ago. Now, here we are, making it as easily as we make our tea."

"Not that easily!" Pahòke chuckled. "A particle collider is not the same as a teapot. An atom is not like a leaf of tea." He sat deeper into his chair and laughed some more, his head swiveling back and forth in amusement. "You are so funny sometimes, my old friend!"

"But perhaps my Father has a point," Sakima spoke up now, having allowed the Elders to say their piece, out of respect. "Isn't it just the problem of creating an environment that can contain the antimatter? Look at the cages our ancestors built for the monsters—"

"—with the help of the *Alànëmëskat*," Takachsin said. He was only reminding her, though, not correcting. This he hoped he communicated to her by nodding his head and allowing a slight smile to surface on his face. "But I'm sorry I interrupted. Please go on, Sakima."

"Thank you, *um*, Dad. Sachem. Thank you for the reminder. Yes, our ancestors worked alongside the People Who Fell From the Sky. Our forefathers were there too, learning and passing on that knowledge to each subsequent generation—down to us, at this table today."

"That may very well be, my dear," said Professor Winkalit. "But it has never been done. It is, frankly, one of the most confounding problems in physics, maintaining antimatter once it's been created. Never been solved. Never will." He shook his head solemnly, like respecting the memory of the dead. Then he raised both arms up, palms facing out as if to say, "That's enough."

Sakima hesitated, allowing the mumbling in the room to quiet down a bit. "While what you say is true," she continued, nodding with deference to Professor Winkalit. Then she turned to address the full table of Elders. "But none of the technologies we use today would have been considered a possibility in previous epochs. From the simplest matter heater to our most complicated portal that takes people to *Mënatink Ohëlëmi* are. Yet here we are, and we accept it as we do the oxygen we breathe. It's part of us and always will be. Until there is no longer oxygen in the air."

Takachsin made thoughtful noises, rubbing his chin and staring at the desktop. "What do you think, Pahòke?" he finally said, gazing across the table at his friend. "Is such a thing even possible?"

"Remotely? Maybe. We're talking a very, very remote chance here. I mean, TeeTee," Dr. Pahòke relaxed into his chair, clearing his throat. "At best, it's somewhere between a complete fantasy and an unattainable dream. That's what I say." He nodded with confidence, crossed his arms, and glanced around the room with pride.

"So," Takachsin said, clapping his hands together with glee. "Not impossible. Good!"

"Well, I meant, I thought I made it clear... " Pahòke mumbled and then coughed, his face turning red. He unfolded his arms and reached out to shuffle papers on the desk in front of him in a bumbling and distraught manner, despite trying to appear serious and purposeful. "Thought I made myself quite clear."

"Surely, this is a *kèpchat's* errand," Professor Winkalit said, ignoring Dr. Pahòke's fretting.

"Can we consider using the tech that is now holding the monsters in check?" Sakima said. There were a few nods and head shakes, with a mixture of under-the-breath agreement and outspoken naysaying.

Sakima plowed on. "Well, I think we can, because the technology has been proven for centuries. As you said, developed with the Star Walkers' guidance." She observed the Elders at the table. "It's at least worth a shot, isn't it?" Her voice came out more meekly than she intended.

Her father's slim smile grew wide. "Yes, of course, it is! Pahòke, why don't you take lead on this, my friend?" Takachsin reached over and patted one of Pahòke's hands, which shuffled his paper around with no clear objective.

"Assign the impossible task to your trusted sidekick, is that it?" He smiled benignly. "Fine, fine. Your daughter speaks the truth and argues like her father. Gentle hand in an iron glove. All right then, let's do this impossible thing. Timeline?"

"Give us some initial report in, say, two weeks?"

"It doesn't matter if you say two weeks or two centuries, I'm afraid I must predict now that the results will not be promising. Because there won't be any results."

"Keep an open mind, Pahòke!" Winkalit said with a chuckle. "Objectivity is the definition of scientific inquiry, is it not?"

Pahòke nodded. After a bit, he gave a sheepish grin.

"What's next on the agenda?" Takachsin said, slapping one hand cheerfully on the desk.

Another scientist, Elder Olsen, who was this meeting's note-taker, read from the list glowing on the panel embedded in the desk. "Um... it says here for item six, the last topic for the meeting is something called a mechSuit? *Mechakgilik?*"

Sakima smiled to herself. She had added that item to the agenda during the meeting while others were deep in discussion on topics that followed the original, unaltered agenda.

"Yes!" Sakima said cheerfully, acting as if this final talk was always meant to be. "That's me."

"What is this?" her father said, peering around at the rest of the Elders with a confused look on his face. "I saw it on the schedule, too a few minutes ago, frankly I have no memory of approving this subject."

"New business, Dad. This is my pet project. You say that you don't remember it every single time I bring it up." She smiled at her Father. "I'm talking about my idea for creating an Mp-built suit with Mp-based weapons. That's why I wanted to introduce the topic in the last agenda item just now, 'New Uses for Mp.'" She let her smile fade. "This suit will be enormous, the way I envision it," she continued. "Real gigantic, like a walking tank!"

"'Designed to contain a single warrior,'" Professor Winkalit said, reading from the spec sheet Sakima now passed to each of the Elders "'*Mechakgilik*: Built to turn any *ilaok* warrior into a super-soldier. Unstoppable, impervious to the strongest weapons in the known multiverse,'" He cleared his throat, slightly embarrassed that all eyes were on him now. "'Stylish, too,'" he said, quoting again from Sakima's brochure. "'Blue, red, and green—the traditional colors—identify various components, while the shiny titanium-Mp everywhere else creates a pleasing overall effect to all who view or wear the suit.'"

There was a lengthy silence, broken only when Sakima laughed. "Guys, I'm kidding about that last part! Kishelë! It's a joke; lighten up. Anyway, I'd like to continue, if you don't mind, Professor?"

"Please do, Sakima."

"Okay. Okay, let's see here. Oh, right! *'Controlled by joysticks, pedals, and verbal instruction. Capable of reaching walking speeds of just under ten miles an hour and sprinting speeds—double that. Constructed to enable leaping abilities up to ten shaèk in the air, to move with ease past fallen military vehicles—'"*

"Wait, wait," Takachsin said. "Why did you insert this into the agenda for today, Sakima? What is this all about?" He returned his gaze to Sakima's handout on the table before him and slapped at it with his hand. "Why are we even discussing this?"

"The future, Dad. I'm thinking about the future!"

CHAPTER 39

akima slumped against an elm tree, among the assorted types of trees that lined the border of Sheep Meadow in Central Park. She sat with her forearms on her knees and played with an arrow in her hands. She slid her hand back and forth across the feathers of the fletching as if petting a cat. Lost in thought, she didn't notice her allies floating slowly down from above on their skyboards. Each kept a respectful distance from their pensive, odd new friend. They were all quiet too, looking down at the ground, trying to come to grips with everything they'd just experienced.

Sakima sighed deeply as she talked to herself in a nearly inaudible whisper. "Why?" she said to no one.

She felt alone, even with the four friends who, for reasons Sakima could not begin to fathom, had risked their lives to help her. She asked under her breath for guidance. She wondered how she could go on; she had failed to save Tangetta and was unable to kill the fiendish beast or threaten it. It had vanished. The worst thing of all was the fact that she had been hellbent on doing this herself, to prove she was the greatest warrior the Mannahatta had ever known

—the greatest of all Algonquian tribes. If she hadn't been so prideful, none of this would have happened.

If only I had told the real warriors of the clan and the Elders, instead of keeping it to myself. The warriors would have successfully stopped the monster, saved Tangetta. Everything I could not do. Tears filled Sakima's eyes, and she cried hard sobs that made her shoulders shake.

I'm so sorry, my little Tangerine. I am very sorry that because of me you are no longer here. You have become a spirit that I can never mention again—as is the Mannahatta way.

She wiped her nose with the back of her hand. Then she pressed her palms to her eyes to make her tears cease. It didn't help; she could not stop sobbing. Janie Jones came over and plopped down beside her. After a second or two, she put her arm around Sakima. That only made it worse, and Sakima lost all control.

Janie Jones tried platitudes like: "It will be all right," and "Don't worry, things will work out." But it was no help and just exacerbated everything. So she said nothing more, keeping her one arm wrapped around Sakima, petting Sakima's knee with her other hand. Then tears flowed down her own face, and Janie Jones bit her lip to stop crying. Her cheeks puffed out with her efforts at suppressing herself until she started wailing, too.

This outburst, of course, caused Sakima to cry even harder. She wept because she needed to cry, needed the comforting, and because it was so sweet that Janie Jones was trying to comfort her. Sakima also cried all the harder because she hated herself for needing comforting. *Warriors don't need to be comforted. Warriors never cry.*

Next, Sakima heard MJ across the way crying too. *For Kishelë's sake.* When she picked up the sounds of both Blue and Curly sniffling, she stood up, gently releasing herself from Janie Jones.

"Okay, okay. Enough!" she said, dusting off the bottom of her pants. She had to almost shout to ensure the words would come out as actual words and not choking sobs. "This is not going to get us anywhere." Sakima wiped her tears away and sniffled loudly. "I needed to be the great conquering warrior, and I met that goal. I wanted to come here and destroy that monster, and I guess I did. I'm something of a warrior now. But my sister is gone. I couldn't save her, and I'm probably responsible for her death. So, actually, I botched the only task that mattered."

Sakima sniffed and rubbed at the tears that were distracting her from her speech. "But there is still one more monster from Mannahatta that must be dealt with. It is the responsibility of the good Mannahatta people to kill him. As a warrior and Mannahatta, and the only Mannahatta who cares here on *Mënatink Ohëlëmi,* your Manhattan island, it's my quest, and I accept it completely: to slay Machto Pequonitto. Or be murdered by him in the attempt."

She peered around her, looking for nothing. MJ met Sakima's gaze, but Blue stared at the dirt while Curly flicked at his fingernails as if he weren't hearing what was said. Behind her, Janie Jones pumped her small fist into the air, a huge smile on her face.

"I have to finish this," Sakima continued. "For Tangetta. I don't expect any of you to go with me. I would prefer it if you didn't. You've done enough—and witnessed too much—making for a lifetime of nightmares. No, this is my fight and mine alone. Farewell, and I wish you all the best."

As she glanced around the little group, even though it'd been only hours, she realized she would miss them and how they had helped her on her mission—a sensation she was unfamiliar with until now. She'd always been opposed by everyone, but today, for some reason, she had a crew who believed in her.

Then the small team fidgeted and moved back. After a short pause, Blue stood up, dusting himself off as Sakima had done. "You're not going anywhere without me," he said. "What else am I supposed to do, now that I've watched your sister die?"

"No, Blue, you don't have to—" Sakima said.

"Me, too," said MJ. "That's non-negotiable." She slapped palms with Blue. He then grabbed her hand and gently twisted it to pull her toward himself. They kissed.

"Come on, guys, seriously," Sakima said. "There's no need—"

"Count me in, regardless then, need or no need," said Curly. He gradually raised his hand as if volunteering for an unwanted but necessary toilet cleaning detail. In reality, he was offering to potentially sacrifice his life to help a stranger in trouble. "What about you, Janie Jones?" he asked, turning to look at her.

Janie Jones's eyes traveled from face to expectant face in the loose circle of people surrounding her. All damp eyes were on her. She took a deep breath.

"Well, what do you think, motherfuckahs?" She laughed with unexpected joy. "Of course I'm in!"

Wùnita gave a sad sigh and pushed her chair away from her worktable. As she rose up, she said a silent prayer that Sakima would stay strong and survive. That she would be able to rescue her sister. Wùnita did not care if Sakima conquered the monster and brought it home, or if she killed it and left it there. She just wanted her daughters—both of them—to return home, safe and unharmed.

She marched slowly to the bathroom, like a woman leading a funeral march. When she passed through the decontamination barriers and into the women's room, she stopped to stare at her reflection in the large mirror. She studied her face and her body for a while. Her face looked mostly like it had always looked, as if it were morphing into her own mother's face—a wrinkle here, a sag there. She was still pretty, but she wouldn't deny that the bloom had begun to fall off the rose. Her body was still slender and attractive, but it had a bit of a stoop to it. As she inspected her image in the mirror, she forced herself to stand more upright, pulling her stomach in and pushing her shoulders back.

In a flash, she shot one foot far in front of her, instantly forcing herself into a kind of "battle-ready" pose. Her arms rammed out perfectly, the muscle memory moving each to the required position: one arm straight out, the other toward the side and back. She looked as if she held an invisible spear.

Wùnita pulled her arms back, crouching further, and then with a familiar force, she slammed the make-believe spear through the air in front of her, deep into an imaginary foe. She turned her head to view herself in the mirror in full battle pose. *I still have it.* She smiled, straightened back up, and strode proudly out of the bathroom.

Back in the area under repair, Takachsin was busy pulling cable from a spool. He ran it into a steel conduit in the wall. One end of the cable would need to be threaded through the portal, the other end into the electrical system in the basement. Takachsin made sure to guide a substantial length of the cord down the conduit into the cellar. He took what remained on the spool and worked it into the metal frame of *Skontay Chìpilësu*. He lowered himself from his knees down to his stomach, sliding his body and the cable along the ground. Creeping past dry dust balls and the occasional mouse pellets inside the portal's wood, stone, and metal frame, he strung the wire until it reached the connection point, where he snapped it into place.

Takachsin wished that the work would go quicker, that *Skontay Chìpilësu* worked perfectly when they'd finished with all the repairs. He couldn't speed up time, with time travel being one of a few things that the Star Walkers, the *Alànëmëskat*, hadn't yet figured out. He couldn't pass the knowledge of it to his people, though they were able now to travel through a limited subset of universes.

But time travel was still far too complicated, even for that advanced race of people. For now, even with the finest brains of Mannahatta scientists and their deep understanding of the knowledge left by the original *Alànëmëskat*, time travel was a future dream.

Suddenly, a loud explosion shook the room, bringing Takachsin back to reality. He instinctively covered his head with his arm.

"Oh, hell!"

Takachsin lowered his arm and scurried out from behind the portal, slinking back through the open vent. He stood up and peered through the flying sparks and smoke that filled the room at the object on the floor across from him. The large alien power source—the substance known as *mpoalonium* (Mp)—or what was left of it, sat in pieces against the wall.

"Takachsin!" someone yelled. "There's been an accident! A miscalculation. The *mpoalonium*. It's... it's been destroyed!"

CHAPTER 40

"Well, this is just too easy, frankly."

Sakima spun around to see Machto and a new henchman, mysteriously carrying long cases of some kind that were probably holding something heavy as the two men leaned over toward the side holding the cases. The two stood about ten feet away from her, both grinning with the same self-satisfied smirk.

"Machto!" Sakima hissed. "This is all your fault!" She reached for her bow and her arrows and prepared to nock and release them when the two dipped into their bags and quickly extracted large metal devices of a type she'd never seen before.

"These are weapons, Sakima. Weapons here on Manhattan are called guns," Machto said, trying not to laugh. "I can kill you, your friends, all the birds, and squirrels, everything here, in the blink of an eye. An incredibly loud and blood-filled blink of an eye. So, fight if you wish to with your silly arrows. No matter how you set them, no matter which target they track and what's hidden in the arrowheads, you will all be dead before they leave your bow. You'll be blown apart with hundreds of nasty holes covering your bodies."

He and the man next to him raised their guns and waved them at Sakima and her recently acquired squad.

"Allow me to demonstrate, in case you don't quite get it yet," Machto continued. With that, he fired with a tremendous racket into the trees and bushes on either side and above the small group. Sakima's friends ducked instinctively as branches, leaves, and a couple of dead birds tumbled to the surrounding lawn. Janie Jones covered her ears, and Blue stepped out in front of MJ to protect her.

It grew quiet again except for some late-landing tiny branches ticking and clicking onto the asphalt path.

"I believe I have your attention now," Machto said. "And I sincerely hope you and your gang of idiots are smart enough to know you can't win."

But while he was bragging, Sakima had finished nocking the arrow in her bow and had taken aim. She pulled the string nearly taut, aiming for Machto's neck. She intended on splitting it in two, severing his carotid artery, then his head from his body.

"Don't even think about it, Sakima," Machto said, slowly pivoting to look her in the eyes. "It will only mean the death of everyone here, people that I assume you care about. Your death, too. You and I might trade deaths and both be killed at once. My new partner here, Keith, will cut your buddies down without hesitation. Is that what you want?" He swiveled his gun so that the barrel now faced her. "My friend and I come in peace, but that is up to you. We only need that thing," he said and motioned at her cuff with his head. "then we'll be on our way."

"You'll not take this cuff," Sakima snarled. "Asshole."

"The bitch has teeth!" Machto laughed. "But we're getting your cuff off, either while you're still breathing or not. Your choice."

"Not while we're here." Blue took an aggressive step forward.

"This your boyfriend?" Machto said. With that, he raised his AK-47 and pulled the trigger.

Before a single shot flew out of the chamber through the barrel and into the air, Sakima's cuff released a hazy blue concave dome of energy. It covered Sakima and all four of her friends. The convex, rounded side, like the top of an open umbrella, faced toward Machto and his minion. The bullets he fired didn't bounce or deflect away. Instead, the bullets simply vanished, disappearing into the blue haze, reduced to their subatomic components, and absorbed into the quivering shield.

"What the hairy fuck?" Machto said, almost under his breath. "Um, Keith? A little help?" He nodded toward Sakima's force field. The other man acted like couldn't care less whether the blue buffer was magic or technological; he would destroy it either way. Machto's henchman blasted away nonstop at the group of friends, to similar useless results. Then he split from Machto and circled the team, firing mercilessly at the sides and back of the protective bubble. Machto joined in, continuing the attack from the front.

The cyan shape expanded, growing wider and taller as needed to protect the team of young friends. Machto and his henchman discharged their weapons until they were empty. They reloaded, shooting again, but all for naught. All that firepower expended without making so much as a scratch on Sakima or Blue or any of the others.

Finally, they ceased and lowered their weapons, which were as spent as both the men were. Immediately upon the attack ending, the cyan haze disappeared. Sakima had no idea how it had initiated, nor how it went away. She looked up from her cuff at Machto and his sidekick, wondering what they had planned next. Apparently, they assumed having these strange weapons would be plan enough—no contingency needed.

Seeing that the bright force field was no longer activated, Machto ran at Sakima, pushing Blue out of his way and pinning her to the ground. The cuff did nothing.

What is with this thing? Sakima thought as she struggled under Machto. *It's there when I need it and not there later when I* still *need it!*

Unable to move with Machto's weight on her, she stared into his angry face. He glowered back at her with a furious expression. "You are so stupid, Sakima, always thinking you're the best, that you can be a warrior. Well, spoiler alert, sweetheart; you ain't either. Now hand over the freakin' cuff before I chop your arm off and take it!"

Sakima tugged the cuff closer to herself, but she couldn't move it far because Machto pressed both her arms into the ground. He eased up slightly, long enough to switch his grip to the cuff and get a firm hold on it.

"Let me go, Machto! Stop this! I can hardly breathe. Let me up, you son of a bitch!"

"Son of a bitch, am I? Well, that would make me your mother's son. So, it will add a nice, weird layer to it when I have you for myself, as soon as I find you alone."

"That will never happen. Never!" Sakima shouted. She tried to draw a deep breath, but because of the pressure of Machto sitting on her, she could only take a shaky, shallow one instead. She narrowed her eyes, feeling herself overflow with anger. Her mouth tightened. "You are disgusting. You sicken me so much. I don't know how you hypnotized my sister into marrying you, but it must have been some strong, dangerous magic. Some deal you made with Matantu, the devil!" She spat into his face, but the spittle shot from her lips above her, then arced back onto her own hair, which was spread out on the grass.

"Oh, is that right?" Machto said, a strange grimace etching itself onto his face. "We'll see about all that." He leaned forward, tongue out, as Sakima struggled and turned away. Then he licked her again, the same repulsive, unwanted lick that he'd forced on her yesterday near *Tèkëne* forest.

"*Maluwe*—damn you, Machto!" she said. *This ass-wipe won't quit.*

"Let her go!" Janie Jones yelled, running over and trying to push Machto off Sakima. He swept his large forearm straight across, knocking her off her feet. Blue tried next, grabbing Machto around his throat, but Machto struck back over his shoulder. Blue stumbled back, one hand covering his nose.

"Keith! Keep these morons at bay. *Now!*"

The lackey stepped forward, loaded his weapon, and aimed it at the four friends. Curly lifted his palms up in front of himself. "Chill, man," he said. "We're cool."

CHAPTER 41

The night had fallen with full confidence. Thanks to where they'd landed after falling off of Yakwahe, Sakima's team had had the terrible luck to be off the usual trails in the park. They were in the shadows, out of range of the large lights lining most of the paths and roads.

Far in the distance, Sakima could still hear the sirens in the New York City night, but none grew louder, meaning none were headed in Sakima's direction, to offer the chance of stopping or capturing Machto and his lackey.

Machto tugged at Sakima's cuff. With a sigh of resignation, she stopped struggling, unwilling to fight an unwinnable battle. She felt as if her arm was about to be yanked from her shoulder. Although there were no obvious straps or hooks to hold the cuff on, it could not be removed without Sakima's say-so. Sakima let go of all resistance, relaxing the tension in her body. The cuff seemed to interpret that to mean it could be released. It did, sliding off her wrist and over her hand with Machto's next tug.

"Ah-ha! Told you I'd take this cuff off of you, Sakima. One way or another!" He turned to show his friend without leaving her. He waved it over his head in his outstretched arm. "Whoo-hoooo! Whoop! Whoop!" he yelled, like a crazed renegade. His cohort whooped loudly and danced awkwardly in a circle.

"Okay, okay," Machto said, finally getting up off of Sakima. He stood over her. "Remember who is your better!" he shouted. Sakima looked away from him, disgusted. "I'm your superior, your Great Spirit! You know why? Because I'm invincible. Also, I know everything, and I am never wrong. Say I'm your better, your god. Say it!" He screamed this last bit even louder, practically apoplectic.

Sakima said nothing. She kept looking away, toward anything other than Machto above her.

"Do it, bitch!" Machto said, grabbing Janie Jones and pulling her to his side roughly. "Do it," he said, withdrawing a metal weapon from his back waistband and clicking it with his thumb. He pushed the thing against the rear of the head of a startled and crying Janie Jones. "Say it, or say goodbye," he said between gritted teeth.

"Enough!" Sakima said, raising herself up on her elbows. "Leave her alone, put the gun down. Fine. Fine." She made a dismissive motion with her hand and her voice dropped to a whisper. "You're my... better."

"I'm the Great Spirit. I'm your god. Repeat it back to me!"

Sakima rolled her eyes. "Okay, fine, you're my 'god,'" she said in a flat, emotionless voice. "Let go of her. Now!"

Machto pushed Janie Jones away so hard she stumbled and fell to her hands and knees, scraping them on the pebbles of the path. Blood seeped from the minor scratches caused by the fall.

"Pig!" Janie Jones said, not looking back up at Machto.

"So we're all clear. Your Mannahatta 'leader' here sees me as her god. If you follow her, you follow me." He gestured to his henchman. "Let's get the hell out of here."

As Machto passed around Kieft to lead, he slipped the cuff on. Then, as if he had a brilliant thought, he swung around and pointed his cuffed arm at Sakima.

"Let's see what this thing can do, shall we?" he said, cackling.

He pressed the turtle gem. Nothing happened. Then he smashed his finger repeatedly on the wolf gem. Still nothing. He angrily slammed his fist again and again on the turkey button and then across all the buttons, back and forth, up and down, over and over. No activity at all. No lasers. No bombs. No shields. Zero. A truly epic fail.

Machto snapped his arm like he was cracking a whip, violently trying to shake it into action. The cuff simply would not respond to him.

"What the hell is going on? What have you done, Sakima? Turn it back on! Unlock it now!"

He kept hitting the jewels, practically punching himself in his forearm. "Show me how. Show me what you did to shut it down!"

"I didn't do anything." Sakima sat up.

"*Liar.* You changed something. When you were struggling to keep it from me, you hit a switch or set some kind of lock sequence. Tell me how to override it or I'll kill you!"

"I'm telling you, Machto, I did nothing. I let you take it. I didn't set anything or—"

Machto swung his AK-47 and slammed the butt of the gun into Sakima's face. She fell back hard, blood gushing from her nose.

"We'll take her with us. Force her to show us how she blocked the cuff," Machto mumbled in disgust. He cocked an ear and looked south. "Sounds like these feather-brained New York cops are finally on their way here." The men put the big guns back in the cases but kept their handguns out, loaded but hidden. "Time to split."

Kieft flipped his case over his shoulder and roughly raised Sakima to her feet.

"Wait, wait," Machto said, coming to a sudden stop. "Take those other girls too." He waved contemptuously toward Janie Jones and MJ. "Sakima might hold out until she dies. She's the stubbornest bitch I've ever known, but she won't let them be killed."

"What about those guys, though?" Kieft motioned to Blue and Curly.

"Don't be stupid, boys," Machto said. "You come after us, you talk to the cops, and your friends here die. You want to be heroes, go ahead. I'll destroy you both because I can." He shook his head and chortled to himself. "Sometimes I worry that I might be too smart."

Kieft nudged MJ and Janie Jones in their backs with his handgun, forcing them to walk with him along the path to return to Columbus Circle. Machto now held Sakima by the arm with a gun in her back.

Curly and Blue watched them leave and then turned and stared at each other.

"What do you think we ought to do, Blue?"

"How am I supposed to know? I need to think."

"Should we follow them? We can ride high above the trees. They'll never see us. We can track them easily."

"But if they do see us, MJ and Janie Jones are dead. Sakima too. How does that help anybody? No, we can't take that risk. I can't think right now. This is too much, too fast, and I—"

"Here come the police!" Curly shouted. He glanced back at a group of NYPD officers headed toward them from the opposite direction. Then he peered back at Blue. "They can help, right? This is good, isn't it? What should we tell them?"

"Tell them? We tell them nothing," Blue said. "We get out of here, pronto."

With that, they both hopped on their hoverboards and sped off into the park, away from the boys in blue and from their captive friends.

CHAPTER 42

Janie Jones had always been a troubled child and would awaken screaming—every evening, often several times a night. Nothing helped. Not feeding, not rocking, not cooing, not diaper changing. Janie acted spooked—as if she could see ghosts. Even during the day, she'd cry and point and screech.

One day, the screaming suddenly stopped. Janie still didn't sleep well, but instead of waking up crying or yelling in fear, she would coo all by herself in her little nursery room, as if she were being entertained by little visitors. She would fuss but not cry. Even when her mother, Samantha, checked in on her, Janie didn't seem to want her attention. She just seemed to want the lights switched off again.

A year or so after that, when Janie was almost three, she slept through the night, as if she no longer had imaginary visitors. Janie was talking by then, and perhaps that had something to do with it. Now that she had someone to converse with in the real world, maybe she didn't need her imaginary conversations.

When Janie reached her fifth birthday, it started again. This time, she wouldn't just talk while the rest of the family slept at night. She began chatting with her "friends" in the middle of the day, at the table as she ate breakfast by herself or with her parents, as well as when she played by herself in her room or the den.

She even started to include her mother in some of the conversations, telling her that so-and-so told a funny joke or that such-and-such said that Janie's mommy looks pretty. Although her mother wasn't a fan of Janie acting like this, she loved her child's vivid imagination. Perhaps she'd become a great actress on Broadway or a successful author. Her books could fly up the bestseller lists and stay there, with movie offers coming in as regular as rain. There could be worldwide acclaim, travel, and television appearances. Her mother liked the idea of that.

In their darkest moments, Janie's parents would fret about Janie, worrying that their only daughter wasn't quite "right." But those moments passed as quickly as they appeared because Janie was one of the happiest kids around. Janie seemed genuinely content. Her parents concluded this was just the way smart people acted when they were young.

By the time she was about to turn "sweet sixteen," Janie could understand herself in a way no drugs or therapy had ever allowed her to. "Mom," she said one afternoon while they sat in the local coffee shop, sipping coffees—her mom had a cappuccino, and Janie had a frappuccino with double caramel and extra whipped cream— "so, um, you know all the talking I do, right?"

"You mean every single day of your life?" her mother said with an ironic laugh.

"Mom, seriously. At night, only. Well, yeah, okay, daytime too. You know what I mean. When I'm alone, when nobody else is there… "

"Yes, I do, honey," Samantha said. "God, you've done it almost since birth."

"But I want to tell you something, Mom: I never knew who all those people were. They just seemed like regular people. There were lots of them. I could see them in the background, milling around. Sometimes I'd talk to a couple of people, grownups at times, sometimes teens. Occasionally little kids. In some instances, I'd speak with only one other person. At other times, there were crowds of people."

"Honey, we're talking about imaginary people. Right?" Her mother, Samantha, squinted a bit at her daughter. "We've talked about this. We've discussed it with each of your therapists, this new one included. Imaginary friends. Right? You agreed."

"Mom, I didn't agree. You all agreed, not me. Because they are real, as real as you and I. They are on a different... plane or or universe or something. It doesn't matter. I know who they are now. I've figured it out."

"Well, who then, Janie? I mean, I'll play along here. Who do you think they are?"

"They're dead, Mom. I can look into heaven. I can see who lives there now. In the Land of the Dead!"

Her mother tightened her lips and put her cup down with a bang on the table.

CHAPTER 43

"Wake up, bitch," Machto said between clenched teeth, slapping Sakima lightly on her cheek.

Sakima winced, her eyes still closed, and slid her tongue inside her mouth along the cheek he'd slapped, searching for damage. She heard the drip, drip, drip of water falling somewhere to her right. She smelled a strong perfume, the scent of roses and vanilla.

Sakima opened her eyes. She was in a nearly all-white bathroom. The lights practically blinded her. She blinked and closed her eyes for a second. When she opened them again, she noticed that the drip was coming from one of a pair of sinks on the vanity behind Machto. A nearly empty air-freshener candle sat flickering on the vanity, which explained the smell. A stack of hand towels was piled next to it.

She returned her gaze to Machto, who stood directly in front of her with his hands on his hips. In one hand, he loosely held the alien cuff. He stared at her with unblinking eyes, chewing rapidly on his lower lip like a deranged chipmunk gnawing on a nut. Behind him were the two guns propped up against the wall.

Sakima understood the visibility of the guns for what it was: a deliberate display to intimidate her.

Her back was wet and cold, and she couldn't figure out why at first. Until after a minute, she realized they had tied her to the bathroom's toilet tank: an insult to injury. Sakima shook her head, trying to focus on the here and now, but it wasn't easy. Finally, when she felt alert enough to speak, she stared directly into Machto's eyes and said, "Wish people would stop telling me to wake up." It was more of a mumble instead of the authoritative command she'd hoped it would be. She decided to try again. "Come here, you," she said in a softer voice, giving up authority for what she hoped was seductiveness.

Machto stopped gnawing on his lip and leaned toward her, too close for polite conversation.

"I especially wish," Sakima said after he'd positioned his head right where she wanted it to be, "all you assholes would stop calling me, 'bitch,' you bitch!" With that, Sakima headbutted Machto as fast, as hard, and as accurately as anyone who'd recently been unconscious and who was currently strapped to a cold toilet could do.

Machto staggered backward, screaming in an unexpectedly high pitch. "Oh, you freakin' b—"

"Don't say it, Machto. I'm warning you." Sakima's face was defiant, her lips pursed, her eyes squinting.

Machto stood as still as a stick for a few seconds, holding his forehead. Then, in a sudden flash of rage, he swung back and struck Sakima hard in the face. She yelled out once, and her upper lip began immediately to swell.

"*Këlulël*, Machto! Go to hell." She spat to the ground, intending it to make herself appear tough. Instead, it mostly dribbled to the toilet seat between her legs, making her just look sad and defeated.

She heard an unexpected intake of air from her blind spot. She turned her head and observed the second idiot, whoever he might happen to be, crouching there like an eager frog on a lily pad. He had an excited look on his face, eyebrows up high and mouth catching flies. Realizing she was staring at him, he quickly recovered and stood up. "Nice punch, Machto!" he laughed.

"Thank you, Keith. I appreciate that, as one artist to another."

Sakima looked back toward Machto, having had as much as she could stomach from his lackey.

"You are such a sadistic *kèpchat*, Machto. You and your girlfriend, Keith."

"It's Kief—"

"Yeah, well, serves me well at times like this," Machto said, interrupting Kieft's constant attempt at correcting his name. "Now, no more bullshit from you. Just show see me how to activate this thing"—he held up the cuff—"and we can both be on our merry ways."

"I don't know what you need, Machto. Other than a lobotomy."

Machto hesitated as if contemplating hitting her again. "Enough with your brave act, Sakima. Why are you holding out? Just tell me, and you can leave here. Proceed. Tell me how to fire it up, and while you're at it, how to use the stupid device—that laser thing that my man Keith informs me it can do." He then slid the cuff onto his arm and waited, hand poised above the row of jewels. "Well?"

"*Maluwe*! Screw you!" Sakima spat again, with more force, blood splattering onto the white tile. "I don't know, okay? I just wear it, and it works. There isn't an off button or startup sequence. I slip it on my forearm, and it goes!"

"Well, I've put it on a dozen times now," Machto said, theatrically waving at the cuff as he executed a slight bow. "And it does not 'go'!" He raised the arm which was not wearing the cuff to strike her again, then stopped at the last second. "Look, there's no reason for you to resist. I don't enjoy having to hit you, Sakima. It's not my style to beat a woman so much. I'm not that kind of guy. Make it easy on yourself, instruct me how you do it, and then I won't need to strike you again. Simple."

Sakima peered up at him in disbelief. She could hear his sidekick giggling and made a disgusted face. *He's mad,* she thought. *Maybe taunting him wasn't the wisest move.*

"Machto," she said with a sigh. "Let's take it down a notch, yes? Let's talk."

"You don't talk, little woman, you chatter, you *kpakuwe*. This is all on you, all your fault. I didn't want this. I just wanted an answer to a simple question."

"Fine, Machto. Let's work together. If you'll allow me to propose a potential solution, here's what I have in mind. You let me put the *tëpinxkèpi* cuff on. I will see if I can figure it out." She nodded as if showing Machto the way he should react to her suggestion. "Okay, untie me first."

Machto, without warning, struck her again, but with not quite the fury as he'd done a few minutes earlier. It was no love pat, either.

"You think I'm a fool, don't you?" he said.

Sakima had, all this time, determined to stay unruffled by Machto's display of aggression during the interrogation. She would not cry, not give him the satisfaction. But as hard as she fought it, she could not keep the tears from flowing. Sakima was forced to face a fact that the universe seemed viciously intent on driving home a particular message the past few days: that she was not the warrior she'd thought she was or could be. Perhaps she was no warrior at all. Now, to add to her misery, the room spun and went black.

"Get her out of here. "Take her into the bedroom," Machto said from what sounded like a mountaintop in the next county. "We'll start again with her later."

Kieft quickly untied her as Sakima slipped nearly into unconsciousness. He grabbed Sakima beneath her armpits and dragged her through the bathroom door into the adjoining room. Machto followed. They dropped her unceremoniously on the floor by the bed. Then they left the room, slamming the door loudly.

Sakima lay like that, staring at the ceiling in the filtered light of the room, trying to not feel or think. She was trying to get back to the forest with its lovely trees and flowers and animals with the unicorn and the Grandmother. And Pat, sweet Pat.

She closed her hurt eye but used her "good" eye to continue to stare up at nothing. She wasn't crying anymore and wasn't feeling sorry for herself. She no longer cared about her own safety or even that of her friends. Or about the fact that Tangetta had disappeared with Yakwahe, the giant hairless bear.

She only thought about one thing now: destroy Machto and his dumb friend. It gave her a bit of pleasure in this world that had gone dark and terrible.

She wanted to slay them with her bare hands so she could feel them die, then stare into their eyes. She couldn't wait and knew in her heart that the moment she daydreamed of would come soon. A slow, satisfied smile grew on her face as she imagined a future moment of sweet vengeance.

Something had happened to her in the past two days, which she wasn't even fully aware of yet. Sakima had seen too much and felt too much. She felt herself changing, turning into something she had always hated. She was becoming cold, emotionless, without pity, without remorse.

Like Machto.

CHAPTER 44

n the kitchen, Machto and Kieft enjoyed a late breakfast meal of coffee and bagels which Machto had delivered from a local shop. And beer, lots of beer, with its sour smell evaporating into the air from the various spills. Their gun bags were fully restocked and sitting by the front door. The sun shot brightness into the living room like disinfectant.

Machto lifted his arm up and examined the cuff he'd taken from Sakima.

"How the hell does this thing work? I mean, where's the on/off button? Or the bio-print mechanism?" he said to no one in particular. "Because if there is a fingerprint reader or eye scanner, I'll chop all her fingers off, remove both of her eyeballs, and take it all with us."

"I don't think it uses biometrics," Kieft said. "Perhaps thought waves; that's the shiny new thing in tech these days. Probably it's like a command you have to concentrate on to get it started. Easy."

"Let's beat the thought out of her head then, Keith," Machto said. "We almost broke her, I know it. Won't take much more."

"No, that's not necessary at all. We don't need the exact

command. We'll dismantle the cuff, like I said, reverse engineer it and then create our own activation word. Not a problem."

"Then we're good to go, right? Got what we wanted. Funny, though… " he trailed off.

"What?"

"We didn't need to torture her at all, as it turns out, haha. I enjoyed it. I'm enjoying the memory of it, even more now, knowing that it was completely unnecessary!" He slapped the table a couple of times with his hand, hooting loudly, splashing a small puddle of beer. He chugged down the contents of the rest of the bottle and slammed it down with a bang.

"Yeah, man!" Kieft said. "Totally worth it!" He laughed along with Machto but with his mouth flat. He peered over at Machto every few seconds to ensure that he should still be laughing. After a minute or so, Kieft stood up. "We should go see my friends; it's all arranged. They're into it."

"Yep," Machto said, standing up and moving close to Kieft so he could tower over the white man and remind him who's boss. "I say, it's time for us to move. So, *shëwanahkòk*, where to?"

"A little north of the city, a place called Nanuet. Forty minutes by train, maybe less. Easy."

"But why the train?" Machto said. "Why not just steal a car?"

Kieft chuckled and shook his head. "You're a riot. Not a clue." He stopped, chuckling when he realized he was the only one amused. "Rush hour, man. You understand?"

"No."

"It will take us freakin' forever to go by car. By train, we'll get there fast and with no problems. Easy."

"I get it. I don't care how we get there; let's just get there. First, we got to handle the girls."

Kieft had a quizzical look on his face. "What about them? What are you planning on doing?"

"Sakima won't last long," Machto said. "I'm not sure she'll ever wake up again. So she's no longer a threat."

"And the other two?"

"Kill 'em. Who cares about them, anyway? They were for insurance, and we don't require them anymore."

"I don't know, Machto, here? In this apartment? I expect it will bring security, the police, and everything. Why don't we leave 'em? They won't say anything. All the same, I think we should take one of them along, to be safe."

Machto almost giggled with joy. "I'm loving this idea! Just the one girl. It's been a long time. Go get the sexy one, man, with the sensuous mouth. Not the chick with the funny eyes." Machto crossed his eyes and stuck his tongue out clownishly. "Nobody needs a girl with eyes that jitter around like that. It would ruin the whole thing."

"But what about Sakeemer?" Kieft asked.

"She'll be dead by tonight," Machto said with a shrug.

Kieft imitated Machto's shrug and then strolled down the hall toward the bedrooms. He returned, pulling MJ behind him. She seemed confused and disoriented. She had been sound asleep only minutes ago.

Speaking slowly, her brain still mostly in dreamland, she said, "You bastards better leave me alone! No matter what you have planned, when my boyfriend gets here—"

"Shut up," Machto snapped. Then to Kieft, he said, "We ready to go then?"

"Ready."

"Don't let her out of your sight," Machto said, pointing at MJ. "No bathroom, no other reason whatsoever to be alone." He thought for a second and then quietly said, "Wish we had handcuffs."

"My grip is better than any handcuffs," Kieft said, squeezing MJ's wrist tightly.

"Owww-wah!" MJ yelled. She tried to pull away, tears of anger welling in her eyes.

"Perfect," Machto said. "Just like that."

They picked up their weapon cases, Kieft never loosening his searing grip on MJ. He spoke to her through clenched teeth, like he'd seen Machto do. "Not a peep, you hear me? Or, well, you don't want to know."

MJ resisted at first, even though Kieft was pulling her through the open doorway. From behind, Machto rapped his knuckles against her head.

Despite the pain, MJ said nothing. She wouldn't look at either of them. She just stared at the floor as she was pulled and prodded toward the elevator. If they could have seen her eyes, they would have noticed they were filled with something new—pure hatred.

CHAPTER 45

The field of grass rippled with the breeze. Ten-year-old Sakima picked a daisy and held it to her nose, breathing in the wonderful scent. She closed her eyes as she sat there, legs outstretched, and turned her face up to the sun. The heat felt so good after the recent cold spell. Spring was finally here, and summer was not far off. The air fresh and almost glimmering, renewed after last night's thunderstorm.

"Achoo!"

Sakima opened one eye and gave her mother, Wùnita, a sideways glance.

"Sorry, honey, pollen," her mother said. "You know how I get. I think it's time to refresh my allergy device."

"You need the pills," Sakima said.

"Thank you, Dr. Sakima."

Sakima giggled. "Mommy, you're being silly. I'm not a doctor! And besides..." said the young girl, stretching her hands high above her head luxuriously. She dropped them back to her sides before she continued. "I want to be a warrior."

"Honey, I appreciate that," Sakima's mother said. She no doubt meant to sound cheerful and encouraging, but her voice betrayed the fear inside that she felt for her daughter and her chosen fascinations.

"Here, have some more. " She held out a shallow basket to Sakima, who took a chunk of fry bread and jammed it eagerly into her mouth. "Have a strawberry, too." Sakima didn't mind if she did, popping a strawberry into her already full cheeks.

"Yum!" Sakima said. She looked around the field, edged by hundreds of trees, many of which had a perfect—and enormous—target attached to its trunk. These were at just the right height, which happened to be Sakima's standing eye level.

Sakima skimmed her hand across the short grass beside her, feeling the heated blades and closer to the ground, the cool dampness. "I should get back to practicing. Still not good enough, I think."

"You're very talented, Sakima. I think you drive yourself too hard for someone so young. What do you say we take a walk? We can hold hands through the forest to the waterfall. You love it there."

"Yeah, it's nice," Sakima said, standing up and stretching. "But I like shooting arrows better." She reached down for her bow and her quiver of arrows, trying to keep her knees locked and her legs straight, just to see if she could do it. She could, of course. Sakima straightened up and held her hand above her eyes and watched a falcon soar through the air searching for food. "I like falcons, Mommy. I wish to be strong like them. Observe everything like they do. Attack like them."

"That's good, honey," her mother said, a smile growing on her lips. "Oh, Sakima, before you get started, I have something for you. "

"Another bow? You just gave me my favorite bow of all time for my birthday. I don't need more bows, Mom. Unless it's an even better one!" Sakima laughed loudly, the music of it twinkling through the spring air.

"Not another bow," her mother said. "It does have to do with archery, though." Wùnita removed a thin parcel from the picnic bag she used to carry the blanket and food.

Sakima jumped up and down with excitement. "What is it? What is it!"

"Close your eyes," her mother said. Sakima did so, feeling like she was floating right off the ground with the nervous anticipation. Her mother unraveled the silky headcloth that surrounded the thing, revealing an arrow of unusual color. "Open," she said.

Sakima's eyes instantly popped open. There on the grass, resting on a large section of wheat-colored fabric, was an arrow. It was unlike any she'd ever seen before. There were three things about it that were not to her liking.

First, the shaft of the arrow was pink. Not a crazy bright pink like in her "appropriate lipsticks for young girls" set. This was more of an almost transparent color, laid over white—still pink but subdued. Second, the fletching was rainbow-colored. Not with every feather dyed like the rainbow, but with each feather a distinct color of the rainbow. One blue, one yellow, one green, one orange, and one purple. Third and last, the arrowhead itself was a ghastly sparkling pink-gold color. Sakima wasn't sure if they made it from gold or just gold-plated, but she didn't care.

"Mother! I can't possibly be seen with that arrow!"

"Well, why not?"

"Everyone teases me as it is. Some boys are really mean. Ow!" She slapped at the mosquito feasting at the back of her young neck. She swept the crushed bug away, leaving a little smear of blood. Sakima made an annoyed face because of being bitten and because of this dumb gift. She pulled her upper lip toward her nose and put her hands on her hips. "They say I'm too girly to be a fighter. They laugh and point and tell me to go play with my dolls and my makeup."

"That's not fair—"

"I couldn't possibly have that arrow in my quiver, and I

couldn't possibly ever shoot it. Ever!" Sakima scratched at the itchy mosquito bite with one hand. She lowered her voice and gritted her teeth a bit. "It's silly, and they would all say that I am a silly girl. Even the girls who call me a half-boy!"

"They shouldn't say things like that… "

Sakima's mother peered up at Sakima and Sakima down at her mom. They looked at each other in silence as the falcon circled above them, still searching for a reason to swoop down to Earth.

"Sakima, honey. Can I tell you a story about this special arrow?"

Sakima made a face of irritation, rolling her eyes and opening her mouth to exhale loudly. Her mother waited patiently for her to finish and to say yes or no, which she eventually did, in a way.

"I guess."

"Thank you. When I was a little girl like you… " Sakima hated these stories. They were *so* boring. She listened anyway because she knew her mother liked so much to tell these to her. "I had a visit from my grandmother. Well, not my grandmother. The Grand-mother. I don't think you're old enough to understand the differ-ence yet."

"Yes, I am." Sakima squished her face. "I am too."

"Okay, well, let me be the judge of that, would you please?"

Sakima kept making the same expression, her mouth twisting tinier by the second, like it was being sucked into her face. "What was her name? 'Grandmother.'"

"I mean, I guess she had a name, but I never learned what it was."

"You don't know your own grandma's name?"

"I knew where she was from, which was kind of like her title."

"What was it?" Sakima folded her skinny arms across her chest.

"The South. She was called Nuhëma Shaoneyunk. The Grand-mother of the South. The Creator of Flowers. Some other titles, too."

"Why?"

"I don't know. That's what they named her. Forever."

"Well, why 'south?'"

"Because it is said she brought the warmth with her after wintertime when she arrived."

"I like that," Sakima said, a big smile popping onto her face where the puncture-wound of her lips had formerly resided. "I like it when it's warm!"

"Me too," her mother said. "So anyway, on this one visit, she gave me this same arrow, the arrow you've rejected."

"I need to practice." Sakima drooped her body, folding into herself.

"I know. I'm almost done." Wùnita cleared her throat. "So she presented me with these two pink arrows, and she told me not to use either of them. That one was for me and the other for my daughter, not yet born."

"Then why did she give them to you in the first place, if she wouldn't let you use them?"

"She wanted me to have them, Sakima. Like I want you to have one now too. Then we'll each own one, a connection. She instructed me—and I'm telling you now, the same thing—that you should not use the arrow until you're positive the right time has come."

"When did you use it?"

"I didn't, honey. The Grandmother said they were for that one special moment. That I'd know the hour when it arrived."

"Why?"

"She didn't say. All she said was not to use the arrows until the time WAS right."

"Well, I can do it now, if I want to. Can't I?"

"Sakima, honey, weren't you listening? No, you can't at this time. What she meant was, there will be a very important moment, and you'll realize it when it happens. You'll know that the time has arrived for you to use this special pink arrow."

"I don't understand," Sakima said. "How can you possibly know something like that?"

"You will feel it in your heart, honey. We both will." Wùnita pressed her fist against her heart. "You need to take this seriously, hon. I have the feeling that what the Grandmother of the South was implying was that this arrow might save your life when nothing else can help you."

"Okay, Mommy, I'll wait until I feel it right here," Sakima said, beating her small fist against her chest with a soft thud.

"Good girl, Sakima."

"But I don't think that I might ever feel it here," she said as she tapped her chest again, "because it's pink, and I don't want to shoot it. Just like you."

"Well, wait... what?"

"You never used it either, right? I think you didn't because it's pink with rainbow feathers."

"No, that's not correct. The moment never came—"

"But wait! I just thought of something. Why did South Grandma give you two arrows? You're a girl, silly. You're not a warrior man!"

"Well, that's true."

"How would you even know how to shoot it?" Sakima tossed her head back, laughing, proud of the observation she'd made. "That's silly of South Grandma!"

"I can shoot an arrow, Sakima."

"No, you cannot, Mommy. I've never seen you do that."

"Well, just because you've never seen me do that doesn't mean I don't know how."

"But girls aren't supposed to shoot arrows. That's for boys. You and Daddy always tell me that."

"Well, yes, that's accurate. I shot arrows when I was your age, Sakima. Then I grew up, I became a young lady, and I didn't want to play with bows and arrows anymore."

"That's not a true story," Sakima said, giggling heartily. "Who would give up arrow shooting?"

"You will, honey. When you become a young woman and become interested in womanly things. Like gardening and sewing and nice young men."

"Well, I don't believe you." Sakima's mouth tilted up toward her left ear.

"That's fine. Put this arrow in your quiver all the same, and keep it for that special day, like I said to you. Like the Grandmother told me."

"Let's contest for it!"

"What are you talking about?"

"Whoever shoots an arrow best wins. We each take one arrow. If I win, I don't have to carry that dumb arrow around. If you win, then fine. I'll put it in my quiver with my real arrows."

"You're on."

"One shot each."

"Fine," her mother said. "But I haven't shot an arrow in… well, I can't even guess how many years…"

Sakima laughed again. "Then I'll win easily, and you can keep that girly arrow."

"We'll see."

"Yes, we will!" Sakima shouted with glee.

"Okay, honey. How about you go first? I need to practice a bit with this bow with no arrows." She picked up Sakima's older bow, the one Sakima was using earlier this year.

"Sure," Sakima said, struggling not to laugh. She took an arrow from the quiver on her back, placed it in her bow, and pulled the bowstring with practiced confidence.

Her mother watched as Sakima released the bowstring, sending the arrow spinning across the field toward the tree. It penetrated the bullseye with such force that the target, although twice regulation size, rocked with the impact.

"You lose, Mommy!" Sakima said, trying to wink at her mother but just squeezing her chunky cheeks, making both eyes close and open a couple of times.

"Could be," her mother said. "That was an amazing shot."

Wùnita selected an arrow at random from Sakima's quiver and nocked it. Then she stepped to the same spot where Sakima had taken her shot and carefully lined it up. She pulled the string to her face, eyes focused sharply ahead on the bullseye where Sakima's arrow stuck. Then she let it fly.

The arrow raced like an attacking falcon through the warm spring air until it slammed straight into Sakima's arrow, splitting it down the middle, sending feathers fluttering to the ground.

Sakima stood there, mouth slightly open, staring at where the two arrows were embedded into the exact same spot.

"What… how… ?" the young girl tried to say, barely getting the words out softly from her mouth, which was mostly agape.

"Skill and confidence," her mother said, picking up the pink arrow and slipping it gently into the quiver still strapped to Sakima's back. She gave Sakima a little pat on her shoulder. "And years and years of practice."

CHAPTER 46

Alone in the dark, locked bedroom, Sakima awakened. Every inch of her hurt. Her skull throbbed and her stomach roiled. She felt poisoned, destroyed. Her eyes, nose, and lips were swollen, and they ached as if she'd walked into a stone barricade.

Sakima gazed about, confused. Where was she? Light from the street outside sliced through the gaps in the vertical blinds, striping the bed with parallel lines like prison bars.

A strong odor of pine wafted through the room. Sakima realized it was the result of a cleaning solution coming from the hallway across from her. She forced herself to sit up, pushing her hands against the polished wooden floor and her back up against the garishly painted red wall. She arched her back first, trying to counter the pain she suffered there. Next, she pressed herself into the wall to force her spine to be as straight as it could.

She flexed both arms, feeling her small but powerful biceps contract and release. Doing so made her feel like herself: strong, capable. She rolled her neck to the right, then down, then to the left, and finally both up and back at the same time. She completed this cycle again nice and slow and then one final time faster than the first. Sakima heard and felt the cracking noises as the vertebrae in her neck realigned. Then she took some slow, exaggerated breaths, breathing in through her mouth and out through her nose. She did this routine three times as well.

As she forced herself to do her daily set of pushups, Sakima thought about the events of the past couple of days. How normal her life had seemed to end just twenty-four hours ago. In an instant it had all changed.

Because of Machto. She sneered. Then she remembered why she was here: to kill any and all monsters, including the worst one of all: Machto.

She flipped onto her back and started her core routine as best she could. Even as hurt as she was, she was not willing to give that up. Lifting her legs and crunching her abs, Sakima remembered causing the Yakwahe to vanish with the help of Grandmother Nuhëma. Then, with a gasp, she dropped her feet to the ground, remembering again that Tangetta was gone, dead. Sakima squeezed her eyes shut and lay on her back as still as a corpse, taking jagged breaths. Instead of processing all the emotions cascading on top of her, she fought to send them deep inside herself, far away from her consciousness. She kept her eyes closed tight, her lips taut with the struggle of trying to escape all that emotional pain.

Eventually, she sighed loudly as her mind drifted to the last few seconds of her battle with that impossible horror. How close she had come to dying. How she had found four friends who'd risked their lives to help her save her kid sister.

Where are they now? Probably safe in their own homes, their own worlds. Maybe, wondered Sakima, *maybe not. Perhaps telling people what took place, what they witnessed, what they took part in. Or better still, and wisely, keeping it a secret between themselves, never to be mentioned again.*

I can't blame them, though, thought Sakima. *I might've done the same if some strange woman unexpectedly materialized on Manhattan, with odd clothing and makeup, as well as weapons, telling a wild story of saving her sister from some mythological behemoth. Then they had fought against that monster, to help me while risking their own lives. Until they witnessed my utter failure and Tangetta disappear into nothingness, into death.*

Well, maybe I would hide all that, too. Keep it concealed from my family, friends, the press, and the police. I don't think I'd say a word. I'd feel sorry and sad for the mysterious alien girl and her tragic loss. I will tell no one about it, forever.

Sakima moved her head slowly, glancing up at the ceiling, absentmindedly following the crown molding with her gaze. She reassured herself that she was still here, alive, and with a purpose. She was a warrior, here to save this world and its people, even if she could no longer rescue Tangetta. She knew that this was true because of Nuhëma, the Grandmother. She'd come to Sakima in a vision and she'd helped her in the real world when she'd returned from that dream, that involuntary vision quest.

But Sakima was puzzled, even as she took solace in that visitation. She wondered why the Spirit of the Grandmother had visited her at that time. She'd never seen her before or even heard her voice. Because she was called the Grandmother of the South and because of the stories she'd listened to since childhood, Sakima had assumed the Grandmother would be a very old woman. She was not. She appeared so young and so beautiful.

But why me? Sakima thought. *Plenty of warriors have died in battle and ambushes.* As far as she knew, Grandmother Spirit had never saved or even appeared to anyone else, other than Sakima's mother. Sakima had never witnessed even a single old warrior tell the story of how the Grandmother came to him at a critical moment and saved him from certain death.

The Grandmother had saved her in what she could only imagine had been seconds from dying. Sakima had felt her own demise was certain and possibly even foretold. It hadn't turned out that way.

Perhaps I wasn't meant to die then. Maybe I wasn't even dying at all. Lack of oxygen can cause the brain to produce odd images.

Sakima remembered the vision of the pink unicorn she'd had while passed out. And Pat—Apatschin! She let loose a small, loving laugh—but it immediately vanished into thin air, as if it had never happened. Because she had suddenly recalled, with an expression of horror on her face, the maggots. Nauseating, writhing worms.

Sakima shook her head to get those images out of her mind. She made a face and pulled her knees up near her chest, her heels pushing against her bottom. She peered around the room. The memory of being tied to the toilet came to her. She recalled seeing her own blood, experiencing the sharp, explosive pain of being hit, again and again.

She shuddered. Instead of being filled with fear, she felt furious. She was bruised and bloody, yes—but not defeated. The body can heal. Her spirit was not broken.

She wondered if the Grandmother would visit her again, here, and help her one more time. Regardless, Sakima could take care of herself. This was just a momentary pause in her quest. Her chin stuck out a bit as she pushed her chest out, strong and defiant as any Mannahatta warrior had ever been.

Sakima fumed on the floor of the bedroom, staying put. She refused to make herself comfortable, to get up and walk over to the bed and lie down. To even go to the large, luxurious-looking chair across the room and plop down on it and relax. She wanted to keep sitting there, uncomfortable, feeding the pain and anger, ready for whatever came next, and to meet it with dignity, bravery, and determination.

Sakima adjusted her position. She scooted around about 180 degrees, from an angle looking at the furniture to the vantage point of facing the door. She changed from sitting over to a squatting pose, set for action. If Machto returned, she'd be fully prepared and alert. She would be psychologically and physically strengthened so she could kill him—and anyone else with him. She would not be taken by surprise again. Even if those two marched in with their loud fire-shooting weapons, she'd be prepared to overtake them, primed for victory and willing to die. No matter what happened next, she would not be staying here, a captive Mannahatta.

She squinted at the door, muscles tense.

In the gloom, the beeping sounds and the occasional siren from the streets outside filtered up to her ears from far below. She waited, locked in, focused. Her eyes nearly burned a hole in the door, her mind on her plan of attack. Should no one appear for hours, or even days, she would still be ready. She would not rest or sleep until she had killed Machto and anyone who tried to help him, then set herself free.

Sakima did not have to wait long. In less than thirty minutes, the moment she had waited for came. A soft tap at the door, followed by a brief delay, and another quiet, timid rapping at the door.

This is it. I will snap Machto's collar bone like the cougar when it drops its huge, heavy paws against its victim's spine. I will lock his slimy, betrayer's neck in the crook of my arm; my other hand will pull the noose of my elbow tight. Finally, I'll thunder to the floor fast and hard, crushing his windpipe—a painful, appropriate death for his crimes.

She lifted herself up into a more compact crouch, one hand and the opposite knee touching the ground. Every muscle in her body was as tense as a steel spring or a sapling tied down and bracing to snap. To kill.

The door opened gradually, slowly creeping and creaking a bit wider each second, like a puppy or a baby was pushing it open, not a man. Sakima flexed her muscles, ready to pounce and end a mean, nasty, worthless life.

The door swung wide. Sakima jumped straight at it, a bat out of hell, right for...

Janie Jones?

CHAPTER 47

Sakima felt stunned at first, realizing that she'd nearly killed one of her new best friends.

"Janie Jones, how is it you come here now? How did you get in here?"

"I think we're in Machto's apartment, or maybe one he's broken into. Not sure what the situation is… " Janie Jones pointed down the hallway from where she'd just emerged. "MJ and I were each in separate bedrooms, so I figured they had you in yet another. I mean, there's like hundred bedrooms here. As soon as I heard them leave, I peeked into one room and then another until—ta-da!—you!"

"How did you determine the passcode?" Sakima said.

"What do you mean, passcode? There was no passcode."

"For the keypad?"

"Um, no. Sakima, this is an apartment, not a fortress."

"Ah, I understand. Standard key, then."

"That's just it. They didn't lock any of the doors. I guess they figured we'd all be too scared to do anything. They sure underestimated us, didn't they?" Janie Jones reached over and pulled back the curtains and flipped the blinds to allow the light in. When she turned around toward Sakima, her hands shot to her mouth. "Oh my god, Sakima! What have they done to you!" Tears filled her eyes.

"I'm fine, seriously. However dreadful it looks to you, I assure you I can handle it. Machto and his sidekick thought they'd sent me to my grave. I believe they were even ready to light the ceremonial red cedar sticks on fire!" She laughed loudly and shook her head with amusement while Janie Jones looked on in silence. Sakima grew serious again. "But they overestimated their own fighting abilities and underestimated their opponent. Me! Well, actually, us!"

The sun shined brightly through the window. Sakima was taken aback by how beautiful and different this world appeared compared to her homeland of Mannahatta. She peered past Janie Jones out at the skyline. She watched as a small hawk glided through the cerulean-blue sky at what she guessed to be many hundreds of feet in the air. *So the building she was in might be taller than Òhchu Peak back home,* she thought.

Realizing that Janie Jones still needed reassurance, she stepped closer to her. "Nothing to worry about," she said, giving her a hug. "Seriously, it's only some minor injuries. I'll heal. Where's MJ?"

Janie Jones wiped her eyes as carefully as she could so as not to smear her eye makeup. "I haven't found her yet. I still have a few bedrooms to go. " She sniffed and blew her nose using a tissue from a box by the bed.

"We need to find her and get out of this place while we can. Janie Jones...?"

"Um, yes?"

"Thanks for looking for me and not just saving yourself."

"Why would I do that? You're my Mannahatta friend, Sakima. Friends stick together."

"You are right, of course." Sakima paused, feeling the bumps and scratches on her face. "Hey, would you give me a sec?"

"Sure, of course."

Sakima walked into the bathroom to ascertain the damage. Surprisingly, she had partially recovered already. She smiled. Had the cuff given her special healing powers, too? So that after all that, the most Machto could do to hurt her was not really that bad. He couldn't even beat up someone correctly.

She washed up quickly, marveling at how clean and clear New York City water was and how it tasted as fresh as if it were from a babbling brook on her Mannahatta.

As she turned to leave the bathroom, she caught the biting stink of the bleach that had been used to clean up her blood. She froze, enduring again a momentary flashback of having been tied against the toilet. She closed her eyes and took a deep breath. Even though she'd taken it well and was already healing, it remained a terrible thing to have experienced. She shuddered, then pulled her shoulders back. *They will never stop me. None of them. Ever!*

Sakima returned to Janie Jones, who stood in the hall by the bedroom door. She gave Janie Jones a reassuring smile as she passed.

"We have to be on our way," Sakima said.

They began their hunt for MJ. As they searched around, Janie Jones shyly continued the conversation.

"Sakima..?"

"Yes?"

"Uh, I have something I need to tell you."

"Sure."

"I kind of have these, I don't know. Powers, I guess?"

"Yeah? Cool. So, uh, what powers exactly?"

"That's a bit hard to explain. Do you know what 'clairvoyant' is?"

"I think so. You can see the future or something?"

"Right, exactly!" Janie Jones said cheerfully.

"So, you're a clairvoyant," Sakima said. "Good for you."

"Well, no, not exactly."

"Then what?" Sakima said, looking over at Janie Jones and tilting her head slightly.

"Okay, okay, I'm a kind of clairvoyant, in a way. I can see dead people… "

"That is awesome," Sakima said, smiling indulgently. She opened the door to the next bedroom, stepped in quickly, and glanced around. She gave Janie Jones a head nod to indicate "moving on."

"No, no, that's not what I—I'm not saying this right!" Janie Jones said, following Sakima to another bedroom down the hall. "Darn, I'm not very good at talking about this." Janie Jones stomped her foot in frustration and crossed her arms over her chest. "It's that I see people who aren't dead," she stammered, dropping her hands to her side with a loud sigh.

"Janie Jones, I hate to break this to you, but I can see people who aren't dead too." Sakima laughed and patted her friend on the shoulder gently. "Not a special power."

"What I mean is," Janie Jones said, taking a deep breath to calm herself and holding out one hand in front of her like she was directing traffic to come to a stop. " I can look into the places where the dead travel through. Purgatory and Limbo and stuff like that. Even Hell, if I have to."

"Okay. I know what you are trying to say," Sakima said. "Those are not the names of locations I'm familiar with, but I get the picture."

"Where the deceased go; where they pass on to."

"Oh." Sakima nodded. "We call that place the Land of the Dead. It is more like a subdued version of your heaven. Our 'hell' is different too. It is a limited engagement of torture by Matantu— whom you refer to as 'Satan,' I believe. After that, the evil ones are dumped back in the Land of the Living as mosquitoes and ticks and leeches. It's a fine spot to be, with the word 'dead' meaning the opposite of living. Not the opposite of good or happy or whatever your people might picture when they hear the word 'dead.' Then there's the Land of the Dead—"

"The Land of the Dead! That's what I call it too," Janie Jones shouted. "But everyone tells me that's wrong, that there's no such place." Her mouth turned down, and Sakima half expected Janie Jones to stomp her foot again.

"There sure is such a place, so don't worry about it," Sakima said as she opened another bedroom door, walked around inside really quickly, and then at her signal, the two moved on to the next room.

"All my life," Janie Jones continued, counting her years on her fingers, "I could see people who were dead. I assumed they were friends or visitors and that everyone could see them. When I got a little older, six or seven, I realized that I needed to keep my special powers to myself. Another thing I was able to do after I became… you know, after I got these… " she pointed dramatically at her chest. "…is that now I had the ability to visit the dead."

"Yeah?" Sakima said, dismissing the fourth bedroom they'd checked. "So, what does that mean?"

"It means that along with having these spirits visit *me*, I could go visit *them*. In my mind, of course, my visions. Not with my body or anything, haha. Nothing physical."

"*Hmmm*, believe it or not, I completely understand."

Janie Jones smiled and nodded. "Good," she said.

They continued searching for MJ while Sakima attempted to digest all the rather bizarre information Janie Jones overwhelmed her with.

"Okay, that is it," she said. "That is the last of the bedrooms on this side. There are two other doors across the living room we still need to investigate. So anyway, go on…?"

Janie Jones cleared her throat. "I—I went there just before, Sakima. That's what I'm trying to tell you. Before I came looking for you and MJ… well, I didn't find her there!"

"Find who?"

"Your little sister."

Sakima stopped in her tracks. She stared at her friend and breathed in and out slowly a couple of times.

"You had better start over, Janie Jones. I do not think I like what you are saying. "

CHAPTER 48

From their vantage point above the street, Blue and Curly could smell the unmistakable odor of hotdogs cooking and pretzels heating, as well as exhaust fumes, pizza, and the boiling tar where the road was being repaired. The sun was fierce on their heads and necks.

Curly regretted not having one of his favorite bandanas with him, which would cover not only his head but the back of his neck as well. His number-one pick was the one with the skulls on it. His second choice was the black bandana with the devil making the horned "rock 'n' roll" finger gesture with both hands, tongue hanging out. His third favorite was his Rolling Stones "lips" one that his father had given him from his personal collection.

The two friends swung their hoverboards up and down Broadway, still searching for MJ, Janie Jones, and their new friend, Sakima.

"Where should we go next? I feel like we've been everywhere in this city," Curly said, trying not to sound too hopeless. Blue and Curly swerved their skyboards a few stories above the car and pedestrian traffic, and the increasing police presence from squad cars to SWAT trucks. "Although maybe not everywhere, just Manhattan. We haven't been to the Bronx yet. Not Brooklyn and Queens, neither."

"Be reasonable," Blue said. "The girls and those jerks, they were all on foot. Even if they somehow hopped onto mass transit, they'd be lucky to have gotten more than a few blocks from here. I mean, two thugs obviously dragging three girls against their will. Well, carrying one and dragging the others, cause that one guy knocked Sakima out with the butt of his gun and—"

"Yeah, you're right. I mean, I know we were wasting our time going crosstown and then downtown, but I was hoping to catch a glimpse of them. Some kind of commotion in a crowd that would turn out to be them. Okay, that was dumb; I see that now. They must've been heading to some hangout pretty close to the park. Stay on the road, find their hideout, and get there quick."

"Yet here we are, in Midtown," Blue said. "A couple of idiots without a clue."

"It was somewhat nearby, and anyway, I took a chance maybe MJ had gotten away," Curly said. "I wanted to come down here understanding that, after her apartment, this would be the next place she'd go, knowing that I would check it."

"I guess. Somewhat BS reasoning, but that's fine. We're grasping at straws here as it is."

They hovered above the dense crowd in Times Square. Vast groups of people being shepherded to, or blocked from, various streets and intersections by either the NYPD or the National Guard. These thousands of people, however, couldn't be bothered to gaze up at two teenage boys on their skyboards, suspended way above Broadway. Although Blue considered that normal behavior for other parts of the city with predominantly local populations, here in Times Square, the Mecca of tourism, it was an anomaly. Virtually none of the characters down there at street level were native New

Yorkers. They were mostly from other countries and the middle and western sections of the United States. They hadn't seen it all; they hadn't seen much of anything. Two boys this high up on skyboards should've at least prompted a glance or two, but there were no glances or pointing fingers.

Blue and Curly zipped by giant LED digital screens, some as wide as 200 feet and as tall as seventy-five feet. All of them displayed talking heads with scrolling text underneath, with various versions of "Is New York City currently under domestic and foreign terrorist attack? Perhaps so!" Then some would cut intermittently to "live action" reports from across the boroughs. One of the biggest of the screens in the middle of Times Square changed to display the face of a beautiful and quite different looking woman. The same face then appeared on various screens. Then the news broadcasts were replaced on every single LED screen by this woman's countenance.

At first, Blue and Curly thought the woman was Sakima, but they quickly realized this woman was older and that it was only a resemblance. Blue and Curly studied the crowd below, but again, no one seemed to take any notice. Surely this was a strange enough occurrence that it would make at least a few of the jaded seen-it-alls below take a gander. Certainly a majority of the not-seen-all-that-much-at-alls. But no one peered up. No one but Blue and Curly appeared to have taken note of the mysterious, identical images.

The woman spoke—not some commercial or political message, but a personal word directed at Blue and Curly. "My brave and loyal friends, Michael "Blue" Biehn and Charles "Curly" Benbova. Please pay close attention to what I am saying. You do not have much time. Sakima Tamanend needs you. And so do Alice "MJ" Tiptree and Janie Jones. The all require your presence."

The boys stared at each other, back at all the screens seemingly everywhere, then again at each other. They each had one eyebrow raised and eyes wide.

"Do you hear that?" Curly said.

"Do you see all that around us?"

They returned to staring at the gigantic LCD billboards and attending to the woman's message.

"My name is Nuhëma Shaoneyunk. I am known as the Grandmother of the South," she continued. "You need to head to the Grand Central Temple, beyond. Sakima will be there very soon, and so will your friends, MJ and Janie Jones. And all three will all be in terrible danger."

It was strange to see this woman's giant face, multiplied by a hundred times, as she mentioned them and their friends by their given names. The two young men reacted by momentarily not moving a muscle, including any activity at all in their brains.

"I know this is a lot. I am sure you are thinking that you are either dreaming or hallucinating or perhaps have gone mad. I do not have the luxury to explain who I am or what I am doing here or how you can see me like this. I might never be able to contact you again, and I am sorry, but I call for you to help Sakima."

The boys hung there as still as statues, confused and unsure if they should do what this mysterious woman told them to do. Was it a trap? Was it a super-customized advertisement? They stored endless bytes of data on you nowadays; they could target your buying habits with surgical precision. Then again, what exactly was being sold here?

"I need you both to leave right away, and I require you to do two very important things," the Grandmother said. "First, it is extremely important that you deliver a message from me."

The two continued to stare, motionless except for Blue blinking his eyes very slowly and Curly licking his upper lip.

"It is a message of life-and-death importance. My sweet *Wematë-gunis*, you need to inform her—"

"What was that? What did she say? Wemmy what?" Curly asked.

"I think it means something like 'sweethearts,'" Blue said. "She's trying to be like a nice grandmother—"

"No, no, I think she said, 'sweet angels.'"

"Sweet angels? Why?" Blue shook his head sadly, his first physical motion in the past few minutes. "Why would she call us 'sweet angels?'"

The Grandmother stared blankly at the two boys from a thousand flat-panel screens and cleared her throat to gain their attention.

"It means, 'forest elf,'" she said. "I was calling you my little forest elves, a term of endearment." She twisted her mouth into a half-smile showing a bit of both love and frustration.

"Why?" Curly said.

The Grandmother smiled. "Never mind. Remember this: Tell Sakima that to travel to where Tangetta is, she must press *tulpe, tulpe, tulpe.*"

The boys looked at each other again, making confused faces, their eyes crinkling and their lips stretching about nervously.

"What did she say?" Curly asked his friend. "Tool-pay? What does tha—"

"Turtle-turtle-turtle," the Grandmother said, some impatience in her voice now. "She must push the turtle gem three times."

"I'm not completely sure what you're saying," Blue said. "But we'll give her your message as soon as we find her."

"Good. She'll know precisely what it means; do not worry. You must also tell her—this is extremely important—that she must press *xinkwtëme-xinkwtëme-xinkwtëme* to return to—"

"Wee choochoo weeum, what… ? Come on!" an exasperated Curly said.

"Wolf, wolf, wolf. Oh, and I almost forgot. She will need this too."

"Need what? Oh!" Blue said, as a beautiful, green feather somehow materialized in his hand.

"She will know what to do. You have to tell her it only works one time," the Grandmother said. "That is all. Now hurry!"

All the enormous screens in Times Square blacked out for a few seconds and then returned to how they were before the woman took them over.

Blue and Curly hesitated only long enough to just barely process what had happened. Blue shoved the feather in his pocket, and they sped off with renewed purpose.

CHAPTER 49

"No, no, it's good news, Sakima! She's not in any of the Places of the Dead. At least, I couldn't discover her there."

Sakima sighed. "I… I do not understand. Can you possibly—?"

"She isn't dead, Sakima. She can't be!" Janie Jones gave Sakima a warm smile. "Don't you get it? I would've seen her there. Yes, I asked around. No one had spotted her. See? That solves it. She's not gone!"

Sakima studied Janie Jones for a long minute, while Janie Jones continued to smile at her with all the joy she could muster.

"If you weren't such a sweet person, Janie Jones, I would assume you were messing with me. I think I might just have to punch you in the nose."

"No, you don't need to punch me! Because I'm not messing with you! See?"

Sakima moved her gaze to the floor and said slowly in hushed tones, "She's dead, Janie Jones. My little sister is dead, and I'm the one who killed her."

Janie Jones retracted her smile. She peered at Sakima as if seeing her for the first time. "No, you didn't, Sakima. I don't even think you killed that monster."

Sakima looked back at Janie Jones and stared at her with a look of confusion.

"You only made it disappear into some other dimension where it won't harm anyone anymore: a place of not-death and not-life. I don't understand it, but I'm thinking that's what your cuff did: sent the two of them somewhere, some not-dead place. You didn't kill it. You didn't kill either of them."

"I do not know…" Sakima swallowed hard. "I am not sure what to think." Now it was Sakima's turn to wipe the tears carefully from her eyes. "Let us keep looking for MJ. It will give me time to consider what you are saying."

"Sure, sure," Janie Jones whispered. She reached out to pat Sakima on her shoulder, but at the last second, she withdrew her hand.

They crossed through the dining area to check the last rooms. As they passed, Janie Jones spied a wet rag draped over the edge of a pail by the front door. The filthy cloth still dripped a few last drops of near-transparent pinkish water onto the floor. She identified it as probably Sakima's blood, from an attempt somebody made to clean the mess.

But Sakima wasn't paying attention to Janie Jones or the bucket. Instead, she was studying the table in the center of the room. She suddenly detected the aroma of coffee still hot in the pot on the counter.

"*Hmmm, kàpi!*" Sakima paused. "I could use a big cup of that *kàpi* right now."

Then, as if spotting an old friend, Sakima saw her bow, arrows, and quiver resting there and cried out with both joy and relief.

"My bow! My arrows! Thank Kishelë!"

Sakima dashed to the table and immediately picked them up and threw the bow over her shoulder. She grabbed her quiver to load the arrows, but noticed something was wrong. Each of the arrows had been snapped in the middle, the broken arrows scattered callously across the large dining room table.

"Oh no! Sakima!" Janie Jones gasped as she came up behind Sakima and noticed the arrows. Sakima's demeanor didn't change, though; she didn't get angry or upset. She simply picked up the halves of one arrow and held the damaged ends together with one hand. Then, with the other, she pressed a switch buried in the feathers of the arrow's fletching. The arrow started to repair itself. A field of blue electricity danced over the breakpoint until the shaft healed into one again.

"Um, wow," Janie Jones said. "That's amazing. And I thought *I* had special powers."

"It is not me; it is the arrows. It is a function they have. The function was developed for release 2.2.3. These I have here are version 10.3.1. That is like the least they can do. Almost literally the least." Sakima continued to "heal" the other arrows and load them into her quiver. "Okay, last of the bedrooms. We retrieve MJ and then leave this place of darkness forever."

But the final rooms did not yield MJ.

"They must've brought her with them, those two evil jerks," Janie Jones said despondently, her eyes wide and filled with tears. "What do we do, Sakima?" she pleaded, bringing her fists up to cover her chin as if protecting herself from bad news.

"We will do what must be done: Track them down. Find them. Rescue MJ. Then after that comes the moment when I terminate Machto and send him and his sidekick straight to the place you call 'hell.' Back among the devils—mahtan'tuwinink!"

"But how?" Janie Jones cried, her face crumpled with despair. "How? How do we know where they've taken her?"

"Well, we could wait here and do nothing, I suppose, but would that feel like the right thing to do?" Sakima asked.

"No, I guess not. Of course not. But how can we possibly locate them?"

Sakima kept staring at Janie Jones while slowly raising one eyebrow.

"What?" Janie Jones said.

"I'm wondering… How far do your powers go? I mean, do you see only the dead and the 'not-dead?'"

"What do you mean?"

"I mean, if MJ is still alive, could you locate her?"

"Frankly, it'd be easier if she was dead."

"Easier, of course. Would finding a living person be beyond your supernatural abilities?"

Janie Jones locked a blank expression onto her face.

"Come on. Let us stay positive here, Janie."

"Jones."

"What? Oh, right, Janie Jones. Stay positive. We *will* succeed. Good over evil; light over darkness."

Janie Jones looked up at Sakima with the loving eyes of a puppy.

"So," Sakima continued, "do you suppose you could bend your powers, modify them, or something? To find our lost MJ?"

CHAPTER 50

"I don't know, Sakima. I'm not sure." Janie Jones let her worries dominate her expression. Then she straightened her shoulders and stood up as tall as she could. "But I can try! It never occurred to me to ever attempt that, but why not? Maybe I can… " She stroked her cheek and was quickly lost in speculation.

"Does this perhaps involve a trance or something?" Sakima said, smiling benignly, coaxing Janie Jones along.

"What? Oh no, sorry, no, it just happens. First, I start pondering things, like I just did, and kind of meditate. Then I end up there, virtually. You know, with the dead, or in this case maybe the living —if we're lucky." ·

"Okay?"

Janie Jones took a deep breath and closed her eyes. "Yeah, I go there, but not in a trance or anything. More like playing the *PlayStation 12VR*. I'm still here. You can see me, right? But it's also like I'm not here. You understand what I'm saying? Sort of like our conversation here. I talk to one of the dead in the same way I'm talking with you. I… that's it! I've got it!"

"Got what?"

"Well, I'm guessing I can't detect an alive person because I'm not that kind of clairvoyant. But..."

"What?"

"I bet one of my dear friends, who has passed on to the next realm, can help me determine MJ's whereabouts. They get around, see? They have a network—a sort of social media—but where everyone's dead."

"All the same... " Sakima hesitated, unsure what Janie Jones was saying. "Do you suppose you could give it a try?"

"Already there." Janie Jones made the "quiet please" gesture, her finger to her lips. Then she winked at Sakima before continuing. "Hello there, Mrs. Archambeau! How are you? Me? I'm fine. Except for being attacked by giant monsters and kidnapped by insane creeps." She paused. "Thank you! You're looking pretty good yourself, considering that, well, you are a spirit."

Sakima leaned against the arched opening between the dining room and the kitchen, her arms crossed, engrossed.

"Listen, Mrs. Archambeau, could I ask you a big favor? Wait! Where are you going? Come back; don't be like that. It's an easy favor I'm asking of you. I need your help finding someone." Janie Jones paused, her palm in the air as if attempting to keep the spirit from running off. She lowered her hand. "No, no. She's a living person. Sorry, I guess I should've said that up front. Anyway, her name is MJ. You know who I'm talking about? Yes, yes, my friend. The girl you see me always hanging around with—her and my boys." She waited for a second to see if there would be a response. When there wasn't she wrapped it up: "Yes, that's right: MJ!"

She grinned and gave Sakima a thumbs up, which Sakima returned with enthusiasm, though she didn't know what it meant. Janie Jones was smiling, so Sakima smiled, too.

"Okay, check around, ask your friends, and—what's that? That's very interesting. You sure about that, though? Yes, sorry, of course you're sure. Okay, Mrs. Archambeau, thank you! Nice chatting with you. Tell Mr. Archambeau I said, 'hi.' Bye now!"

She turned to Sakima and mimed wiping sweat from her brow. "Whew! That was a bit much. She's in a terrible mood. Anyway, um, what were we saying?"

"MJ. Where is MJ right now?"

Janie Jones stared back blankly at Sakima.

"What did you learn?" Sakima said, raising her eyebrows and leaning in toward Janie Jones. She spread her palms up and out in front of her and waited. "Well?"

"Oh, right! You couldn't hear any of that, could you? The other side of the conversation, I mean. I forgot about that! I was wondering after you spoke, 'What in the world is Sakima talking about?' Ha ha ha!"

Sakima put her hands on her hips and tilted her head, her smile gone.

"I thought, 'Sakima's standing right here! Of course, she listened to the entire thing!'" Janie Jones laughed.

"No, Janie Jones, I could not hear any of it. I am not a reverse-clairvoyant or whatever you are."

"Grand Central Terminal."

"What is that? You are a 'grand sensing'… *what?*"

"No, no. The big indoor train cathedral, midtown. The place they call Grand Central. They're at the station buying tickets, according to Mrs. Archambeau. I guess they're heading out of the city?"

"We have to stop them—if it is not too late." Sakima suddenly felt sad and strangely hopeless. Janie Jones might be right about MJ's location—which, frankly, she doubted. She was not buying the whole "talking-to-the-dead" act. If they didn't get there in time, MJ would already have left. Once gone, another person under Saki-ma's "protection" would be as good as dead.

MJ and Tangetta. Sakima sighed. Perhaps I'm not the warrior I had hoped I was. This many people shouldn't be dying with a real warrior around to supposedly protect them.

"I don't know what you're thinking, and I don't care," Janie Jones said. "But we need to go right away!"

Sakima straightened up, a look of fierce determination coloring her face and altering her stance. She held her chin high, eyes narrowed, legs apart and bent ready to spring. "Right, do not mind me. After-effects of being tortured nearly to death, I guess. Regardless, we go now."

With that, they both darted out the exit and down the hall on their way to save MJ and to, maybe, kill a couple of *mahchikwi lënuwàk*—terrible guys.

CHAPTER 51

"*Maaa-chto!*"

Sakima's voice echoed in the massive amphitheater on the main concourse of Grand Central Terminal at 42nd Street in New York City. The cacophony of thousands of people talking, shoes tapping, and suitcase wheels clanking on the marble floor nearly blocked out her loud shout. The air ducts' fans blowing and the near-constant announcements on the public address system reduced Sakima's cry to just another element of the general commotion. A handful of faces glanced at her as crowds rushed through the terminal or rested in seats or waited idly for a train or a friend to arrive.

Sakima hovered above them all on Blue's skyboard, having just fortuitously met up with Blue and Curly right outside the building. Curly and Janie Jones floated close by on his board.

Sakima nocked her bow with a standard heat-seeking arrow from her quiver in a single fluid motion. She aimed it precisely at Machto's black heart, maneuvering the bow away from MJ and Machto's sidekick, Kieft. She would deal with him next. The arrowhead automatically ticked through settings to locate and store Machto's unique heat signature.

"*Let. Her. Go!*" Sakima cried out.

About half the interested faces became bored, their owners returning to their business at hand. They recognized a publicity stunt when they saw one, and almost nobody spent any more brain activity wondering about what this circus might be promoting.

Machto, however, froze, staring up at Sakima. He took a moment to evaluate the situation, to plan his next move. While he did so, the rest of the New Yorkers and visitors moved on with their lives.

"Sakima!" he hollered up to her. "I see you don't learn your lessons very well. Back for another round? Or are you here to 'rescue' your girlfriend?" Machto yanked MJ's arm and positioned her out in front of himself like a shield.

While Machto continued taunting, Sakima caught Blue's eye. She tilted her head to signal him to descend closer. He understood and did so with Curly and Janie Jones following close behind.

"You are a terrible teacher, Machto; you're bad at everything," Sakima said. The combined odor of the crowds with various food smells, mixed with the scent of the recently applied floor wax, reached her nose in a bouquet of strange aromas.

Machto took a couple of steps toward Sakima and stopped, still looking up at her. "Come down here, fight like a man: the man you wish you were."

"You have got it wrong; I do not wish to be a man, and I am very good at being a woman. What I want is to be better than ordinary men. A true warrior!" Eyes shining, Sakima relaxed, smiled, and pulled back on the string of her bow. Without any hesitation, she let the arrow fly, knowing it would strike Machto, and only Machto.

However, Sakima's arrow smacked loudly into the ground instead, shattering the point. All of Sakima's arrows, including that one, were programmed to drop out of the sky should any non-targeted lifeform come between it and the intended target.

"You took the coward's way out, Machto, using MJ like that. No surprise."

She selected another arrow, nocked it, and set it again for Machto's heat signature. This time, she disengaged the self-destruct fail-safe and reset the targeting function. No margin for error, but this new setting emphasized pinpoint accuracy. The arrow should hit the mark using coordinate-measuring precision. It should pass right by MJ and leave her without a scratch, with a safety gap of less than 0.00001 Bohr units, to find its way to Machto. Sakima let loose her second arrow.

Machto once again grabbed MJ and held her forcibly as he ducked down behind her. He was outsmarted by Sakima's smart arrow. It found its mark: an inch or less of Machto's exposed shoulder, which was not completely hidden behind MJ. The arrow struck hard and buried itself in his arm.

"Damn it!" he yelled, stepping back and inadvertently releasing MJ from his grip. "*Këlulël!*"

MJ stood there stunned for an instant by her sudden freedom. Then she bolted towards Blue, Curly, Janie Jones, and Sakima. "Blue!" she called out, waving to her boyfriend. Before she could get far from her captors, a hand shot out and pulled her back as she struggled to free herself.

"Gotcha, bitch!" Kieft, Machto's henchman, snickered. "Nice try." He turned to Machto. "You all right, man?"

Machto sneered, his face red. He drew a quick breath and released it loudly between clenched teeth before speaking. "What do you think?" Before he could say another word, a second arrow ripped into Machto's chest. It entered a bit off-center from his heart and managed to miss all vital organs.

This was not a standard arrow but chosen deliberately by Sakima for Machto. It was a special "poison" arrow. She wasn't exactly sure what it did, but she knew that it contained an ingredient that caused immediate drowsiness and weakness of the muscle. It rendered any opponent virtually and instantly defenseless.

Hovering with Blue on his board at a safe distance, Sakima studied the scene and waited for Machto to topple. He didn't. He just glared angrily up at the woman he blamed for everything as he jerked at the arrow until he got it free. He screamed at the pain, but he never stopped staring at Sakima, his eyes red and bulging with fury. At last, his eyes froze and rolled slowly up and back.

Finally, thought Sakima, *the drug is working. Not as fast as I expected, but I will take it.*

But Machto didn't pass out or lose muscle coordination. His skin became strangely even darker than it was. Sakima didn't understand. While she'd never struck with this type of arrow before, she knew well its capabilities and the symptoms it should produce. Turning skin inky wasn't on the list.

She watched more closely. Machto's skin wasn't merely changing shade; it seemed to be morphing, the result of his veins turning a deep blue and bulging out from his skin. The effect wasn't restricted to the points of entry. It covered his entire body, especially his neck. The veins and capillaries appeared to squirm as they fattened, doubling in size. The arteries ran thickest across his face, intertwining in ways that didn't resemble anything Sakima had ever seen before.

The arrow tip seemed to be triggering an allergic reaction of some kind, unintended by Sakima. Her next thought was that there was something wrong with Machto. Something in his blood already which interacted unexpectedly with the knockout drug in the arrow.

Then the veins and arteries began to shrink back. Machto seemed to return to a normal sense of awareness when it all subsided. The only remaining effect of the arrow's drug was an odd little twitch in his right eye. Staring at Sakima and without breaking his gaze, he yelled at his helper, "Kill the bitch!"

Machto laughed. At first it was a slight chuckle, then an outright cackle, then a near-hysterical guffaw that caused his shoulders and chest to bounce about.

What the hell? Thought Sakima. *This idiot, this* kèpchat, *is out of his mind!*

CHAPTER 52

''ve got this, Machto," Kieft shouted. "Allow me to demonstrate my secret weapon to you on the field of battle! Hurrah!" He turned his head to stare at Machto with the exuberance of a zealot. "You know," he continued, dropping his voice down to a whisper, "the ray gun I described to you when we first met? Call this a demo, if you will. I truly think you're going to like it." Turning back to Sakima and her friends, he shrieked, "Behold!"

The man strutted forward, a nasty grin on his face. He reached into his jacket pocket and pulled out an odd-looking weapon. It was small enough to fit in his hand without much of it reaching beyond the boundary of his palm. It was flatter than expected for a gun and looked more like a smartphone. Except for the barrel, which was red and had three globular bubbles along its length like an old-school water pistol. The largest of the bubbles was closest to Kieft's hand, decreasing in size as they arrived at the business end. It had a blue handle with a yellow trigger. The "cell phone" part of the pistol featured several graphs and readouts, supposedly to tell the user when the target was in alignment. Or perhaps the strength of the weapon's ammunition. For this beta version, those screens merely displayed:

This screen will contain data.

He raised the gun and pointed it at Sakima, staring through the red plastic crosshairs at the tip of the barrel. "Bye, bye, honey," he barked. "I won't say it's been nice to know you because it hasn't!" He chuckled for a second at his own wit, peering back at Machto for agreement. Getting none, he returned to carefully checked the info screens that were scheduled to be operational soon. After a painful few seconds, he recognized that there would be nothing to see there until the next software update.

While Sakima and her allies could not help but watch dumbfounded, the henchman put his fingertip on one of two touchpads on the device. He swiped right, indicating he accepted the target as shown. A deep buzzing sound emanated from the pistol, and it started to shake. He steadied the weapon by grabbing it with both hands. He kept the bright red barrel, the color of a child's toy, pointed at his enemies.

Kieft smiled as he watched a brilliant oscillating wave escape the gun. It was bluish white, like glacial ice. He followed the pulse as it rippled slowly through the air, headed for the four people hovering above on their skyboards. Then he observed as they frantically tried to decide in which direction they should flee. He laughed harder as his advanced prototype of the diabolical weapon worked perfectly for the second time in two days.

All four skyboarders suddenly found themselves frozen in place, hanging in midair, unable to move. Sakima attempted to stretch back to reload her bow from her quiver, but she couldn't make her arms do anything. She struggled to yell to Curly for him to reach up and grab an arrow and hand it to her, but she was incapable of using her mouth or vocal cords. Then she realized her eyes weren't able to refocus on any of her friends. She was forced against her will to stare only at the belligerent smirk on the face of this despicable man, Kieft.

She was incapable of defending herself or her companions. They were sitting ducks, waiting to die. Hanging in the air like sculptures, the friends fought to break free of the grip of the strange device.

What kind of magic is this? Sakima thought. *Is this Iroquois? Mohican? Worse? Someone has made a pact with Mahtantu, the devil. That is the only way to explain such impossible physic.*

Next came a sputtering bang, like a car backfiring, and without warning they broke free, dropping a few feet lower on their boards.

"What just happened?" Curly said.

Below, Kieft wondered the same thing. The good news was that he'd found a preproduction bug—an error in the software or hardware. The bad news is that the defect caused Phase 1 of the attack to lose its "freeze" power and release those captured by it. He knew this because he could see the four talking, pointing, while the boards they rode bounced gently in the air.

Kieft proceeded to invoke Phase 2 manually. On a different touchpad, to the right of the first, he swiped again, this time to the left. "I reject you, bitch," he said under his breath. The weapon shook again, so roughly it practically jumped out of Kieft's hands. He held on tight with a look of determination, his gaze locked and his jaw set. A tiny grin slithered across his lips.

"We need to get out of here!" Sakima shouted far above him. "*Go!*"

The two boys, although free from the weapon's strange grip, looked to be in a stupor. After a bit, they snapped out of it.

"Yeah, yeah," Curly said. "Go, right, good idea…"

"Going now," Blue said and went nowhere.

A piercing sound unlike any normal tone on Earth filled the station. Then, from the odd, bubbly red barrel, distinct waves rippled out, like a stone makes when dropped into water. Concentric circles grew bigger and wider as they rolled closer to the four allies. Free of the physical grip of Phase 1 of the device, they now appeared to be ensnared in a new, psychological phase.

"What the hell is all this now?" Janie Jones said, pointing to where Kieft held his gun pointed at them. "It's like magical donuts in the sky!"

"Not magic donuts." Curly raised his eyebrows high and his recent grin vanished, replaced by a grimace. "Sakima, any ideas?" he said, glancing over at her.

Sakima thought for a moment, puzzled by it all like Curly and the rest of them. "None, because I don't understand what in the world is going on." She watched the see-through, glowing ovals make their way toward them through the space above the concourse, spirals traveling with steady, deadly determination.

Kieft slapped at the weapon repeatedly, seeming to be as perplexed as Sakima as to why the rays of his ray gun traveled as slow as marshmallows through Jello. He pivoted his eyebrows into a "V" and sneered even more nastily. "I'm going to engineers' hell!" he mumbled.

CHAPTER 53

Back on their skyboards, Team Sakima had still not moved out of the way. They were too mesmerized by the absolute weirdness of the wobbling, clear, hula-hoop-shaped objects slowly headed toward them. Finally, she spoke, as if in a trance.

"Only my cuff can do that, those circles... " Sakima said, confused. "Nothing else has that ability. At least, I didn't think anything could." Her face scrunched up like someone was working strings on her lips, pulling them up. Sakima squinted an eye as if squeezing it might make sense of all the confusion.

Blue dropped the skyboard that he and Sakima were on straight toward the ground, since heading downward was easier and quicker than going up. Curly followed Blue's lead with Janie Jones hanging on tight, her arms wrapped around his waist. All four were nearly touching the floor now, ready for the next required evasive maneuver. Second, the ceiling above exploded as invisible waves hit the dome, obliterating the painting of Pegasus, the mythical creature that had, mere seconds ago, been flying proudly in the center of that blue-green plaster ceiling of Grand Central station.

"Some kind of strange, negative ripples, right?" Blue said to no one in particular. "Invisible, like sound waves."

"Except I didn't hear any sounds!" Curly said. "Until things exploded."

"Where'd that come from, that kind of power?" Blue mused. "I mean, we use sound waves a lot these days, instead of TNT. Only in a controlled environment with the public far away, and with demolition and explosive professionals, as well as acousticologists in attendance."

"Acoustic-olo-*what?*" Curly said.

"Acoustic experts: people who understand constructive and destructive sound wave technology."

"And those sound wave machines," Janie Jones chimed in. "They're huge, the size of buses. I saw it on a documentary my Mom watched. Not anything you could hold in one hand like this guy has. Not even close."

"I've seen this before, though," Sakima muttered, searching her brain for the answer, not wishing to waste energy on talking. "But it's not tech I've ever encountered outside of what my cuff is capable and besides—*Blue! Need to move! Now!*"

Blue turned, finally getting his head out of the clouds to discover at the last second that another wave of see-through ovals had almost reached them. He and Curly sent their boards zipping through the crowds at ground level as Kieft attempted yet again to destroy them. The LCD screens listing train departure and arrival times wobbled fiercely before disintegrating into nothingness.

"Holy shit!" Curly gasped.

"Jeez!" Janie Jones joined in. "That is so not cool!"

Curly and Blue circled the boards back to face Kieft and Machto again, from farther away and quite a bit higher. Their heads nearly touched the curved, teal-and-turquoise ceilings of the terminal. They all hovered there, as if waiting for direction on how to proceed from Sakima.

"That's enough," Sakima said. She bit her lower lip and gazed down at the men and women scurrying for cover from whatever the heck was happening all around them. "He's going to seriously hurt somebody. These people are all innocent, defenseless. I won't allow it!" She breathed in hard and pushed her chest out. "Warriors don't bring trouble; they end it." Her face was stony, her eyes set.

Is now the time? Sakima thought. *Mother, why aren't you here to tell me? Is this that moment you told me about so long ago? The one where I would quote-unquote, "just know?"*

With her lips tight and her jaw firm, Sakima whipped a specifically-not-pink arrow out of her quiver, nocked it in her bow's string, and set it free. All the motions executed like a ballerina, twirling and jumping and landing soft.

The arrow sailed through space. It was no special projectile, this arrow. Not heat-seeking, nor DNA-identifying. Nothing was scientific or magical about it. Not pink with rainbow fletching. It was a plain arrow, one of a dozen in Sakima's quiver, which she used regularly for target practice. An ordinary arrow flying along on an extraordinary day.

The arrow hit its spot as if programmed to do so, and not because it was controlled by software, because this arrow wasn't, but because of Sakima's great abilities. It bit into Kieft before he had a chance to comprehend that death was coming for him. It sliced through his larynx and lodged there.

Kieft dropped the ray gun prototype and fell to his knees. He tugged at the arrow, the ordinary arrow with the perfectly normal arrowhead. He gurgled, blood pumping from his neck, his eyes bulging as he struggled for air. Then he went down face forward, dead, the criminal with his multimillion-dollar ultimate weapon defeated by the female warrior and her ordinary arrow—but extraordinary skills.

Machto lurched to his feet, his skin having taken on a bluish-green hue. He grabbed at the cuff, which had begun to itch horribly, and threw it angrily at the ground. "Useless piece of shit doesn't work anyway!" He backed away, clutching MJ around her bicep.

"Leave the girl!" Sakima shouted. She stared down an arrow shaft suspended in her tautly pulled bow directly at Machto's face. With a curse and a shove, he released MJ and then realized the girl had been his only chip in the negotiations.

MJ sprinted toward Sakima and Blue as Sakima let the arrow go straight at Machto. *You don't get rewarded for being forced to do the right thing, especially when that was to "un-kidnap" the young woman you stole,* she thought. *No, you get stopped so you can never do such a thing ever again!*

The arrow cracked against the marble of the wall where Machto had been standing, but he had already disappeared down a large corridor.

MJ ran to where Blue had landed his skyboard. Sakima stepped aside and backed away as Blue jumped off and MJ jumped into his arms. They hugged for a long minute before separating far enough so that they could kiss. When they'd finished, MJ, still holding onto Blue, whispered, "Thanks." She burst into tears and buried her face in Blue's chest. He kissed her on top of her head and let her have a good cry.

CHAPTER 54

Sakima looked away, catching Curly's eye, who nodded. She smiled and peered over at Janie Jones, who stood behind Curly. Janie Jones peeped around him while being protected by his body, like a bunny peeking out of the safety of its burrow. Sakima winked at her; Janie Jones smiled back and mouthed, "Thank you." She pressed her face against her boyfriend's back and cried.

Sakima stood and stared at her own feet, then up at the ceiling where it had been broken, and before anyone could notice her, she jogged over to the spot where Machto had jettisoned her cuff. She wanted more than anything to have a good cry, but a warrior would not and should not do that.

As she slid the cuff onto her arm, she wondered why she was here. Was it only to have these short, half-won battles? That didn't seem very epic. Although the clash with the monster, Yakwahe, had had those qualities—impossible odds, monumental courage, skill, and a dash of luck. All the same, it wasn't at all what she was hoping being a hero would be. Especially given how close to defeat she was constantly, as well as her complete failure at saving Tangetta.

Sakima believed the life of a warrior meant fighting alongside comrades-at-arms. The four friends who aided her were great. While it was wonderful to have allies who had your back while you fought demons, they weren't warriors or street fighters. Just friendly people trying to help a newcomer in need.

Sakima realized something else as she dusted off her cuff and verified that the jewels were still fully attached and functional. In her fantasies, she always did monumental, heroic deeds. What made her first battles as a true warrior different was that there were no witnesses. Yes, her new friends had seen some of it, but then again, not her initial encounter with Yakwahe. They weren't Mannahatta, which wasn't essential, but which would certainly help.

For some reason, Sakima had expected huge cheering crowds. Flags waving. Trumpets blaring. She wasn't prepared for the loneliness. She hadn't known that being a warrior, an *"Ila,"* would be such a hard, solitary thing. You fight with everything you have. You are either killed or you do the killing, to live another day to do it all over again. There was no end to being a champion because there was always some evil to combat. Only when you were old and ready to die could you put down spear, knife, and bow, then say that you would "fight no more, forever."

Until then, you battle one demonic creature or person after another. Sakima felt as if she'd lived this scenario out in microcosm these past few days. Destroy or be destroyed. Terminate or be terminated. No medals, no parades, no honors. Even if there had been, she was pretty sure that the pomp and circumstance wouldn't matter a whit; that the fight was over, and with all non-*ilaok* not understanding. Then it's back to the war front to kill again.

Sakima sighed, feeling suddenly exhausted. She glanced over at Kieft's dead body. She had never killed a human before, or any actual living thing, just bioMechs. Taking a life felt worse than she could ever have predicted it would. She didn't feel proud and strong or like she wanted to celebrate. Rather, she felt small and stupid like she'd made a huge, irreversible mistake.

The funny thing was, she had been looking forward to it for so long. Desperate for the "real deal," after years of shooting at inanimate targets and moving mechTargets and recently taking down bioMech animals. She couldn't stand the waiting, knowing that as a warrior, she could slay living and breathing beings, and with luck and a lengthy career as the first woman warrior the Mannahatta had ever known, she might eventually kill hundreds of her enemies over time.

She had imagined it to be more like a celebration. Dancing, shouting, hands in the air—a truly wonderful sense of elation and pride and accomplishment.

But Sakima felt none of that right now; only hollow, empty—a stranger in her own body. She didn't know who she was or where she stood. For a moment, she became dizzy and weaved in place briefly. She turned her gaze away from the corpse lying in its pool of darkening, sticky blood to study the curious crowd closing in, being held back by men in blue, arms outstretched.

He'd been a human just minutes before, this Kieft person. An unpleasant individual, but still alive and real. Now, he seemed like nothing. An empty husk. No history, no future. As if he'd never existed, never spoke. Never lived or loved, never experienced pain or joy. He might've had a wife and children, who'd now never see him again. It was all Sakima's fault.

"Grandmother," she whispered, feeling her world collapse around her, as if her dreams had gathered together and were crushing her, as if she were trapped at the bottom of the ocean or beneath an avalanche. Tears crawled down her cheeks like forlorn spirits in a futile slither to the grave. "Help me, Grandmother," Sakima reflected. "I need you!"

She took a heaving, giant sigh. She clenched her fists, trying to contain her emotions and man up. Warrior up. *Woman* up. Then she noticed that the gems in her cuff glowed, faintly at first, then stronger. This distracted her, but just for a second.

So it works just fine, but for me only, I think, and for nobody else.

In a slow weaving fall, Sakima collapsed to her hands and knees. Barely able to hold herself up off the ground, Sakima's hair dragged on the tile. Then she vomited onto the beautiful, ice-cold marble floor of Grand Central Terminal.

CHAPTER 55

"Sakima?" Blue said, turning around to look at her. She was already back to standing up, although shakily, thanks to an assist from Curly and Janie Jones. "Um, sorry, but did you say, 'grandmother?' I mean, right before you fell down and barfed… ?"

Sakima held her palm against the front of her forehead and concentrated on the faces around her while she breathed carefully in through her nose and out through barely parted lips.

"Jeez, Blue, leave her alone, will you?" Janie Jones said. "She nearly passed out. She's having a hard time dealing. Can't you see?"

Janie Jones put her arm gently around Sakima's waist. She wanted her arms to instead surround Sakima's slightly quivering shoulders, but she couldn't reach that high even on her tiptoes. Janie Jones's short stature made reaching Sakima's shoulders too much of a reach.

"It's all right, Janie Jones," Sakima said in a soft, almost frail voice. "I'm okay now… Blue? You were saying something?"

"Yeah, so, your grandma South came to see me and Curly before, and your grandma—"

"Sorry, but she's not *my* grandmother. She's *the* Grandmother. The Grandmother of the South."

Blue looked confused, unclear on the distinction, or if there even was one. "Um, okay. So *the* Grandmother," he said, overemphasizing the word "the" as "thee." "She instructed us, Curly and me in other words, to tell you—"

"Wait a minute. Wait, wait!" Sakima held up her hand toward Blue like a traffic cop. "Are you telling me the Grandmother of the South showed herself to you two non-Mannahatta boys?"

"Well, why not?"

"I have about a million reasons, if you have the time…"

Curly and Blue glanced at each other, then back at Sakima. "Okay, then! Anyway, she said—"

"'She' said? So, you actually saw and heard Nuhëma Shaoneyunk? That is, well, interesting," Sakima said, rubbing her cheek in thought. "Because I have only met her in my dreams, and I am a full-blooded Mannahatta. She appears to very few of us to begin with." She narrowed her eyes. "But two random white guys from a land that is not Mannahatta. She is cool with just—*POOF!*—appearing to you?" Sakima tilted her head to one side, pursing her lips. She relaxed and said, "I apologize, but I am finding all of this hard to take in. And I guess I'm a bit jealous. So where did this miracle take place?"

"Um, Midtown. You know, Times Square."

"What's 'times square?' You mean, mathematically—times squared'? Or something times something, squared? I do not get it."

"First of all, none of that's a real thing, Sakima," Curly said. "Times Square is this, uh, I don't know, four or five connected blocks? With lots to do, shops and stuff like Madison Square Garden, Ripley's, Tussauds Wax Museum—"

"I have no idea what the interest could conceivably be for a museum devoted to wax. Is there a String Gallery? And a Lint Library?" She folded her arms across her chest.

Curly shook his head and glanced at Blue, who then gazed over at MJ with one eyebrow up, who in turn peered over at Janie Jones. MJ shrugged her shoulders, raised her palms up, smiled, and blew her bangs up out of her eyes.

"Doesn't matter," Blue said. "Big festival. Let's call it that. Does that have meaning for you?"

"Sure," Sakima said.

"Okay. Well, this area has all these gigantic screens around it, a couple of stories high and some higher, showing ads and stuff."

"I'm going to say I understand what you're talking about."

"Good," Blue said.

"Even though I don't."

"That's fine. Well, you're—sorry, thee—Grandmother showed up out of nowhere and popped onto every one of these screens. Her face mostly. She said, 'Hey, Blue and Curly! Up here, sweeties! Yoohoo!' or whatever."

"That's not exactly how it happened," Curly said, giving his friend a disapproving shake of his head.

"Close enough," Blue said.

"Hey, guys? I'm thinking we'd better get out of here before we're questioned or maybe even arrested," MJ said. She motioned her head sideways at the crowd and the medics and the police. "We kind of stand out, don't you agree?"

A cop glowered at them from the other end of the expanse and then spoke into the two-way radio attached to his shoulder. An unusually high number of NYPD personnel moved about the terminal, some running, some meeting up to talk, and some circling on police hoverboards. There were even some wearing flak jackets and carrying rifles. The battle minutes ago between Sakima and her friends and Machto didn't seem to be the sole reason for this influx of militarized law enforcement. The news of the monster in

Manhattan had clearly been received and was being taken very seriously across the borough.

"Let's get moving," Blue said, waving the others on as he and MJ headed toward the eastside exit. "Carry the boards, less conspicuous."

They weaved and nudged their way through commuters and panicked onlookers. All the different body odors and colognes in the crowd merged into one generic unpleasant waft of stink. They emerged at last through the chaos with a view of the exit doors.

"What did Nuhëma say to you through all of these big screens?" Sakima asked Blue as they cleared the bulk of the crowd. "Do continue." She pursed her lips, still skeptical.

"She said to inform you that to rescue your kid sister you've gotta smash turtle-turtle-turtle, like that, and also—"

Sakima leaped forward past Curly and MJ so her face was nearly touching Blue's. "You'd better not be messing with me," she said through clenched teeth.

"Please, Sakima, calm down," Janie Jones said, catching up from behind. She tapped her on her wrist. "Okay?"

"Yeah, jeez, girl. We're not fooling," Curly said. "Why would we joke about something like this? We know how serious this is for you. For all of us."

Sakima continued to stare unblinking into Blue's eyes, her hand having slipped down onto the handle of her favorite knife, *chessi*. Without moving any other part of her body, she shifted her head and her steely gaze oh-so-slightly to peer over at Curly. He gulped but held her gaze for as long as he could. When he blinked, Sakima backed off Blue, deciding to take the word of her new friends.

"Okay, sorry," she said, slowing her pulse with deliberate breathing. "I suppose I should trust you all. I mean, I do trust you. "

"Sakima?" Janie Jones said.

"What is it?"

"Your sister. You remember I told you that, well, she's not dead, right?"

"Yes, of course," Sakima said.

"Well, um, she's still not dead, so don't worry. But... I don't know how to say this!"

"Just say it, Janie Jones," Sakima said.

"Your sister. Tangetta. She's in the in the dead place now! And not just any dead place—the worst dead place!"

Sakima stared at Janie Jones, trying to comprehend what in the world she could possibly mean. Then she turned to Curly. "Okay. What was that pattern again? The key sequence? Give it up."

"Not a sequence," Curly corrected her. "The same button: turtle, three times. You know, one, two, three." He held up a finger for each number. When he finished, he just stood there, hand and three fingers frozen.

"Oh, crap, I almost forgot!" Blue interrupted. "She told us to give you this." He reached into his pocket and pulled something out. "She said if you hold it tight or something, it will be useful."

"In what way, useful?" Sakima asked, snatching the feather from Curly's outstretched hand.

"Funny. She didn't say."

The group stepped through the doors and out onto the sidewalk and into the sunshine. It was scorching hot, but after the over-air-conditioned indoor environment, it felt wonderfully warm on Sakima's face. Even the stink of hotdogs and old garbage was a kind of relief. Real air, real smells.

Ambulances sped through the intersection as fast as traffic permitted, inching through the gridlock, then screaming away once free.

NYPD cars and even trucks zipped by, some pulling up to drop officers off, others to pick them up. A SWAT bus rumbled by, followed by a dark green military truck, each leaving the strong stench of diesel exhaust. The side of the truck was stenciled in white with NATIONAL GUARD | NEW YORK.

The sound of sirens in the background was a cacophony of overlapping rhythms and discordant keys. Low flying helicopters roared by, kicking up garbage and dust and stopping the conversation.

Sakima and her friends marched around a small construction site where workers poured asphalt into a pothole, filling not only the hole but also the air with the smell of warm tar.

"Well, that's interesting because I don't," Sakima said. She tucked the turkey feather into her knife sheath that hung on her waist. "For that button sequence, I just do it…"

"Not a sequence—"

"Like this?" She tapped the turtle button very deliberately three times with a slight pause between each push.

Instantly, Sakima appeared to be more of a projected image than an actual person, shimmering like a reflection in a bright, rippling pool. Then she faded away, right before their eyes.

"Sakima!" Blue shouted. "Use the other button to return! The same way!"

The glittering image of Sakima tilted its head as if hearing the message but not comprehending. Then she was gone.

"The wolf one! Wolf-wolf," Blue yelled, his voice fading a bit with each "wolf" until it ended with a final whispered, "wolf?"

The group stood there, staring in disbelief, alone on the corner. They didn't say a word. Curly held his skyboard vertically between his right foot and his hand like a surfboard. Blue switched his skyboard to the top of his shoulders like the wings of an airplane, gripping each end. They both wore a look of total defeat.

Cars, taxis, buses, trucks, and thousands of people of every size, color, nationality, and gender swarmed around the four friends as if nothing unusual had happened. As if the world hadn't just ended.

CHAPTER 56

Samantha Jones pushed herself hard on the treadmill to complete her workout. Seven miles on the "hilly" program, and some of those damned artificially created hills were mountains. On one virtual mountain, she felt like she was running straight up a cliff for a mile without a break.

Her thighs hurt, her calves ached, and she was covered in sweat. She had never felt better. Sam Jones loved the feeling of completing a great workout—not because the routine was finally over—but because it gave her a sense of victory.

Yes, she did it to lose weight and keep it off, but she also cherished the feeling of strength and courage. Samantha Jones liked to imagine herself as a warrior. Running into battle, racing toward ultimate victory. She felt like a fighter: strong and capable of anything. Of course, once the session was done, the mood faded over the next few hours until she was "just Sam" again: a middle-aged divorcee with an unruly daughter and a love life deader than the broken equipment stacked in the club's basement.

She had to admit to herself, as she stepped off the treadmill and wiped her face with a small white terrycloth towel, that she was now officially worried. She wondered why her daughter wasn't answering her VRfone. Why she hadn't turned the beacon back on so Sam could see where in this great big city her daughter hung out.

She climbed in the shower and went through the motions, her mind a thousand miles away. While she dressed, she thought about how this morning she'd woken up with a positive, devil-may-care attitude. She had made Janie's favorite breakfast of all time: strawberry pop tarts with strawberry icing and an iced almond-milk mocha latte. All made with the full expectation that Janie was already at home and in bed asleep or would come strolling in through the front door any minute.

Samantha stared at her image as she put on a fresh face of makeup. She rolled up the expensive lipstick in its gold case that she'd purchased the night before. She adored the bright color and was convinced that the lipstick would simultaneously make her more confident and relaxed. Samantha grabbed her purse and her gym bag and tossed each over a shoulder.

Outside, the day was beautiful, the best in a while. Perfect blue sky, warm with a bit of a breeze, and sunshine like on her favorite beach in Miami. She slipped on her sunglasses and smiled as a row of NYPD squad cars zipped by her, sirens blaring and lights flashing.

Despite her new lipstick, her fierce exercise routine, and the amazing weather outside, she was starting to freak out about her missing daughter. She stopped smiling, took her VRfone out of her purse, and dialed 911. She held the phone flat in her palm. A police officer's head appeared in 3D, hovering over her screen in a blinky, desaturated, see-through hologram image. Even with the bulky headset he wore—enormous audio cups completely covering each ear and the large mic in front of his face—the young fellow struck her as quite good-looking.

"Stay aware of the latest warnings. Stay within guidelines," the man said, flatly quoting the marketing message of the week for the

NYPD. He cleared his throat. "Officer Rick Ya here. What's your emergency, please?" He was clearly fielding multiple calls at one time, as well as operating a few data terminals.

"My name is Samantha Jones. You may call me Sam," she smiled flirtatiously. "Um, so, I want to report a missing person."

"Really, lady?"

"What's that now?"

"We've got bigger things to worry about at this time. Haven't you seen the news? Or does this have something to do with the attacks?"

"Look, I have no idea what you're talking about. My daughter is missing, and I demand that you find her!"

"Because of the attacks? Is that what you're saying?"

"No, what? Of course not! Wait, I mean, I don't know. What are these attacks you keep droning on about? Anyway, I don't think so. I hope not—"

"Okay, tell you what. I'll take your info, but we are swamped here. Every cop is fully engaged in the ongoing crisis."

"That's all fine and good, but I still want to make a missing person report."

The officer sighed, rolling his eyes. "Okay. Let's make this quick, ma'am. Who would you like to report missing? How long has it been?"

"Uh, oh, well, it's my baby girl. Since yesterday."

"Okay, her name?" He hadn't looked at her once, Samantha realized. He'd been looking down the entire time. She wondered if was checking reports, entering info, or just watching the game.

"Jones, Janie," she replied, a bit miffed.

"Age?"

"Sixteen."

Finally, the officer had the manners to take a second and glance up at her.

"Sixteen?"

"Yes, and a half, but—"

"Ma'am, sorry, what's your name again?"

"Um, Sam. Samantha." She beamed and pursed her lips.

"Ma'am, here's the thing. These reports of teenage runaways are more common than you might think. Teens run away from home all the time these days. We get a mill—"

"Not my Janie!" Sam yelled, interrupting the officer's speech. A part of Sam recognized, deep down in a section of her brain she hated to visit, that she couldn't blame Janie if she had run away. Sam had been so disengaged lately. That thought was quickly replaced with one much worse: that if she hadn't run away, she might be in serious trouble. Or dead.

Samantha Jones burst into tears then and clicked her phone off. The cop's avatar wiggled and sparked and faded away. She pulled a few tissues from her bag and dabbed at her eyes. She flipped the tissues about in her hands before reaching up and blowing her nose, strong and loud, while glancing absentmindedly across the intersection.

Diagonally across the street from her stood Janie, along with her three best friends, involved in an animated conversation. Sam couldn't believe her watery eyes. She blinked hard and stared again. *It was her daughter.*

Samantha sobbed loudly one last time like she was gasping for air. She collected herself and waved, slowly at first, and then more and more frantically. Then she got up on her tiptoes and yelled.

"Janie! Janie Jones! Over here! It's your mother!"

The traffic noises, already loud, increased significantly as an ambulance threaded its halting way through the intersection, blocking Sam's view for a few seconds.

When the ambulance had finally moved on, so had Janie.

A helicopter, sweeping low, produced a windstorm that ripped the wet tissues right out of Sam's hand and swiped the look of joy off her face.

PART THREE
HADES

CHAPTER 57

Sakima stood in a world of fire. All around her flames leaped fifty feet high. The sky seemed a writhing inferno, and rivers of lava roiled past in all directions. Everything in the landscape appeared bright red and orange like molten steel in a steel mill, or else blazed with fury.

Sakima felt roasted in the hottest oven ever made. Her flesh seemed to sear right off her body. Sweat gushed from every sweat gland. Within seconds of arriving, her skin glistened, and her hair dripped as if she'd just stepped out of the shower.

The stench of sulfur and the sickening miasma that reminded her of burning hair—a repugnant combination—overwhelmed Sakima's sense of smell. The lava reeked of boiling metal in a smelt, with hints of rat feces mixed with a dash of vomit.

Her sweaty body smelled funny, too, in a way it *never* smelled before. Even when she trained her hardest in the blistering summer sun, she believed she gave off a nice, fresh scent, like wet grass. Here, it seemed like every evil thought, every negative rumination, every last, horrible nightmare strained out through her skin, along with all their associated odors.

Sakima glanced around worriedly. No paths, no roads, no way to tell in which direction to head. If Tangetta was down here in this world of endless flames, Sakima couldn't imagine how she would ever find her, or how Tangetta could ever survive.

She picked up the sound of screaming off in the distance, the most wretched and forlorn sounds she'd ever heard. Screams of agony coupled with moans of hopelessness and despair seemed to fill the air, audible above the roaring noise of the flames and the bubbling undertones of the lava streams.

She squinted through the haze of black smoke and soot to see how she might begin her travels, her search for her little sister, but she found no clues. As she peered into the far reaches, still trying to get her bearings, she tilted her head with confusion.

There appeared to be a giant towering above, somewhere up ahead. Sakima tried to focus better, but her eyes watered from the heat and gasses. There was no mistaking it, however. Perhaps a mile away, a colossus with bright red skin stood twenty feet tall. He, or it, slashed a whip of fire through the air, snapping it at an area below him that Sakima couldn't quite see. She identified it as the place where the screams and moans were coming from. Over and over, the colossus snapped that whip, and a crescendo of shrieks echoed each time it thrashed down. The gigantic crimson monster cackled and shrieked something that sounded like "sinners!"

Sakima found herself unable to move. She felt a fear she'd never experienced before, which froze her heart and soul despite the overwhelming heat. She felt sick to her stomach. How would she get out? More importantly, how would she ever find Tangetta and free her of this place—wherever in hell it was?

A thought flashed through Sakima's brain. *Hell. I'm in hell. That otherworldly location Janie Jones tried to tell me about. The dwelling of the dead, the worst of all possible ghastly realms.* She shuddered as she considered her revelation. *Nowhere could be more loathsome than here, and my poor sister is somewhere amid all this misery!* She sighed deeply.

At the same time, this realization hardened her resolve. *My actions resulted in Tangetta being brought to this terrible world. I will not fail her a second time.* Sakima marched off into the inferno, fists bunched, back straight. Her eyes squinted from the intense heat and the ash-filled atmosphere, but they were focused unblinkingly on saving Tangetta. And getting her free of this living nightmare. No matter the cost.

Striding carefully between the burning lava flows, the licking flames, and the steaming hot boulders, she was determined to find her sister and spirit her to safety. Even if it meant she, Sakima, might be left behind in this horrid place until the end of time.

She marched on, the heat unbearable and forcing her to stop and rest every dozen or so steps. It was like making her way through a live volcano for infinite miles in all directions. Sakima could feel herself drying up with each step, in such need of water that she thought she'd go insane if she didn't have some soon. A mere teaspoon of liquid would be the most wonderful thing.

Sakima could feel her skin blistering, especially her lips, which were already peeling, the skin as dry as an old callus. Her tongue was both drying up and getting bigger, like a thick, leathery steak in her mouth. She was sweating so hard that the sweat off her forehead poured into her eyes, aiding the billowing black fog in obscuring her view. Sakima struggled to lick what slight drops of moisture made it down from her eyes to anywhere near her lips and tongue. It was hardly anything at all because virtually all of it steamed away, fizzing into nothing before it reached her mouth.

She felt as miserable and as lost as she'd ever been, but she soldiered on nonetheless. She forced herself to put one foot in front of the other, again and again. She made slow progress, but at least it was some kind of momentum.

In her mind, it seemed as if she had been going on like this for hours, maybe days, the heat shriveling her body, destroying her will to live. The horrible howling and wailing from afar beating her soul down until she had no spirit left, no confidence, and no faith. Still, she trudged on, barely able to see in front of her. Searching for her lost sister, not daring to hope she might find her. Or that either of them—assuming Tangetta existed somewhere in this horrible place—would ever escape.

"Grandmother of the South!" Sakima cried out in anguish, her voice a throaty, dry crackle. "Why have you forsaken me? Why have you led me here? What do you expect me to do? How can I find my sister here in this fiery, endless pit? Nuhëma Shaoneyunk, help me! Please!"

Overhead, Sakima spotted winged demons swooping and diving in the fiery sky, shrieking at whoever they tormented far beneath them. She couldn't see anyone or anything more than a few yards ahead of her, let alone the place a half-mile or more in the distance where the monsters circled.

She could barely make out some other terrible, dark creatures in the space between where she shuffled along, burning and dying, and where the flying demons soared through the sky, if you could call it that. It was more like an ocean of lava that had somehow been smeared across where a sky should have been.

"Nuhëma!" Sakima muttered. She knew she was dying; it was only a matter of time. Sakima thought she was losing her hold on reality, starting to hallucinate. Through smoke and flames and waves of heat rippling in her vision, she could have sworn she spied a cage suspended in midair.

A huge, black metal enclosure swung somberly back and forth on a rusty chain—a warning bell in the scorching, murky air. As far as Sakima could see, the chain continued upwards hundreds of *shaèk* into the flaming atmosphere, with no anchor in sight. It hung there; the cage attached below twisting in the heat, just a few feet or so above the highest of the spurting flames, as if it were a cooking pot steaming the night's dinner.

She worked her way closer. It required so much strength and

energy and force of will; it was as if Sakima dragged a barge full of bricks behind her. The sweltering white heat battered her, making her feel sick with the worst headache she'd ever had. She moved on anyway, driven to discover what might be in the cage she had spotted—or imagined—hanging there in fiery space.

As she came closer, her curiosity peaked, because now, inside the black, burning cage, she thought she could make out a figure. There seemed to be a droopy shadow moving in a lethargic and mournful way from one side of the enclosure to the other. It would occasionally sit and then get back up again to repeat the ritual.

What is that thing? Why is it trapped in such a hovering jail? Sakima thought. *When will I, mercifully, be allowed to die?*

She inched her way along. If she had the capacity anymore to experience surprise, she would have wondered where her strength came from, where her spirit found the will to continue. Because most of her mind, Sakima understood completely, wanted her body to drop where it stood, to fall over, fall asleep, and never wake again.

As she grew nearer and nearer, step by trembling, painful step, Sakima realized it was no shadow in the hanging pen. That impression was generated by both the distance and the blazes and soot. It was a little person—and truly small—not just her eyes playing games with her.

It wasn't a trick of the fire and the smoke and the sizzling torrents of heat that first created this mirage. *No,* Sakima realized as she got closer; *no generic diminutive creature occupied that cage. It was a little girl.*

It was Tangetta.

CHAPTER 58

Takachsin had convinced Wùnita to go home with him, to take a break. Women from the village had arrived at the facility to help her at last, but she had insisted on pressing on, working herself to the point of exhaustion.

"Come with me, hon. You need to rest, have a bite of food, and drink some tea."

After many such offers from her husband, Wùnita finally agreed, her head throbbing and her hands stiff from the repetitive work. So he took her away in a small, open-air hovercar—*pèmitàn mpàki*—across the magnetic roadway. In minutes, they were home where Nimàt and Amimi met them, as Takachsin had requested.

While Wùnita and Mimi prepared and served the tea and snacks together, Takachsin wandered into Sakima's bedroom, lost in his own thoughts. He stopped at her doorway, struck by how quiet and still the room was, as if her life force no longer existed there. It seemed to be more like a museum made in Sakima's memory than a young woman's room.

Takachsin strode over to where Sakima had propped her childhood quiver in the corner. He removed an arrow and examined it, rolling it between his thumb and fingers. The arrow was standard in terms of technological upgrades. It was also about half the size of a regular arrow. He twirled it slowly in his hands, remembering teaching the very young Sakima to shoot. Takachsin recalled how Sakima had been such a natural right from the start that it had shocked him that day, her seventh birthday.

How can she be this good on her first day of lessons? Where does she get this from? Takachsin had thought then. *Certainly not from me; I can't shoot the side of a longhouse at ten paces.*

The air conditioner kicked on. Already set too cold, the atmosphere soon became as icy as a mausoleum. He stood up, still holding the kid-sized arrow. Before he left, he stretched down and absently smoothed Sakima's bedcover where he'd been sitting. Then he made his way wearily to the living room.

Wùnita hunched on the couch with Mimi perched next to her, attempting to comfort her. The baby, Mimëntëta, cooed in her cradleboard next to the large picture window. Wùnita held in her palm one of Tangetta's little homemade dolls, made of sticks and cloth, with a crudely drawn face. Nimàt sat in a chair across from her.

Takachsin walked past Nimàt and lowered himself into the armchair closest to his wife. He could smell the mint, raspberry, spruce, and snowberry wafting up from her tea on the table by his arm. He reached out and touched her knee encouragingly. The electronic kettle was still active for some reason, clicking on and off as it modulated the temperature of the ready-to-pour hot water. It was as if someone was dialing a number again and again, with no one ever answering.

Mimi picked up a cup off the tray and handed her father fresh, steaming tea. This blend of tea was nearly all she ate or drank nowadays. She was trying to lose the last of the weight she'd gained during pregnancy. She used to look quite a lot like Sakima, but lately, after the birth and her years of marriage to Machto, she looked older, heavier, and sadder.

"Father," she said while looking instead at her mother. "I didn't want to mention this with everything else going on, but… "

"It's fine, Mimi, my daughter. You can tell me anything. Please, what is burdening you?"

"Machto."

Takachsin beamed. "How is Machto? Good man, that one." He blew on his tea and sipped it.

Mimi paused as if unsure how to proceed. She appeared to change her tack. "Well, that's part of it," she said. "He's gone. He went missing about the same time as Sakima."

Takachsin's knitted his eyebrows. He placed his teacup on the table, mouth downturned. "Are you implying that they—they ran off together? I know he pays her a bit too much attention, but that was just Machto being Machto. I—"

"What? No, Father. That's not at all what I am saying. I mean, he's gone, and I'm concerned. More than that, I… I think he might be responsible for the creature breaking out of its cage—"

"Oh, yes, yes, I see! You're worried he's left to help Sakima. Is that it? To save the day? Yes, that sounds like Machto. Something he'd do, yes." He picked his teacup up cheerfully and drank from it.

Mimi and Wùnita exchanged a glance. "Never mind, Father. Maybe we can talk about this some other time."

"Sure, sure," Takachsin said, sipping his drink with a self-satisfied smile. "Of course. Anytime."

Wùnita studied her husband, her eyes blank and moist, the surrounding skin red and puffy. She peered over at the statue of Kishelë, awkwardly glued together as best she could do after Sakima had run off that night. At the same time, Takachsin, lost in thought, focused on the hummingbirds outside who fed from a strangely coffin-shaped feeder Sakima had built. It was meant to look like a house, and she'd painted it bright pink and hung it there herself. The hummingbirds hovered in midair, as if by magic, before darting off to the next feeding option on their route.

"Taka," Wùnita said without looking up, her voice quiet, almost inaudible.

Takachsin put his hand on hers. Nimàt put his hand on her other hand, the one holding the doll. "Taka, I don't think we'll ever see her again. I couldn't take it; not another child gone." Takachsin wasn't sure if she was speaking of Tangetta, Sakima, or both.

"We must keep hoping, my love, continue to have faith. That's all we can do." He squeezed her hand, but she didn't respond. Instead, she closed her eyes and said, almost to herself, "It would kill me, I am sure, to lose one more child, let alone two more. Losing Hìtami, my little Tommy, already nearly put me in my grave."

Her husband nodded, unable to speak for a second.

"Our daughter has always lived under a curse, feeling the need to replace Tommy in our hearts. Or to at least live up to his legend," Wùnita said, more to herself than to Takachsin. "What could we do?"

He studied her face, desperately searching in his head and heart for the best thing to say.

"It did not help," Wùnita continued, "that on the same day that Tommy traveled to the Land of the Dead, Sakima chose to be born." She sobbed.

The three, possibly the only remaining members of the Tamanend family other than baby Mimëntëta, came together around their matriarch. Takachsin dropped to one knee in front of Wùnita. Mimi had scooted over closer to her mother, and Nimàt leaned way forward, also with a knee on the floor. They formed a circle of love and despair, trying to hold themselves—and their family—together.

Then the video phone blinked, accompanied by a quiet but cheerful chime, breaking the moment to pieces. The family tried to ignore it, to let it go, but it flashed and rang, an insistent child.

Takachsin glanced over with some reluctance. It was a line from SOW, the Shawken Obroa Wîkëwam building where the portal was under twenty-four-hour repair. He turned away and involved himself in the family hug again, closing his eyes. The phone stopped, but thirty seconds later, it started again. This cycle repeated twice until Takachsin spoke.

"I must answer this, my love," he murmured to Wùnita, who acknowledged this with a nod.

He extracted himself from the group, stood up, and strode the few steps over to the vidPhone.

"Yes, hello, this is Takachsin," he said, instantly activating the video screens at both ends.

"TeeTee, I hope I haven't called at a bad time," Pahòke said.

"There is no good time, my friend, not until Sakima and Tangetta are returned to us."

The men shared a minute of silence. Then Pahòke continued.

"You might consider coming on down here, TeeTee. We are almost done, and everything has been testing out well so far." He hesitated, expecting Takachsin to speak. When he didn't, Pahòke continued. "Also, the *mpoalonium*, it… has healed itself! I've never seen anything like it. We collected all the pieces and when they were near each other on the bench, the bigger pieces pulled the broken sections together toward an invisible center, back into one solid chunk of the element. Incredible." He paused at the memory of it. "Anyway, I thought you and Wùnita would prefer to be here when we switch the portal back on. It's ready."

Takachsin didn't speak; he just stood staring at the screen, evidently stunned at this sudden good news and the report on the *mpoalonium's* amazing self-reconstruction.

"Or not?" Pahòke said shyly, as he'd apparently expected a loud cheer or at least a positive comment from Takachsin. "Up to you."

"We'll be right there," Takachsin said, hanging up the phone with a wave of his hand. The image on the other end of a confused-looking Pahòke staring straight ahead faded to white.

Takachsin turned to inform Wùnita as to what was happening, but she had already heard. Instead of tears of grief and despair, tears of joy streamed down her cheeks. Nimàt and Mimi helped her to her feet.

"Taka, this could be it!" She let loose a heavy sigh. "Let me first grab a couple of things." She glanced away and then down at the floor. "I will, um, yes. I will meet you all down there. Soon."

"No, Wù, we'll wait for you," Takachsin said, grinning slightly and unsure why his wife would want to delay this glorious occasion. "That's not a problem."

"I need a few minutes alone, Taka, don't worry. I'll take the very next *pèmitàn mpàki* hovercar, I promise you."

Takachsin squinted a bit at her and was about to argue, but Mimi spoke up. "Let's give Mom a minute, okay?" She lifted Mimëntëta up and onto her shoulders. "I think she wants some time alone to reflect, to pray."

Takachsin, at last, realized he was on a fool's errand to convince her to leave with them. "Okay, my dear," he said. "I understand, I guess. Are you sure you will be all right?"

"Of course, yes. Now run along. Don't make any decisions until I get there, though!" she said, making a weak attempt at sounding cheerful. She walked her family through the foyer to the front door. As she shut herself in, Takachsin glanced back with one eyebrow up.

Once the others had left, Wùnita stood in the entry for a minute, alone. She gazed at the large tulpe painting on the wall, remembering how harshly she'd reprimanded Sakima for leaning against it. She wished she could take that moment back, the last with her daughter. She had her reasons for protecting the art. There was a chance of it receiving unintentional scratches and other damage. Because of that legitimate concern, the entire family knew to give that side of the hallway a wide berth, coming or going, and by habit, they always did so.

But Wùnita had a more important reason for instilling that behavior. She pressed the upper left foot of the turtle twice, then the lower right leg three times. Each time she selected only one oyster shell piece of the many used throughout the artwork.

With the sound of a small electric motor purring, the tulpe painting slid up into the wall above. It revealed a locked door about a *shaèk* wide and a half a *shaèk* tall at Wùnita's eye height. She leaned close into the bioScanner, which read her iris like a finger-print. After a brief second, the metal door also glided out of sight with a quiet whoosh.

As Wùnita studied the contents of her large, secret closet a smile grew on her face. She wiped away the few remaining tears still lingering on each cheek. Then she reached deep inside the cubby, grasping an object made of wood in her left hand and another of cloth in the other, dragging them both out together, pulling them out into the light.

CHAPTER 59

Sakima stopped in her tracks. She squinted across the heatwaves and smoke and dust and leaping flames. It was Tangetta, without a doubt. Of course, there was a chance her sister might be part of the hallucination of the odd floating cage and its never-ending chain.

She realized then how dog-tired, *mwekane*, she had become. Her muscles weighed her down, old leather bags filled with sand. Her bones literally creaked—she heard them. All due to the insane heat and her dehydration. Her tongue was swollen, desiccated. Her eyes were so dry she couldn't blink.

Regardless, she knew she must press on somehow. If this turned out to be Tangetta, great. If not, that would have to be that. Because either way, Sakima wouldn't survive this place much longer. She recognized she'd be almost dead by the time she rescued her sister—if the person she was looking at even was her sister. If this was nothing but a horrible illusion messing with her mind, it would usurp the remaining bits of her courage and strength. Suck it all to dust. She'd die there in the non-shadow of the non-cage not holding Tangetta.

She forced herself to keep moving her legs, to trudge her husk of a body forward another inch through flame and ash and misery. Each step required monumental effort; everything hurt so much, and it all seemed pointless and impossible. Sakima wanted to cry, but she had no tears; her entire being was parched and brittle. Sakima knew it wouldn't be long until her blood, her actual real blood coursing thickly inside her actual physical body, started to boil.

She couldn't believe any of this was possible—that she was down here, dying. Then again, she wouldn't have imagined everything that had previously taken place. None of it seemed real. Part of her brain, in a very faraway place, remembered that it was only yesterday that she had run through the moist fields of grass on verdant Mannahatta. The breezes blowing the sweet smell of jasmine and pine through the air, with birds flying free, swooping and diving in the blue sky. Before that, the rain—amazing, refreshing showers. She had taken rainfall for granted and had assumed moisture would always flow from the clouds. She recalled how it had genuinely annoyed her, wondering when it would quit so the gleaming sun could dry the grass and warm her skin.

Sakima snapped back to reality, as her swollen tongue smeared across her dusty, cracked lips. She coughed a sharp painful hacking that cut her throat. She reached out, her hand quivering high toward the suspended cage. She was too weak to hold her arms up for long, and they soon slumped against her sides like dead birds falling from the sky.

When they dropped, her fingertips scraped against a white-hot boulder, the texture of an unpolished tombstone. Sakima didn't feel the pain she should have because nothing registered anymore—except for the never-ending, unbearable heat of a smelt, of a furnace, of being burnt alive.

Somehow, in her dazed and dehydrated confusion, she had nearly reached the suspended jail. It swung gently backward and forward in the middle distance, buffeted by heatwaves. In a few more agonizing steps, Sakima arrived, peering up with waterless, papery eyes at the cage suspended ten feet above the flames.

So it was true. Sakima was sure of that now. She wanted to yell out, to ask Tangetta—if that was her she'd seen, if that was anyone at all she'd seen—too show herself. To call down here from that jail cell and prove that Sakima hadn't completely lost her mind. But no hand appeared, no little face, no tiny voice.

Sakima couldn't move; she had turned to stone, burning rock set to ignite and then explode. *So this is the end: this strange hell. This is how I die,* she thought, unable to lower her head. It was as if every muscle in her neck had morphed to iron and might never yield again.

Sakima didn't care. She understood it was over. She knew she had lost. *Why did I come here? Why did the Grandmother of the South instruct me on how to get to this horrid land? Was it just to die?* Sakima had these thoughts with no emotion, like reading a random list of words someone else had written centuries ago.

She picked up a sound coming from far away: a distant, dream-like voice that called her name.

"Sakima!"

Sakima couldn't blink or move her head. Her ears still worked well enough and required no manual adjustment. She stood there, a statue, listening. Then she heard it again.

"Sakima, Sakima! *Save me!*"

Before she realized it, Sakima saw that sweet face, peering down at her from the rim at the bottom of the horrific cage.

"Tangetta," Sakima whispered in more of a cough than a comment. "How are you? Are you okay?" It astonished Sakima how seeing and hearing her sister made so much of her fear drain away. She swallowed hard, and it hurt. "I have come to take you home. "

"Goody!" Tangetta said softly. She raised herself all the way up and clapped her soot-covered hands together, making little black clouds of dust cascade all about her. "Can we go? Please? I want to be back home with Mommy and Daddy."

"Me, too. First I need to get you out of that cage. *Hmmm*, let's see." Sakima staggered around the pen, still gazing up with her neck locked in place, using up the last of her strength. "I don't imagine you have a rope, or a ladder, or something in there with you, do you?"

Tangetta laughed. "You are funny; I have nothing up here with me! No dolls, no snacks, no favorite books."

"Well, that's not good, is it?"

"No."

"Let me think a bit, okay?"

"Okay!" Tangetta smiled and got down on the floor of the cage again to watch her sister walking below. "What are you looking for?"

"Some latch or hatch or door we can open, maybe? But all I see is a rusty old lock on the door and that big chain that holds you up in the air." Sakima thought for a second. "That gives me an idea. "

"What?"

"I'm going to try something."

" 'k."

"Do not be scared."

"I am scared already, though."

"Well, you can stop being frightened; I'm here now. So, relax a little and be a brave girl, okay? Here we go."

" 'k… "

Sakima removed her quiver from her back and searched her supply. There it was: what she'd been looking for. Sakima nocked the projectile and aimed with care. She shouted, "Tangetta, stay down. Don't get up!" Then she let the arrow fly.

The missile hit the chain about two *shaèks* above the roof of the enclosure to wedge itself within a single link. It whirred loudly as soon as a miniature spinning saw emerged from the tip of the arrow. It was deadly action for any enemy unlucky enough to be impaled by the arrow, yet extremely useful in this situation.

The arrow sawed away, cutting through the thick, rusty chain link bit by tiny bit. At last, the buzzing stopped, its energy used up. Sakima stood prepared. She had a second saw-arrow fed into her bowstring. She pulled back, aiming precisely. The string snapped, sending the arrow flying straight into that same chain link, biting into the arrow already there, which split apart and tumbled to the ground. Once it made contact with the fiery floor, the arrow burst into flames and was gone in seconds.

"Get ready to hang on, Tangetta," Sakima called out. "You will fall but not that far. Then I will be able to get to you, free you."

" 'k, Sakima, I am ready."

Sakima smiled for the first time since entering this furnace world, as she imagined Tangetta forming her hands into tight little fists making her most determined face. Meanwhile, the second arrow continued its work on the link. A loud crack ensued, and the cage dropped with a dramatic clang. However, after all that, it had moved by only two inches. The arrow ground away until another bang rang out, followed by a descent of a few more inches. Finally, the arrow was through, separating the link completely from the rest of the gigantic, endless chain.

"Any minute now, Tangerine! Hang on!" Sakima said.

One chunk of the link dropped to the burning ground, the other remained stuck in the chain. She'd done it! She'd broken the chain. Why wasn't the cage descending? With her neck still locked, she stared up, trying to understand how gravity worked in this horrible nightmare. Then she noticed the pen was falling, about a foot a minute—sinking at an almost imperceptible pace, a pebble through week-old pudding.

Slowly and with care, Sakima lowered her head and massaged the back of her neck, looking down. She worked the muscles and ligaments so that they might act as if they belonged to a neck again, and not an oak tree. She gazed around as she did so, absently scanning the scorched landscape.

That's when she spotted them: The *manëtu*. Demon creatures.

They were on the horizon, crawling over the scorching rocks on all fours without flinching. Their eyeless, hideous faces were bent up in a way that should be anatomically impossible, as if their heads rode on hinges instead of on necks.

And they were headed directly for Sakima at an incredible speed.

CHAPTER 60

If Sakima had had any energy left, she would have shrieked. As it was, she hardly moved a muscle. She stood as motionless as stone, watching these abominations—eyeless things, with mouths full of teeth that seemed to cover more than their muzzles—headed toward her. They passed through currents of steaming lava as if it were a cool stream over red rocks, as if traversing fresh, dewy grass.

Sakima glanced up at the hanging metal jail. It made slow, steady progress toward the flames dancing on the ground beneath it. *Come on, hurry. Speed up.*

She switched her gaze over to the approaching demon creatures, the *manëtu*. They were so much closer now. She had to free Tangetta from that cage and try to find the path out of this horrible place. She needed to do that right now.

"Tangetta! Run to the back, will you do that, please?"

"Yes, Sakima." Tangetta stood up carefully and sped to the other side, then stared at the locked door. "I did it! I'm ready again, Sakima."

"Good girl!" Sakima sighed. There was a chance Sakima could

crack the lock, a chance worth taking. Then what? Even if she could somehow break it off, Tangetta wouldn't be able to push that heavy metal door open.

She'd have to wait until the small prison had dropped a lot further. The one thing she didn't want to do: stall or delay. Speed was of the essence—hustle and action. Instead, Sakima was forced to linger in standby mode. To do nothing but wait as that pack of death-bringers crept closer and closer, while watching the cage fall oh-so-strangely out of the smoke-filled atmosphere.

Well, I will not do that, she decided. She locked an exploding arrow into her bow, the only arrow of that type in her quiver. She sent it flying at the lock, as the cage dropped to just above her eye level.

The arrow exploded and thankfully, so did the padlock, splintering into a hundred pieces. Sakima took three agonizing steps backward. Then, with every ounce of her remaining strength, she ran and leaped as high as she could. She managed to grab onto the gate and pull herself up. At first, nothing happened.

She called out to Tangetta. "Come here, my little Tangerine. Come to Sakima!"

With a few additional tugs, her left foot on the side of the cage next to the gate, it swung open just enough for Sakima to reach in. She grabbed Tangetta, who had run toward her, filled with joy at the whole thrill of it all, as if they weren't both about to die in the most horrible manner.

Yet Sakima found it impossible not to laugh because of Tangetta's giggle and the small arms that her little sister squeezed tightly around Sakima's neck.

"Okay, okay," Sakima said, chuckling. "Here we go!" And with that, she jumped the remaining four feet to the ground, Tangetta clutching to her with all her might. Sakima groaned from the pain of the landing, not because it had been any great distance, but because her entire body already ached beyond comprehension. She caught her balance and straightened up. "You good, Tangerine?"

"I'm a good girl!"

Sakima smiled. "Well, I know you are. What I meant was, are you okay? Did you hurt yourself when we hit?"

"No, Sakima. I'm good! The other kind of good like you said." Tangetta busted out a belly laugh at her own cleverness. "And I hate these monsters! See, Sakima? I told you there were monsters!"

"Yes, you did. I'm glad you're okay, though." She stopped talking, staring straight ahead.

The demons were only a few paces away. She could see the slime on their enormous teeth, their huge steak-tongues licking their unexpectedly wet lips. She could smell their nasty stench—a foul reek, an animal corpse rotting in the sun, a repulsive smell.

There were too many. She couldn't defeat them all. She wasn't sure she could beat any of them. Could these things even be hurt—killed? Or were they beyond that? Supernatural beings?

Sakima closed her eyes and exhaled, trying to find courage through concentration. Then she remembered: the feather, the gift from the Grandmother. She drew it out from where she'd stuffed it in her sheath.

"Don't let go of me, Tangerine."

"I won't."

"And it would be better if you kept your eyes shut nice and tight. No peeking, okay?"

" 'k."

Sakima gripped the long green feather and jammed it into her thick hair just above her ear. She looked down at Tangetta, but she had disappeared. So had Sakima's limbs. She put her hand in front of her, but there was no hand. She and Tangetta had become invisible.

Sakima breathed the putrid steam through her nose and clenched teeth as she watched the minor demons approach them now. A couple of them had stopped in their tracks, sniffing the air. A few others wandered about, confused, only a foot from herself and Tangetta. *For once since I entered this terrible, rancid place,* she thought, *I might have the advantage.*

Sakima randomly pushed the buttons on her cuff. She hoped and prayed it would take her and her sister far from the nightmare they were trapped in. She pressed the *xinkwtëme* button and paused for a beat. *Xinkwtëme* again. Paused again. Nothing.

How can this be? Sakima thought. *Did Blue remember the directions wrong? It is wolf, isn't it?* She tried again. Still nothing.

It must be the demons, Sakima suddenly realized. *They are too close. All that evil is somehow interfering with the cuff's powers. We need to separate ourselves from them.*

The *manëtu* sniffed around, confused, trying to track down the missing humans they'd sensed seconds earlier. Perhaps a superior sense of smell compensated in some form for their eyelessness. The feather's magic seemed to hide both the scent and sight of the two sisters. Then a demon made an abrupt stop, swinging its hideous head in Sakima's direction as if it could see her, vision or not.

The hell-beast made a horrifying screech to summon the other *manëtu,* who sharply snapped their heads toward Sakima as well, followed a high-pitched screaming mixed with a distorted growl. The demons howled and snarled with the cacophony of a hundred insane, dying dogs. Sakima had never heard a more sickening and frightening sound in her life.

CHAPTER 61

The *manëtu* slowly circled Sakima's position. These horrors were much bigger than she'd expected: more like small horses than big dogs. With Tangetta stuck to her hip, Sakima snatched her knife and slashed at the things. Tangetta screamed, still keeping her eyes shut as tight as she could make them.

Sakima took a quick break from hacking monsters to give pressing the buttons on her cuff once again. She needed to believe this would work; it had to work. She pushed the wolf button. Paused. Wolf again. Paused. Before she could press the *xinkwtëme* gem a final time, a beast caught the cuff in its rotting teeth.

Whether or not it did this intentionally, Sakima had no way of knowing. She yanked her arm hard, but the demon dog tore the cuff painfully off. Sakima watched as that monster trotted off with her cuff, the disobedient pet. It seemed to laugh, too, if you could call it that; a disgusting utterance.

Sakima stood frozen in horror. The freaks had found her and her sister. They had the cuff. She glared at the demon as it scrambled off with it in its grotesque muzzle, chased almost playfully by some of the other *manëtu*. Watching, she felt as if her soul, not her cuff, had been stripped from her.

She understood how terrible this defeat was. How she'd failed to be the hero, to be the warrior, by botching her attempt to save her sister for a second and final time.

On each recent occasion in which she thought she had what it took, it was as if the universe slapped her down and mockingly said: "No, you don't have what it takes at all, *SUCKeema*. Not even close."

One of the remaining demon beasts growled with the sound of sand in a grinder. It flexed its muscles, squatting halfway on its haunches as if ready to launch. Sakima instinctively understood what it was planning. The monster would attack her and Tangetta, then rip their throats out and eat them alive, even though the two sisters were completely invisible to the eyes and noses of normal creatures.

The *manëtu* then attacked, streaking through the air, screeching and snarling, hideous rows of fangs fully exposed and drool flying behind it from its gigantic mouth.

Sakima drove her knife deep into the chest of the nightmare beast in midair, falling to the ground under its ghastly unconscious body. She tried to shove the beast off her, but it was too heavy. Then she realized with a shock as she struggled and pushed: Tangetta had become visible again. She'd lost physical contact with her sister, and the monsters could sense her once again.

Frantically, Sakima kicked and shoved, but she couldn't get the dead monster to move, to fall off her. She was trapped and power-less to help her sister. Other hell-beasts circled Tangetta who, surprisingly, wasn't crying. Instead, she looked incensed.

"Sakima!" she cried out. "Time to kill more monsters!"

Her hands were balled up into fists, and she stood her ground, feet apart to steady herself, in the same style she'd seen her big sister do it.

Sakima forced a sliver of space between the creature and the surface and fought her way onto her stomach. She determined the best course of action was to crawl from under the hell-beast, rather than trying to hoist it off of her.

While two of the *manëtu* circled, still unsure of the situation or perhaps suspecting a trap, the creature farthest from them began its attack, aiming to kill the child. The monster was in a crouch, low to the rocky surface, ready to pounce, acid-drool dripping onto the steaming ground. In a sudden flash, it bolted through the black, sooty air over burning pumice and bubbling lava, fat limbs pumping up and down. It growled loudly as it approached, its tongue flailing about behind it. It jumped, howling, less than two *shaèk* from Tangetta. Sakima managed to escape from under the belly of the beast, leap to her feet, nock her arrow, and send it flying. Then a second. Then a third. She drilled them into the monster's flesh again and again.

It fell to the ground, and as she watched it disintegrated swiftly, becoming part of the sooty atmosphere. She twisted to face the last of the beasts, loosing arrows into it repeatedly until it turned to ash and its dust fluttered into nothingness.

Sakima spun around to study the monster that had stolen her cuff and gotten away. Her face fell into grim lines. Her eyes narrowed and her eyebrows tightened. She peered off into the fiery distance as her mouth curled slowly and determinedly down.

"Stay right here," she said to Tangetta, who nodded, her eyes wide.

Feeling the return of extra energy from the adrenaline surging through her body, Sakima began to jog, and then miraculously, to run. She could hear the *manëtu* cackling and growling and screeching as she chased after the thing carrying her cuff. She wondered how she was even moving, let alone sprinting, over the lava flows and glowing charcoal-rocks, through the quivering waves of heat and billowing soot.

As she ran, she nocked an arrow, holding her bow steady, the string pulled halfway taut. She aimed. She waited. It had to be a kill shot; she would not get a second chance. It moved too fast and was far ahead of her. Sakima paused as the beast quickly approached the limits of her bow's range. Then she stretched the string to her ear, pulling it so hard her arms shook, and then she let the arrow fly.

The arrow seemed to whistle through the air as it carved its course through the extreme heat and smoke. It hit exactly where Sakima had aimed: the rear of the creature's head. She didn't hear it hit; the beast was much too far in the distance. But the arrow must have embedded itself in the creature's skull because she then witnessed the *manëtu* topple.

As Sakima ran to catch up with the beast, she saw it rearing onto its back legs and crash face forward to the ground, its hind parts flying up behind it. She observed its jaw release the cuff as its skull cracked open from the combination of the arrow and crashing into the hard, scorching ground. She caught up to it just as it slide across the molten surface and came to a halt.

Sakima swaggered up to the beast and noticed the heart of this creature from hell continued to glow, showing signs of life beneath its gelatinous, murky skin. She withdrew the blade from her waist and straddled the monster. Then she grabbed the beast by its patchy fur and yanked its head off the ground. In a single, swift, determined motion, Sakima slit the demon's throat.

The blackish blood from the *manëtu* sprayed out in an arc, sizzling and steaming as it splattered on the scorched rocks and pumice. She watched with horror as maggots and worms wriggled out of the deep neck wound. Cockroaches fought their way through next. Sakima felt the urge to throw up again at the sight, but she forced herself not to. *That has got to be the most disgusting thing I've seen in my entire life,* she thought, as the creature turned into dust and soot and ash.

She stood up slowly, turned, and walked a few steps in Tangetta's direction. As she made her way through the ash and flames, she reached up and grabbed the feather from her hair and returned it to her knife sheath. After a few strides, she casually bent over to pick up her cuff lying there. Oddly it was completely unharmed—there were no chew marks, no burnt spots, and all the jewels were still intact. She slid the cuff onto her arm and continued walking back to Tangetta.

"Are you all right?" she asked her when she finally got to her little sister.

Tangetta sniffed uselessly to stop the snot tears running out her nose and streaming onto her upper lip, where it dried out immediately.

"I want to go home, Sakima. I mean it. I do not enjoy it here!"

"I know. Me neither, my Tangerine. Come here." She held her hand out to her kid sister. "Come on."

Tangetta took it, nestling her hand into the much bigger palm of her sister's. Sakima smiled.

"Now, hang on tight, yes?"

" 'k."

Sakima tapped the bright blue wolf button on her cuff three times: *Xinkwtëme. Xinkwtëme. Xinkwtëme.* Then she and her sister vanished.

CHAPTER 62

"I don't understand what just happened," Janie Jones said.

"Neither do I," Curly said. "I thought the turtle-turtle-turtle thing would cause a map to display or something. Or even her little sister to sort of pop up here out of nowhere."

"Me, too," Blue said. "I didn't expect Sakima to disappear into thin air!"

The four gazed about them as if expecting to see Sakima looking out of some window at them.

"We can't hang around here waiting, though," MJ said. "It's not safe with that evil dude still here somewhere. Speaking of popping in out of nowhere, that's something that asshole would definitely do."

A long tandem bus approached, beeping at the car parked in the bus stop lane. The bus driver honked repeatedly, but the vehicle didn't budge. The thumping of the music inside was so loud it sounded like an open speaker. Huge crowds swept past them—a river of people talking. Some stopped to snap a selfie. Others tapped messages on their cellphones. A few of them beamed holograms of their loved ones from the VRphones in their outstretched hands.

Random folks waved and shouted here and there. Some were right by the friends, while other wavers and yellers were across the street. Emergency and military vehicles were everywhere, including the sky above them. It was chaos.

An ambulance approached the intersection blocked by taxis, SUVs from New Jersey and Connecticut, and a red double-decker bus, the tour guide within it pointing out to the tourists in their seats the statue of the Greek God Mercury on top of the Grand Central terminal building. It seemed tourism continued despite the crisis, or perhaps because of it.

The tour bus tried to pull over with a blast of diesel-scented smoke that smelled like a full-on oil refinery, but it had nowhere to move. The ambulance somehow increased the volume of its sirens. Some cars in the intersection crawled out of the way to create a narrow, temporary path through the traffic. Carefully, the ambulance made it through and on to the next junction, only to be met with more of the same problems beyond.

When the noise had abated sufficiently, the four friends could speak again. Janie Jones spoke first.

"What about Sakima? Where did she go? Who told you to tell her 'turtle-turtle-turtle?' What's going on? Where are we? Who am I?"

Her face froze in an expression of complete bewilderment as she scratched her head, her shoulders slumped and her eyes glassy.

"And also," Curly said, ignoring Janie Jones, "don't forget… "

Blue and MJ ceased staring at Janie Jones, turning to Curly as he continued talking.

"We said, 'wolf-wolf-wolf' too, you know," Curly added. "Exactly as her pretty grandmother told us to. We were a little late informing Sakima, but still… "

"*The* Grandmother," MJ corrected him.

"Yeah, right, *thee* Grandmother, whatever that means."

"And she was telling you to do all this from... what again? A billboard?"

"No, all the billboards. I mean, not billboards. All the screens in Times Square."

"How is that possible?" MJ said.

"I don't know," Blue jumped in. "It just was."

"Wait a minute," Janie Jones said, coming out of her self-induced trance of confusion. She scrunched her face, tilting it slightly toward the sun, which made her squinting eyes press together even tighter. "Wait just a gosh-darn minute." She paused again as if trying to solve a puzzle in her mind.

"What is it?" MJ glanced over at her.

"If *the* Grandmother was only on the screens, as you said, only being broadcast somehow..."

"Yeah?" Blue said.

"Then how in the blazes did she give you that feather?"

Blue huffed from frustration. "I don't know, Janie Jones. She just did."

"That's not a very satisfactory answer."

"Well, but that's the truth."

Curly spoke up. "She said, 'Give this to Sakima. It's important.' Or something like that. Then: *ala kazaam!* The feather was floating there, inches from us."

"I grabbed it out of the air. At first, I thought it was a hologram."

"Yeah," Curly interrupted. "Perhaps she used a type of super-advanced hologram technology."

"She transported it somehow," Blue continued. "From wherever she was broadcasting herself. From another dimension or something."

"I think it's simple," MJ said.

"Yeah...?" Janie Jones and Curly said in unison.

"Magic."

Curly smiled and looked at Blue. He was grinning too.

"You know," Blue said, "that's the perfect word for it. It describes everything that's happened here and to us since we first caught sight of that monster and saw Sakima get thrown through space and into all that scaffolding."

The other three nodded.

"Well, good magic and bad magic," Janie Jones said. "Wouldn't you say?"

The others looked at her, their smiles fading slightly.

"What do you mean?" MJ said.

"Yeah," Curly said, not following either.

"Well, all the positive magic from Sakima and her—I meant, the Grandmother."

"And the bad stuff?" Blue said.

"The negative energy from those guys with that weird weapon. Well, from that enormous monster, of course. Wouldn't you agree?"

"For sure," Curly said, nodding.

MJ and Blue both said, "Yeah." Blue continued, "But it's feeling as if that's the end now. That all the magic has stopped."

"What are you talking about, baby?" MJ said. She leaned into Blue as she peered into his eyes, as if to better understand his point of view. She put her hands on his bicep and squeezed; she loved doing that and found it very comforting. MJ laid her head on Blue's chest and heard his heartbeat through the soft Sex Pistols T-shirt.

"What I mean is, what happened to Sakima?" No one said anything for a few seconds so Blue continued. "She could be gone, forever. Maybe she's not coming back. Maybe she's dead. Maybe—"

"Don't speak those words!" Janie Jones shouted, alarmed.

"We just don't have any idea, Janie Jones. We don't know a lot of things!" He threw his hands in the air in frustration. "Where did that monster take Sakima's little sister? Are they in some evil alternative dimension together? Is that where Sakima took off to? Are they trapped there now, forever?"

A heavy funeral shroud of silence fell over the group.

After a lengthy pause, Blue spoke again. "Janie Jones, what I'm saying is, can't you tell us if Sakima is… well, dead?"

Janie Jones studied Blue for a second while everyone else stared at her.

"OMG. You're right! What am I doing?" She smacked herself gently on her forehead. "Okay, okay. I can do this!"

She closed her eyes, and then she immediately opened them.

"Too much noise; too many people. Can you guys make a circle around me? I don't feel safe doing this while just standing out in the open here."

None of them had to be asked twice. Blue and Curly formed a "V" in front of her while MJ went over and stood back-to-back with Janie Jones.

"Better?"

"Totally."

"Excellent," MJ said. "Now get started!"

"I'm on it," Janie Jones said.

She shut her eyes again. After a short delay, she hummed softly and then, almost imperceptibly, swayed.

"I'm in," she whispered. "Looking around now and… *oh my god!*" she yelled. "This is a horrible place! This is a gruesome, disgusting nightmare! *EEEeeee!*"

"What's happening?" Curly called to her over his shoulder. "You all right, Janie Jones?"

"No, I'm not the least bit okay! I've never experienced a world like this! It's so terrible. *Oh god, oh god, oh god!!*"

PART FOUR
THE RETURN

CHAPTER 63

They waited patiently while Janie Jones hyperventilated. They had seen it before and knew it would pass. Classic Janie Jones.

"I've only been to the Land of the Dead, a quiet place," she continued. "But this... This is full of flames and blackness and dreadful sights. I can't stay. Nope, that's it. I'm leaving!"

"But is Sakima down there? Can you see her?" MJ said. "Can you try to find her before you leave, please?"

"I don't see her, that's it. She's so not here. I'm out! Can't stay!" She snapped her eyes open, unblinking, like she'd seen a ghost, but not a friendly one. She bent over and inhaled deeply, her hands on her knees.

"Easy, easy," MJ said, turning around to rub her back reassuringly. "Breathe, babe, breathe. "

"I'm okay," Janie Jones said after a minute. She took another full breath, exhaling hard, then straightened up. "I'll tell you, though… I think I can safely say Sakima wasn't there."

"That's good."

"Or if she was, she is in terrible danger, and there's nothing we can do about it."

"What? That's awful!"

"Oh, the horrors! This terrible, terrible world! The worst place of the dead… "

"Um, Janie Jones?" Curly said, trying to quietly interrupt her rant.

"The wretchedness! The screams! The pain!"

"Yo, ah, Janie Jones! You might want to peek over there."

"A living nightmare. Flames, black smoke, demons!"

"Stop, Janie Jones. Look!"

"Oh, what a place… Wait, what?"

"Just turn around," MJ said, pointing.

Janie Jones did.

And there stood Sakima with Tangetta holding her hand.

"Hi, guys," Sakima said, letting a radiant smile take over her face. "I… I got her. I did it."

The four flung themselves at Sakima and Tangetta with hugs and kisses and rapid talking.

"Where were you?"

"How did you get back?"

"How did you ever find her?"

"So wonderful to see you again!"

"So glad you're safe! You, too, little one!"

"We were so scared for you!"

"We missed you!"

MJ picked Tangetta up, gave her a tight squeeze, then transferred the child to her hip. She gently patted Tangetta's head and played with her hair. "How's my brave girl?"

Tangetta smiled and shrugged her shoulders.

"Just a second," Sakima said. "Here, Tangetta. Hold still." Sakima pressed a pair of jewels on her cuff and pointed it at Tangetta. "Ask her again, MJ. Should be good now."

MJ raised an eyebrow, a bit confused, but she did as Sakima suggested. "I was saying, little one: How's my brave girl?"

Tangetta giggled. "That's better! I understand her now!" She pulled her face in real close to MJ's. Then she put one small hand on each of MJ's cheeks and gave a little squeeze before saying, "I'm good! Sakima told me I was good!"

"Yeah," said Sakima. "She's very good, a strong and brave girl."

"Well, okay!" MJ said, laughing. "Okay. That's what I would have guessed, knowing Sakima. That strength and bravery runs in the family." She patted Tangetta on her head as Sakima looked on proudly. "And you're proof of that."

All six of them hugged. Sakima, MJ, and Janie Jones all tried, mostly without success, to keep from crying.

After a bit, they separated, wiping eyes, standing back, hands on hips, patting Tangetta, unsure what to say.

"Whoa! Too much, man," Curly said. "Too much." He sniffled and then looked over at Sakima. "Now what, boss?"

She stared at him and then gazed at everyone and said, "You guys ready?"

"You bet we are!" Blue shouted, the others yelling various forms of the affirmative.

"Great," Sakima said, adjusting her knife belt at her waist and her bow over her shoulder. She gazed into their eyes, one by one. Then she grinned and winked.

"Let's end this."

The small group cheered.

"Let's go get that bastard once and for all," Sakima continued, yelling over their cheers. A big, confident smile exploded across her face. The cheering slowed down and things around them grew quieter.

"But first, does anyone have some water?"

CHAPTER 64

"How exactly do we go about ending this, Sakima?" Blue said.

"We need to locate Machto, and then we must finish him. Only after that can this nightmare finally end." She turned to look at Janie Jones. "Do you think you will be able to locate him? Are your powers capable of that?"

"I'm not positive, Sakima. It's not something I do. I mean, I guess if he's near some people who are very recently dead, maybe."

"How did you do it with MJ, when we needed to find her?"

"Again, I don't know. Maybe because she and I have such a strong bond? Plus, I had help from my dear friends in the Land of the Dead."

"True. Could you try, perhaps?" Sakima said.

"I guess I can try. It could work to ask again, but I don't want to be a pain in the you-know-what," Janie Jones mused. "So yeah, let me attempt it, but no promises."

She closed her eyes, searching whatever part of her had these abilities.

Janie Jones journeyed to the Land of the Dead, asking all her acquaintances there for their help. She visited people she'd met from many different cultures. Hindus in Trāyastriṃśa awaiting reincarnation. Chinese Taoists in Tian, Buddhists in Svarga Loka hoping for entrance into Nirvana. Christians in Heaven and Limbo, Muslims in Dār al-maqāmah, and Jews in Shamayim.

But in none of these worlds could she find a path to the living. In none of them could any of her friends, some of whom she'd known since she was a baby, help her as much as they wanted to. Maybe it was the inherent evil in the person she was searching for that blocked his aura or soul from being seen by the kind people she knew. Janie Jones kept trying.

Before she could stop herself, she had left the lands of hope and light and found herself somehow back in the terrible world of fire and brimstone. She had entered the other place, known by many names: Naraka, Xibalba, Sheol, Hades, Diyu, and Jahannam. She had returned to hell.

It was like swimming to the bottom of the ocean in a thunderstorm—dark, difficult to move, and impossible to see anything. The heat and pressure crushed her, made it tough for her to breathe. Janie Jones fought against the feeling of being trapped, of desperate hopelessness, of never leaving this godforsaken world. Then as she floated through that terrible place in her spirit form, she spotted something: an opening, maybe a passage. A strange light appeared to filter down from high above.

Janie Jones followed that light to the path, through the portal, and up into a series of dark tunnels. The route led her mind and soul higher and higher still until she finally burst through into the sunshine. Bright blue skies, beautiful buildings shimmering in the sun. She'd come back at last to New York City: the Land of the Living.

Everywhere was noise and life and crowds. Huskies, Golden Retrievers, those little sausage dogs. Mercedes and Porsches along with beat-up, 20-year old Hondas, some of which had plastic wrap on side windows and dangling rear-view mirrors. Restaurants wafting every possible smell combination from all cultures and nations. Clothing stores, cellphone stores, food vendors. Janie Jones spotted signs for the opera and ballet and jazz across the street from where she stood. People carrying instruments in protective cases hurried past. Then she saw him.

Machto.

CHAPTER 65

Machto appeared blurry, out of focus, as if she were still in the underworlds studying him from another dimension. She sensed something next to him, a dark, enormous, malicious entity. Janie Jones couldn't make out any details or even the outline of its shape. Then she realized it wasn't standing beside him, but it seemed to be hovering over him, casting a gigantic black shadow over Machto. The shade didn't feel foreign and singular. Instead, it appeared to mingle with him, as if they were of the same evil spirit.

Janie Jones felt frightened, more scared than she'd ever been. She perceived her life to be in extreme danger, even though only her mind or some strange part of it had found this location, had entered here. She understood in a horrifying moment of clarity that she was not physically here. Yet being this close to the evil, although only by mental projection, had put her very soul in serious jeopardy. Janie Jones then realized that the dark thing that stared at her from far away could *see* her. She needed to flee as fast as she could.

But it was not so easy to control her own powers, and she didn't know what to do next. Even though she could sense the hateful entity reaching out to her, getting closer. She screamed.

"Janie Jones!" Sakima said, shaking her. "Janie Jones, return to us!"

She felt like a burlap bag of corn cobs in Sakima's hands. Janie Jones's limbs were loose, her head drooped to one side. She moaned. She twitched. Sakima held onto her while her friend spasmed. Then Janie Jones screamed again.

"My Kishelë!" Sakima said. "Janie Jones, wake up! Please!"

Janie Jones opened her eyes and kept them wide open, unblinking.

"Lincoln Center," she said. "But there's something… " She stepped to the curb and sat down, head in hand. "There's danger there, Sakima, a great evil."

"I can handle it," Sakima said, standing up taller. "You have no idea what I've seen and been through."

Janie Jones sighed, fighting back the tears. "I think I do have a slight idea." She sat in silence.

Sakima waited, not wanting to push her too hard, understanding that Janie Jones had witnessed terrible things while she'd been in that trance. She reached out and gently touched her Janie Jones' hair, but she didn't react, and her breathing stayed loud and unsteady.

After a moment, Janie Jones sniffed, shook herself a bit, and stood up. "When do we leave?"

Sakima grinned. "Right now. Before he disappears from there and hides from us again." She glanced over at her little sister who amused herself by watching a group of pigeons scurrying haphazardly along the sidewalk. "But we need someone to take care of this one."

"Janie!" said a loud voice not too far away. "Janie! It's your mother!"

Dashing through the intersection, knitting her way through the gridlock and waving her hands above her head like a maniac, came

Janie Jones's mother. She was laugh-crying, her expensive mascara smeared on her eyelids and cheeks.

"Jaaaaa-nie!"

The group stared at each other and then at the yelling woman. Tangetta laughed out loud and pointed at her.

"Sakima, look at that lady! She's silly!"

"I've been so worried, Jane!" her mother said, running up to her and giving her a big hug. "Where have you been?"

"Been really busy, Mom, but I'm fine. Honest," Janie Jones said.

"Well, you look terrible, honey! Have you even brushed your hair today? Let me see." She took a large brush out of her purse and ran it through her daughter's tresses.

"Mom, stop. It's fine. Don't fuss like that." She waved her hand around her, trying to deflect her mother's grooming.

"Oh, all right, I'll leave it. You do it, then." She stuck her arm out, brush in hand, and waited. Reluctantly, Janie Jones took the brush and slowly stroked it through her mane, rolling her eyes while she did so.

"Janie, honey, introduce me. Who are your new friends?"

"This is Saki—" Janie Jones started.

"Who is this precious little girl?" her mother interrupted. She squatted down to Tangetta's height, balancing on her high heels. "Aren't you an adorable thing!" She held her hand out to Tangetta. "Pleased to meet you. My name is Mrs. Jones, but my first name is Samantha. You may call me Auntie Sammie."

Tangetta hid behind Sakima's leg, eyes wide.

"What's your name?" Mrs. Jones asked her, waiting for a handshake. "Come on, don't be shy." She smiled at Sakima and then returned her gaze to the child.

Tangetta said nothing. She peered wistfully up at her sister, who beamed broadly at her and nodded.

"Go ahead, tell her your name. It's all right. She's a friend. That's her mommy." Sakima pointed to Janie Jones. "And Janie Jones is really nice."

Tangetta peeked at Mrs. Jones then up at Sakima then over at the woman, who by now had withdrawn her handshake so as to not worry the young girl.

"My name is Tangetta," Sakima's sister said at last, in such a shy whisper it was barely audible.

"What was that again, little one?"

"Tangetta," she said, even more quietly than before, which meant almost no sound at all.

"Lately she prefers 'Tangie,' short for Tangerine," Sakima said. "She likes that."

"Tangie! Oh, that's pretty. Tangie?" Mrs. Samantha Jones put on a serious face. "May I please hold your hand?"

Tangetta reached her hand out tentatively and Samantha snatched it up.

"Good, good, Tangie! And do ya know what?"

"What?"

"I think we are going to be fast friends. I feel it. I have a good sense about these things: a kind of intuition."

" 'k."

Samantha stood back up, still clutching Tangetta's tiny hand.

"Well, where are you all off to on such a beautiful day?"

"Mom, we were right in the middle of something. Um, so..." Janie Jones said, hesitating. "We'd like to know if you could watch Tangetta for a short time."

Sakima jumped in. "Just for an hour or so, maybe less. Would that be too much of an imposition?"

There was an awkward silence. Then Samantha said, "Well, kids, I'm not sure that's such a great idea."

"Mom?" Janie Jones pleaded.

"Janie, I'm only kidding! I would kill to spend time with this little brown nut!"

"Jeez, Mom! Please don't call her that!" Janie Jones's eyebrows shooting up her forehead. "But anyway, thank you for taking care of her."

"So what were you all doing before I arrived? What's so important that you need to rush off like this?"

"Doesn't matter, Mom. Tangetta can't run with us. That's the problem: she's too young."

"But I want to go!" Tangetta stomped her foot. "With my sister! In case the monsters come again and put her in a cage. So I can save *her* this time!"

"Monsters and cages." Samantha chuckled, shaking her head. "What an imagination!"

"Kids, haha!" Sakima said, trying to join in convincingly. "The things they say!" She shrugged as if she had no notion what Tangetta was going on about. Then she cut a quick look at Tangetta, who stared up at her, her small face red with anger.

Mrs. Jones scrutinized each of the friends in turn. "You're all hiding something," she said. "And you… " she swung her gaze to Sakima. "What's your deal?" She glanced at Sakima's outfit curiously. "Why all the weaponry? Is it real? Or is it part of your costume or what?"

"The 'weaponry?' Sakima asked, leaning forward slightly to understand what Janie Jones's mother was saying.

"You know, the knives and bows and all that." Mrs. Jones passed her hand up and down in front of Sakima as if blessing her.

"Oh, that!" MJ cut in as Sakima collected herself. "That's exactly what we were in the middle of doing when you showed up! We were headed to Central Park. Big archery contest today. Costume judging. The whole nine yards. She's been practicing for weeks. Haven't you, Sakima?"

Sakima's head jerked backward, and she gave MJ an incredulous stare. She knew nothing of any archery or costume contests, and her recent practice had been no different from any other week.

MJ winked at her. Unsure what that meant, Sakima awkwardly winked back.

"She's shy," MJ said. "But only because she's so good. Hates to show off."

"Exactly, Mom," Janie Jones jumped in. "She loathes all that bragging stuff. I despise it too. Actions speak louder than words; that's my philosophy."

"They didn't cancel?" Mrs. Jones asked.

"What do you mean, 'cancel?' Why?"

"Hello? We're under attack from outer space aliens or something, like in the movies. You're saying you didn't know… ?

"We should get going," Blue interjected apologetically. "Hop on, MJ."

MJ jumped up behind Blue and wrapped her arms around his waist, locking her fingers on top of his chest.

"Janie Jones?" Curly said.

"A minute, Curly." She shifted toward her mother. "Mom? Is it all right if we take off now? Can you watch Tangetta? Please?"

"I'm not sure, sweetheart. I only now found you, and I don't know her very well. What if she… ?"

"We can have your favorite French dinner. You love it when I make it, Mom. How's that sound? As soon as we're done kill… killing it at the archery contest, I'll come right home."

"Oh, okay, okay. I'll watch her. Promise to come straight home when you're all done? I'll be there with my new best friend."

"Of course, Mom. I promise!" Janie Jones hopped up on her skyboard.

Sakima bent over to address Tangetta. "You be a good girl, okay, Tangerine? I will be back real soon to get you." She ruffled her sister's hair and then got on the board behind Janie Jones. The group lifted their skyboards a few feet into the sky. Janie Jones peered down at her mother and smiled and waved.

"Don't be too late, honey. I'll be waiting!" Mrs. Jones called up to her. She smiled and gazed down at Tangetta. "Want to go get an ice cream sundae with your aunt? I know just the place!"

"Ice cream!" Tangetta yelled. "I love ice cream!" Then she turned to stare up at her big sister who still hovered above, although she had traveled higher away. "Sakima, what is ice cream? Do I love it?"

Before Sakima could say anything, Samantha said, "Oh, you sweet girl, you are in for a treat! Ice cream is the most amazing delicacy, and there are simply hundreds of flavors! Once you have some, you'll want it every day, forever. In fact, you'll have to visit a gym every day forever because of it."

"Sakima, what's a gym? Do I like to have the gym?"

"Come along, Tangie," Janie Jones's mother said. "Let's get you your very first bite of ice cream!"

"Bye, Sakima," Tangetta said. She waved a happy goodbye to her sister. The last thing Sakima saw as she glided up above the crowd was her kid sister skipping alongside Janie Jones's mother, talking excitedly.

Sakima realized then that it could very well be the last thing she'd ever see her do and that they might never see each other again.

This knowledge made her angrier than she'd been in a long time. *How dare these monsters do this to me? How dare they strip me of my life, my family, and my youngest sister? How dare they threaten my friends and menace Manhattan, the Land Below?*

She curled both her fists into balls and tightened the muscles in her stomach and her arms and her legs. She stared off to the northwest, toward Lincoln Center, with a steely-eyed expression.

Then she spoke to her friends-in-arms, calling out above the thumping of helicopter blades passing by and the sirens of emergency vehicles in the near distance.

"Let's go kill some freakin' monsters!"

CHAPTER 66

"This way!" Sakima shouted as they sped along, eager for the fight, hoping to bring the horrible adventure to a quick finale. They turned the corner, speeding and weaving twenty feet above the city streets on their hoverboards.

The team burst up Broadway to West 64th Street and then bounded and floated up the wide cement stairs to Lincoln Center. They came to a sudden stop across from a large, bubbling water fountain that filled the air with the sounds of splashing and the faint odor of chlorine. They lowered their skyboards with care so that Sakima could hop off.

A vast throng of frightened people congregated around the outskirts of the plaza. Police had set up metal crowd-control barriers along the exterior of Avery Fisher Hall, with a line of Humvees parked beside the south wall. One hundred or more cops armed with rifles and pistols crouched behind by clear, bulletproof shields. A scattered few held megaphones to their mouths, barking out orders.

A National Guard battalion, outfitted with machine guns and rocket launchers, hunkered down against cement and metal barricades protecting the Metropolitan Opera House. Another brigade was stationed by Julliard. Still, others congregated between Lincoln Center and Fordham University. Equipped with much of the same weapons and gear as their counterparts, this group also navigated more than a dozen armed drones over the scene. These flying predatory machines soared up and down and back and forth across the entire location like a frenzied flock of raptors at feeding time.

Snipers lay prone and ready in position on top of the buildings in the immediate vicinity, their scopes gleaming in the sun. Medical personnel, firefighters, and other early responders hollered commands and hailed one another from the perimeter of the commotion beyond the cascading water fountain near Broadway.

There, in the middle of it all, was Machto with his colossus of Mannahatta myth.

Sakima could not believe what she saw, yet she knew exactly what it was. She was momentarily frozen. *How could this be?* Yakwahe, the gargantuan monstrosity had somehow returned from whatever hell she'd sent it to, using her cuff's alien technology and the Grandmother's magic.

Yakwahe glared at Sakima and her backup crew with its oily, red eyes. It let out a loud, piercing screech as the crowd below her pushed and yelled, seeming to regret staying to view the behemoth. Beside this hideous monster stood Machto with an automatic weapon pointed directly at Sakima.

She did not hesitate, bolting for her enemies with no fear on her face or in her heart. Machto didn't shoot at first due to the unexpected shock of her attacking instead of running. In the milliseconds it took for him to snap out of his stunned state of disbelief, she sped toward him as if she were still riding a skyboard.

Machto narrowed his eyes. As soon as she reached him, he thrust both barrels of the guns against her stomach. Before he pulled the trigger, however, Sakima snatched her knife, chessi, from her waist, then jammed it as strong and as deep into Machto's chest as she could. From the looseness in the shaft as it dug in, she realized the blade had missed all the vital organs. He squealed in pain but was able to give her a solid smack with the side of his weapon.

Sakima dropped hard and howled when she hit the cement. Machto smashed the butt of his gun down where she'd landed, but she'd already rolled away. His lips pulled back in frustration, he shrieked at the hairless behemoth, "Kill her, damn you—wèkwite-hook—kill them all!"

Sakima had already sprung to her feet. She bolted over and slashed Machto again, this time across his thighs, barely missing the sure-kill spot of his femoral artery. He fell to his knees, dropping his gun, which skidded away from him through the plaza. Face contorted in fury, he leaped at Sakima, knocking her to the grass and dirt, screaming a blood-curdling cry as he did so. He beat her again and again, shrieking as if he'd lost all sense. Yet to Sakima he still sounded like the Machto she knew: a terrible person who only now, here on this strange land, revealed the true depth of his evilness.

"Bow down to me, bitch! I'm your god! Say it!" He hit her again, harder. "Say it, you damn ugly bitch!"

"Say what, now?" Sakima said, smiling. Something about this repetition of an earlier moment, instead of frightening her, struck her as funny. Her smile grew to a huge grin. "Oh, you mean, 'Fuck you?' Happy to: Fuck you, Machto!" And with that, she drove her second knife directly into his groin.

He squealed at a pitch Sakima would have thought he was incapable of hitting. His blue veins, which had throbbed unnaturally earlier, had grown three times the size of ordinary veins, running throughout his body, his neck, and his face. The veins pulsated horribly as if snakes danced inside his skin. Machto's eyes bugged out, doubled in diameter. As he choked, his tongue lolled out, spit dripping from his mouth.

Her repeated knifing, along with the poison in the arrow tip she'd launched into him at Grand Central Station, seemed to be joining forces to produce this grotesque reaction. Sakima also suspected for a long while that he dabbled in perverse black magic, here and back on Mannahatta.

Such a misguided indulgence could never be good, she thought. *An evil force might very well have something to do with this—what?—transformation?*

Machto forced himself to stand up, screaming, his arms flopping about involuntarily, his legs wobbling from the wounds. A strange cracking noise, like the sound of far-distant thunder, matched what appeared to be black sticks pushing their way out through the sides of his head. These resembled the early horns of a young stag, mere knobs, horrific as they burst through Machto's skull. He screamed and flailed about in agony as expressions of shock flashed across his now ghost-white countenance: mouth open, eyes wide with terror. Then his whole body stretched, first his limbs, then finally his torso. He was already a foot taller than what he was seconds ago. Six feet, seven feet tall, and still growing.

What is happening? Sakima thought, stunned and afraid. *What kind of curse is this? What level of nightmare?*

She felt queasy as she witnessed Machto transforming bit by horrifying bit into some sort of man-monster, with elongated limbs and sharp teeth. Then, impossibly, he stopped screaming and snarled, a wretched smirk on his lips.

That's when Sakima recognized what Machto was becoming. Something like Mhuwe, the man-eating giant of the myths whom other nations knew by the name of Wendigo.

"*I am your god!*" he yelled, cackling insanely, his voice garbled and distorted. "*The Greatest Spirit!*" He gazed down at his strange body and reached up to feel the protruding nubs on his head. He flexed his muscles, enjoying their new, animalistic size and strength.

Sakima, despite it all, had found the wherewithal to nock her bow with a fresh, jet-black fire arrow. She aimed it at the contorted version of Machto and let it fly. "As I was saying, and just in case you did not hear me the first time," she taunted him. "Fuck you!"

The arrow drilled itself through the air at this Machto-ish abomination.

But the projectile bounced off him like a toy ball against a brick wall, impotent against the monstrous thing Machto was turning into.

What? That's the deadliest of my arrows. Nothing can stop it! Well, until now, anyway...

Commands of strategy roared out of bullhorns, shadows cast by drones swept darkly past her, guns cocked menacingly, and large engines somewhere revved in anticipation of imminent action.

But nothing happened. Not a single person or machine came to her aid.

Military and political leaders were lost in intense debates about how to put an end to these invaders without blowing Lincoln Center and half of the Upper West Side of New York City into bits.

"There are innocent lives to consider—voters' lives," the Mayor argued.

"Buildings, too, many of which are historical," a council member added. "Consider the expense of replacing just one. And the media outrage!"

"None of that will matter if we don't take this beast out," a colonel in full uniform hissed. "Let's drop the biggest bomb we have on the motherfreaker, and let the devil take the hindmost!"

These debates and the officials having them left Sakima to stand before an insane, deadly freak-show all by herself, as if forgotten, as if unseen.

She stood there, her head tilted to one side, wondering what to do next when she suddenly remembered the Grandmother's instructions for using the cuff. The green *tulpe* twice; the blue *xinkwtëme* twice; and finally, the red *tschikenum* two times. She jabbed that pattern on her cuff.

Bright blue concentric circles warped out in waves, growing larger and larger as they wobbled through space at Machto. Once they made contact, his limbs pulsated. As his head vibrated, he looked as if he realized he might be in serious trouble. He appeared to be suppressing the pain and becoming more arrogant with his emerging powers. So, he began to taunt Sakima one last time.

"Ah, you got a little fight in you yet, I see," Matcho shouted. "Well, bring it!"

He started toward her on his long, unstable, evolving legs. Then, understanding as he teetered along that he was in no position to counterattack, he changed his attitude.

"Well, perhaps later, you ridiculous Mannahatta 'she-warrior,' haha! After I figure out what these new amazing powers I've been granted can do, we will meet again, and you will be mine!"

With that, he turned, and managing a sort of galloping stride, headed swiftly toward the rear of the plaza. Once there, he leaped over the tall grass mound known as the Tisch Illumination Lawn.

"Come back and fight, you coward!" Sakima hollered after him as he disappeared down to the street below. Before she could pursue him, Yakwahe circled around and blocked the way.

Too bad for you! Sakima laughed, surprised by her unexpected lack of fear. *I've destroyed you before, and I'll do it again!*

But the beast charged at her so fast she had no chance to plan a defense, let alone attack. She was aware only of the stench of open sores as the hideous creature towered over her, wrapping her in its shadow of death.

Sakima stared up at the monster, unblinking, her face a mask of both pride and fierce determination.

CHAPTER 67

Lumbering thunderclouds drifted across the sun, plunging her living room into darkness. Wùnita drew items from her secret space and carried them over to the couch. She closed the door, and the painting slid quietly into place to hide the cubbyhole once again.

Before she could contemplate what her actions truly meant, she caught a noise behind her, a sound similar to the faint sound of breezes through the leaves of a cedar tree. A soft silhouette played against the wall next to her, the top rippling like tall grasses flowing gently in the wind.

Wùnita froze, not moving a muscle, staring straight ahead at the shadow on the living room wall.

A gentle whisper called her name, but Wùnita did not turn around.

"It is time," the voice said.

"I thought it might be," Wùnita said.

"As I have always promised, your opportunity to prove yourself has come."

Wùnita sighed. "I just didn't think it would come so late in my life," she whispered with a shrug. "I mean, you made that promise to me when I was twelve years old."

"It was never the right moment, my dear. Until today."

Wùnita took the packages she'd removed from the hidden cubby off the couch and brought them into her bedroom. She uncovered the contents of the first bundle, dressing with deliberate swiftness in what she retrieved.

"But Wùnita, my sweet spirit," the voice said gently, "there is a price."

"I know," Wùnita murmured almost without sound. "Can I at least say goodbye?"

"That remains to be seen."

"I just want them to be safe, happy. That's all I've ever desired. I wanted that for my Tommy, too…"

"I appreciate that, Wùnita. But that was not in the stars."

Wùnita said nothing while she finished dressing. She took the other objects she had retrieved and clutched them in each hand.

"I would've liked to have seen them grow up," she said. "To see what they might grow into. Especially Sakima. I worry about her so much."

"You need not fret any longer, my dear. Sakima has become who she was always meant to be. You should be proud."

Wùnita released a short, involuntary laugh, even though there were tears in her eyes. She swallowed hard and then she said, "I am ready."

"I have prepared everything," the voice continued. "You will arrive at exactly the right time and in precisely the right place."

"You have seen her? Have you talked with her?"

"You must leave immediately, Wùnita, my darling girl. Time is not on your side. There are many dangers, much new evil. You have prepared for this your entire life, though. You will know what to do. Remember your lessons. I shall see you soon in the Land."

"Goodbye, Grandmother," Wùnita said, finally finding the courage to glance over at her, but the Grandmother of the South had already moved on.

CHAPTER 68

Yakwahe swept Sakima up with its gruesome paws and hurled her across the plaza, high above the National Guard troops, and through the tall Opera House windows. Sakima smashed to the floor and slid along the carpet, her arms and legs covered in small cuts, sharp fragments of glass everywhere around her.

Knowing she had to escape quickly, she rose to her knees in a daze, lacerating her palms on the shattered glass. As she fought to stand upright, blasts of hellfire flames roared in from out of nowhere. She flattened herself again, cutting herself even more.

This is unexpected. Sakima's mental flash hardly registered as awareness. *Yakwahe must have picked up this new power from whatever place I sent it,* she thought.

Sakima dodged and rolled as incoming flame-bombs in rapid succession destroyed the area where she had been. She raced to the other side of the building, smashing the closed metal door out of her way, and entering the outdoor plaza again, both knives drawn.

The monster's gigantic paws snatched her into the air once again. This time it flung her across the square, all the way to the ballet building. This would have been a killing blow, had Blue and Curly not intercepted her in midair. It hurt her when they grabbed her, surrounding her like a human net. The pain would not compare to what she would have experienced had she crashed into the cement from that height and at such a speed.

Embracing each other, the three followed a loopy circular path to the walkway. There, they somehow managed an acceptably soft landing. Blue and Curly laid Sakima down as gently as they could before they both collapsed onto their backs. She wanted to cry out from the intense pain, but the breath had been knocked out of her. She shook her head to revive her senses, then got laboriously to her feet. With a nod of thanks to the boys, and without a second's hesitation, she ran off again to deal with the creature.

Sakima pressed the turtle/wolf/turkey button sequence once more, shooting bright blue concentric circles at Yakwahe—the same destructive *mpoalonium* waves she had sent at Machto, which had nearly torn him apart.

For the monster, the waves had no more adverse effect than shining a flashlight on a mechBear. Yakwahe roared, stomped over to her, and picked her up for a third time, slamming her to the ground as hard as it could. She smashed not into a concrete slab but onto the softer grass of the Tisch Lawn.

Sakima writhed in agony as the monster raised its fists high over its head and hammered them down. She rolled aside at the last minute, a small part of the behemoth's paw barely brushing across the side of her head. The rest of the force of the impact bludgeoned a hole next to her six feet deep. Even so, contact was enough to cause blood to splash from her mouth and nose. Sakima realized with alarm that she couldn't focus her left eye and that a loud ringing echoed in her left ear.

Sakima lay in terror and defeat as she heard the sickening behemoth roaring above her. *I can't fight this monster*, she thought. *It's too strong for me alone to defeat it, and my cuff is useless against it now. I've failed once again. It's over, and I have failed to save this world and its people from an evil Mannahatta monster. I am afraid this fate will be the same for my beloved Mannahatta and Mannahatta. Most importantly, I cannot protect my family, my Mother, my Father...*

Then, very un-warrior-like, she sobbed. *I've tried my best,* she thought. *I tried everything. I know this is not a coward's death, nor a loser's, but a true warrior's.* She sniffed and wiped at her nose. She noticed that her finger was smeared with blood as her hand fell back onto the grass. *Not every warrior can win every battle. Many die trying.* She spat up some blood, and the ground felt as if it rippled under her as the sky closed in. *I stayed brave until the very end; I did not dishonor my family's name or the Mannahatta people.*

"I am finished," she said, her voice scarcely audible, her chest heaving with despair. She shut her eyes, perhaps for the final time. "This is the end."

"Sakima, this is not the end for you. Not today, my love."

The Grandmother of the South's statement seemed to fill the entire plaza, but Sakima realized it existed only in her mind.

"To win this one, you need the right combination. That is, press twice on each jewel, and two times through. *Tulpe-tulpe;* then *xinkwtëme-xinkwtëme;* then, finally, *tschikenum-tschikenum.* Immediately after, you must do that same pattern a second time."

Sakima listened to the Grandmother say these words from the Spirit plane to the depths of her soul, as her brain slowly processed them. She struggled to rise, knowing that at any moment another blow would come, and understanding that she would not survive that final hit from Yakwahe. She studied the beast with hazy concentration as it hovered above her. The colossus balanced on its hind legs, bellowing at the crowd and waving its front paws about, almost as if bragging. *A last-minute, pride-fueled display before it completes my public execution,* Sakima thought.

But she concentrated more, forcing her vision to focus again, the Grandmother's directive virtually echoing in her ears. She pulled herself up and rested on her elbows, studying the scene with clearer eyes. She was wrong, it turned out. The creature wasn't gesturing and bragging; it was swatting at Blue, Curly, MJ, and Janie Jones. The beast swiped and swatted, but her companions stayed just out of the monster's deadly reach on their hoverboards.

Sakima scanned the cowering crowd in the near distance. Some covered themselves with their arms or hands or shopping bags. Some were in tears, some in shock. The hordes of people here when her friends and she first arrived had fled for their lives when the fighting began: when it became obvious Sakima would not prevail.

The National Guard and the NYPD held back, powerless to attack because Sakima and her four allies were all in the line of fire. So they waited. Would they wait until she and her companions were killed?

"Remember, Sakima, two times. You must do this now and do it perfectly. Be brave." The Grandmother's voice in her head faded away slowly.

Standing on shaky limbs, her body aching, and her mind in a fog, Sakima tapped out the sequence. She then went through it again, as the Grandmother had so explicitly instructed. A blindingly blue beam shot from her cuff directly at the beast's face and hit it in the forehead, right between the eyes. No floating circles this time. It was a bright shaft of light in the form of an angry *mpoalonium* falcon attacking its prey.

Yakwahe didn't bellow because the ray hadn't damaged it as it entered its body and flew out the other side, where the blue, transparent falcon dissipated in the air. The monster dropped back on all fours and lumbered to and fro, caught in an invisible trap. It kept looking straight on as if its head had been stuck on a stick and frozen in place. Because of this light that had torpedoed out of her cuff, the beast could no longer turn its head in any direction. It could move its body all around and as much as it needed to, but its face was locked in by the beam to peer only directly ahead.

What good is this? Sakima thought, exasperated. *Great, I have a magic beam that makes monsters unable to look left or right or up or down. How very powerful a weapon I have. The 'mighty' Sakima conquers all with her face-locking powers. Èchei!*

Powerless to take its gaze elsewhere, Yakwahe's only focus became Sakima, so it charged at her at full speed. She dropped and laid flat, hands locked together over her head, hoping the creature would gallop past her in its frenzy. It skidded to a stop and grabbed her by her clothing with its slimy teeth, tossing her around, an enormous dog playing with a cheap and easily mutilated toy.

Sakima felt her brain was about to explode and the excruciating pain caused her to consider that perhaps she was losing her mind. *This is the end*, she thought. It was the only conclusion that made sense to her.

Not that she was giving up; but she just couldn't keep on in this manner anymore. Blackness met her in the spinning world of suffering she found herself in, life slipping out of her. This time it was truly the end. There was no way out, and she knew it.

Then, from somewhere beyond the throbbing hurt and the increasing darkness, she caught the sound of someone crying out from far away, a familiar voice from the void. A voice filled with anxiety, but with love, too.

"Sakima! My dearest, sweet Sakima!"

CHAPTER 69

"TeeTee, yes, good, you're here."

Dr. Pahòke waved his friend over to him. Takachsin gazed about at the improvements in the lab as he strode along. Nimàt and Mimi—with baby Mimëntëta strapped to her—left their father to his discussion and wandered off to check out the changes for themselves.

"Look around you, yes? What do you think? Almost done, right? Looking good, no?" Pahòke continued, hyped up on too much strong *kàpi* and not nearly enough sleep.

"Yes, I can't believe all you've accomplished—what the entire team has done—in such a brief time." Takachsin slapped the man on the back to congratulate him. "When do you expect to run tests, though?"

"That's the thing, isn't it?" another Mannahatta scientists, Professor Winkalit, interrupted. He approached them, carrying a clipboard, flipping through the sheets, and checking an item off the top page. He put the pen behind his ear. "Things appear to be in order, without question. When we've run the mechanical tests and electrical tests, it's all checked out okay. As for the software testing

—unit tests, stress tests, regression; white, gray, and black box—they've all completed too. No problems."

"That's great news," Takachsin said.

"Hold on, tell him about the atomic field test," Pahòke said.

"That's just it, TeeTee. After the *mpoalonium* somehow reformed itself into one piece again, after having been shattered, we ran tests. Seventeen tests completed successfully. The atomic and neutronic tests didn't finish; they just broke. Every single time."

"It's like a program crashing," Pahòke added. "We can't get proof positive that the transport system works. We can't isolate the issue."

"Might never be operational, in other words," Professor Winkalit said.

"Can we run a real-world test?" Takachsin said.

"You mean put an animal in and see what happens?"

"Yes. A small animal. A rat or a squirrel."

"I understand what you're suggesting, TeeTee. It wouldn't give us usable data, even if it appeared to enter the portal successfully."

"Why not?"

"Because we can't know whether it got through safely or whether it exploded en route."

"Can you put a tracker on the animal, perhaps?"

"Can't track across universes in that fashion. If only such technology were available, we could pinpoint your daughters' location using a device like that."

"How would we possibly know if it works? How will we ever be sure it's safe to travel through? Or even acceptable to use anywhere?"

Professor Winkalit ran his hand back and forth across the top of his head agitatedly. "Yeah, there you go, right? What we need are the original designers, the Ones Who Fell To Earth. The *Alànëmëskat*."

Takachsin nodded gravely. "They designed this thing. They built it. They made sure it would last forever."

"Correct," Winkalit went on. "Kind of genius, if you think about it. Except that they didn't plan for a gargantuan, enraged monster to crash into the portal, ripping it almost to shreds with its enormous size and weight."

"They created it specifically for Mannahatta and *Alànëmëskat*," Pahòke added. "They engineered for those passengers, they based the design specifications on them—"

"For four, no five hundred, years," Takachsin said, "it quietly purrs away here, idle and waiting. Year after year, decade after decade. Century after century. No one using it. No one ever traveling to *Mënatink Ohëlëmi*—the Land Below—or even wanting to." He sighed and wiped his hand across his mouth and chin. "Until my daughter did. The first Mannahatta to use this alien tech as designed. The first one brave enough, or dumb enough, to do so."

"Well, technically, TeeTee, both your daughters were the 'orginals,' so to speak. Didn't Sakima travel through it to try to save Tangetta, your youngest?"

Takachsin nodded slowly. He still was having trouble absorbing that reality—coming to terms with the fact that both his daughters might never return. Departed to *Mënatink Ohëlëmi*, assuming they'd even made it there. If they hadn't, then they were either lost within the multiverse forever or dead. Both amounted to the same thing. "Yes, you're right, Pahòke," he said, at last, sounding defeated.

"I appreciate you need to get down there as fast as possible, TeeTee. It's what I'd want too, if they were my kids. But: patience. We have to run some more tests, tweak additional settings. I know we're close, though. I mean, look at it!" Pahòke gestured grandly toward the portal, *Skontay Chìpilësu*. "We got the whole thing repaired, rewired, running smoothly, except for the MTS, the *mpoalonium* transport system. As soon as I can make that operational again and with positive test results, I'll be the first to say, 'Send our warriors through to the rescue!' However—"

"What?" Takachsin said wearily.

"It occurred to me right now, um, a slight issue I'd like to bring forward for discussion—"

"What is it?"

"Since, as you know, we've never sent a warrior to the other side of the portal before," Pahòke bit his lip. "It also means we've never brought a warrior back."

CHAPTER 70

Takachsin closed his eyes. All this was too much. He just wanted his daughters to return safely to Mannahatta. He no longer cared about the science and the physics, or even the odds for success anymore. He needed the nightmare to end. Takachsin sighed. No matter what, he was the tribe's Sachem, their leader. And he must lead.

"Okay, I understand. Are we certain we can do that? Or is this all merely a shot in the dark?"

"It's funny you ask, TeeTee. While we were reconstructing this entire portal, we referred over and over to the Xuwi Lèkhikàna, the Ancient Books. There, we discovered an interesting set of things we'd never comprehended before."

"Yes? And that was...?"

"Volumes of drawings and diagrams and hieroglyphics and instructions. All written in antiquated Mannahatta words, along with the language of the Star People, the *Alànawènik* of Eldëror."

"Yes, yes, Pahòke. That is not any kind of breakthrough, I am sorry to say. I am well aware of what the Ancient Books contain. We have all been cognizant of that sacred information for centuries.

What it all amounts to, I'm sorry to say, is a hill of corn and lima beans. Last I checked, it's not much more than 'jump on through that great big portal hoop over there!'"

"Yes, that's very true, TeeTee." Pahòke nodded. "But we kept digging, not wanting to miss some essential knowledge regarding the repairs already underway. Then it revealed itself to us as if a message from the Spirit World. Toward the end of Volume 17, the last book."

"I await this revelation."

"Step-by-step instructions on how to complete a successful crossover. It took the AIAM—Artificial Intelligence & Analysis Machine—multiple passes, but it was able to finally piece it together."

Takachsin began to speak, but his friend raised his palm up to cut him off.

"And it deciphered something else, TeeTee, just as important, perhaps more so."

"Please spell it out."

"The instructions for returning. We have them at last."

"Are you sure? That seems impossible. How could we have missed it all these centuries?"

"Our AI systems have been evolving over all that time. We're only now, in our lifetimes, reaching the capacity with the AIAM to accurately analyze these ancient Alànawènik texts."

"So, my old friend, I must ask: do you believe it will work? Do you honestly think we are capable of pulling this off?"

"Okay, so I can present both good news and bad news. My question for you is, which do you want first?"

"Give it to me, I do not care in what order," Takachsin said, his shoulders slumping. He sat down on the nearest swivel chair and rotated it a bit as he listened.

"Okay, okay. So, returning is relatively easy. I mean, as easy as a procedure involving wormholes, black matter, chaos theory, and the Many Worlds multiverse can be. So, not exactly like press the big 'CLICK TO RETURN HOME' button or anything. The physics of the design does seem to work in 'reverse,' if you want to put it that way."

"I assume that's the good news?"

"Haha, yes, of course. What else would it be?" Pahòke laughed. "It means we can absolutely and without a doubt bring your girls back!" He paused and chewed at a fingernail for a second. "Well, in theory, anyway—"

"All right. Sure, whatever. So tell me, Pahòke, what is the bad news?"

"They must position themselves where they 'landed' in the parallel universe. Precisely the same spot, at exactly the correct millisecond."

Takachsin stood up and stretched backward, feeling a vertebra or two pop along his spine. He suppressed a yawn. "Well, I hate to say it, old friend, but I can identify a big flaw in this already," he said. "Sakima and Tangetta crossed through separately. At different times. So, there'd be no 'exact spot.'"

"Not a problem, not a problem. You see—and here's the beauty of how the *Alànëmëskat* designed the system—it doesn't matter! Anyone can be in any of the locations. Or all of them! Their departure sites are all automatically geo- and universe-coded into the portal system's memory. *Skontay Chìpilësu* knows precisely where to look and what needs to be done. Ain't that sweet?" Pahòke flashed a bright smile.

"Yeah," said Professor Winkalit, rejoining the conversation, his checklist completed. "The only requirement is for your kids to get themselves to one of their entry locations and boom, they will register in our sites now that the system is up and running again. We don't need to find them; in fact, we technically can't. Then, we send warriors down to retrieve them at that very spot and they all return here." He crossed his arms over his chest and then shrugged his shoulders in a fake-humble "I can't help it if I'm a genius" motion.

Takachsin pondered this for a moment. Then he let a small smile trickle across his face to match the little glimmer of hope in his heart. "Okay, I see. Yes." He nodded, hand on his chin. "We can't locate them, but in a manner of speaking, they can find us. Correct?"

"Exactly."

"So how long, by your calculations… " he looked from Pahòke to Winkalit, "before our warrior volunteers can pass through the portal and retrieve my girls?"

"A month, maybe two, and that includes about two weeks for the drop training."

"Two months? Are you mad? I don't want to wait two seconds!" Takachsin slammed his hands down on the workstation table in front of him.

"Well, if it helps, the training can be implemented simultaneously with the final testing of the portal system, maybe?" Winkalit suggested. "Shave off a couple of weeks."

Takachsin stared at the man as if studying mold on bread. "No," he said sharply. "That doesn't help."

"There is no other way, TeeTee," Pahòke said sadly.

"You are wrong, all of you educated, talkative men. There is another option," a woman's voice called out behind them. "I will go. I will leave today."

CHAPTER 71

Takachsin turned to see his wife, Wùnita, standing before him. She was dressed in a style he couldn't remember having seen before, carrying things he wasn't sure he'd seen her carry in all the years of their marriage. After a stunned moment, he said, "No, you cannot do this! The system is not fully operational. It's not stable. It could kill you."

"It will be all right, Taka."

"No, my love." Takachsin studied his wife's eyes. The expression there was as old as time, but he did not recognize it. "Wùnita?"

She walked up to him and gave him a strong hug, and then she kissed him hard on his mouth.

"I will miss you, my darling," she whispered, a tear in her eye. "But I want you to remember I will always—always—be with you."

"Wùnita. What in the world are you talking about?" Takachsin said, but he got no answer. "Wùnita?"

"I love you, Takachsin Tamanend. I'll love you forever."

With that, she stepped into *Skontay Chìpilësu*. A flash of jagged, bright blue lightning sparked and popped with a deafening boom. Wùnita vanished.

"My god, TeeTee, you shouldn't have allowed that!"

"She's gone, Pahòke," Takachsin said. He cleared his throat, having caught his heart there. "She's gone to save her children."

There was a long pause as the workers and scientists and villagers and Takachsin glanced around at each other in the sudden silence. No one knew what to say or what to do. Nimàt and Mimi came running over from the far end of the enormous room.

"Daddy," Mimi called out to him. "Daddy, what happened? Where's Mom?"

"My daughter, my son," he said in a hushed tone. "She had made up her mind to travel through the portal herself." He wiped at his eyes for a moment. Then he gazed over and pointed to the information flashing on the massive arch. "The settings, see? *Skontay Chìpilësu* is unstable, untested since the monster smashed it. They changed when she went through." He paused. "She may not be heading toward where she thinks she's heading. She... might never make her way home."

Mimi's eyes opened wide, and she was on the verge of tears as Nimàt put his arms around her.

"She'll make it, though. I know she will," he said, which made a slight grin appear on Mimi's lips. "With the help of Kishelë—and all Grandmothers and the Grandfathers—she'll get there. She'll get back. I'm sure of it. Safe and sound and with Tangetta and Sakima in tow!"

"She has to," Mimi said, her voice trembling, her shoulders pulled straight as if her posture might help her to be brave.

Baby Mimëntëta suddenly burst into a loud, wailing cry that echoed throughout the gleaming glass and metal laboratory like a warning bell.

CHAPTER 72

From out of nowhere, Sakima's mother appeared, flying through the air above Sakima. She had launched herself off the top of the Metropolitan Opera House. As she descended, she nocked an arrow that had a pink shaft, a rainbow fletching, and a golden point.

And she looked more beautiful and more powerful than Sakima had ever known her to be. She was wearing an outfit like Sakima's, only old-school. While Sakima wore black pants with mechLeather protective "battle" patches, her mother sported a white traditional skirt that fell below her knees. While Sakima had on a top, also black, that exposed her strong arms and taut stomach, her mother's top covered every inch of skin.

Wùnita sent the arrow flying with such authority that Sakima wondered how her mother could shoot so well. As far as she was aware, her mother didn't practice at all and had often told Sakima that she was no longer any good at archery.

The arrow soared, straight and true, finding its home in the pale blue dot that the beam painted on the face of the beast. The monster was unable to turn away. Instead, it stumbled backward a dozen steps, nearly losing its balance.

It's been injured, Sakima thought. *I can't believe it; the monstrous fiend can be hurt!*

Yakwahe regained its footing and immediately changed focus. It stopped trying to overcome the blue ray and Sakima's attack and instead concentrated on the new, dangerous arrival.

The hideous beast charged at Sakima's mother where she'd landed on the concrete pathway after sending her arrow into the creature. Before Wùnita had a chance to flee, it reached her and viciously stabbed a single claw of its paw into her chest. The tip was covered not only with sharp scales but what looked almost like shark's teeth. These instantly chewed into Wùnita's body while she writhed in unimaginable agony.

Sakima lay there, immobile from the shock of what she was witnessing, crushed by the realization that her failures had led to this. She was forced to see her mother being tortured in front of her.

Wùnita thrashed about, struggling to tear the claw from her chest. Then Yakwahe ripped its hideous talon out, and she howled in pain.

Despite all the aching Sakima felt from the incredible beating she had just endured, she shifted over and painfully rose to her knees. She managed to stand up, weary and dizzy. Sakima headed off to confront the beast again. She approached it, torn apart, bleeding from cuts everywhere, her head throbbing. She was suffering so much she almost wished she would die.

But two factors overpowered her temporary desire to escape pain and sorrow. She needed to save her mother, and she had to slaughter this terrible monster once and for all.

Yakwahe repositioned its body, ready to drive its claw once again through Wùnita's rib cage. Before it could attack again, Sakima's mother yelled out to her, using the last of her strength.

"Shoot, Sakima. Fire that arrow I gave you—the one you hate!"

Sakima was so beat up and exhausted, she barely comprehended what her mom told her. *What arrow do I hate?* Then she remembered: that ridiculous arrow her mother gifted her long ago. She gave it to her when she left the house that fateful night to travel off through the portal.

"You'll know when the time has come to use this. You'll use it then, not before," she had said.

That horrendous pink- and rainbow-colored arrow, the one she'd been too embarrassed to carry. Sakima had been so angry then she hadn't made a mental note of her mother sliding that arrow into her quiver as she'd stormed away. She'd figured she would pull it out and toss it aside as soon as she was out of her mother's sight. In her anger, as she'd stalked away that night, she'd completely forgotten to do that. Now that same "ridiculous" arrow slept in her quiver, awaiting the right moment. This moment.

Sakima reached speedily for the arrow, as fast as her beaten body let her move. She picked the odd object from her quiver and threaded it into her bow as Yakwahe raised its huge paw to obliterate her mother forever.

"You must split my arrow, Sakima!" her mother cried out again, sputtering blood as she did so. "Slice it down the middle precisely or it won't work! Nothing will happen—"

Wùnita didn't finish her sentence because Yakwahe had snatched her up, lifting her off the ground and pulling her up to his mouth. Sakima couldn't believe her eyes. The demon monster intended to eat her mother alive.

She aimed at the spot the light blue beam made, where her mother's arrow had pierced the monster's skull. She was more than prepared to shoot, but now her mother hovered there, blocking the face of the colossus. *Not again! Why does this keep happening to me?* Her hands shook. She shut her eyes to concentrate.

Then, in her mind's eye, or perhaps in some other universe, she saw him: Apatschin. Her Pat. He seemed to materialize before her from nothingness.

Apatschin, the boy she couldn't save, stood smiling at her. As his smile grew bigger, he nodded and simply stated, "You got this, Sakima, you are brave, strong, and true. I believe in you, and I love you still, although we are no longer in the same universe."

Sakima wept.

Then she pulled herself together and wiped away her tears. The noises and sights from the horror around her filled her senses again.

She stretched the bowstring further than she ever had, stressing the wood and *mpoalonium* of the bow to such an extreme extent it was in danger of snapping in the middle.

Then she let it go.

CHAPTER 73

The bow flopped about viciously in her hand, but Sakima held it tight and didn't allow it to drop.

She watched as the arrow hurtled like a bird of prey over her mother. It weaved past her friends, who swooped about in the air in an attempt to distract the monster to keep it from swallowing this second strange visitor who resembled their new friend.

Sakima's at last arrow hit the tail end of her mom's arrow, the one embedded already in the monster's forehead. It split the fletching of the initial arrow, sending the rainbow-colored feathers fluttering to the ground: red, yellow, blue, orange, green, and purple.

Yakwahe screamed angrily and appeared ready to massacre Sakima, Sakima's mother, all the kids on the hoverboards—everyone in sight.

But Sakima's arrow continued its path, even after splitting the shaft of her mother's arrow. It drilled through it, carving it in two. Yakwahe could not look away or get that tractor-like blue beam to detach itself from his face, no matter how many times he batted at it. He could not put a stop to whatever magic this was that held its head unmoving and staring at the Mannahatta warrior girl.

Helicopters and drones circled above shining spotlights into the shadowed area where the monster stumbled about. Sakima's arrowhead violently pierced the first arrowhead, cracking it open and shattering it to pieces. Her arrow then entered Yakwahe's skull almost surgically, following the path created by the original arrow.

It penetrated the monster's brain matter, and it did not stop until it went out the rear of its head. The arrow stuck two inches out of its skull there, having, at last, put an end to the monster from Mannahatta legends and myths.

Then Yakwahe appeared to melt into the Earth as it was sucked back into the hellish world where Sakima recently journeyed in search of Tangetta.

As the monster was dragged out of this universe into the other nightmare place, every part of it disappeared until only its upright arm was showing. Then only the hand that clutched Wùnita. Then even that was gone, finally releasing Sakima's mother, who rolled a few feet in Sakima's direction.

Sakima rushed forward, sliding onto her knees. "Mother! Mother! Are you all right? Get up!" She noticed that the whites of her mother's eyes were red. Her face and neck were swollen and badly bruised.

"My darling, Sakima," Wùnita's voice was a hoarse whisper, but a slight smile played gently on her lips as she spoke.

Sakima leaned in closer and cradled her mom's head in her hands.

"I don't have much time, and I must tell you something important."

"What is it?" Sakima asked softly, tears welling in her eyes, her lower lip trembling.

"Bring Tangetta here, in exactly the same position where you saw me appear on the roof." She coughed and let her eyelids fall.

"Mother?" Sakima swallowed hard. "Okay, sure, I'll do that. But why?"

"The only way, my love, for you and your sister to return safely to Mannahatta is to be in that spot… " She opened her eyes again, forcing herself to stay conscious and focus on her daughter. "It must be the exact same location, for when your father uses the portal to bring us back."

"Okay, I think I understand. So, Mom, how about I help you make it up there, okay? And you wait for me to return with Tangetta."

"Sounds like a plan, my darling." She gasped weakly. "Sakima?"

"Yes?"

"Hold me for a second. Let me look at you. Lean closer. I want to kiss you."

Sakima watched her mother gaze up at her as the sounds of the shouting and the helicopters and the sirens faded far into the background. She bent down even closer to her mother. Wùnita lifted her head and kissed Sakima on the cheek.

"I love you, Sakima. I always have and always will… Sakima?"

"Yes, Mom, what?" Sakima spoke as softly as she could.

"I am so very proud of you." It was the merest wisp of a whisper, the last words Wùnita Tamanend would ever say as she closed her eyes forever.

"Mom?"

She rocked her mother gently. "Mom? Wake up… Mommy!"

PART FIVE
HOME

CHAPTER 74

The cheering and the music and the dancing were one thing —the fireworks another. Drums beat out rhythms and songs while rockets arced and exploded in the night sky.

Men and women hopped and skipped to the traditional dances wearing the ceremonial outfits of their ancestors. Their singing, chanting, and shouts of joy filled the air. A huge fire roared in the middle of the village where table after table groaned under the weight of all the festive food. There were trays of bioVenison, bioBuffalo, bioBeaver, and other bioMeats, as well as bowl after bowl of apples, pears, peaches, grapes, and tangerines. Numerous other delicious foods, such as stew, succotash, cornbread, and fry bread covered many other tables. The desserts were well represented too, with even more tables holding big and small cakes, candies, and other delights.

The ceremony in Wùnita's honor went on all day, with mourning and speeches and various rituals, both spiritual and celebratory. Her family took time by themselves in the funeral longhouse to gather around, surrounded by flowers. White, cream, and soft yellow gardenias—Wùnita's favorites taken right from her garden. The family all held hands and remembered Wùnita as a wife, mother, and grandmother. No one held back the tears or the smiles the memories brought out.

But tonight was a night to rejoice. No more sadness, not even from Takachsin—already suffering from guilt over his prior, wrong-headed assessment of Machto. When he'd heard of his wife's brav-ery, it stunned him and made him proud and joyous.

Her way to the Land of the Dead would be a glorious one. He believed his wife had reunited now with their warrior son, Hìtami, as well as with the Grandmother and the other protective Spirits.

Takachsin was terribly sad, but he also understood the love of his life had made the ultimate sacrifice to save her children—their children. He knew she had accepted her destiny freely and gladly, that she would have had it no other way. It seemed selfish to be depressed because her sacrifice meant that his daughters were now home, safe, and reunited with their father.

Still, Takachsin missed her so much and couldn't imagine a day when his sadness would leave him. At that moment of sorrow, he was startled by a tremendous cheer welling up from the enormous crowds around the entire village. The drums beat more rapidly and louder than they had all evening.

There she was. *Sakima.*

She walked through the entrance on the main road. Sakima wore a beautiful traditional gown of white. Blue and green designs intertwined throughout the dress, speckled with jewels and shell pieces, which shined from the glow of thousands of minuscule frag-ments of *mpoalonium.* On her right shoulder, Sakima sported her first tattoo. It was the Mannahatta pictogram for monster-killer, the monsters drawn symbolically as intertwined snakes with a blade slash across them all, showing that they were defeated. Across her forehead, a beaded headband displayed a single feather. Around her neck, she wore a hoop of copper and a necklace of braided silver which held at the bottom the Mannahatta symbol for kishuxa: the moon.

Takachsin beamed as his beautiful daughter approached. Sakima held Tangetta's hand as her sister walked beside her proudly, wearing a simpler but matching outfit. Takachsin couldn't hold back any longer and dashed across the village center to his two daughters, disrupting the ceremony of the Warrior's Welcome.

"Dad!" Sakima said. "We're right in the middle of—"

"I don't care!" he shouted. With tears in his eyes, he hugged Sakima tight and kissed her on her cheeks. Then dropped to his knees and hugged and kissed Tangetta, too. Finally, he stood up, laughing and crying simultaneously, and then looked his middle daughter straight in the eyes.

"Today is the proudest moment of my life, my daughter, Sakima. You have brought so much honor to your family, your village, and your nation!" Tears rushed down his face. He wiped his eyes and blew his nose with the cloth he whipped off his neck. When he finished, he nervously stuffed it into his pocket. "Come, come," he said. "I've something to show you."

"But, Daddy, the ceremony! I have to—"

"It can wait. You come too, Tangetta."

"Okay, good!" Tangetta said, reaching up and taking Sakima's hand again with her left hand and her father's with the other.

The three walked happily together through the crowd, past the food and the dancers and the drummers, to the very center of the village. They proceeded up a wide set of marble stairs, where they were joined by Nimàt, who also gave Sakima a strong, quick hug.

"Hey, sis."

"Hey, Nimmy."

At the very top of the steps, Sakima's sister Mimi stood with her baby, Mimëntëta, in her arms. They were both next to a large object on an even larger platform. It was covered with a huge ceremonial Mannahatta cloth that rippled gently in the evening breeze.

"What's this?" Sakima said, smiling and waving the tips of her fingers at her little niece, Mimëntëta, who giggled and gurgled at the sight of Sakima.

Her father called out then to no one that Sakima could see. "Now's good, new friends. Come on out!"

From behind the large cloth-draped object appeared Sakima's friends from what she and they now knew to be the Land Below—*Mënatink Ohëlëmi*—MJ, Janie Jones, Blue, and Curly.

"What?" Sakima shouted her surprise and took a step backward, covering her mouth with her hands.

CHAPTER 75

"The biggest night of your life, Sakima. Of course, we sent warriors down to retrieve your new friends!" Takachsin said. "We felt strongly they had to be here, after all you had told us about them! With the system upgrades, we found them with no trouble."

Janie Jones ran up to Sakima and gave her a bear hug, with no intention of ever letting go. "Hi, my Mannahatta friend!" she shouted.

"Hey," Blue said, waving to Sakima from where he stood, insisting on being all cool and casual about it. In contrast, Curly shot her a big, goofy smile and an exaggerated and somewhat theatrical thumbs-up sign. The smile Sakima understood. What the thumb signal meant she had no idea, and she didn't even attempt to interpret it, though she sensed it was a good thing.

MJ strolled over to Sakima like it was no big deal and stood in front of her. She shrugged and said, "Hey, girl."

Sakima wasn't sure how to react or what to do, so she stayed standing there with Janie Jones stuck to her like a burr from white-bear grass.

A moment passed. Then with a shout of "Oh, screw it!" MJ threw herself at Sakima, and they both hugged and laughed and cried together.

"You've all ruined my makeup," Sakima said, dabbing at her eyes. "Idiots."

MJ and Janie Jones giggled, then MJ said, "Mine's been ruined all freakin' day, Sakima, so I don't want to hear your sad story."

Sakima grinned, looking at the friends she'd grown to love.

"But wow, Sakima," MJ continued. "What a place you have here, this Mannahatta. I like it! But I don't even know what to think about it and how we got here. Or is it 'up' here? And how we managed to survive all the crazy shit that happened to us together!"

"Me neither," said Sakima, smiling affectionately at MJ a bit longer because she couldn't believe her eyes. "But Dad." She turned to look at him, "I don't understand, I mean, how—?"

"I know they aren't Mannahatta, and they may or may not be *Wematëgunis*—Mannahatta helpers of our mythology—but they are our very special guests of honor tonight!"

"These guys? Honor?" Sakima looked incredulous.

The four friends looked around at each other, puzzled, then at Sakima, only to catch the twinkle in her eyes. They immediately broke out in huge peals of laughter, with Sakima and her family joining in joyously. As the hilarity slowly subsided, Takachsin spoke up.

"Now," he said, addressing Blue and Curly, who stood on either side of the huge, curtained object. "Time for the big reveal!" He waved his hand straight down like a flagman signaling the start of a race.

Nimàt and Blue worked some hidden ropes together, pulling the large fabric up and off the object.

"Kishelë!" Sakima said softly, cupping her hand over her mouth and bending a bit at the waist as if she'd been lightly punched.

"What? What is that!" She stumbled backward, almost losing her balance.

"Sakima, it's a statue, sculpted by our ancestors and the *Alànëmëskat* over 300 years ago." He paused. "Look familiar?"

"It's... *me*," she breathed, letting her hands drop. Her eyebrows made their way up higher on her forehead as her mouth opened in astonishment. "I don't see how."

"We never showed you this statue. That would be against all our teachings and sacred instructions. It was designed and chiseled using the combined magic of Grandmother Nuhëma and our *Alànëmëskat* benefactors, the Star Walkers. All this time, no one knew who this woman was that they had carved together—a female warrior in full fighting gear."

"*Èchei...* wow," Sakima whispered.

"This statue is what inspired your mother to want to be an Ila, a warrior, believe it or not, on the day I first showed it to her. It was against the rules, but I wanted her to see it. She chose to raise a family instead, which takes a different kind of warrior's heart!" He winked at Sakima before continuing. "But you, your desire to be a warrior, a hero, came from deep within you. You had no sculpture to inspire you, no role models to imitate. It has always been all you."

Sakima hesitantly strode up to her likeness in stone and touched it on the shoulder, staring at the face, studying it. "But how? How can this be?"

The monument was unmistakably her: the same outfit she'd worn to the Land Below. The same quiver, the same belt holding the same knives. On one arm, positioned in the same way with buttons facing up, was the mysterious *Alànëmëskat* cuff with its line of turtle, wolf, and turkey jewels. On the other, an archery cuff. Her entire adventure foretold in sculpture.

Her father approached her and saw the obvious concern—or was it wonder?—in Sakima's eyes.

"My dear daughter, let me tell you a story. It's time you heard it."

CHAPTER 76

"What story?" Sakima asked.

"The legend of how the Grandmother and the *Alànëmëskat*, as well as how your cuff—our whole way of life—came to be."

Sakima glanced over up her father, unsure what was coming next.

"Okay, I guess…"

"A spacecraft belonging to the *Alànëmëskat* crashed through multiple parallel universes in the Many Worlds to get here to Mannahatta on that fateful and historic day. They taught their alien technologies and knowledge to our *Lëpweichik*—the Wise Ones—and our Spiritual Guides, such as the Grandmother of the South, Nuhëma. Over the years, decades, and centuries, they gave much, and we learned much. Together they designed a new world of endless possibilities."

Sakima nodded. "I know this, Daddy. We're taught it in school, of course. Everyone knows the story."

"Not this next part," her father went on. "Nuhëma worked with the Star Walkers to create this cuff just for you, knowing that you would be ready for the challenge once you were old enough. Your mother knew this as well as I, but we didn't want it to be true, for you to be the one. We didn't want to lose you. Because you see, we thought it was a statue created in memoriam—as a monument to your sacrifice, your death."

"I don't understand," Sakima said. "How could they have known what I would do and who I would become—centuries before I was born?"

"They were from a future time, the Star Walkers. Of course, Nuhëma Shaoneyunk knows all time—what has been, what is, and what is to come. So she designed the cuff to fit you perfectly and to function for you and you alone. She appreciated what would be your mischievous nature and knew you wouldn't be able to resist trying it on. It was foretold. As was the fact that you'd be able to intuitively—and with a little help from Nuhëma—figure out how it worked, how to activate it. How to use it to save the Land Below."

"This is so strange, Dad. Why didn't someone else try it? How did she know that another wouldn't steal it at some point in all the years before I was even born?"

"They did! Many tried. But, my daughter, the cuff does not work for anyone else. They constructed it to respond only to you. For half a millennium, others have examined, touched, and explored the cuff. It did not react to their touch or thoughts, so all Mannahatta considered it nothing but a beautiful relic, part of the myths from long ago. Until you finally came along, as the sages had predicted."

"It was meant to be!" Janie Jones intoned in awe, nodding somberly.

Sakima smiled at her and then addressed her father solemnly. "Anushiik—thank you—Daddy, for telling me that." Then she stared at the limestone likeness of herself, lost in her own thoughts.

Takachsin grinned with pride and pulled his daughter in close for a hug, but he could tell her mind was elsewhere.

"What is it?" he asked.

"Father. What's that?"

"What's what?"

"In 'my' other hand," she said, gesturing toward her stone image. "That strange object there."

"I have no idea. Something tells me you're going to discover just what it is, though. One day soon."

Deep in thought, Sakima looked at her family, her new friends, and the villagers everywhere enjoying themselves at the celebration. When she turned her gaze back to the sculpture, she saw her mother and the Grandmother smiling down at her from above and just behind the statue. They shimmered, as if from a haze, but they still seemed quite real. Then she understood.

Everything had happened exactly as it was supposed to. She'd have to learn to stop worrying and trust the universe and her guiding Spirits.

Most of all, she understood that she was someone special now, a warrior—the first Mannahatta woman ever to be so.

In some strange epiphany, she also knew she was a legend in the making. She raised her fist high in the air and let loose the loudest whooping yell she'd ever hollered in her life.

"Whooo!" Sakima laughed. "Forget the ceremony. Let's party!"

MANNAHATTA WORDS
LANGUAGE SPOKEN ON SAKIMA'S PLANET

Mannahatta words are shown *italicized* in this novel, except for the names of people and pets.

A

Ahi Manunsko (*AH-hee Mahn-oonx-su*). The most senior Elder of the Mannahatta people, known as Elder Manunsko. His name translates to "he is a very angry man."

ahoaltuwi (*ah-HO-ahl-tu-wee*). Means "loving one." Aunt Ahoaltuwi is the wife of Takachsin's best friend, Lippoe Pahòke.

ahpòn'tëta (*ah-pahn-TEE-tah*). Cookies.

aimalàxàmuk (*ay-mah-LAX-ah-mook*). Bitches (negative use); female dogs (normal use).

Alànëmëskat (*ah-lah-nuh-MISS-kaht*). The Star Walkers, the multiverse/wormhole-traveling people. This word is a combination of *alànkok*, stars, and *pèhpëmëskat*, walkers. From the Mannahatta myth of the People Who Fell From the Sky.

Alànkok Luweyunk *(ah-LAHN-goke Loo-WAY-oonk)*. The North Star.

Amimi *(AH-mee-mee)*. Sakima's older sister. Her nickname is Mimi. Means "little dove."

ànkùntëwakàn *(hank-oo-tah-WAH-kahn)*. Blessings.

ansikëmès *(ahn-SEE-kah-mess)*. The maple tree.

Apatschin *(ah-PAT-sheen)*. The name of Sakima's childhood boyfriend, "Pat" for short. Means "he who has gone."

B - E

chesimus *(chess-see-muhs)*. Means "little brother." chessi *(chess-see)* is the name Sakima has given her favorite knife.

èchei *(uh-chay-YEE)*. "Wow!" or "Gosh!" or "Cool!" Alternate spelling is "ekee ay," which is a phonetic spelling as well (for that alternate).

Eldëror *(el-door-roor)*. Home planet of the Star Walkers; thus the beginning of the "Elder" council. Name is a tribute to Princess Leia's home planet, Alderaan, and the home planet of the Ewoks, Endor.

F – I

Gegeyjumhet *(gee-gay-JOOM-het)*. Means "leader" and the rule of law, similar to Sachem.

gischileu *(gee-she-loo)*. Means "true." Lèke Gischileu is Sakima's love interest in the series. His name means "Loyal and True"; in other words, one who is very faithful and real.

Hìtami *(hee-TAH-mee)*. Sakima's older brother, whose nickname was Tommy. Means "the first" or "the one who came before."

ilaok *(eee-LOWK)*. Warriors.

J – K

Kahèsëna Hàki *(kah-hee-sen-ah HAW-kee)*. Mother Earth.

kàpi *(kah-pee)*. Coffee.

këntkatàm *(ken-kah-tohm)*. Let's dance!

kèpchat *(kef-chaht)*. A fool.

kèpcheonkèlët *(kep-chay-OON-gah-let)*. Insanity; an insane person. Often used with "rage" to indicate steroid-like chemical-induced anger and out-of-control violent behavior. See also: wchètahsën.

Kishelë *(key-shell-luh)*. God. One of many names for the Creator, which also include Ketanëtuwit and Kishelëmùkònk.

kitahikàn shohpe *(tee-tah-EEK-cahn show-PAY)*. The seaside or seashore.

kpakuwe *(kuh-coo-wuh)*. Chatter, also a chatterbox.

kukhus *(kook-hoos)*. Owl.

kwèn'shùkwënay *(wen-SHOOK-wen-nie-ah)*. This is the name for mountain lion, bobcat, or cougar.

kwèhkwès *(KWAH-quaise)*. A large, crow-sized woodpecker with a prominent red crest (top of its head) and a vocal noise that often sounds like a child laughing. Also known as a pileated woodpecker.

kwëshkwësh *(koosh-KOOSH)*. A single pig. Pigs (plural) is "kwëshkwëtët."

L

Lapowinsa *(lah-pow-IN-sah)*. A great leader from Mannahatta history.

Lèke *(lay-kay)*. The loyal one. Lèke is an up-and-coming warrior and Sakima's love interest. Full name is Lèke Gischileu *(GEE-shah-loo)*, which means "he who has proven himself to be true."

Lenape *(len-AH-pay)*. One of many tribes akin to the Algonquian nation along the northeastern seaboard of North American. The Lenape were the original people of the island of Manhattan on planet Earth.

lënu *(LEN-oo)*. A man.

lënuwàk *(LEN-oo-wahk)*. Men.

Lëpweichik Èlikhatink Mannahatta *(lep-wah-EE-cheek el-ee-KAH-tink len-ah-pay)*. The Mannahatta Technology & Research Center. Literally, the wise ones + the village + Mannahatta = Village of the Wise Ones.

M

Machto Pequonitto (*MAHCH-toe pay-quo-NEE-toe*). Sakima's brother-in-law. Means "evil spirit."

maluwe (*mah-LOW-way*). Damn it, or darn it. Means something similar to "Dammit!" or "Curse it!"

manëtu (*mahn-AY-too*). Demon monsters.

Mannahatta (*man-nah-HAHT-tuh*). Mannahatta is the planet in an alternative universe where Sakima and her family live. It means, "beautiful land of many hills." Mannahatta is also the name of the people on the planet as well as their language.

Matanto (*mah-TAHN-toe*). The Mannahatta name for the devil.

màxkwi (*mahx-kwee*). A bear.

mechakgilik (*mek-ah-GEE-leek*). The mechanical/robotic super-suit designed by Sakima. The word means "great big suit." Often referred to as a "mechSuit."

mechmàxkwi (*mek-MAHX-kwee*). A part-machine, part-living-creature lab-created bear. Also known as a mechBear.

Mënatink Ohëlëmi (*mah-NAH-ting OH-lay-may*). New York City, most specifically Manhattan. Literally, "the far away island" and means the Land Below.

Mhuwe (*muh-HOO-way*). A man-eating giant of Mannahatta folklore. A creature with horns and patchy fur that can grow twice as tall as a human.

Mimëntëta *(mee-mee-ahn-TAY-tah)*. Sakima's niece and her sister Mimi's daughter. Literally means "baby," but in this context, "Little Mimi."

Moskim *(moh-skeem)*. The Rabbit Hero of myth. Also known as Tschimammus *(chuh-mah-muss)*.

mpoalonium *(bow-LONE-ee-um)*. A powerful element from another world given from the Alànawènik. Literally translates as "Power from the Gods." The element is written as Mp on the Periodic Table of Elements; atomic number 111, atomic weight of 333.

mwekane *(mm-WAY-cah-nay)*. Mannahatta word for dog. The diminutive form, mwekanètët, means "puppy."

N

Nagatamen Mùxul Allanque *(nah-gah-TAH-men mah-HOO-lay ahl-LEN-kay)*. The alien spacecraft driven by the Alànëmëskat, the Star Walkers. Typically referred to simply as NaMùxAll. It means, "the Trusted Starship."

nahënëm *(nah-hoom)*. Raccoon.

namès *(noh-MAY-uhs)*. A fish; namèsàk (noh-MAY-sok) is the plural for fishes.

nikanixit xkwe *(nee-kay-nee HUN-kwah)*. Another word for queen; a female leader. See also: kittakima.

Nimàt *(NEE-mat)*. Sakima's slightly younger brother. The word literally translates to brother.

Nink Shawi *(ning SHAW-wee)*. The edge of the Mannahatta world, a magical location with clear views from Mannahatta to the Land Below.

nshawësi xkwe *(jah-WOO-see whay)*. A derisive term for women in general as the weaker sex, the "weak woman."

Ntite Pìkchëlhe *(nee-tay pik-shell-AY-ah)*. The Think & Draw 2000 (the number 2,000 is *tèlën txën nisha*). A talking, meeting-facilitating electronic whiteboard.

Nuhëma *(new-HEY-mah)*. The Grandmother of the South. Her full name is Nuhëma Shaoneyunk.

O – R

òwkës *(OH-kwes)*. A natural (not machine) fox.

òhchu *(oh-choo)*. Òhchu Peak, the tallest mountain top on Mannahatta. Means hill or mountain.

òpalanie *(oh-pah-LAH-nee-ay)*. Bald eagle.

òpinkwinakwsu *(oh-pink-wee-nok-soo)*. Opossum.

Pahòke *(pah-HO-kay)*. Means friend or friendly. It is also the last name of Takachsin's best friend, Dr. Lippoe (meaning "wise one") Pahòke, PhD.

pèmitàn mpàki *(pay-MEE-tahn moke-kay)*. Mannahatta word for their hovercar. Literally means "floating vehicle."

phwit *(phweet)*. Nonsense; B.S.

punkwës (*pohng-WIS*) / punkwsàk (*pohng-WIS-ick*). Mosquito/mosquitos.

pupukwësh (*puh-PUH-koosh*). Quail.

S

Sakima (*sah-KEE-muh*). The heroine of these tales, the first Manna-hatta female warrior and a woman of legend. The daughter of Takachsin and a member of a family of great honor.

salàpòn (*suh-LAH-pahn*). Frybread. A traditional bread made with flour and salt and fried in butter or fat.

sànkweyòk (*san-GWAY-oh*). Weasel.

shaèk *(SHY-ak)*. Measurement similar to a yard or meter; roughly three feet in length.

Shatemuc (*sha-TEE-muk*). The Mannahatta word for the Hudson River. It means "the river that flows both ways," which might refer to the fact that the Hudson contains both salt water and fresh. Also referred to as *Mahicannituck*.

Shëwanahkòk *(shah-wah-NAH-coke)*. White people, or people of European descent.

shiki skixkwe (*SHEE-key SKEE-sksay*). A beautiful young woman.

sisilieyòk (*see-see-lee-A-ohk*). Bison.

Skontay Chìpilësu (*SKOON-day chee-pee-LIS-su*). Name of the portal to the multiverse. Means the "dangerous doorway," the "exciting passageway." In common usage it means simply "portal."

T

Takachsin *(tuh-KUH-shin)*. Sakima's father. Means leader. His nickname is "TeeTee" (for T.T.) and his wife calls him "Taka."

Tamanend *(tuh-MUH-nend)*. Sakima's family name. A well-established name in Mannahatta history.

Tangetta *(tan-JET-ah)*. Sakima's younger sister, whom she affectionately calls "Tangerine." Her name means "short, small, and sweet."

tànkamikàn (tah-mah-MEEK-ahn). A spear.

taonkëlàxàm *(tone-GLAHK-um)*. Bastard. Literally translates to "stray dog."

tèchitaku *(tetch-TAH-koo)*. For fuck's sake. Literally, "oh no, absolutely not, no way!"

Tèkëne *(TAY-kun-nee)*. The forest. This is the massive, ancient forest near where Sakima lives.

tëmakwe *(tah-mah-KWA)*. Beaver.

tëme *(TEM-may)*. Coyote. Also written as *tëmetët*.

tèpahtu *(tay-pah-TOO)*. Stupid.

tèpahtu lënu *(tay-pah-TOO len-oo)*. Stupid man.

tëpinxkèpi *(tah—pinks-SKEP-ia)*. Sakima's cuff.

tëta *(tah-tay)*. Where. Wherever.

tschikenum *(CHEE-can-um)*. Turkey. The Turkey Clan is one of the influential clans of the Mannahatta, it symbolizes good luck and fertility. Sometimes spelled *chikënëm*, pronounced the same.

tùkwsi kishux *(toke-say kee—SHOO[wah])*. Full moon.

Tùkwsitàk *(too-SEE-tuck)*. The wolf. The Wolf Clan. One of the influential clans of the Mannahatta, it symbolizes courage, strength, and loyalty.

tulpe *(TOOL-pay)*. The turtle. The Turtle Clan. One of the influential clans of the Mannahatta. It symbolizes wisdom and loyalty, as well as stubbornness.

U, V

There appears to be no Mannahatta words beginning with U or V.

W

wanìshi *(was-NEE-shee)*. Thank you; thanks.

wchètahsën *(wahk-sah-tch-CHAY-shen)*. Literally, "stone muscle." A dangerous and addictive steroid-like substance. See also: kèpcheonkèlët.

wëlìsëwakàn *(well-ees-ah-WAH-kahn)*. A beautiful woman.

Wematëgunis *(wem-ay-tay-GOO-nees)*. The little people of the forest. They are elf-like mythological people who help any Mannahatta who might find themselves lost or in trouble in the forest.

wëshkiyëm *(wesh-KEE-um)*. Refers specifically to whiskey but can mean any strong alcoholic liquid.

Wickquasgeck (*WIK-quash-jeck*). The long, wide trail built by the Mannahatta people and which in the Land Below is called Broadway.

wikëwam (*WEE-ka-wahm*). A house.

Wîkëwam Shawken Obroa (*WEE-ka-wahm Shaw-ken Oh-bro-wah*). The Mannahatta Science, Research & Technology building. Named using the Mannahatta word for house/building (*Wîkëwam*) plus nods to two Star Wars planets—*Shawken*, famed for science and tech, and *Obroa*, known for its vast libraries and medical centers.

Wikhakamik (*wee-kah-kah-MEE-kay*). Being there when the End of the World has arrived.

Winkalit (*wing-GAH-leed*). Last name of a scientist with long gray hair. Means "best friend."

wichëmil (*wee-CHAH-meel*). Means "Help!" or "Help me!"

witatschimolsin (*wee-hat-scheem-OHL-seen*). Means "wise advisor." Rita Shim Olsen is a near synonym of witatschimolsin.

wulit (*woo-leet*). Suffix or prefix that means "the best."

Wùnita (*woo-NEE-tuh*). Sakima's mother. It means "she who knows," or "she who is able."

X, Y

Xahèli Pili Hàkink (*ha-HAY-lee PEE-lee HAW-king*). The Many Worlds. Literally, the Many New Worlds.

xàskwim (*HUH-skeem*). Corn.

Xinkwi lè Mushhakunk *(kzhing-wee lay moojsh-HAH-koon)*. Big Event in the Sky. Refers to the White (or European) Year 1609 A.D., which was known to the Mannahatta as the Mannahatta Year of 10,609.

xinkwi tàmahikàn *(kZhing-wee dah-mah-HEE-kuhn)*. Big machines. Refers to the high-tech machines brought to Mannahatta by the Star People.

xinkwtëme *(zing-TWAH-meh)*. Wolf.

xkwe *([h]'a-kway)*. A woman.

xkweyòk *(see-kway-ohk)*. Women.

Xkwithakamika Shawi *(xwee-hah-kay-MAY-kah Shah-WEE)*. A location in Mannahatta that translates to "the Edge of the World."

xwisëmësa *(wee-sah-MEE-sah)*. (My) little sister.

Yakwahe *(yuh-KWAH-hay)*. The giant hairless bear monster of Mannahatta legend that attacks New York City in the Mannahatta series Book 1: *City At My Feet*.

Z

There appears to be no Mannahatta words that begin with the letter Z.

ABOUT THE AUTHOR

THOMAS MORE developed a fascination with science fiction during his childhood years. This early passion evolved into a life-long love of both reading and writing, eventually leading him to an advanced degree in creative writing.

When not crafting stories, Thomas More enjoys playing guitar, piano, drums, and trumpet, and reading new and classic sci-fi books.

Born and raised in NYC, he lives in Manhattan.

———

FOLLOW THE AUTHOR

amazon.com/author/thomasmorewriter

goodreads.com/ThomasMoreWriter

instagram.com/thomasmorewriter

facebook.com/thomasmorebooks

x.com/thomasmorebooks

pinterest.com/thomasmorewriter

tiktok.com/@thomasmorewriter

ACKNOWLEDGMENTS

Special thanks to Matthew Turano for his wonderful, creative, and impactful developmental editing for this series. Thanks, too, to Lisa Hannan Fox for her perfect copyediting and proofreading. With gratitude to my online teachers including David Farland, Brandon Sanderson, Chris Fox, and most especially Holly Lisle. And finally, thank-you to Alex Newton for creating the amazing book description used on the back covers and book listings.

9 781942 947561